The Sisters Weiss

Also by Naomi Ragen

The Sisters Weiss

Naomi Ragen

ST. MARTIN'S PRESS   NEW YORK

This is a work of fiction. All of the characters, organizations, and events portrayed in this novel are either products of the author's imagination or are used fictitiously.

THE SISTERS WEISS. Copyright © 2013 by Naomi Ragen. All rights reserved. Printed in the United States of America. For information, address St. Martin's Press, 175 Fifth Avenue, New York, N.Y. 10010.

www.stmartins.com

Library of Congress Cataloging-in-Publication Data is available upon request.

ISBN 978-0-312-57019-4 (hardcover)
ISBN 978-1-4299-5779-3 (e-book)

St. Martin's Press books may be purchased for educational, business, or promotional use. For information on bulk purchases, please contact Macmillan Corporate and Premium Sales Department at 1-800-221-7945, extension 5442, or write specialmarkets@macmillan.com.

First Edition: October 2013

10 9 8 7 6 5 4 3 2 1

To my daughters, Bracha and Rachel,
who continue to inspire me with their love of life,
sense of adventure, and loving kindness

My spirit had brought me here. My spirit bore me and lifted me on imaginary wings, up and outward without end.
        —Sarah Faiga Foner, *Memories of My Childhood Days*

PART ONE

1

Williamsburg, Brooklyn, 1956

Years later, when the terrible sins—both real and imagined—they had committed against each other had separated them seemingly forever, the sisters Weiss would remember that night very differently.

What really happened was this.

It was a Friday night. Crowded around the enormous, dark walnut dining room table that took up the entire living room were the immediate family (except for their two eldest brothers, Abraham and Mordechai, both off learning in an upstate yeshiva), a distant cousin who had just come over from Poland, and the usual pale, eager Talmud students who changed from week to week. Shining in their Sabbath finery, everyone sat up straight waiting for the meal to begin, hungrily eyeing the two large, handmade challah loaves—kneaded personally by Rebbitzin Bracha Weiss—resting in their place of honor covered by a gold-embroidered velvet cloth so as to shield them from the insult of the wine being blessed first.

Their mother, Rebbitzin Bracha Weiss, her arms filled with baby Duvid, settled Pearl, barely three, on the opposite side of the table from her in one of the big dining room chairs, although the child's feet barely reached the edge.

"Really, Mameh . . ." their father, Rabbi Asher Weiss, remonstrated, shaking his head warningly. "You're asking for trouble."

He was a big, heavy man with a serious paunch who dressed in the black garb of the Hassidim, although he wasn't a Hassid. But, by adopting their distinctive clothing, he felt that much closer to a holiness that secretly—and to his everlasting shame—consistently eluded him. Most importantly, he enjoyed covering himself in an outer shell that advertised to all his utter alienation from what he felt was the too-easy American lifestyle with its careless acceptance of life on earth, a life he was convinced was a heavy responsibility, a burden to be borne until he could, with thanks, relinquish it entering the World to Come.

Pearl squirmed. Ever since the baby had usurped her mother's lap and arms, not to mention her crib, she had been indulging in strange outbursts of unpredictable behavior. Just the other day, she had absolutely refused to have her hair brushed and curled, compelling her exasperated mother to hold up scissors and threaten her with baldness.

"I can't help it, Tateh," Rebbitzin Weiss answered, not without her own doubts. "I just can't squeeze her into that high chair anymore. She's just too big. Besides, the baby is going to need it soon enough. She has to learn to behave herself sometime . . ."

They both looked anxiously at Pearl. But she seemed perfectly steady, perfectly content.

Walking around the table from child to child, Rabbi Weiss laid his large hands on their heads, murmuring a prayer. Rose nuzzled into them like a warm blanket of absolute love and protection: "May God make you as Rachel and Leah. May God bless you and watch over you, may His eye shine down upon you and give you peace," he whispered, his eyes closed, his heart open. When he had thus blessed all his children, changing the prayer slightly for his sons (asking that they be blessed like Ephraim and Menashe, the sons of Joseph), he slammed his open palm against the table the way a judge uses a gavel, signaling that the meal could begin.

"*Shalom Aleichem,*" he sang, joined by the others, a prayer bidding farewell and thanks to the angels who had accompanied the men home from their synagogue prayers. Each verse was repeated three times, making it feel interminable, especially to the children and those whose stomachs grumbled with hunger. That was followed by *Eshet Chayil mi Yimtza,* "who will find a virtuous wife," which sounded like a question but wasn't.

> *Her price is far above pearls*
> *Her husband's heart trusts in her . . .*
> *She saved for the purchase of a field and bought it*
> *She planted a vineyard from the work of her hands.*
> *Charm is false, and beauty is worthless.*
> *A God-fearing woman is to be desired.*

The song in her praise momentarily distracted Bracha Weiss from her worries on whether she'd flavored the chicken soup with enough salt or added enough water to the chulent to keep it from scorching overnight on the hot plate (a sojourn necessitated by religious strictures against cooking or heating food on the Sabbath). A small, satisfied smile played around her thin lips, her tired eyes lighting up. The young men joined in shyly, swaying slightly, their eyes closed as they imagined their future wives.

As the last notes faded, Rabbi Weiss lifted the crystal decanter of red wine, pouring the thick red liquid into an ornate silver wine cup given to him on his wedding day by a rich uncle who had engraved it with his own name, lest his largesse ever be forgotten. As was the custom, it was filled until several drops overflowed, running down the sides, striping the chilled, moist silver. Balancing the cup in the center of his palm, he carefully rose. Everyone immediately followed, except Pearl. Before anyone even noticed, she'd slipped out of her seat, rushing to her father's side.

"*BARUCH . . .*" Rabbi Weiss said, his eyes closed in concentration, swaying slightly as he chanted.

"*Baruch . . .*" Pearl repeated.

He opened his eyes, surprised, staring down at her, then eyeing the rest of the table, especially his guests. Catching the tentative smiles that moved fleetingly across their faces, he allowed himself to exhale.

"*ATA . . .*" he continued nervously.

"*ATA . . .*" she repeated, louder and more insistently, intent, they all soon understood, not in participating but in taking over the ceremony. The warm smiles froze.

Had she been a boy, the scenario would have been quite different. Perhaps one of the men would have lifted him up onto a stool. Perhaps Rabbi Weiss would have allowed him to touch his arm, looking at him encouragingly, and everyone would have been delighted at this display of early saintliness on the part of a child so young and so eager to perform a religious obligation. But as it was, it was viewed as a sign of bad character and, even worse, bad upbringing, a female putting herself in front of a room full of men in a wanton and naked display of desire to be the center of attention—an anathema to any truly religious girl from a truly religious family. People sucked in their breath and wondered. Immodesty and brazenness were sure signs that Gentile blood had found its way into one's veins.

Red bloomed in Rabbi Weiss's pale cheeks as he sent a swift, accusing glance in his wife's direction, then looked down at the child, shaking his head in stern warning.

"*Adonai . . .*"

"AHH . . . DOUGH . . . NOI!" Pearl shouted, oblivious, hopping from foot to foot as she claimed the spotlight, finally grabbing for the shiny magic cup filled with its delicious elixir. With a sudden, harsh movement, her father nudged her aside. Whether she grabbed his trouser legs to keep her balance, or lost it and fell heavily against him, the sudden shift caused the cup of wine to teeter sickeningly until collapsing on its side, splashing red, sticky liquid all over Reb Weiss's elegant satin waistcoat, the white tablecloth, and, most of all, Pearl's head.

The smack, swift and resounding, on her behind sent her howling around the table. She headed not for her mother's fully occupied arms but for Rose. Pressing her small head into her six-year-old sister's stomach, her short, chubby arms embracing her fiercely, she sobbed dramatically. Rose said nothing, hugging her back with all her strength. Then, she took a cloth napkin and tried to wipe down her sister's dripping head.

"It's forbidden on the Sabbath to use cloth!" her mother warned, giving her no other instructions.

Obediently, Rose put down the napkin and, without being told, led Pearl off to their bedroom, where they sat holding each other, rocking to and fro.

"*Sha, sha shtil* . . ." Rose whispered, until Pearl's screams softened into sobs and then hiccups.

"Sticky hair!" the child moaned.

"It's Shabbos. I can't wash it. It's not allowed."

"STICKY HAIR!" the child wept hysterically.

"You shouldn't have bothered Tateh during kiddush. It was very naughty," Rose scolded.

Pearl's cries redoubled, more indignant than pained.

"Well, if you stop crying, I'll brush it for you," Rose told her, even though that too was technically not allowed on the Sabbath since it was forbidden to pull out hairs. But the wide-toothed Sabbath comb would simply not do the trick, she realized, as she gently brushed the sticky purple knots from the long, blond strands, trying her best not to tug them too harshly.

"Tell me, Mamaleh," Rose said softly, using her mother's diminutive term of endearment for them both, "what were you trying to do?"

"To make kiddush and drink . . . the whole cup, like Tateh!" Pearl sobbed.

Rose put down the brush, her large, brown, intelligent eyes serious. Then, suddenly, she smiled, a small, secret smile of understanding and collusion. "You were thirsty?"

Pearl stopped crying. She nodded.

"If you let me change your wet clothes, I'll bring you your chocolate milk. All right?"

The child nodded, sucking on her thumb.

Ever since Rose could remember, Pearl had been her special responsibility. They shared a room, the only two girls in a family with four brothers. She was an expert in preparing the drink, without which Pearl refused to go to sleep, knowing the exact ratio of cold milk and hot water to be added to the sweet chocolate powder. In addition, she knew just how to shampoo Pearl's hair without getting soap in her eyes (she told her to look at the birds on the ceiling) as well as the exact spot that, when tickled, would send her into paroxysms of giggles, distracting her from the tantrums to which she was sadly prone.

Struggling with the buttons and zippers on her sister's dress, Rose finally slipped the wet, cold garment down her arms and up over her head.

Pearl shivered. "Shoshi!" the child sobbed, using the family nickname, a short version of the Hebrew word "shoshana," meaning "rose." "Shoshi, bring pink pajamas. With the bunnies," she demanded sleepily.

"In a minute." Rose disappeared, returning with paper napkins, which she used to sop up the liquid still dripping down Pearl's arms and back.

"Sticky!"

"I know. But you can't take a bath; it's Shabbos. Come into the bathroom, and I'll rinse you off by the sink."

But the water was cold. It was forbidden to use hot water on the Sabbath or to use a washcloth or sponge.

"*Gevalt! Gevalt!*" Pearl screamed each time Rose cupped her hand with cold water and attempted to wipe her down, until Rose finally gave up, toweling Pearl off and bringing her pajamas. Gently, she pushed her little sister's small limbs through the openings, finally closing the snaps. Tucking her into bed, she said: "I'm going to get you your bottle, Pearl. Just stay here and wait." She tucked her gently into bed.

"Hungry," Pearl said, throwing off the covers and standing up.

Rose hesitated, then took her hand and led her into the kitchen, hoping her parents wouldn't notice. Sitting her down by the small kitchen table, Rose moved a stool over to the stove, then climbed up. Lifting the lid off the boiling pot, she felt the hot vapors scald her face. Bravely, she extracted a piece of chicken and some liquid, which she ladled into a bowl along with a carrot and some egg noodles.

"Here," she said, carefully blowing on a spoonful, then offering it to her sister.

Pearl stubbornly clamped her lips shut. "By self!" she demanded.

Rose nudged the bowl in front of her, then handed her the spoon. "Here, take it, but eat slowly," she warned, sitting down beside her, trying to forget about her own growling stomach.

"Oh, so there you are!" Rebbitzin Weiss exclaimed as she came into the kitchen. "You *chutzpadika* girl!" she exclaimed, wagging her finger and head at Pearl. "You don't deserve *any* dinner! Such a thing! To interrupt your *tateh* in the middle of kiddush! To spill the kiddush wine all over the table!"

Pearl put down her spoon and howled into her soup.

"Oh! So now you're crying? *Vi m'bet zich ois azoi shloft men.* When you make your bed, you sleep in it! Come, enough already with you tonight," she said, scooping her up.

"But Mameh, she's hungry!" Rose pleaded, following anxiously behind as a kicking Pearl was put down in her bed.

"Ach, she got wine stains all over your dress, too!" Rebbitzin Weiss said to Rose. "You see? You ruined your sister's clothes and her Shabbos dinner, too! Such a naughty girl! Why can't you be more like your sister?" she scolded Pearl, who in response suddenly stopped crying, bunching her small mouth together defiantly, her eyes slits of fury.

"Ach. What am I going to do with you? Never mind. Come already, Shoshi. Eat something."

Reluctantly, Rose turned away, taking her place uneasily at the table. The fish and soup had already been served and cleared. She reached for the large steaming platter of chicken and roasted potatoes.

"She didn't hear kiddush," Shlomie Yosef pointed out. As a bar mitzvah boy in training, he was very *frum*.

As everyone knew, one couldn't eat before hearing the blessing over the wine, and since everyone at the table had already heard it, no one could make it for her, as it would be taking God's name in vain.

It was a problem all right.

"Tateh?" Bracha Weiss beseeched.

Rabbi Weiss looked out the window into the apartments of their neighbors to see whether any of them could still be joined for the blessing. But all around them, Sabbath *nigunim,* which preceded the final Grace After Meals that signaled the conclusion of the meal, were already being sung.

"She'll have to make it for herself then," he said irritably. Girls were not supposed to make kiddush for themselves, certainly not girls who were not even bat mitzvah yet, and certainly not in front of a room full of men, some of them strangers.

Refilling the silver cup, he handed it to her along with a prayer book, which he opened to the correct page, pointing to the words. Rose took the book in one hand and the moist, slippery cup in the other, steadying her trembling hands as she looked at the sparkling wine that teetered so close to the edge. She would die if she spilled a drop, she thought, panicking.

"*Baruch Ata Adonoi . . .*" she began, slowly at first, then growing more confident. She had been learning how to read and write Hebrew since kindergarten but had never dreamed of saying kiddush on a Friday night in front of a room full of people! When she finished, a large "amen" resounded around the room.

"*Nachas.*" Her father beamed, getting up and patting her on the head. "Now, take a sip, *nuch*!"

Just as she put the cold, smooth rim of silver to her lips, she saw Pearl standing in the hallway, watching her, a look of envy and betrayal contorting her features.

"MINE!" the child roared. "MINE, MINE."

2

Williamsburg, Brooklyn, 1957

The High Holidays were a difficult trial for four-year-old Pearl. For weeks before the New Year, followed by the Ten Days of Penitence and culminating in the awesome and terrible Day of Atonement, she hardly saw her father, who seemed to live in the synagogue or study house. And she had learned better than to approach her mother, who, burdened with endless days of cleaning, shopping, and cooking, not to mention getting everyone's holiday clothes ready, was an irritable nervous wreck.

When the holiday finally did arrive, Pearl found herself bundled off to bed after a light supper in the kitchen, as her parents, older siblings, and family guests participated in the enormous holiday meals that went on and on into the night. Lying in bed, she'd listen to the clicking of plates and the thud of heavy platters being added to the groaning table; to people laughing at a joke she couldn't hear; and singing songs she knew and would have liked to sing, too. She imagined with envy the heart-shaped cubes of sugar and platefuls of chocolate delights being handed out generously, mourning her fate. Why had she been born too late? She would never, ever catch up to her sister Rose . . . never . . . she would repeat in her head until—overcome by the fatigue of the long day spent running around the synagogue corridors and courtyard playing tag in her heavy holiday dress and tight new patent-leather shoes—she reluctantly gave in to sleep.

In the morning, she found a cloth napkin on the dresser. When it was carefully unwrapped, she found two sugar cubes, a piece of crumbling chocolate cake, and three almond cookies inside, tidbits Rose had squirreled away for her.

"Thank you, Rose!"

Rose smiled. "It's a little crushed and dry but still tasty. And next year, you'll be old enough to stay up."

That had not occurred to her! Her sister would always be older, but she too was growing! It filled her heart with sudden joy, as did the weeklong festival of the Feast of Tabernacles, or Sukkot, in which even the youngest children were allowed to participate, helping to decorate the pretty little booth that her father and Shlomie Yosef and Mordechai, home from yeshiva, built of wood in the backyard and that the girls and their mother decorated, hanging colorful chains of pretty paper, shiny red apples, and bunches of grapes from the ceiling of palm branches that formed the roof. Abraham, recently married, would be spending the holiday with his in-laws in far-off Monsey, as was the custom for newlyweds.

Sukkot was a holiday that started and ended with Sabbath-like holy days, but in between had ordinary days that even the most ultra-Orthodox men used to take a religiously mandated vacation, spending time with their wives and children on rare and joyful outings.

This Sukkot, it was the Bronx Zoo.

"But what will we see there, Rose?" Pearl asked anxiously, settling into her sister's lap as the crowded subway car with its rancid odor of oil, old rubber, and scraped metal careened down the dark tracks.

"Lions and tigers and monkeys," came the excited reply.

"Wild animals? Like the plague in Egypt?" Pearl questioned, horrified. Animals in general were feared by religious children, and benign pets virtually unknown. Dogs especially were considered impure and contaminating creatures whose mere presence made it impossible to pray or say a blessing of any kind. And only those with a mice problem among the very poorest of families kept cats.

"No, not like the plague . . ." Rose struggled to explain. "Beautiful creatures like the ones God saved from the flood. Remember the pictures in the book Tateh gave you? The one about Noach and the ark?"

The tall giraffes and the lions, all walking docilely in pairs into the strange wooden boat.

"They don't bite?"

"One bite? You they'll chew up and swallow as soon as you walk in! Such a tasty little morsel!" Shlomie Yosef told her wickedly, unable to resist.

Pearl froze, then burst out in wails. "I want to go home!" she sobbed, until the other subway passengers in their workday clothes turned to look at her and, in so doing, rested their gaze longer then they'd planned, staring at the strange, foreign-looking family dressed up in holiday best on an ordinary Tuesday afternoon.

A teenager in a black leather jacket looked at them insolently: "HYMIES!" he called out, just before the subway doors slid open and he jumped off.

Rabbi Weiss's cheek twitched. He adjusted his large black homburg hat, his eyes lowered.

"Stupid *shegetz*," eighteen-year-old Mordechai said bitterly.

Rabbi Weiss threw him a cold look of warning. "No matter where we are born or where we live, we Jews will always be strangers because our laws and our God are strange to those around us. We must never provoke them."

For the rest of the ride, no one said anything.

"Tateh, it's the next stop," their mother finally whispered. "Help me."

"Hmm . . ." he uttered distractedly, lifting the carriage out to the platform and up the stairs to the street.

Their steps were heavy as they neared the ticket booth to the zoo. Rabbi Weiss took out cash and gave it to Mordechai. "Go, buy the tickets."

Rabbi Weiss sat down on a bench nearby. He was not used to being seen together with his wife and children in public. It felt demeaning somehow for a Torah scholar to be involved in such frivolous activities. In fact, were it not for the fact that what they were doing was in honor of the holiday, and thus a mitzvah, he might have considered the terrible insult on the train a just punishment from God for going to the zoo in the first place.

"I also want a ticket!" Pearl wailed, refusing to budge, feeling deprived and belittled.

"You don't need one. You get in free," her mother scolded. "Go under the turnstile! *Nu* already?"

"I'll give you my ticket, and I'll go under," Rose said, taking her hand.

"This is allowed?" Rabbi Weiss asked the ticket taker, who shrugged and waved them through.

Pearl took her father's hand. "Tateh, why did Hashem save the *vilde chayas* from the flood? Why did He put them in the ark?"

"Some *people* are worse than *vilde chayas,*" Bracha Weiss interjected with a conspiratorial glance at her husband. "He keeps *them* alive, too."

"Because He made all creatures, and there is no end to His compassion," her father said gently, suddenly gaining back his good humor.

"Tateh, is it maybe because they are so beautiful?" Rose asked, taking his free hand and looking up at him earnestly.

He squeezed his daughters' hands affectionately, then lifted Pearl into his arms. "As it is written: 'But ask now the beasts, and they shall teach thee; and the fowls of the air, and they shall tell thee: Who knoweth not in all these that the hand of the Lord hath wrought this?'" he said in Hebrew, walking through the leaf-strewn paths, staring with childlike delight at the creatures behind the bars as he pointed them out to his little girls and his sons and wife.

"Look, Mameh, the monkey house!" Rose shouted, running ahead.

"Go away from there, quickly," her mother called back.

"Mameh, it's all right. The children can look. You go sit down."

"Why doesn't Mameh like the monkeys, Tateh?" Pearl wanted to know as they went into the elaborate Beaux-Arts building.

"It's not that she doesn't like . . . it's . . ." But he didn't continue.

"It's because she thinks she might be having another baby and if she looks at a monkey, the baby will also come out looking like a monkey," Shlomie Yosef whispered into Rose's ear.

It was Rose's turn to be horrified. But soon she forgot everything as she stared at the strange creatures that looked so familiar with their expressive, almost human faces and delicate pink hands. She watched, filled with compassion and delight, as a mother chimp cuddled her baby.

"Look, Pearl, see the baby chimp?"

But Pearl couldn't get beyond the dark strangeness of their skin, the way they hooted and swung so fast from the bars and ropes.

"He has a *tuchus,* a naked *tuchus.* It's not allowed. We can't look . . ." she said piously, turning away.

"Very good! She's right!" their father agreed. "It's indecent. Let's go to the birds."

Rose reluctantly dragged herself away.

"As it is written: 'Curse not the king, no, not in thy thought . . . : for a bird of the air shall carry the voice, and that which hath wings shall tell the matter,'" said Rabbi Weiss as he entered the aviary.

Rose felt breathless as the birds circled above her with their wide wings, wishing she could tear off the roof for them and let them soar into the sky. The more she looked, the more she resented her father's attempt to lock them into some kind of pious context. Who had the right to label them, to reduce them into something controllable, useful, and convenient?

The reptile house was next. Pearl, terrified of the snakes, had to be taken outside. But Rose lingered, studying with fascination the intricate designs and patterns of their skins. God could have made one snake, with one kind of skin without designs of any kind, like the skin of humans, she thought. Instead, He had chosen to do this. Her child's heart filled instinctively with love and admiration for the abstract, unseen God she blessed in her daily prayers, for His endless creativity and sense of beauty, which touched something deep inside her.

"Such a big place," her mother sighed, fanning herself. "I'm *shvitzing,* and my feet are killing me. Soon we'll eat. Are you hungry?"

"But, Mameh, we just got here!" Rose implored, disappointed, anxious to get in as much as possible before they packed up and went home.

"Your *mameh* is right!" Rabbi Weiss affirmed, ending all discussion.

Food. It was always about food, always about when they were going to eat, Rose thought with uncharacteristic resentment. How could you stop to sit and chew when faced with such miracles?

Tired of looking for a picnic table, they spread a blanket on the grass. Mrs. Weiss took out the chicken-on-challah sandwiches she'd prepared and wrapped in waxed paper for the youngest children and herself, the jars of sliced fruit and pieces of leftover honey cake and apple-noodle kugel—snacks she'd prepared for her husband and sons, who were forbidden to break bread and eat a meal outside the sukkah during the holiday. Someone went to buy drinks. They lay in the grass looking up at the trees and sky.

Pearl squealed, pointing to the ground.

"It's just an anthill," Shlomie Yosef said, lifting his foot to crush it.

"NO!" Rabbi Weiss grabbed him. "You must never be cruel to any living creature, even an ant. As it is written: 'Go to the ant, you sluggard; consider its ways and be wise! It has no commander, no overseer or ruler, yet it stores its provisions in summer and gathers its food at harvest.'"

He sat on a rock, looking like a raven in his dark, festive coat, Rose thought, watching her father as Pearl climbed into his lap. Rose sat down beside him in the grass. "Come here, Shlomie." He beckoned kindly to the boy, who was still sulking from the reprimand, touching his son on the shoulder. "The pain of a man and the pain of other creatures is the same; there is no difference. A mother's love and tenderness comes from her heart, her feelings, not her mind. All living creatures have such feelings." Overcome by his own words, he suddenly hugged Pearl, who leaned into him, allowing herself a moment to claim him as her own, and hers alone, as she basked in this rare display of tenderness. Rose watched, touched by a sudden envy. The older she got, the less her father touched her.

"That is why the Holy One, blessed be He, forbids us to wear leather shoes on Yom Kippur. As Rabbi Moses Isserles, the blessed Ramah, states: 'How can a man put on leather shoes—for which it is necessary to kill a living thing—on Yom Kippur, a day of grace and compassion on which "His tender mercies are over all His works"?'"

"But is it not also written: 'Conquer the earth and subdue it'?" asked Mordechai, a serious, quiet boy already being praised by his teachers as one of the most promising scholars in his class. "Is not the whole earth man's to do with as he pleases?"

"Quite right, Mordechai. But for the glory of God, my son, not our own, and with restraint," his father answered him, nodding affectionately. Soon they would find him a match, a girl from a wealthy, pious family who would be able to support him as he labored in the study halls to reach his full potential as an authority on Jewish law, a *posek,* who would help the Jewish people submit to God's will by answering the serious questions that arose in each generation on how to adapt modern life to the Torah's ancient, unchanging laws.

The soft winds of the Indian summer sent a leaf falling from the sky, which tangled in the thick curls of Rabbi Weiss's beard. Rose leaned over, plucking it out.

He smiled, taking it from her hand: "As it is written: 'And the dove came in to him in the evening; and lo, in her mouth was an olive leaf plucked off; so Noah knew that the waters were abated from off the earth.'"

"Do you know the whole Torah by heart, Tateh?" she asked in wonder and admiration.

"I know what I know, but not as much as I should know. Not as much as your brothers will know," he said with a proud look at his sons.

"I will also study the Torah and make you proud, Tateh," Rose whispered, leaning against him.

"You will make your parents proud in other ways, child." He chuckled affectionately.

"What ways?"

"You will be obedient and *frum,* and keep the laws stringently so that God will send you a great scholar for a husband, who you will work for and support, and in that way share his reward for all his Torah learning, and in that merit Hashem will grant you sons who will be great Torah scholars . . ."

"But I can also learn things myself, Tateh!"

"Then learn to listen and to be an *eshes chayil,* child, like your mother." He smiled, nodding at his wife, who smiled back. "That's all the *Rebono shel Olam* asks of you."

Pearl drank in her father's words, but Rose was troubled.

3

Williamsburg, Brooklyn, 1959

"Time to get up, *maidelehs*!"

Sunday mornings were always hardest. While the rest of New York slept on quietly through a two-day weekend, the day after the Sabbath was simply another tedious weekday for the Weiss family. Rose dressed quickly in her school clothes, the long-sleeved blue blouse and long pleated navy skirt, pulling the brush fiercely though her hip-length brown hair, which she then expertly braided. As she did every morning, she went into the kitchen and waited for her mother to outline her preschool chores.

"Go down to the grocery and get bread, milk, eggs, some butter . . . and maybe a little jam. Tell her to write it down."

Rose tensed.

"And hurry. You still need to help Pearl get dressed."

She lowered her eyes. "Yes, Mameh."

She walked reluctantly down the steps, dreading the lingering stare of the nasty woman behind the counter as she took out her little pad and penciled it in. Always, Rose worried if her parents had actually paid last month's bill or if this time the woman would shout at her, chasing her out in humiliation.

It would never have occurred to nine-year-old Rose to complain. Life was hard and full of things you didn't want to do but did anyway, whether because they were the right thing to do, or because there was no alternative. Her father set the example, rising before daybreak to purify himself in the cold waters of the ritual baths—winter or summer—before saying his morning prayers in the synagogue. Only then did he begin his long day's work as a bookkeeper at the yeshiva. Her brothers too spent long hours studying Talmud, while her mother not only took care of the house but worked part-time selling tablecloths and towels in a local shop. Even six-year-old Pearl struggled with the demands of her first-grade teacher, often sitting in the corner as punishment for talking too much or forgetting the words to the blessings. Even little Duvid was not wholly exempt, spending his mornings in endless recitations of the Hebrew letters in cheder.

Rose never considered her life harsh, having no inkling that other girls her age had indulgent mothers in white aprons tenderly combing their hair and making them breakfast. But even had she been aware such things existed, it would have seemed like a story in a book of fairy tales she'd once taken out of the local library, which—while tempting—were utterly foreign and forbidden, like delicious food displayed in the window of a nonkosher restaurant.

The streets of Williamsburg were quiet, the spring leaves abundant as they swayed above her in the warm wind of May. If she finished quickly enough, there was always the possibility of stopping off on the way home at the candy store to look at the magazines. *Life* and *Look* fascinated her most, with their full-page color photographs. Last week, Marilyn Monroe had been on the cover of *Life,* chewing on one diamond earring while the other dripped down from a frothy wave of platinum blond hair. There had been something disturbing to the girl about the way the woman's white teeth clamped together, something she couldn't quite explain to herself as her stomach went queasy with excitement. *Look* magazine had also had a woman on the cover, a brunette with painted red lips and blue eyes, her photo covered by circular bands of red, white, and blue next to the words "the case for the American woman." She'd stared at the photo, shifting the basket of groceries from hand to hand as the handles cut into her tender flesh.

Mr. Schwartz, the store owner, busy behind the counter serving scrambled eggs to Gentiles, was always kind to her, never yelling at her as he sometimes did to other kids, demanding they buy something or leave. Once, he had even given her a magazine for free. "They left it out in the rain, the morons. Here, take it."

Aside from several pages that had been stuck together, it had been perfectly wonderful. She kept it hidden beneath her mattress.

She lifted her legs, hurrying. But the line in the grocery was long. She would have to skip the candy store today, she realized, disappointed.

"You went to milk the cow?" her mother scolded when she got home. "Hurry and dress your sister! She won't have time to eat."

Pearl was still sleeping.

Rose tickled her nose, then pulled her arms up from under the blanket, shaking her gently into consciousness.

"No!" Pearl whined, burrowing back beneath the covers.

"Look, Pearl, be a *tzadakis* this morning, won't you? Don't make me late again. My teacher said the next time she will punish me. And your teacher will yell, too, remember?"

Pearl reluctantly sat up, biting her lips. She was afraid of her teacher, who liked to smash heavy rulers and pointed sticks against their desks to get their attention.

"Come, I'll help you."

She brushed the child's beautiful blond curls with pleasure, the way you would comb a doll's hair, thinking how she preferred Marilyn to the all-American woman. Even though Pearl had not only gotten the hair but the large, clear blue eyes that ran in her *tateh*'s family, while she'd gotten stuck with her mother's rich, dark brown in both, she was not envious. Female physical beauty was not a quality her family or her culture lauded or prized. In fact, a really beautiful girl was considered flashy and somewhat immodest, calling undue attention to herself. Her sister's face was too pretty and angelic, a perfect oval with perfect small lips and a tiny nose. She herself looked decidedly plainer, with her narrow cheekbones, large, full lips, and very Jewish nose. But her eyes, despite their color, were beautiful, too, she realized: sparkling dark ovals that thankfully called attention away from the other, less wonderful elements of her face. They were the first thing anyone noticed about her.

"No tights!" Pearl complained, wriggling away. "It will be hot!"

At least three times a week, if not more, they had this fight. Ever since Pearl had turned six and started school, her parents decided the stringent laws of modesty should be applied to her as well. But sometimes, Rose knew, if Pearl threw an especially tiresome tantrum, her mother would give in and allow her to wear socks like many of the other girls in her class, whose parents were less meticulous about the laws of modesty for little girls. Tired and rushed, Rose gave in, helping her on with her socks, then helping her to lace up her shoes.

Their mother, who usually had more patience, noticed immediately. "What's this? Go put on tights and don't you dare open your mouth to say another word back to me!"

Duvid was sick, again. He had kept her up all night. The child lived on antibiotics. On top of that, Rebbitzin Weiss had an appointment with her gynecologist to take a test that would ascertain if the last few days of throwing up was a flu she had caught from her son, or something she had gotten from her husband. Not being allowed to use birth control because of religious stringencies, she was never quite sure. The "blessing" of pregnancy always hovered over her, and would until the change of life made it impossible.

Without a word, Rose dragged her sister back into the bedroom, pulling off the socks and pulling the tights up forcibly around her waist, Pearl all the while struggling against her with all her might.

"Stop it already, Pearl!" she demanded, wiping the beaded sweat from her forehead.

"Come eat already. You'll both be late," their mother called from the kitchen.

"Mameh?" Rose said reluctantly.

"What now?" said her mother.

"The teacher says we have to bring in a quarter to school today."

"A quarter? For *vus*?"

"I don't know. The teacher said."

Reluctantly, her mother opened her purse, digging into her change.

"If the teacher said . . ."

The institution of school had its own sacredness and authority that her parents never questioned. Still, she knew her mother never liked to part with money, and she felt unhappy in making such a demand, even if it was only a quarter. She placed the money carefully in her pocket.

Pearl complained all the way to school, dragging her feet as Rose tried to hurry her along.

"It's too hot in tights! Why did you get a quarter and not me?"

"Because the teacher said. And if you stop complaining, I'll play a game with you."

"What?"

"I'll pick a color, and you and I will think of all the things that are that color. And if you can think of more things, then you'll win."

"What color?"

"Well, what about blue?"

"No, no," the child complained. "White. White is better."

"All right then. White."

"A wedding dress. Now it's your turn."

"Clouds."

"Frosting on a wedding cake."

"Cotton."

"Wedding shoes."

"Pearl, can you think of something that doesn't have to do with weddings?" Ever since their brother Abraham had gotten married the year before, Pearl had been enraptured, talking of little else.

"For *vus*? Don't you want to be a bride, Rose?"

For some strange reason, the question sent a chill down Rose's spine. To her, her sister-in-law Gitel had seemed like a doll, all dressed up in silly clothes and led from place to place, first by her parents and then by her groom. She hadn't even been allowed to dance. They put her in a special chair, and there she sat, her elbows resting on the arms, a silly smile pasted on her too-rouged face, while all the women and girls danced rings around her and brought her cups of cold water as they fanned her sweating brow. What was fun about that?

Rose didn't answer, kissing her sister's hot, sweating forehead with compassion before reluctantly leaving her at the entrance to her classroom and to the mercies of Mrs. Abramov, who stood waiting with a large wooden ruler tapping against her palm. While boys were regularly hit by their rebbes, the girls seldom were. Still, the noise of a ruler smashed against the old wooden desks was shattering. It was too bad she had missed out on having Mrs. Geller for her teacher, a beautiful young rebbitzin with sparkling dark eyes and a lovely smile who had not been teaching long enough to have lost her enthusiasm and patience.

It made her sad to see Pearl so unhappy. But what could she do? Even with Mrs. Geller, the child would have had problems. She had no self-discipline. Her teacher sent home notes complaining at least twice a month that she talked nonstop to her friends and spent the rest of the time daydreaming. Talking-tos followed, and even a rare and occasional spanking, but they seemed to have no effect upon her at all. She was irrepressible, Rose thought with a reluctant kind of admiration as she hurried up the cracked steps of the old stone building to her own classroom before the late bell sounded.

Like most parochial-school buildings in Williamsburg, theirs was a converted apartment house. Old, scuffed chairs and desks filled the tiny former bedrooms and living rooms. There were no lockers in which to store the heavy books that had to be dragged to and from home each day. There was no gym, no auditorium, no cooking class—nothing but blackboards and chalk. There weren't even decorations on the walls: no snowflakes for winter or pumpkins for fall, just bare expanses painted an ugly, institutional green that set her teeth on edge.

While she enjoyed the morning classes in Torah and Jewish law taught by pious rabbis or their learned wives—women in dark wigs and hats and calf-length skirts and opaque stockings—she nevertheless fingered the quarter in her pocket, anxiously waiting for Miss Fischer's afternoon English class.

She was entranced by Miss Fischer, who taught goyim in the mornings at PS 68. She was so young and pretty and wore red lipstick and high heels and did not cover her blond hair with anything at all. Rose loved the assignments she gave out to read stories and to write about them. It didn't even feel like homework but like something she would happily do for fun. Miss Fischer was also a smiler, which the rabbis' wives were not. She had beautiful white American teeth.

"Girls, please be seated. I hope you've all brought your quarter?" Miss Fischer said.

The fortunate ones nodded eagerly, while the others hung back in their seats trying to avoid eye contact.

"Good. Now I have a surprise for you. Mr. White from the Dime Savings Bank of Williamsburg is here to speak with you about a subject that is so very important to your future that even your rabbis agreed he could come in and take up some class time. So please, be on your very best behavior and listen."

They stared at the smoothly shaven, bare-headed Gentile in his seersucker suit as they would have a tribesman from Zululand.

"Hello, my name is Dan," he said, his smile wide, as if he had heard a good joke. It was not returned. He continued smiling, not knowing what else to do in front of a class of foreign-looking, unsmiling little girls. "How many of you have ever been to a bank with your mom and dad?" he asked.

Unsure they were allowed to speak to such a person at all, the girls lowered their eyes. Besides, none of them had either a "mom" or a "dad," and their *mamehs* and *tatehs* were wont to keep money in bills in shoe boxes or under the mattress.

He shifted uneasily. "What? No one? Well, I never . . ." He chuckled awkwardly. "Well, it's like this, see. You earn money, or maybe your parents or relatives give it to you, what's the best thing to do with it?"

Someone finally raised her hand. "Buy something?" she said.

"You could do that," he replied, smiling but shaking his head, his face clearly indicating she'd gotten the answer wrong. "Let's say you've got a dollar for your birthday. You could go to the candy store and fill up a brown paper bag with penny candy . . ."

The girls suddenly smiled and nodded.

"Whoah! I say 'could.' But what will you have the next day if you do?"

They looked at each other in surprise. Who ever thought about the next day when you had a dollar in your hand and a candy store around the corner?

"I'll tell you what! Bad teeth and a tummy ache!"

This was certainly true and no laughing matter. But since their teacher, Miss Fischer, laughed, the girls allowed themselves confused smiles.

"But if you put that money in the bank, the bank will add more money to it, so that you'll have more than a dollar. And if you keep adding all the money you can to that amount, then one day, well, sir, you'll have enough to purchase anything you want. A bicycle, a new television set . . ."

The girls looked at each other in amazement at this startling information. Did the ownership of such things depend merely on having the money to buy them? Or did you need to be a wholly different person, living a totally different life? The boys had bicycles, but the girls? As for television sets, they were unheard of in religious homes.

As they turned their appalled faces to him, it was his turn to be confused. "Well, maybe not those things, but something else, see? You decide what it is you want, see . . . ?" He coughed. "I understand your teacher told you each to bring in a quarter today? Well, we at the Dime Savings Bank of Williamsburg are going to open bank accounts for each of you with that money! We'll give each one of you a little book and write it down. And then we are going to give you each, absolutely free, another quarter, so that each of you will have fifty cents in your account! Every week, your parents are going to give you another quarter, which you'll bring to school, and someone from the bank will be here to collect your money and write it down in your passbook. If you keep adding, then when you get to five dollars, we are also going to give you this valuable gift, absolutely free."

He reached into a bag, pulling out a box about six inches wide and six inches thick, painted black. The sighs of disappointment were audible. "It's a brand-new Kodak box camera!" he explained. "You look in this end, and when you press this button, you can take a picture!"

Rose felt her whole body tingle. Photos, like those in the magazines, she thought, feeling herself fill with excitement.

"How many of you have one of these at home? Or maybe your dad or mom has one?"

Even those who did have cameras at home were reluctant to admit it. Frivolous modern luxuries were considered a moral stain and being well-off a sign of impiety. After all, the men looked up to and admired in their world were scholars who had deliberately chosen to live in poverty in order to spend their time increasing their Torah knowledge so as to better understand and fulfill God's will and inform others how they might do the same.

"No? Well, then, you can be the first one in your family. Now, won't that be swell?"

It took Rose two months to reach five dollars with the reluctant weekly quarter she got from her parents, supplemented by occasional babysitting money from the neighbors. She was given a coupon and told to take it to the bank. Even though it was around the corner from her school, she had never been inside. It was cavernous and dreamlike, with Greek columns and vast swathes of cold, rich marble on the walls and floors. When she picked up her camera, she found that something of the bank's cold majesty had seeped into the little box, making it seem like an artifact from another world, a world of men in light summer suits and straw hats, pretty blondes like Marilyn chewing on earrings with lipstick-smeared lips, a world parallel to their world of dark bearded men in black coats and skullcaps and scrubbed-faced women with dark wigs low on their foreheads. It was another dimension, hovering just above their own, unseen, impenetrable. And now this thing had fallen into her hands as though through some unfathomable crack, linking her to a vast and unknown universe.

It was thrilling.

She held it tightly in her hands, running home in excitement.

"Mameh, look!"

"Vus is dus?" Her mother eyed it suspiciously.

"A camera. From the Dime Savings Bank of Williamsburg. It's free."

"Free?" Her mother arched her brows suspiciously, contemptuously, looking it over.

"If you have five dollars in your bank account."

"You have already five dollars?" Her mother's stern face melted into a grin, impressed. "Tateh, you hear that? Already Rose has a bank account, *nuch,* with five dollars!"

"'She saved for the purchase of a field and bought it, and she planted a vineyard from the work of her hands,'" her father quoted, smiling, coming into the kitchen. "My little *eshes chayil!*" He beamed at her.

She blushed with delight.

"And you know how to use it?" he asked her.

"There is a book, with instructions."

He patted her head.

"A lucky, pious yeshiva student will one day have a wonderful wife, eh, Mameh?" he said, stroking Rose's head.

Her heart overflowed with joy.

"This is true," her mother answered. "A girl who knows how to put one penny next to the other so her husband can sit and learn without worrying about supporting a family is a treasure."

"Let me take your picture, Mameh!"

"What, is this a wedding?" she blustered, patting down her wig and taking off her apron.

"With Tateh!" Rose begged.

He backed off, waving his hands. "No, no. It's *bitul Torah,* a waste of time."

"Come, Tateh. It takes a minute!" Her mother suddenly urged him with uncharacteristic insistence.

He reluctantly stood beside her, careful not to touch her, squeezing his beard in his hand to smooth it down. "Wait!" He went to the closet and took out his large black hat, placing it carefully over his skullcap. "Now!" he ordered. "*Nu,* Mameh. Give a smile!"

She glanced at him, a rare smile lighting up her careworn face.

As Rose looked through her lens, she saw for the first time as if by magic that otherwise invisible bond connecting them.

"Smile!" she said, and the word made her smile as well as she pressed her finger on the button.

But when the picture was printed, the results were disappointing, the photo of her parents dark and blurry, their features almost indiscernible, nothing like she remembered. Still, long after her parents were no longer speaking to her and her own home was already filled with hundreds of the thousands of photos she was destined to take, she kept that one in a special box, treasuring it.

4

Williamsburg, Brooklyn, September 1963

"But who will take me to school in the morning now?"

"Don't be a baby, Pearl! When I was your age, I not only went by myself, I walked you to school! Behave yourself and in three years, you'll also be going with me to Bais Yaakov High School."

"You'll be married by then." Pearl sulked.

"I have no plans like that, believe me. But At Bais Yaakov, they only take the good girls, the ones with the best reputations," Rose warned her. "So you'll have to start behaving yourself, stop rolling up your skirts and wearing bobby socks instead of tights. You'll have to listen to Mameh and Tateh and not talk back to your teachers . . ."

Pearl bit her lip, staring at her sister resentfully. "Like you never do anything wrong."

"What do you mean?"

"I know about the magazines. The ones you keep under the mattress."

Rose inhaled. "You little snoop! I'm not ashamed. There's nothing wrong with them!"

Pearl gave her a shrewd sidelong glance. "So why do you hide them, and only look at them at night with a flashlight, under the covers?"

"Because Mameh and Tateh don't understand about magazines."

Pearl sat down on Rose's bed. "What do you like so much about them, Rose?"

She sat down beside her sister, her eyes looking into the distance, far above Pearl's head. "I don't know. They tell me about things."

"What things?"

"Things! Things that happen to people. Things people do. Places they go to. People that are not like us."

"Goyim?"

"Don't use that word. It makes you sound stupid."

"Mameh and Tateh use it all the time. Are you calling *them* stupid?"

"NO, no. Of course not. Just, they came from Europe; they went through the war. The Gentiles killed their families."

"*Our* family."

"Of course. But Americans gave their lives to stop the Nazis. They liberated the camps . . ."

Pearl began to fidget. "Why can't you still take me to school, Rose?"

"Because—for the millionth time—I have to catch a bus in the opposite direction." Rose reached across to her sister, wiping Pearl's tears away with her thumb. "Why don't you want to go by yourself? Is there something you're not telling me?"

She shook her head.

"I'll talk to Mameh. Maybe she can walk you some mornings."

"She won't!"

They both knew that was true. Mameh had better things to do. Her youngest in school, she was now working full-time as a saleswoman in a bakery. She worked hard and expected the same from her family. She did not believe in spoiling her children by giving into their whims. Besides, the streets of Williamsburg were considered extremely safe and it was not a long walk.

No one would have suspected what lay behind Pearl's insistence. Only a few months before, while she was playing alone in front of the house as everyone was busy with Passover cleaning, a strange man in a pious beard and a black hat like her father's had tried to talk to her and give her a candy, and when she refused, he'd reached out and held her tightly by the shoulder, pushing her into the alleyway. Mrs. Schultz suddenly sticking her head out of the window as she beat the dust from her pillows had made him turn around sharply and disappear. Pearl, convinced it was her own fault for insisting on playing outside while everyone else was involved in the mitzvah of preparing for the holiday, said nothing to anyone.

"Why don't you walk with friends, Pearl?"

"What friends?"

"Malki, Shulamit . . ." They lived on the same street.

"They don't like me . . . they say . . ."

"What? What do they say?"

"That I don't daven with enough *kavanah*."

Rose looked at her solemnly. This was a serious accusation. "Is it true? Do you not mean the words you say when you pray?"

"I pray with all my heart! But I always finish before they do because I know the prayers by heart and my Hebrew is better than theirs . . ."

"Then they're just jealous. So make different friends. There are always new girls that need friends."

Pearl thought about it, wiping her eyes, feeling a little more hopeful. "Can you walk me once a week? I promise to get up really early!"

She shook her head firmly. "No, Pearl. I just can't. You are just going to have to get used to doing without me."

Pearl watched in bitter silence as Rose excitedly dressed in her new school uniform for her first day in high school. She looked older, prettier, Pearl thought jealously. Almost like a *kallah moide*.

"Let me see my Bais Yaakov girl," Mameh said, opening the unlocked door to their bedroom without knocking and walking in as she always did. "*Shaine, shaine. A shaine maideleh,*" she said approvingly, impressed. "You ironed everything."

"Yesterday already, Mameh."

"Very good! You see your sister, Pearl, how she takes care of herself? God bless you! Make us proud, as you always do."

"Yes, Mameh," Rose answered, bending her head to accept her mother's kiss of benediction on her forehead.

Bracha Weiss turned her attention to her younger daughter. "Put away the toys and make your bed, Pearl. Honestly. What is going to be with this child?" She looked up in exasperation, appealing to the heavens.

"I can't walk to school myself!" Pearl suddenly insisted. "I want you should walk with me."

"What? Every day it's another *mishagas* with you!" her mother said, shaking her head.

"She says she's afraid, Mameh," Rose interjected.

"From *vus* is there to be afraid in Williamsburg?" their mother scoffed.

"Bad men. Jews," Pearl finally blurted out.

"What a thing to say, Pearl! There are no bad Jews here. Only God-fearing men like your *tateh* . . ." she insisted. "That is why your *tateh* and I chose to live here, and not on the outskirts of Borough Park with the Italians and the *schvartzes* and Puerto Ricans."

"Please, Rose, please, you take me!" She sounded desperate.

Rose sympathized, but there was nothing to be done. She shook her head no.

Pearl stared at her with daggers in her welling eyes.

"Good-bye, Pearl. You'll find some friends to walk with. You'll be all right," she said, her heart uneasy, avoiding her sister's face. "Good-bye, Mameh."

The walk to the bus stop alone took Rose twenty minutes. It was in the opposite direction from her and Pearl's old school, in an area of barbershops and hardware stores, an area not all that familiar to her. But she sympathized with Pearl.

She too had fears about traveling on a city bus all by herself twice a day, a bus filled with every kind of stranger. But when she boarded, her fears dissipated. In fact, for the first time in her short life, she felt a heady sense of freedom. She was on the cusp of something new, strange, and potentially wonderful, she felt, a sudden, unexpected surge of adventurousness sweeping through her, heightening all her senses. She was alone but in the largest, most interesting city in the world. High school, she hoped, would be different from grade school, larger, more open to the world.

Little did she realize on that first journey into adulthood how fully her wish would be granted, and with what unimaginable consequences.

5

∞

Williamsburg, Brooklyn, 1964

The first year of high school passed quickly. At first, Rose was overwhelmed by the amount of work, but then things began to lighten, the Hebrew verses becoming rote, English and math and science—always her best subjects—bringing to her attention fascinating new areas for her to explore on her own in the library. She became part of the life of her class, an integral, well-accepted member who traipsed with them to collect charity and visited Orthodox Jewish old-age homes to bring cheer to the elderly every Friday afternoon.

The only thing she stubbornly resisted was joining the collective dreams of her peers concerning marriage and motherhood. She could not even explain to herself why, simply imagining it was too early to think about such things. But had she been brave enough to dive down and explore her feelings in depth, she would have had to face the shocking fact that not a single woman in her family or her community embodied the kind of life she envisioned for herself, a life whose outlines were still shrouded in mystery, blurry and indistinct. The rapidity with which that fog lifted, everything coming suddenly into focus, was as breathtaking as it was unexpected.

It began on the first day of her sophomore year, when a transforming new element entered her sheltered and settled life in the person of Michelle "Miriam" Goldband, who landed in her classroom like a tropical bird fallen out of the sky. That which her Bais Yaakov classmates found most shocking and which for them explained almost everything that was strange and wrong about her could be summed up by the startling fact that she was French. Even in a school uniform, she managed to arouse attention and inspire envy by wearing shiny patent-leather shoes with a small heel. While she spoke a number of languages, including Yiddish, she claimed that the Yiddish spoken in America was incomprehensible to her. *"Gai close da vindow,"* for example, or, *"Was hut der mama gemacht fur lunch?"*

As time went by, troubling rumors began to spread. Michelle's father was a beardless professor of French at Brooklyn College who did not attend any of the neighborhood synagogues. Her mother had been seen without a head covering over her flashy blond curls. Why the school had accepted her at all remained a mystery to the girls and their disgruntled parents, the key to which lay with Rabbi Mischkin, the school's undisputed spiritual authority, who had sole discretion in such matters.

While he never said so out loud, it was clear to all that Rabbi Mischkin was reaching out to the Goldbands, whose misguided insistence on living among them had now put the entire community's well-being at risk, unless they could be gently steered into the fold. By accepting Michelle, rabbinical authorities would now be able to exert some influence over the family's behavior by holding expulsion over their heads. As long as there existed a possibility of converting them to the true way, shunning them and thus allowing them to float subversively unmoored thus influencing the pious good people around them with their French ways, was simply unacceptable.

The girl fascinated Rose. So when Mrs. Kornblum, their teacher, asked for volunteers to help tutor the new immigrant from Marseille, Rose eagerly raised her hand. She was the only one. The teacher quickly changed her seat to the one next to Michelle's.

Rose found herself studying the girl for hours, examining everything from the little pieces of jewelry she wore around her neck and on her slim wrists to the exquisite perfection of her hair, plaited intricately from the top of her head. And while the other girls complained they could hardly under-stand a word she said, Rose drank in her accent, enamored by the almost musical way she lingered over some vowels and swallowed others. Often, in secret, she would attempt to imitate the way the girl's mouth puckered as she formed the words, as if getting ready to be kissed.

After school hours, Rose eagerly accepted the task of going to Michelle's home to help her with homework. Before long, she even arranged to pick Michelle up on the Sabbath and accompany her to the synagogue, although it was a long walk from her own neighborhood and meant she could spend no time with her old friends.

"She's not one of us," her mother grumbled. "Aren't they Sephardim?"

"Rabbi Mischkin is a great scholar and a great *tzadik*," Rabbi Weiss said decisively, ending the discussion. But inwardly, he decided the school was going downhill and they'd have to find Rose another one. But in the mean-time, they could hardly forbid her from volunteering to help instill Torah values in a new immigrant, especially since it was the teacher's idea. Again, "the teacher said" held its magical sway over them, and Rose, to her delight, found herself at Michelle's house several times a week.

She lived on the outskirts of Williamsburg in a rare brownstone that stood out like a pretty woman among the drab gray and dirty white apartment houses and tenements. Instead of the cramped, boxy railroad flats most people lived in, the Goldbands had a separate room just for formal meals, which had a large, elaborate table and a huge china closet filled with silver ritual objects. Even more amazing, they had a room they called a library, which was filled entirely with bookshelves containing hundreds of vol-umes in English, Hebrew, and French. It was there they worked on their homework.

"*Vous êtes charmante*," Michelle's father said the first time Rose met him, extending his hand to her for a forbidden touch. He wore a tiny skullcap and a tweed sweater with leather elbow patches. He was clean-shaven and smoked a pipe.

Rose blushed furiously, not knowing what to do. What was he doing home anyway? she wondered. At this time of day, all the other men in the neighborhood who didn't work full-time were in *kollel* or at the synagogue reciting their afternoon prayers.

"*Non, papa,*" Michelle warned him, shaking her head. "It is forbidden for girls to touch a man except a father or brother."

"Ah, I forget. Forgive me, *mademoiselle* Rose." He smiled charmingly, putting his hand inside his trouser pocket. "Well, *vas-y, vas-y,* enjoy your studies."

He soon disappeared, replaced by Mrs. Goldband, who brought a silver tray of éclairs filled with freshly whipped cream and a crystal decanter of lemonade.

"No, thank you." Rose shook her head dutifully, having been forbidden by her parents to eat anything at Michelle's home. As outsiders and newly religious, the Goldbands were not to be trusted as far as their observance of the strict laws of kashrut were concerned.

Mrs. Goldband raised her eyebrows. "It is kosher. I assure you."

She seemed hurt, Rose thought. And wasn't it a worse sin to hurt someone's feelings and embarrass them? Confused, her loyalties stretched and tested, she resisted for several more seconds before eagerly succumbing, reaching out and devouring one.

It was the most delicious thing she had ever tasted.

"Good?" Mrs. Goldband asked, smiling.

"It's amazing!" Rose exclaimed sincerely. Michelle's mother nodded, satisfied, closing the door behind her.

"Take another!" Michelle urged her. But Rose was already feeling guilty she had eaten even one, wondering if God would punish her for her weakness of character or reward her for her sensitivity to the feelings of others.

Doing God's will was never absolutely clear to her, the way it was to others. For who could read God's mind, especially when His commandments sometimes seemed at odds with each other? She would compensate by performing another mitzvah, she thought, opening her book and patiently explaining the Torah lessons and the laws of the High Holidays to Michelle.

"For everything, there is a law," Michelle complained, interrupting her. "A right way and a wrong way. *C'est compliqué!*"

Was it? Rose wondered. Complicated? What other way was there to live, after all?

Michelle rose, stretching her coltish limbs and picking up the empty decanter. "I'm going to get some more juice. Do you want to come with me?"

Faced with the prospect of facing Mrs. Goldband yet again, and thus an unknown cornucopia of other forbidden delights, she declined.

"I'll stay here and wait for you."

Rose wandered around the room, exploring the bookshelves. At first, they didn't seem to be arranged in any kind of order, but slowly she saw a pattern as she pulled them off the shelves for a quick look, hurriedly replacing them. In one section there were novels in French by Balzac, Camus, Stendhal, and Colette, while in another novels in English by D. H. Lawrence, E. M. Forster, and Virginia Woolf. There were dictionaries and thesauruses in several different languages. There were books about art: Chagall, Monet, Manet, Degas. And right next to them were the photography books: Henri Cartier-Bresson, Brassaï, Robert Capa.

One with an especially striking cover caught her interest, Doisneau, the desire to leaf through it irresistible. She sat with it, cross-legged on the carpet, her skirt riding up barely covering her knees, as she slowly turned the pages, lost in the wartime streets of Paris. She followed the eyes of people in a crowd looking upward, their faces filled with fear, wonder, tension. What were they looking at? she wondered. And there was a face peering over the dark glass of a door front, the expression hostile, guarded. Why? A courtyard was littered with paper pamphlets, almost like snow. What did they say? Why had they been thrown? What did it mean? Each photo aroused her imagination. They were like pages torn out from the middle of a book, containing only a tantalizing hint of a life, a time, a place, a story. They made you wish you could enter and live there and explore until you cracked open the mystery like a walnut, getting at its meaty heart.

"Ah, *excusez-moi*. You are still here." Mr. Goldband walked in, smiling as he looked her up and down. "I just need to get something." He reached up and pulled down a book.

She jumped up, blushing, smoothing down her skirt, suddenly conscious of her exposed legs. "I'm waiting for Michelle," she stammered.

He was a young man, she thought. At least, much younger than her own father. Or perhaps his smooth, clean-shaven face simply made him seem so. He had high cheekbones and a wide forehead that reminded her of Clark Gable.

"It's okay, okay, I don't bite." He smiled. The skin around his blue eyes crinkled dashingly. "What are you looking at? Ah, Doisneau!" He pronounced it "dwa-no." "He interests you?"

She nodded almost painfully, her face reddening further. "I hope it's all right. I once had a camera." She had long ago put it away, disappointed and embarrassed by the disparity between her vision and the results she'd achieved. "But the pictures weren't any good. Not like this."

"What kind of camera?"

"A Kodak box camera. I got it from . . . from the Dimes Saving Bank . . ." she stammered, feeling young and foolish.

"Of course Doisneau's photos are better than yours! You didn't have any control! Your camera was a toy. The lens was made of plastic. You couldn't control the exposure . . ."

She looked up, confused.

"I mean, how much light strikes the film," he explained patiently. "You could not focus it. You could not choose to make one part of the picture sharper than another. So unless the person or thing just happened to be in exactly the right spot . . ."

"Everything came out blurry."

"*Exactement!* There are a lot of reasons. Perhaps you did not hold it steady. Or perhaps the people moved, or your film was too slow."

"The people were dark."

"Because it was too dark, and you could not compensate for that with your cheap camera. Doisneau had a Zeiss-Contax or a Leica. Ansel Adams said he preferred the Contax to the Leica. But either one will let you control how much light comes in by opening or closing the shutter . . ."

"The shutter?" she asked, forgetting her shyness, forgetting she was speaking to a handsome adult man, the father of her friend, lost in fascination and curiosity.

"Patience. I'll explain everything."

"Nothing looked like I thought it would."

He smiled, nodding. "Ansel Adams stressed a photographer has to visualize in his mind what he wants the photo to look like before he presses the shutter release. You have to find a new way of seeing. You have to see what is in front of you with a frame around it. Here, look at this." He opened the closet and carefully took a camera out of a box. "Careful now. It's a Contax Three. Slowly, *doucement*. Now, look through this. What do you see?"

She held it up to her eye. All she saw was Mr. Goldband's midsection, and the books behind him. Quickly, she lowered it.

"Not a pretty picture, my stomach, eh?" he laughed. Slowly, he walked around behind her. Putting his arms lightly around her shoulders, his chin just above her head, he enfolded her hands in his, helping her to position the camera in front of her eyes. Slowly, his chest touching her back, he turned her toward the window.

"*Voilà!* Look out into the street, into life. Find something that fascinates you, that tells a story. After that, you will worry about how much light strikes the film. You see this?" He pointed with his forefinger at a small black dial. "This is the aperture. Think of it like . . . say . . . the pupil of your eye. It gets very small in the sunlight, no? And opens wide in a dark room."

She felt her body growing warm and strange, the touch of his arms electric.

"This is the aperture, like window blinds that open and close. You decide how wide with these numbers here. The larger the number, the smaller the opening. Then, there is the shutter speed. That you set over here, on this dial. The two means a half a second. A very long time. That is how fast the curtain is opening and closing."

She nodded now, almost faint as his warm breath caressed her cheek.

"Now, the focus."

She felt his fingers touch hers insistently but gently.

"Turn this wheel on top. In the center you'll see the two images overlap; that means it's perfectly in focus."

She fingered the camera, her grip tightening beneath his hands. "How much does a camera like this cost?"

"Oh, that is the question!" He smiled, suddenly dropping his hands to his sides "Two hundred dollars."

The relief of being set free was offset by this disappointing news. Her heart fell. He might as well have said a million.

"But you don't need this camera, Rose! May I call you Rose?" he said tenderly.

She nodded, everything about him electric and sharply in focus.

"You can get a Kodak Argus for . . . fifty dollars. If you learn to use a light meter, to take your photos outdoors, and are not in a rush to use a flash it will be more than adequate."

"Can you show me how to use a meter?" she asked, shocked at her own boldness.

Before he could answer, the door opened.

She watched him put his hands hurriedly into his pockets and take a step back, increasing the distance between them, and the movement made her feel suddenly ashamed, as if she had something to hide.

"I am showing your friend how to use a camera, Michelle. Are you also interested?"

"No, Papa."

"Michelle likes paint and brushes, *n'est-ce pas, ma petite*?" He smiled, smoothing down her hair. "Well, I am off to work, girls. But when you come again, I am happy to talk to you more about photography, Rose."

She cleared her throat. "Thank you very much, Mr. Goldband."

"And if you want to borrow the book about Doisneau, please, take it home."

"Really?" She was thrilled.

"Of course!"

She brought it home that evening in her school bag, standing on a chair to hide it behind her extra blankets, high on her closet shelf.

"What's that, Rose?" Pearl asked.

Rose took a breath. The entire experience of the afternoon welled up inside her with all its dangerous and thrilling complications. She felt slightly feverish and sickened, filled with the kind of energy that demands some kind of release. "None of your business, Pearl!" she shouted.

Her sister's face screwed up in resentment and insult.

"It's a book from Michelle . . . her father's . . . library. I borrowed it. It has pictures of Paris."

"*Vus is dus?*"

"It's a city, far away, on the other side of the ocean."

"I also want to see the pictures!"

"This is not for you! You might ruin it!"

"I won't! Why do you treat me like a child! I'm going to be bat mitzvah soon!"

Rose hesitated, suddenly feeling sorry for her sister, wanting to include her. "But you can't tell anyone about it, Mameh or Tateh. You promise?"

Pearl picked up on her sister's uneasiness with that peculiar radar that exists between siblings who live together closely and have scores to settle. "Why not? What's wrong with it?"

"Did I say anything was wrong with it? There is nothing wrong with it.

Nothing. Just . . ." She hesitated. "There are some things that Tateh and Mameh wouldn't like you to see."

"And they like you to see?" she answered shrewdly.

"I'm older than you, Pearl."

"'The beginning of sin is sweet, but its end is bitter,'" Pearl said, repeating their father's mantra. "That is true for you, too. For everyone."

"Why do you think this is a sin?"

"Why are you afraid of Mameh and Tateh finding out?"

"I'm not afraid!"

"Yes, you are! You're trembling!"

Rose looked at her hands. The child was right. She lowered her voice to a whisper.

"All right, all right. You can take a look, but not by yourself. I'll show them to you."

Rose took down the book, sitting down on the bed next to her sister.

Pearl stared at the cover. Men in bathing suits, naked to the waist, were jumping off a bridge into the water. In the background was the Eiffel Tower.

"They are naked! NAKED MEN!" she shouted.

"Lower your voice!"

But it was too late.

"What's this I heard?" Their mother rushed in.

Rose tried to move the book under the bedcovers, but her mother's eye was too quick for her.

"*Vus is dus?* Rose, you give that to me RIGHT NOW!"

"It's just a book of photographs, Mameh!" Rose said defiantly, holding the book behind her back, shielding it with her body.

"Are you speaking to me with disrespect?" her mother asked, flabbergasted at such behavior in her obedient Rose. "Give it here!"

Her heart sinking, Rose handed it over.

Her mother sat down on the edge of the bed, flipping the pages slowly, as Rose moved away, standing by the door watching her, trying to imagine from her expression what she was looking at: The charming photos of laughing children holding on to each other as they crossed a busy Parisian street? Snow-covered statues in the park? Or a man and woman passionately kissing? A photo of underwear in a store window? The photo of a woman staring at the painting of a nude in an art gallery?

Rebbitzin Weiss slammed the book shut.

"Mameh!"

"I'll talk to you later. First, I must talk to Tateh."

"Mameh, please don't show it to him!" she wanted to wail, begging her mother for mercy for the first time in her life. But she couldn't bring herself to utter the words. Besides, what good would it do? Her parents were one person.

"ROSE!" her father called.

She stood up stiffly, walking into the living room as one walks to the guillotine.

Her parents were sitting side by side at the table, the place where usually her father's large Talmud lay taken up by Mr. Goldband's book.

"Sit down!"

She pulled back a chair. Her knuckles were white.

"Where did you get this filth?"

"I . . . borrowed it. From the Goldbands' library."

"This is the kind of book these people have in their house?" her father thundered.

"Tateh, they didn't give it to me. I chose it. You remember, I had a camera once. I was interested. I didn't see all the photos, just a few. They were wonderful. . . . Then, he said I could take it home if I wanted. It's not his fault. He was very kind." Too late she realized that Michelle's father should not have been mentioned at all. But she had never before had reason to lie, and too late she recognized that she suddenly did.

"You spoke to your friend's father? Alone?"

"Just for a minute, Tateh! Michelle went to the kitchen to get water, and I waited for her in the library. Her father came in to get a book and saw me reading this . . ."

"You are forbidden to go back to that house, do you understand?"

"But Tateh, who will help Michelle?"

"You are forbidden! End of discussion."

"But how will I return this to Mr. Goldband?"

"I will make sure the school returns it to Mr. Goldband."

She felt a chill go up her spine.

"Tateh, no!"

"You are forbidden to go back to that school, understand?"

"But where else can I go?"

"You will stay at home until we find another school. A more suitable school. Now go to your room!"

She ran to her room. Fully clothed, she pulled the covers over her head.

"Rose, what happened? What happened, Rose?" Pearl shook her, trying to pull down the covers. Without looking up, she smacked the child's hands away viciously.

"Leave me alone, you brat! You've ruined my life."

Pearl howled, but Rose could not hear her over the sound of her own heartbroken sobbing as she felt her life shatter into a million painful, wounding shards.

6

It was, Rose thought as she sat in the living room surrounded by her parents, older brothers, grandmother, aunts, uncles, and older cousins, like the biblical ordeal ordained for the *sotah,* a woman accused without proof by her jealous husband of committing adultery. When she was dragged to the Holy Temple, the priests would undo her hair and publicly demand answers to horrible and embarrassing questions about her character, her behavior, and her sins. The punishment for lying was a terrible death, one worse than stoning or hanging, your body simply dissolving into a painful and putrid waste.

Mute with fright and confusion, her eyes darted from one accuser to the next as she was pelted with questions that bounced painfully off her heart like sharp little rocks.

How many other forbidden books did she have hidden in her bedroom?
Did the Goldbands eat food without the proper rabbinical hechsher?
Did they eat pork?
How many other books had Mr. Goldband forced on her?
Did Miriam Goldband eat in nonkosher pizza parlors?
Did Miriam Goldband secretly meet boys?

What did she know about Miriam Goldband? About Miriam Gold-band's mother?

And, last but not least, the questions that made her heart stop: What was her relationship with Mr. Goldband? Had he ever tried to touch her?

Had he? She wondered. Tried? Was that what it was, his hands over hers on the camera, the way he stepped back suddenly when Michelle returned?

She shuddered, large sobs finally breaking from her silent lips, her slight, girlish shoulders heaving, her chest rising and falling, bringing the family council to a frustrating and premature end and the consensus that the task at hand was beyond their powers. The proper rabbinical authority needed to be consulted. The Honored Rav would certainly get answers out of her that they could not. And if not, at the very least he would remove the crippling burden from their shoulders of deciding what was to be done next. This alone, it was decided, was worth the shame of involving him.

In the hours that followed, Rose lay awake in her bed, her body trembling as the cold, dark hours of night swept over her in terrifying waves, her imagination conjuring up worst-case scenarios. Had she, without knowing or willing it, done something sinful and shameful? Would she now be sent abroad to the Gateshead girl's boarding school in England, where they reportedly watched your every move and you had hardly any contact with your family? It had been rumored that a girl found smoking cigarettes in the park with a boy had merited that punishment. Married off at seventeen to an English Hassid, she had never been heard of again. What will happen to me? she agonized, until her exhausted body fell unwillingly into a troubled sleep.

"Rose, Rose . . ." Pearl shook her awake. "I'm sorry, Rose, I'm so sorry . . . please, Rose . . ."

Pearl was standing at the foot of her bed, her long blond hair disheveled, sticking to her wet cheeks as she sobbed. She looked abject and miserable, which only made Rose angrier. What did she have to be miserable about, the little snitch?

"Leave me alone! I *never* want to speak to you again, you little *moisar*! This is all your fault!"

Astonished at this vicious response from her kind sister, Pearl stopped crying, wiping her eyes. "But if I'm truly sorry, Rose, and ask you three times, you *have* to forgive me; otherwise, it's *your* sin."

"That's only before Yom Kippur! Right now, I don't have to talk to you at all!"

"Please, Rose!"

Their mother swept through the door like an angry wind. "What are you two speaking about? Rose? Pearl?"

Rose said nothing, pulling the covers back over her head. So, this was how it was going to be, then, from now on? Her mother standing outside her bedroom door like a spy, listening for secret transgressions.

Pearl burst into fresh sobs. "Rose won't forgive me!"

"What is there to forgive? You did nothing wrong, Pearl. Now go get dressed for school. And don't speak to your sister again until I tell you it's all right. And you, Rose, get up and say your prayers with special *kavanna* so the Holy One, blessed be He, might forgive your sins!" Later that morning, sitting between her parents in a chair that made her feel like Goldilocks usurping the Papa Bear's seat, she faced the distinguished and powerful religious authority she had before only glimpsed from afar through the thick curtains of the women's section in the synagogue. His eyes were dark and piercing under his gray, bushy brows; she could not meet them for shame. She lowered her gaze, focusing on the way his fingers clasped and unclasped, the gnarled knuckles like the branches of an old olive tree she had once seen in the Brooklyn Botanic Garden.

It was like facing God, she thought, who could see directly into your heart and soul. All her thoughts and transgressions were laid bare before him. There was no escape.

Suddenly, he leaned across the table, his face stern, but not unkind. "Do you believe, dear child, that our God is a merciful God who forgives transgressions and welcomes back those who stray from the righteous path?"

She nodded sincerely.

"And do you believe that though your sins be as scarlet God shall bleach them as white as snow if you repent?" he continued.

"Yes, *Kavod HaRav*."

He nodded, satisfied, his hands enfolding each other gently. "A good girl does not suddenly wake up one morning and look at forbidden pictures. Tell me, child, whose idea was it to look at that book?"

"Mine! Only mine! I took it off the bookshelf at the Goldbands' house."

"And when you saw the pictures, did you not immediately put it back?"

She hesitated. "No."

Her parents inhaled deeply.

"And why not, child?"

"Because some of them were beautiful!" she burst out, shocked by her own defiance. "They were pictures of children, of the streets of Paris."

"Beautiful! And the others? The immodest ones? Did they also seem beautiful to you?"

What could she say? That they were no worse than the photos in *Life* and *Look* magazines she'd been looking at for years? That she even kept magazines with photos like that under her bed? That, yes, she did think they were beautiful?

"I am interested in photography. I was given a camera in school."

The Rav looked up at her parents in surprise and disapproval.

"It was a gift, from the Dime Savings Bank, years ago, Honored Rav," her mother said hurriedly, mortified.

"She doesn't even have it anymore. It was a toy. She took pictures of the family," added her father.

"M'ken nisht aroifstzen a freshen kop."

A clap of silence, as loud and frightening as thunder, struck them all dumb.

I can't give her a new head.

The Rav turned to her. "Go, wait outside until we are finished."

Her legs shaking, she left the room.

The Rav waited for her to close the door, then turned to her parents, shaking his head sorrowfully. "The corruption started long ago, under your noses."

All the words they had practiced to defend her, to foist the blame on the Goldbands, felt like dust on their tongues. There was nothing left for them to say.

"But what can we do now, Honored Rav?" Rabbi Weiss asked humbly.

"You must send her to a different school, where she will be sheltered from bad influences. How old is she?"

"Almost sixteen, Honored Rav."

"In another year, you'll find a good *shidduch* for her, and she will become a kosher wife and mother in Israel, and leave all this *narishkeit* behind her."

"What school, Honored Rav? She is already in Bais Yaakov."

He smoothed down his white beard. "For someone like your daughter, that is too *frei*. Send her to Bais Ruchel."

"Bais Ruchel?" Her parents looked at each other in alarm. "That is Satmar. We are not Satmar."

"But as the Rambam teaches, sometimes to reach the middle path, a sinner must go in the extreme opposite direction. Bais Ruchel teaches *al pi taharas hakodesh,* a pure holy education. It's what your daughter needs now. Do you have any other children?"

"*Baruch Hashem,* another five, Honored Rav. Four boys, three at *kollel* and one in yeshiva, and a younger girl."

"They share a room, the two girls?"

They nodded.

"Ah, this cannot continue! Rose must be sent away, at least for the coming year, until the school works its influence of purification. They must have no contact, lest the older corrupt the younger."

Rabbi Weiss said nothing, the sharp exhale of a single, hard breath the only sign of the depth of his heartbreak at this ruling. He found it necessary to clear his throat harshly before he could utter a single word. "But surely, the Honored Rav does not mean that Rose should have no contact at all with her family?"

"Like Joseph the *tzadik,* she must undergo this total separation for a short time in order to grow into the pious, good wife and mother she is meant to be. Of course, this is up to you. But if you are strong and are able to resist your natural feelings, my advice will bring blessing to her and your whole family."

"Yes, Honored Rav. Thank you, Honored Rav," Rabbi Weiss said meekly, getting up to go.

His wife followed, her face frozen. Once outside the door, he turned to her in agony.

"How can we send our Rose away?"

Bracha Weiss looked at her husband in surprise. "We have asked the Honored Rav for his advice. And now we must follow it to the letter. As it is written: 'Do not turn from their words either to the right or to the left.'"

"And Rashi says: 'Even if they tell you right is left or left is right . . .'" Asher Weiss grimaced.

The session was over, Rose thought, looking at her parents' miserable faces as they exited. And so is my life.

The next day, her father handed over the borrowed book, wrapped in a plain brown paper bag, to the principal of Bais Yaakov, informing him that his daughter Rose would not be returning. After examining the book thoroughly, the principal agreed. He called in the Goldbands, returning the book and expelling Michelle.

Later that evening, Rose was called into the living room.

"You are going to live with your *bubbee*."

She was stunned. Her grandmother lived in faraway Borough Park, where she knew no one. It was exile.

"But Mameh, Tateh, please, please don't send me away from the family! I'll never do it again!"

"We have no choice," her father said sadly, looking down at the floor, before putting on his hat. "I'm going to *daven Mincha*."

She ran after him into the street, begging, "Tateh, please, please!"

But he was gone.

"Stop making a *tzimmis*! You want the whole neighborhood should hear?" her mother said harshly, grabbing her by the hand and pulling her back up the stairs.

"But Mameh, I . . . you . . . can't. Please!"

"Your *tateh* told you. It's not up to us."

She was astonished. "But you are my parents!"

Her mother held up her hand. "There's nothing to discuss. The Honored Rav said. If you behave, you will be allowed to come back in a year's time," her mother continued, her eyes hard, her lips pinched into a thin line of determination. "There's nothing to talk about. The tighter you hold on to the Honored Rav's *gartel*, the more it will help you."

"He doesn't even wear a *gartel*! We're not even Hassidim!"

"Chutzpah yet! You talk back, yet? *Gartel* or no *gartel*, his Torah knowledge and piety put him in direct communication with the Holy One, blessed be He. He has *Daas* Torah, a special connection to the will of the Holy One. Who are we to argue? Besides, you can help your *bubbee* with her housework and keep her company. It will be a great *chesed*, a way to make *teshuva* for all your sins. Here, I've packed you a suitcase."

"What, you mean now? I'm going now?" She sobbed uncontrollably.

"Stop! Enough already! It will be easier for you if you just behave and listen. Here, I bought you some new things for your new school."

"What? I'm not going back to Bais Yaakov?"

Her mother said nothing, handing her two pairs of stockings and a pair of shoes. The stockings were dense with thick, ugly seams, and the shoes the kind her *bubbee* wore.

"These are Satmar clothes."

"They are called Palm stockings. The Satmar rebbe himself invented them. They brought him samples of stockings, and he would pull them over his own arm, testing them. If he could see his hairs, he said no. Finally, he found this material. Now, every woman and girl in Satmar wears them. STOP CRYING. The Honored Rav said Bais Yaakov is too free for someone like you. Only because he helped us, Bais Ruchel agreed to take you. Say thank you; otherwise, you'd be home and finished with school."

She would not be finishing her sophomore year at Bais Yaakov. She would not be saying good-bye to her friends, or to Michelle. The idea was like a large avalanche that buried her in darkness. It was unimaginable, a plunge and hurtle down a deep pit that seemed bottomless. She wiped her tears. "Do I have to wear them outside of school, too?"

Her mother hesitated. No one in their family wore such stockings, but Rose—by her own choosing—was now a special case.

"You would not want to be thrown out of Bais Ruchel, too. You know what that would mean for your *shidduch,* when the time comes? The matchmakers will never be able to find anyone for a girl who had to leave Bais Yaakov and then was thrown also out of Bais Ruchel . . ."

Matchmakers? She was just a few years older than Pearl, she thought, shocked. "I don't want a *shidduch!*"

"Then think of Mordechai, Shlomie Yosef, your older brothers, their *shidduchim*! Think of Pearl and Duvid! Who will want to marry into a family with such a stain on its reputation? And think of your father! Do you think he will be able to continue working in yeshiva with such a daughter? Stop being so selfish!"

She went to her room, rolling down her beige panty hose and pulling on the new stockings. They were dark, flesh-colored tights with awful seams going up her calves and thighs. She felt like a freak. Then, she slipped on ugly laced-up Oxfords that completely covered her lower foot. They were a perfect match with the stockings, she thought with dark humor. She sat down heavily on her bed. What strange and evil alchemy had transformed looking at beautiful pictures into this ugliness? she wondered, appalled.

On that first night away from home, she sobbed quietly into her bed pillow on the hard bed in the strange bedroom with its ugly drapes, a room that smelled of mothballs and the paraphernalia of the old. Her shelf of books was gone, her toys and games and stuffed animals, and her pretty Shabbos dresses. All of her hair bands and barrettes, except for the plainest ones, had also been left behind. She'd been allowed to take her school bag and some long blue pleated skirts and long-sleeved blouses. She was stranded, like Robinson Crusoe, on a bare desert island with no inkling when the rescue ship would be coming for her.

Without knocking, her *bubbee* opened the door, sitting down beside her.

"Nisht fun kein nacha lebt men, un nisht fun tzores shtarbt men." One *doesn't live for pleasure or die from aggravation!*

"A yung beimelech beigt zich; a alts brecht zich." A young tree bends; an old *tree breaks.*

"Sha . . . sha. It's time to stop crying. Tomorrow is also a day."

She handed her granddaughter a worn, clean handkerchief, and a rugelach, hot from the oven.

Rose sat up in bed, wiping her eyes and blowing her nose with one hand as the cookie melted in the other, filling the room with the tantalizing scent of warm cinnamon and chocolate.

"Come into the kitchen, *maideleh.* I'll make you a glass of tea."

She followed her *bubbee* into the old kitchen with its ancient stove and icebox, sitting down on a chipped wooden chair by the rickety wooden table covered with an old oilcloth. She cupped her hands around the hot glass of amber liquid, dropping in cubes of sugar.

"In Russia, ve put a cube in our mout, den sipped de tea trouh it. Dat vay, you don't need so many."

She popped a cube into her mouth also, filtering the tea through it. It was very, very sweet. She chewed silently on the warm cookie.

"So, you vant to talk about it, *maideleh*?"

"I didn't do anything wrong, Bubbee!" Rose burst out. "I just wanted to look at some pictures in a book!"

"I heard vat kind of pictures."

"But I didn't know . . . I only saw the first pages when I took it home . . . besides, I don't think they were so bad."

Her grandmother sighed, handing her another rugelach. "A lie stays put, but da trut has feet, sometimes it runs avay. . . . De rugelach, dey're good?"

"Delicious, Bubbee."

The old woman suddenly winked. "Gut tings come vidout varning. Now go to bed."

"Thank you, Bubbee."

The old woman followed her into the bedroom, pulling the covers over her, then closing the door softly behind her.

With the sweet taste of sugar in her mouth, she closed her eyes and slept, dreaming of escape.

7

She went into a kind of shock those first few days in Bais Ruchel. Classrooms were in an ancient public school building leased from the city meant to hold half the number of students. Badly and cheaply renovated to hold the overflow, the building even had some bathrooms that had been turned into classrooms, the toilets, basins, and fixtures removed, leaving behind unsightly bumps and bulges beneath the badly cemented walls.

But the biggest shock was the language, the morning's religious studies conducted completely in Yiddish. Yiddish! The secret language of her parents and other old people; the language of tragic old countries long abandoned across the sea for a better home. Even when learning the Bible, they were given no access at all to the actual Hebrew text. Instead, a teacher "explained" the story of the Torah portion of the week to them in Yiddish, thus removing the possibility that they might read the commentaries or question the interpretation of the text in any way. It was like being read a children's fairy story, she thought.

This week it was the story of the plagues of Egypt: "And God hardened the heart of Pharaoh so that He might increase His signs and wonders . . ." the teacher said in singsong Yiddish.

She couldn't stand it. "But Rashi says God only hardened Pharaoh's heart after the first five plagues. Before that, Pharaoh hardened his own heart, because he was wicked," she blurted out, not even waiting to raise her hand and be called upon.

"*Vus?*" the teacher asked, eyes narrowed in suspicion and disapproval, her voice incredulous. "And you are saying there is something the *Eibeisha,* May His Holy Name Be Blessed, does not do? That His will was not on Pharaoh from the first moment?"

"But we were taught we have freedom of will to choose between good and evil, no? Only after Pharaoh kept choosing evil again and again did God take away his power to choose good. As Rashi explains: 'In the first five plagues, it is not stated that God hardened the heart of Pharaoh.' If you give me a *Chumash,* I'll show it to you . . ."

"Silence! Step outside immediately!"

Rose, not exactly surprised, got up with a calmness bordering on insolence, walking slowly out the door, a secret smile playing around her lips as she turned her back on her classmates. She knew the rumors about her had been circulating. Hardly anyone spoke to her anyway. And that was fine with her, she told herself. With each other, they were like puppies: soft, cheerful, full of playful good humor. She wondered if a single one even realized they were all caged pets, whereas to her, the bars became more visible, blatant, and intolerable with every passing day. How could she befriend such girls?

She waited in the ugly hallway, filled with contempt. What could they do to her? Hang her? Cut off her tongue? Send her back to Poland? How much worse could it be, after all?

Rebbitzin Brindel, her teacher, soon followed. Clutching her gray wig at both temples, she yanked it down lower on her forehead, looking sternly into Rose's sullen eyes. "I understand you have been sent here in order to purify yourself so that you might be worthy of a blessed match," she said in Yiddish. "Here, you will be taught only what is important for a woman to know. Do not taint this classroom with impure knowledge you've acquired before coming here. Do you understand?"

Rose stared at her. Is that what I am doing here? Getting ready to be a sacrificial lamb on the altar of some holy *shidduch* to an arrogant yeshiva *bochur* who will do me the big favor of lording it over me and letting me support him for the rest of his life? Her eyes filled with tears.

Totally misunderstanding her distress, Rebbitzin Brindel softened. "*Sha, sha.* Don't worry. Because you are a new girl, you will not be punished this time. But remember that you are forbidden to speak in Hebrew, the impure language of the Zionist apostates. We also do not learn Rashi here. That is for the men. We learn *al pi taharas hakodesh*. In purity."

"Yes, I'm sorry," Rose stuttered, appalled. Rashi, the great medieval Torah commentator who questioned and explained the holy text, making it comprehensible to any intelligent person, for men only? Was she no longer a person, then, but a helpless baby sparrow to be fed knowledge digested and regurgitated?

She returned to her seat. For the rest of the morning, she studied the paint peeling off the walls and the wooden floorboards peeking through the worn linoleum, waiting for the afternoon and her secular studies to begin.

Her relief in having the lessons in English soon faded. While, like Bais Yaakov, Bais Ruchel was supposed to adhere to New York State requirements to teach English, science, history, and math, she noticed the books they were given had pages missing and sentences that had been blacked out. In none of the stories they read did girls and boys appear together. Mostly, they were about boys and horses, or boys and dogs. None of the science or history books mentioned dinosaurs.

She felt her brain shrinking. Just being there made her feel stupider, the subject matter and teaching methods like an ill-fitting shoe that rubbed her mind and spirit raw. She returned to her grandmother's exhausted, her fury against her parents growing, determined to have it out with them. She called her mother. "I need to speak to Tateh!" she demanded. "You have to take me out of this place! I'm not even allowed to learn Torah in Hebrew, to learn Rashi. They won't even let us read from the *Chumash*, or the Prophets! How can this be what God wants!"

But her mother refused to even put her father on the phone. "Your father is resting. I'll tell him what you said. He'll call you back. But remember who made your bed when you don't like sleeping in it!" she added unsympathetically.

Each day, she waited, praying for her father to call, for her parents to re-lent, for something to happen. Weeks went by, her sharp hopes dulling, a gray cloud settling over what was once the clear, blue sky of her understand-ing of life. The warm feeling that had once enveloped her when she prayed, taking three steps backward and three steps forward and bowing to declare: "Oh, Lord, open my lips so that my mouth may declare Your Praise," sud-denly evaporated. "He sustains the living with loving-kindness, revives the dead, supports those who fall, heals the sick, unchains the imprisoned, and keeps faith with those who grovel in dust." The words withheld their mean-ing, becoming gibberish, a senseless song whose tune she remembered but whose words she had long forgotten.

Where was He, that God? That loving, creative, powerful Being she had spoken to every day of her life? Had He too moved away, turned His back on her, for such a silly reason as looking at photos in a book? Was He in league with the Honored Rav, with her parents, then? She didn't want to believe it. But what other explanation was there, after all, for all that had happened to her? As Rebbitzin Brindel declared: "His hand was in everything that hap-pened."

She felt confused, anguished, and full of doubts. The sincere joy she had once taken in learning and praying, in discovering the wonders of the Cre-ator in everything around her, faded and darkened. In many ways, being cut off from God was even worse than being cut off from her family. For had she been able to take Him with her into exile, she would not have been so pro-foundly alone. She would have had her familiar companion and guide and protector. Without Him, she was lost, living in a foreign country.

She tried hard to find her way back to Him, to come home, searching for hidden signposts. But the way offered by her new school and her family and especially the Honored Rav (who she had come to hold most responsible for her plight) was only leading her further away, she realized, deeper into the silence of a Godless wilderness. She, who had always taken her faith as a given, never realized until now how delicate a thing it was, like a tender, newly opened flower so easily trampled and destroyed. Lost and alone, what choice did she have but to become an explorer, to forge a new path, drawing her own map, with only her mind as compass? The only way to do that was to read.

The stringent lectures against the evils of books, magazines, pamphlets, or anything else not specifically approved by the school only made her more determined to get her hands on some reading material not approved by her school. But high on the list of Bais Ruchel's forbidden places—along with cinemas, theaters, and homes with television sets—was the public library. Being caught in one meant immediate expulsion.

At her grandmother's, she found some relief in immersing herself in simple, mindless chores, almost enjoying plunging her hands into hot, soapy water; getting down on her knees to scrub the linoleum; straining her elbow to scrape off the dried beans and potatoes from the Sabbath chulent pot.

But as she scrubbed and polished, she thought of the phrase "dying of boredom." Could it, she wondered, be taken literally? Could the restlessness ballooning inside her finally stretch her heart so thin it would burst? Was it then a matter of life or death, for which even God allowed one to commit transgressions in order that one might live to eventually perform good deeds?

The day she decided it was, everything changed.

"I have a cooking class after school today, Bubbee," she said, telling the first lie in her life. She waited for her body to dissolve into putrid waste. But the only thing that happened was her heart began to beat faster. She felt faint.

"Are you feeling all right, *maideleh*?"

Rose touched her face, which was growing hot. She nodded, stuttering: "I . . . I . . . am in the woman's way."

"Ah." Her grandmother nodded, without further comment. This, like any subject to do with womanliness, intimacy, bodily needs or functions, was best obscured, the way Victorians covered table legs, referring to them as "limbs" so as not to arouse impure imaginings.

That day after school, she walked quickly away from her fellow students and teachers. Not daring to wait for a bus or be seen riding the train, she walked and walked until her feet were blistered and sore. But there it was. The public library! The very shape of the building, with its large windows revealing the treasures inside, filled her with a joy that banished all her fears. Pulling open the large heavy doors, she hurried inside like a pilgrim seeking sanctuary.

She sat on the comfortable chairs, a pile of *Life* and *Look* magazines on the table in front of her, leafing through them the way a sultan counts gold coins. Exploring the shelves, she discovered the *National Geographic* magazine and the *Saturday Evening Post,* which she added to the pile. Drinking her fill, she then roamed the room, finding the books on photography, studying the way the light fell, the way the people stood, the landscape and the composition. Finally, assessing the amount of time it would take her to walk home, she rose. But before leaving, she walked with determined steps over to the librarian's desk.

"Excuse me?"

The woman with her large glasses and tight bun adjusted a plain pearl earring as she studied Rose. She wasn't a St. Rose of Lima parochial-school girl. Those Catholic girls didn't wear stockings, and she'd never seen one with a skirt less than three inches above her knees. She wondered for a moment if the girl was some kind of foreigner.

"I would like to take out a library card," Rose said with an accent that only a non–New Yorker would consider odd, putting the librarian's doubts to rest.

"Your name?"

"Rose . . . Monroe," she stammered, giving an address that she'd written down as she'd walked along.

Having to choose only four books from among the stacks was an agonizing challenge. She finally made her choice, reminding herself she would soon be back to exchange them for four new ones. She hid them inside her school bag.

"You're late! I was worried! So, you cooked something?" her grandmother questioned her when she came in.

"What?"

"In your cooking class?"

"Ah, right. Challah, Bubbee. We learned how to make challah."

Her grandmother sighed. "For this you need to come home after dark? This *I* can teach you, believe me. Go eat something."

"I'll eat, but first I want to do my homework," she said, anxious to hide her treasures in a safe place.

"First, eat!" her *bubbee* commanded.

She ate, tasting nothing, thinking about how only the first lie was hard. The rest came so naturally, it almost felt the same as telling the truth.

That night, and every night that followed during that period of her life, she lay under her bedcovers holding a dime-store flashlight that illuminated rows of words strung together with magical skill. Slowly, they dissolved the fetters on her spirit, which had felt like shoes bogged down with mud from tramping through the jungle. Dried, polished, repaired, she danced with them through the night, slowly at first, then kicking up with joy, roaming freely, transcending the rigid strictures of her life, the little apartment in Borough Park, her family in Williamsburg, Brooklyn, New York, America. She sat cross-legged on a magic carpet that floated over lands and lives so very different from her own.

There, in secret midnight rendezvous, she met Anna Karenina, Madame Bovary, and Anne of Green Gables, standing side by side with them, viewing the world through their eyes. What photos she would take, she thought, of the onion-spired churches of St. Petersburg, the French countryside, or Prince Edward Island as it burst into life each spring!

And that was how one night she met David, the sensitive little boy aching with loneliness and fear in Henry Roth's *Call It Sleep*. For the first time, David saw a coffin. He asks his mother about death, and she answers him: "They say there is a heaven and in heaven they waken. But I myself do not believe it."

Her mind lingered over these shocking words. *"They say there is a heaven . . . But I myself do not believe it."*

It was the first time in her life that she considered such a shocking idea. It was not so much the idea of dismissing heaven, but of disbelieving things that were taken for granted by everyone around you. That you had the right, the power, the freedom *not to believe*. It was a stunning revelation, both miraculous and terrifying.

The next night, she sat in the kitchen watching her *bubbee*'s small, heavy figure bent over the old stove, stirring the contents of a steaming pot with her large wooden spoon. This is real, she thought. This you could know. But as for the rest . . . everyone was simply guessing, rabbis, parents, teachers . . . They believed what they wanted, what they had been taught, what their parents before them believed.

And right then, surrounded by the odors of chicken soup and stewed apple compote and baking challah, her life changed forever.

I do not believe I deserve to be punished for looking at beautiful photographs.

I do not believe the Honored Rav is infallible or that his knowledge of the world comes from God. It that were true, then all of the Honored Ravs in Europe would have told their congregations to escape the Nazis when there was still time. Instead, they told them the opposite. The Honored Rav was wrong to tell my parents to send me away; and my parents were wrong for listening to him. Rebbitzin Brindel is wrong for speaking Yiddish in America, for wearing stockings with ugly seams and old-lady shoes, and for giving us Bible stories, instead of teaching us how to read the Bible and to understand the words of God for ourselves.

And so began her own life, a secret life. She had no idea where it would lead her, but only that she had no choice. Once you see, you cannot unsee. The ends did justify the means, if the alternative was to live a lie rather than simply just telling a few lies yourself. Just how bad it could get, or how far she would be forced to travel, she was in no position at that time to even imagine. Had she seen the future, she would not have been able to imagine the joy, only the terror.

8

Her mother tried everything.

"Come see the delicious cupcakes we bought you in the bakery, Pearl, chocolate icing with sprinkles."

"I'm not hungry."

"I passed by Judith's clothing store and saw this in the window. It's for Shabbos. Look how *shaine*!"

Pearl glanced briefly inside the bag, fingering the pretty, soft material. She made no attempt to take it out.

"*Nu*, don't you even want to try it on?"

"Not now, Mameh. I'm tired."

"It's been three weeks already. Enough!"

Pearl slunk into the room she once shared with her older sister, quietly closing the door behind her.

The pain, Pearl thought. She'd never felt such a thing before. Although her stomach felt queasy and she found it hard to swallow, it wasn't a stomach-ache or a sore throat. It was as if she'd accidentally swallowed something sharp, a fish bone or a sliver of glass, that had lodged deep inside her, tearing into her tender flesh like a splinter under a fingernail, and had no way to pry it out.

The room felt huge and lonely. She had trouble falling asleep, and once she did the night was interrupted by terrible nightmares in which naked men jumped up and down on her bed while her sister stared at her with angry, accusing eyes. In the morning, no one was there to help her get dressed or braid her hair. In school, she found she no longer had any desire to gossip with her classmates, but neither could she concentrate on her schoolwork, her teacher's voice an annoying buzz in her ear. She was tired, so tired, all the time.

"Tateh, I'm worried."

He looked up at his wife, closing the Talmud that lay spread out on the dining room table and kissing it. He pushed his glasses to the top of his head. *"Vus?"*

"You don't have eyes? She's like a skeleton, skinny, pale. She eats nothing."

None of this had gone unnoticed. He was also worried. And he also missed his daughter Rose. Terribly. The fact that she had called to speak to him and he had not called her back cut him like a knife. But he had no choice, no choice. The Honored Rav had spoken, and he could only obey. The medicine was bitter, but to dilute it would simply prolong the illness.

"Did we do the right thing?" she asked him for the hundredth time, she who had been so sure at the beginning.

He shook his head. "We can't question the Honored Rav."

She was silent. What was there to say?

"Is Pearl here?"

His wife nodded.

He got up heavily and knocked on his daughter's bedroom door. "Pearl, it's Tateh. Can I come in?"

"Of course, Tateh."

He opened the door and looked at her.

It was worse than he'd imagined. The sweet bloom of her round cheeks had disappeared seemingly overnight, her rosy complexion taking on a sickly pallor. She sat on her bed, her thin arms folded tensely in her lap, her thin legs dangling listlessly off the side.

"Can we sit and talk?"

She grabbed her heart-shaped pillow—a birthday gift from her sister—hugging it tightly as she folded her arms across her chest. A private conversation with her father was not something that happened every day. She was honored as well as apprehensive. Finally, she nodded.

"Then come into the living room with me."

She followed him.

"Sit."

She looked up at her mother, who stood fidgeting nervously in the corner, pretending to be dusting.

"Mameh, you have something to do in the kitchen?" he said pointedly.

"Oh, yes," she answered, surprised and a bit offended, walking out of the room.

He went to the bookcase and took out two copies of the Bible. "Let's learn a little Torah together, all right?" He opened it to Genesis, chapter 36. "And Joseph was a shepherd with his brothers . . . and he brought their gossip to his father."

Busy reading, he did not notice the dark crimson stain that spread suddenly across her pale cheeks. "And Joseph dreamed a dream and told it to his brothers, and they hated him even more." He closed the Bible and kissed it. "Joseph was his father's most beloved son. But in his youth, he made mistakes that caused his family much pain. But instead of disciplining him, his father continued to spoil him, giving him a coat of many colors. Now, Hashem, May His Name Be Blessed, could see into Joseph's soul. He knew that Joseph was a *tzadik,* but He also realized that Joseph could only reach that height through suffering. And so Hashem arranged for Joseph to be taken away from his family for many years. His father mourned him. His brothers missed him. But for Joseph's own good, Hashem ordained him to suffer enslavement and exile in Egypt so Joseph could become the *tzadik* he was meant to be. In the end, this exile saved not only him but his family. In the end, Joseph and his brothers came together in love. Do you understand, *maideleh?*"

"But I was Joseph! I brought you gossip!" she cried, wiping the tears from her eyes.

Had she not been responsible for Rose's terrible punishment? If only she had never asked to see that book! If only she had kept her big mouth shut! "God should punish me! You should send me away!"

He shook his head, resting his large warm hand over her small, young head, smoothing her hair down tenderly. "None of this is your fault or your responsibility. We are not punished for another's sins. Obey God's will with joy, little Pearl. Pray with a pure heart for your sister's return, and God will answer your prayers. Eat, and rest, and play outside to keep your body healthy, as your body is a gift from God and it is His will that we care for it. As it is written: 'You shall love the Lord your God with all your heart, all your soul and all your might.'"

In his words, she heard the pronouncement of God Himself. To disobey would be catastrophic. Enslavement and exile. "Yes, Tateh. But, Tateh, when can I see her?"

He gnawed thoughtfully on his lips. "We'll see, we'll see. Now go, have a snack, go outside to play. Will you do that out of respect for God and for your parents, who only want the best for you and your sister?"

"Yes, Tateh." How could she refuse?

Obedience became her shield. Where once she was thoughtless and will-ful, she now put aside her childish tantrums, finding that even the most dif-ficult and distressing of life's trials could be accepted once you got used to them. You could find compensations for old joys with new pleasures.

The compensations were many. Her mother, who viewed her as a conva-lescent, began helping her to get ready in the morning, even walking her to school several times a week, while her father continued to lavish her with at-tention, including private study sessions and gentle affection, until one day the ache inside her was suddenly and mysteriously gone. Her fear of sin and repentance over what she had done to her sister metamorphosed into a fer-vent and uncompromising obedience, which expressed itself in the almost fanatical adherence to even the most minor requirements of religious ritual. As long as she obeyed, she was sure that she and those she loved would be saved from the terrible scourge of Divine punishment.

And so she put her right shoe on before her left shoe, then tied the left shoelace before the right shoelace. And when she took them off, she remem-bered to reverse the order, exactly as written in the condensed version of the Code of Jewish Law. She never questioned why. Like the mysterious law of the red heifer, whose ashes somehow purified the Jewish people from sin, she accepted that all her religious obligations were God's will without asking for explanations, doing whatever she was taught by her teachers and her parents, convinced that performing such acts was a way to please Him.

What, after all, did human beings understand about anything? Could anyone really explain how the earth was created or why they were here? Wasn't it better, then, to simply obey all the rules blindly, because asking questions just led to doubt, and doubt led to sin? And how could you sin against an all-powerful God who created you and controlled the universe? A God who would control your fate even after you died, for all eternity? Even if something you were asked to do made no sense at all, wasn't it better to just do it than risk the consequences of defiance? After all, look what had happened to Joseph! And to Rose. It was too dangerous to stray, to think for yourself, to ask too many questions. If she wanted her prayers answered and her sister to come home, she needed to be worthy of God's love by being strictly obedient to His laws.

She took to studying the condensed Code of Jewish Law, memorizing the rules.

It is written (Micah 6:8) "And to walk humbly with thy God." Therefore it is the duty of every man to be modest in all his ways. You should not put on an undershirt while sitting but while still lying in bed, placing your head and then your arms through the garment, so that when you get up you will be covered. One should not say, "Behold I am in the most concealed of rooms, who will see me?" *For the Holy One Blessed be He fills the whole universe with His glory. It is forbidden to walk in an erect posture (for it shows haughtiness) . . . Before praying in the morning, you are not allowed to go to a neighbor or meet him or say "good morning" For why should you honor him before you have honored Me? . . . On saying the praises to the most high God . . . you must remove the phlegm and saliva or anything that tends to distract your thoughts. Then walk three paces backward and say: "Who redeemed Israel," then walk three paces forward, in the manner of one approaching a king . . . It is proper for every G-d fearing person to be aggravated and worried about the destruction of the Holy Temple in Jerusalem . . .*

It was all overwhelming. She had not known! She had been such a sinner, such a sinner! And now, all her transgressions fell on heavily, like boulders. Her teachers had only the highest praise for her transformation. But her parents were concerned. She seemed older to them, her easy laughter seldom heard. But only when they saw her sneak a copy of *Duties of the Heart* off the bookshelf did they finally become alarmed enough to intervene.

"This is not a book for a young girl!" her mother scolded her, and even her pious father agreed. "It is a book for scholars and yeshiva boys who need to repent their sins, a book full of fasts and self-punishments."

"But I want to go up to a higher level, to come closer to God so He won't punish me and He'll forgive Rose . . ."

Her father shook his head helplessly, looking up at her mother. "You don't need this book, or fasts or punishments. Honor your parents and teachers and do exactly what you are told, *maideleh*. That is enough."

But it wasn't, she thought. Her parents had no idea of her numerous, terrible transgressions, which she was now convinced had destroyed her family and separated her from her only, beloved sister. And even though she now believed that this separation was a good thing ordained by God and that her sister and family would ultimately be blessed by it, still it had become necessary because of evil that had been committed, the way Joseph's separation had flowed from the evil he had committed toward his brothers and the evil his brothers had committed toward him.

It wasn't enough to pay lip service. To sincerely repent was to fill your heart with sorrow for all you had done wrong, to feel humbled by your sins and to seek out piety, serving your Creator with all your heart and soul and body.

She tried. And tried. And tried.

9

At first, Rose didn't recognize her sitting on a table in a crowded kosher pizza parlor surrounded by tall, handsome boys wearing colorful crocheted skullcaps and pretty girls in pastel mohair sweaters and short skirts. The intricate braid was gone, replaced by a fashionably teased short bob, her delicate face accented by subtle makeup. She was a knockout, Rose admitted.

"Michelle?"

She turned, a smile forming with infinite slowness on her lips as her eyes focused in Rose's direction.

"*Ma chérie!*" she called excitedly, jumping down off the table and hurrying outside. She kissed Rose warmly on both cheeks.

Rose exhaled, amazed at this reception. She'd been afraid to even look her in the eyes. "I'm so sorry, Michelle. So sorry. It was all my fault."

"Sorry for what?" She shrugged. "I hated that stupid place. It was like the Bastille. I'm in a much better school now, Flatbush Yeshiva. They have the coed classes and a basketball team. I'm even trying out for the cheerleading! There, no one speaks Yiddish, morning or afternoon! They speak English. They even teach French. Imagine!" She grinned.

"You . . . you . . . mean . . . your parents sent you to a freeer school?" It was stunning.

"Well, after I got expelled . . ."

"They expelled you!?"

Michelle grinned wickedly. "Not me exactly. My family. For having a father who reads and has a library . . ." She giggled, pointing her forefinger at her temple and making a circular motion. "Cuckoos, the bunch of them. When my family first came to America, they didn't understand. They thought . . . they wanted . . . a Jewish school. Then, they learned there is Jewish and then there is Jewish. They've also had enough of the black hats and the long beards. So, we moved to Ocean Avenue. My father is much closer to the college; my mother goes to a Young Israel where everyone dresses like her. Trust me, it was a big favor, *chérie*. But what are you doing here? Don't tell me you also got expelled?"

Rose hesitated, ashamed more for her family than for herself. "No. My parents took me out."

"But why?"

There was no way to answer that without causing the Goldbands undeserved pain, she thought, shrugging. "They put me into Bais Ruchel."

"Does that also have a basketball team?"

Rose smiled ruefully. "No, but they have other great things, like classrooms in the bathroom and stylish uniforms." She turned around, pointing to the backs of her legs and the ugly seamed stockings.

Michele gasped. "*Incroyable!* What kind of place is that?"

"It's Satmar."

"I heard about them." She shuddered.

"My parents thought the hats weren't black enough and the beards were too short in Williamsburg." She laughed bitterly.

"Your parents . . . they also moved to Borough Park?"

Rose shook her head.

"So, you travel here each day?"

"They sent me to live with my grandmother for the year. If I do *teshuva,* they'll take me back next year."

Michelle looked stricken; then, she winked. "So, they don't have their thumb on you all the time, *n'est-ce pas?* You must come with me, then, to my classes at the School of Visual Arts in Manhattan. I go once a week for painting. But they have the photography classes, too. You'll adore it, *chérie*. Such fun!"

"Where is it?"

"On Twenty-third Street and the Third Avenue in Manhattan. You just have to change the trains only once."

On the subway, alone, at night, into Manhattan, she thought, the very idea unimaginably dangerous and wonderful. For a brief moment, she allowed herself to float there on her magic carpet. But soon she landed with a thud. "If my parents . . . if Bais Ruchel . . . if they ever found out . . . if they even saw us talking to each other . . ."

"But what they don't know, it does not hurt them, eh? So we make up to meet in the city!"

She shook her head. "I couldn't!"

Michelle searched Rose's frightened face curiously. "Why not, *chérie*? What is wrong with learning art, or photography? Did God not give us our talents? Are we not sixteen years old? In Williamsburg, at seventeen, they already find you a husband. If we are almost old enough to get a husband, we are old enough to decide to take the subway into Manhattan for a class, *n'est-ce pas?*" She reached into her purse, tearing off a piece of paper and writing down her number. "Here, call me if you change your mind. Spring classes start in two months. Good-bye, my friend."

"Bubbee, I think I'm going to sign up for a *chesed* committee, to visit sick people in the hospital, the way I did in Williamsburg."

"This is a very important mitzvah, to visit the sick. Your parents, you told?"

"Not yet. What do you think, Bubbee, is this a good idea?"

"You haf da time? It von't be too hard for you?"

"I have the time, Bubbee."

"I'm sure you do. Dat Satmar school . . . dey teach da girls nut'ting." She shook her head disgustedly, then sighed. "So, if you vant, go. It's okay by me."

"Really?"

She seemed a little bit too delighted, her grandmother thought shrewdly, looking her over. "Dere's a reason you're not telling me?"

Rose swallowed. "Of course not, Bubbee."

"*Abi Gezunt*—in good health. But I'll check with your parents. It's trou da school?"

"No, it's through the synagogue. The one around the corner, where we go for Shabbos."

"And how many times a veek?"

Rose hesitated. "As many times as I want, Bubbee. But I thought I'd go after school on Tuesdays."

"But not too late?"

"No, Bubbee. Not too late."

Her grandmother patted her on the cheek, nodding tiredly. "It's time to put da *bubbee* to bed," she said, shuffling off.

Rose quietly cleaned off the table and washed the dishes. While she was no longer bothered by lies, she still had a prick of conscience each time she transgressed, and was still not above expecting on-the-spot divine punishment. Looking apprehensively around her, she wondered if a plate would fall out of the cupboard on her head, or a glass would slip, cutting her wrists.

Reassured at the uneventful progress of her chores and the absence of divine intervention, she checked her grandmother's whereabouts, ascertaining she was already in bed fast asleep. Hesitantly, she closed the kitchen door behind her, picking up the phone.

"Michelle, it's Rose again. What night is that photography class?"

As expected, her parents thoroughly checked out the *chesed* committee and the hospital visits, going so far as to discuss the whole arrangement with the principal of her school and the Honored Rav himself. Only after all agreed that this was a good sign of a positive change in her character did they all give their consent.

She went every Tuesday after school, handing out little packages of sweets to the old people and their relatives, sitting by the bedside making small talk to those languishing alone. Her mother regularly checked on her progress with members of the committee, even calling to personally congratulate her: she'd heard only praise, she said warmly. After several weeks had passed, her mother relaxed and stopped checking up on her. It was then that she made her move.

"Bubbee, I want to add another night a week to the *chesed* committee, Thursday nights. I feel it would be good for my character."

"*A broocha on your keppeleh!* God should only reward you."

Rose felt a tightening in her chest and an ache in her stomach at hearing these heartfelt words of praise from the old woman. But she had no choice, she told herself. She had started down this road, and to turn back would kill her. Even though she hadn't started the class, she already felt devastated at the idea that it would not happen.

Besides, it wasn't her fault. *They* were the ones who had forced her into lies and deception, after all! If only they had left her alone!

"But Bubbee, please don't tell Mameh and Tateh yet."

Her grandmother's radar hit a bump. She narrowed her eyes. "Why not?"

"I want to make sure it's not too much for me. If you tell them and I quit the extra night, they'll be so disappointed. I don't want them to disappoint them. Not again . . ."

The old woman nodded sympathetically. "*Ich farshteist, maideleh.* It's all right, it's all right. Go, go. It'll be our secret."

"Thank you, Bubbee!" She hugged the frail shoulders, breathing in the flour and cinnamon that rose from her apron, her own special scent. Her heart felt heavy for the deception.

But whatever misgivings still lingered inside her, they were soon overwhelmed by joy when the day finally arrived. She took the BMT line on Fiftieth Street, just as she would have if she were going to the old-age home, but instead of getting off one stop later, she took it into Manhattan, changing trains and waiting for Michelle at the entrance to the Twenty-third Street station.

What if she didn't come? she panicked. What if, instead, some strange man, like the ones who had shouted at them on the subway that day on the way to the zoo, approached her? What if . . . ? Her heart began to drum.

"Hi, sorry I'm late." She wore a short, expensive coat with wooden buttons and a warm fur hat. Like a model, Rose thought in admiration.

They hugged, then walked together to the school. She tried not to think about how she would pay the tuition fees, hoping the teacher would allow her to simply "sit in" for the first few sessions, and afterward . . . well, she would cross that bridge when she came to it.

She was startled when she reached the building, watching the students mill around, giving her surprised looks.

Michelle grabbed her, pulling her into the first bathroom. "You'll have to

do something about that outfit if you don't want everyone staring at you."
Quickly, she pulled out Rose's tucked-in shirt, unbuttoning the first few but-
tons. Then, she rolled up the sleeves to above her elbows. Finally, she grabbed
the waistband of Rose's skirt, rolling it up until the skirt uncovered her knees.
She stood back, inspecting her work critically. "It's those horrible stockings.
They've got to go!"

"But my legs will be naked!"

"No, they'll look like legs, not wooden stumps!"

"Oh, I just couldn't!"

"Fine." Michelle reached up under her skirt, pulling down her own sheer
panty hose and handing them to her. "Here, take mine, *d'accord*?"

"You'll freeze!"

"It's warm in here. We'll switch back before we leave."

Rose went into one of the toilet stalls and changed, stuffing the Palm
stockings into her coat pocket.

"How's this?" she said, offering herself up to her friend's inspection.

Michelle reached behind her, pulling out her braid and hairpins, spreading her long, silky hair around her shoulders. She smiled. "No one will stare
at you now, except in a good way."

Rose looked in the mirror. "Oh, I couldn't . . ."

"Oh, yes you can," Michelle said, pushing her out the door. She took her
hand, pulling her up the stairs and down a long corridor. She pointed to a
door.

"Here, this is where your course is being given. I'm upstairs. I'll wait for
you at the entrance when our classes are over. Have fun!"

She clutched Michelle's arm.

"I have to go! I'll be late. Look, just go in and sit down. You will be fine.
You'll see."

Terrified, she walked quickly into the classroom and sat down. Now it
was her turn to stare, especially at the men and boys with no head coverings,
wearing unbuttoned shirts that showed their chest hair and tight jeans that
boldly outlined their bodies. She was horrified. She jumped up, walking
quickly toward the door, her plan to hide in the bathroom until Michelle's
class was over. But just as she was about to pull open the door, someone
pushed it open toward her and entered.

He was a man her father's age, and thus a man who looked old to her, though he was only forty. She had never seen a man with such a smooth, hairless face, no different from a woman's, she saw, startled. It was round and fleshy with a large cleft chin that would have looked handsome on a younger, thinner man. As it was, it simply accentuated the pounds he'd put on over the years. His graying hair was neatly trimmed, combed straight back from his high, smooth forehead, yet his sideburns were stylishly longer than they should have been for a man his age, she thought. His dark eyes were small and clever and something about the way he looked at her frightened her a little, although she could not say why. Perhaps "frightened" was not the best word, the most accurate word. She reconsidered. Perhaps the word she was looking for but refusing to find was "excited," even "disturbed," as he aroused in her strange feelings with which she had trouble coming to terms.

"You look lost," he said kindly. "Are you?"

"I don't know. Maybe," she whispered.

He raised an amused eyebrow, the smile coming only in his eyes, his lips a straight line, his nose just a tiny bit flared with amusement. You'd have to know what his face usually looked like to even notice it, she thought.

"Are you interested in a photography class?"

"Yes," she said, finding her wits.

"Well, good then, because you are in one! Why not just find a seat and relax?"

People around her tittered. Ashamed, she dropped quickly into the nearest chair.

His name was Vincenzo Giglio, he said, writing it on the board, and he was their teacher. According to the brochure she'd picked up as she'd entered the building, that meant he was an award-winning photojournalist whose work regularly appeared in *The New York Times, Look,* and *Life.* He wore dark pressed pants and a dark sweater from whose collar and sleeves a checked shirt peeked out. He was dressed more like a dentist, she thought, vaguely disappointed. She also decided he was shorter than he should have been, considering the broadness of his shoulders. Like the statue of Michelangelo's *David* she'd once seen in *Life* magazine. But it was a manly, strong body. A competent, powerful body.

He dimmed the lights, setting up a slide show of his work, projecting photographs on the large, blank wall. There in the dark, as the disembodied voice of this unknown man explained meaning and composition, she slowly forgot herself completely, the people around her vanishing along with the walls of the classroom and the city itself, subsumed into a language that held her in thrall. Her sense of sin also departed, taking with it her fears, her excruciating shyness, her insecurities. She felt cocooned in a private world of her own choosing, where miraculously she made the rules. And in this parallel universe, for the first time in a long time, she began to enjoy herself simply because she had ceased to be herself, feeling foreign and strange and other but in the best way possible. Instead of searching for a way back to the familiar, she realized she only wanted to go forward, leaving the familiar behind forever.

When the lights went back on, she looked around shyly. She'd never dreamed of meeting such people, let alone joining them in any shared enterprise other than a random subway or bus ride. There was the black teenager wearing a huge afro and bell-bottom jeans and a tie-dyed T-shirt. There was an olive-complexioned young man wearing leather pants and a pretty blond girl in a low-cut maxi dress, braless, her frizzy hair like a vast halo around her head. By deliberately and freely choosing this activity, she realized, they had now been invited into her world, and she into theirs.

A wave of immense excitement washed through her, followed by a jolt of panic of even greater intensity. She'd been banished from her home simply for looking at a book of photographs! What would they say if they could see her here, now, in a classroom full of indecently dressed Gentile boys, being spoken to familiarly by a beardless man named Vincenzo old enough to be her father, her hair undone, wearing a short skirt and a partially unbuttoned blouse with rolled-up sleeves that bared her white forearms! My parents! My teachers in Bais Ruchel! The Honored Rav! The idea of being caught and judged by any of them in such a state was paralyzing.

". . . And so, your assignment for next week is to choose a subject that exemplifies transition. Begin with a series of outdoor photos and then slowly move on to interiors. Oh, and those of you who have not registered, please go to the office after class and take care of the formalities."

She waited for him outside the door.

"Professor Giglio," she said.

"Oh, hello. You again! You look awfully pale. Are you feeling all right? You aren't going to faint, are you? I don't know what to do with fainting ladies . . ." Again, that barely discernible smile gleaming out of those dark eyes.

"I feel . . . yes. I'm fine. That is . . . I'm just not sure how I'm going to pay for this class."

"Your parents . . . are they poor?"

"NO, no. Not exactly. Well, maybe. But I can't ask my parents."

"Why not?"

"I'm . . ." She swallowed hard. "Not supposed to be here."

"Ah. Tell me more."

"My parents are ultra-Orthodox Jews from Williamsburg . . ."

"Ah . . . okay . . . I get it."

He didn't, not really. Like most people who live in New York City, he had seen the odd Hassid in black garb and sidelocks walking the streets, but, other than knowing that they existed, he knew little else, nor did he want to. "It's a Jewish thing, right?"

"Right."

"So, why are you here?"

Something in the question crystallized for her everything she was feeling. The answer came spilling out, her wild heart finally overcoming her reasonable brain. "Because this is the most important thing in my life right now. I have to be in your class," she said with an outpouring of passion that surprised and embarrassed her. She felt tears well up.

"So, a bad girl, huh? My favorite kind." The laugh lines around his eyes deepened, his lips finally succumbing into a smile. "Look, I can pretend I don't see you for a few sessions, but you'll have to register eventually. There is nothing I can do about that . . ."

"Oh, I understand. I'm sure I will be able to work it out. . . . Thank you!"

"But you do have a camera, don't you . . . ?"

She looked down at her hands. "I am planning to get one."

He was equally annoyed and intrigued. "Well, you won't get much out of this class without one. See you next week."

"Thank you, Professor Giglio! With all my heart!"

"*Professor*," he repeated mockingly, cupping her chin and giving it a playful shake as he looked deeply into her innocent, young eyes. "See you next week, honey," he said.

The impression of his fingers on her skin lingered as she made her way down to the entrance to wait for Michelle. It tingled.

They met at the entrance, then retired to the bathroom to change stockings.

"I've got to buy a camera," Rose told her, calling out over the stall as she pulled up the dreaded hose and handing Michelle the sheer ones under the stall wall.

"I thought you already had one?"

"That was years ago. Your father said it was a toy."

"My father could lend you one. He's got a million."

Rose considered this, but her initial enthusiasm waned as she thought about the implications. "I might break it, or lose it," she answered, but what she was really thinking was: I might have to be alone in a room with your father. I might have to show him my gratitude. He might demand it.

"*D'accord*. Then I'll ask him where you can buy one cheap."

"Ask him, but don't mention me. Say it's for someone else. One of your friends from Flatbush."

Michelle pushed out of the stall, adjusting her skirt. She gave Rose a curious stare, about to question this strange request, but then thought better of it. "Where will you get the money, Rose?" she asked instead, changing the subject.

Rose said nothing. What could she say, except that she still believed in miracles?

10

It was only in bed that night, tossing and sleepless, that she remembered her Dime Savings Bank account. Miraculously, the passbook had been in her school bag when she left home, ready for the following day's deposit. No one had remembered to take it out. She jumped out of bed, putting on her flashlight. She opened the passbook: $520.00!

A fortune. Her hands shook as she considered the possibilities.

The next day, she walked into a local branch with it. Presenting it to the clerk, she felt like a bank robber. "I want to withdraw the money." She took a deep breath. "All of it."

"Do you have some identification?" the clerk asked.

She took out the copy of her birth certificate that her mother had inserted into the passbook, suspicious that the bank might one day try to cheat them by questioning ownership of the account.

"Special occasion?" the clerk asked, counting out the money.

"Very," Rose answered.

Too excited to wait for Michelle's father's advice, she immediately went to several camera stores to shop. But none of them took her seriously, trying to sell her Polaroids and Brownies. They refused to even unlock the cases holding the more serious cameras so she could look at them. Frustrated, she called Michelle.

"My father says he'd be happy to lend you one. That you should just come over . . . But if you don't want to, he says you should go to the Wall Street Camera Exchange. Ask for Alan."

She missed her library night, looking up on a subway map how to get to Wall Street.

"Could I speak to Alan?" she said timidly to the busy, bored man behind the counter, whose face suddenly took on some interest.

He shrugged. "That's me."

"I'm a friend of Mr. Goldband's," she said, then blushed furiously, correcting herself. "I mean a friend of his daughter, Michelle."

"Ah, the Frenchman. He's a good customer. And how can I help you?" He smiled.

"By not trying to sell me a Brownie, or some other kid's camera. I'm going to be a famous photographer and win awards," she told him boldly. "So when I tell everybody I started off with a camera from your store, which one is it going to be?"

He took a step back, blinking. "What you need, of course, is a Nikon F."

"How much will that cost?"

"Four hundred dollars just for the body, without any lenses . . ."

She shook her head sorrowfully.

"Okay, so here's the next best thing: a Miranda Sensorex. *Popular Photography* rates this as almost as good as the Nikon—almost. It doesn't have all the Nikon's features, but the price includes an excellent normal lens. It's a great camera to start a career off with.

"Or"—he reached to the shelf behind him—"there's the Canonflex, their latest after the sensational Canonet. It's got an interchangeable pentaprism viewfinder, a completely automated aperture control system, and an externally coupled selenium exposure meter. There are lots of lenses available too, from thirty-five millimeter all the way to one hundred and thirty-five millimeter. It's a whole system. It will never be obsolete."

She lifted the Canonflex to her eye. The heft was impressive. Her fingers curled around it. "How much?"

"Three hundred dollars, and for another fifty, I'll throw in a zoom lens."

"I'll need some film," she said. "Fifty rolls. And I want you to throw that in, too, free of charge." He shook his head. "You're killing me. Half-price. I can't do better than that."

She considered it. "And a discount on developing the rolls whenever I come here?"

He shrugged, amused. "For a world-famous photographer to be, how can I say no?"

As she counted out the money, her hands shook. Her name was on the passbook, but it was her parents' money. She felt like a thief. But a happy, successful thief, she told herself, rejoicing in her momentous victory, and a deep-seated satisfaction in her revenge.

It took her three wasted rolls until she finally figured out how to use the camera, but when she did, the results were breathtaking: faces in a crowd waiting for the light to change, their expressions unguarded, wistful, and revealing. Two little girls playing hopscotch on a chalk-marked sidewalk, their limbs loose, their hair flying. And then there were the interior shots taken while her grandmother took her afternoon nap: a study of a well-used pot misted in rising steam that gave it mystery, the arrangement of simple ice cubes on a platter that looked like a work of modern art, she thought. But her favorite was a self-portrait in the mirror as she blew bubble gum, her eyes obscured by the camera, her fingers aloft. She loved hiding behind the camera, the gum the only hint of her age and personality.

Of course, the photos could all have been improved, she realized. She would have liked the shadows to have fallen less harshly in some, more illumination and less ambiguity in others. But she adored her new camera. Adored it, suddenly feeling, for the first time in her life, that she and the world were one, awash in possibilities.

"So, you're back," said Mr. Giglio. "I thought I'd frightened you off when I didn't see you last week. My heart was broken," he said with that familiar gleam in his eye.

"No, I just . . . now . . . got a camera and did the work, so . . . I had to skip last week."

"Let's see what you've got, kid." He reached out to her.

Scared and hopeful, she handed him the envelope with her photos, then watched as he flipped through them silently, her self-confidence deflating, until she noticed that crinkle near his eyes. "Love the bubble gum, Miss . . . ?" He glanced at the registration list. "Monroe?" he questioned. "Really?"

"Yes," she lied.

She had paid the tuition and was now officially enrolled for the entire semester, until the summer, at which time she could transfer to the summer classes. She had money left over for that, too.

"Does that mean they're good, Professor Giglio?" she asked, barely daring to hope.

"No, not really."

Her heart fell.

"But they do show originality of thought, and that is what is most important in any artist. By the end of the term, we shall improve your technical skills to match your talent. Deal?"

"Deal," she answered, her heart leaping up with joy. Artist. She was an artist.

And so began a new rhythm in the life of Rose Weiss. She lived for the days she went to the library, and the day she went to her photography class, and in between for the times she could read her new books and take her photos. The strange fiction that comprised her days in Bais Ruchel, her exile from her family, her life with her grandmother became more of a footnote to her real life, something that had to be endured to make it possible. The more she poured into that real life, the stronger and less vulnerable she felt against the abuses of the life forced upon her, her spirit growing until she felt and saw glimpses of her old faith breaking through the dark clouds. Despite her sins, God had helped her. God had reached out to her and given her a new chance to be happy. He had lightened her punishment when no human had been willing to reach out to her and do so. He had had compassion for her weaknesses, and sympathy for her plight.

Again, she felt the pull to the sacred words of prayers, words of praise, thanksgiving, and requests. He was out there; He was listening, even if her parents and teachers were not.

If only this idyll could have lasted a few more months, she often thought, looking back years later. Perhaps disaster could have been averted, the terrible break avoided altogether, jumped over, like those deep crevasses that climbers reaching for the peaks manage to somehow circumvent. But then again, perhaps not. It was there, waiting for her, and she stumbled. What followed was as life-changing and tragic as it was inevitable.

11

"When am I going to see my sister?" Pearl wailed.

It had been six months, and the child's plaintive entreaties had been growing stronger and stronger. Despite all the attention and gifts lavished on her, which had had some effect, Pearl's longing for Rose was beginning to take its toll. Her whining was almost constant now. Her parents couldn't stand it.

"Get them together for a little while," her father told her mother.

"But the Rav . . ."

"The Rav said it was up to us!" he answered, annoyed. After months of adhering strictly to the guidelines, he was beginning to feel the stirrings of regret and something else. It was very easy, he thought resentfully, to give advice, especially if you didn't have to live with the consequences. Even his iron-willed, pious wife was beginning to buckle, but not for the same reasons. Early on, the glowing nature of the reports had roused her suspicions and her anxiety. Satmar schooling had to have been a shock and a trial to her bookish daughter. And for the last few months in their weekly phone conversations, Rose had sounded positively happy, her complaints gone. Butter wouldn't melt in her mouth. Could it be that her will had been totally broken? Or more ominously, her mental stability? Bracha Weiss was also anxious to check up on her daughter firsthand.

"I have an idea," she told her husband.

"*Nu?*"

"She volunteers at Beth Abraham once a week, on Tuesdays. We can go there at the same time. We can take Pearl."

"Excellent. Find out what time she starts." He was happy and excited at the prospect of seeing his daughter. "We should bring her something, Mameh," he told his wife. "A present. She deserves a present. She has done so well. Everyone says so."

"What should we bring her?"

He thought about it. "Maybe a new Shabbos dress?"

She nodded. "I'll take Pearl shopping with me. We'll pick it out together."

The mother sifted through the racks, wondering exactly what size to get. Her old size was a four, but perhaps she had grown? It had been months, after all. Better to get a six. It could always be taken in.

"Here, here!" Pearl called excitedly, pulling a pink dress with sequins off the rack. "Like a princess dress."

"No, it's too fancy-shmancy," said her mother, amused, thinking "too showy" and, most of all, too expensive.

Pearl pouted. "It's a present. For Rose."

"Come, look some more. What about this?" It was a simple gray dress, but with a stylish overskirt of filmy chiffon that was also lightly beaded and embroidered.

Pearl looked it over. It was pretty. Not as pretty as the pink. And certainly not as pretty as her own dresses, especially the latest violet one her mother had bought her just two weeks before. She thought about it. Rose would look pretty, but not prettier.

"Yes." She smiled, nodding.

The only thing left was to ascertain exactly what time to show up.

"Bubbee, it's me. Tateh and I want to visit Rose, surprise her. We want to meet her at Beth Abraham, where she goes to volunteer. What time should we go?"

"Tuesday or Thursday?" the old woman asked.

"Bubbee, she only goes once a week, on Tuesday."

"Oy," the old woman said. "I forgot."

"Forgot when she goes?"

"No. Forgot I vasn't suppose to tell you vhat a *tzadakis* you have. Vhat a wonderful daughter you have trown out of your house . . ."

"What are you talking about, Bubbee?"

"She decided to volunteer tvice a veek. On Thursdays also. All her school-work she does, and my floors and the chulent pot she scrubs, and also she volunteers, two times a veek. *Vus mere vilstah?* Vhat more you could vant?"

"I didn't know. Why didn't you tell us?"

"She said she vasn't sure. Maybe it vould be too much. She didn't vant you to be disappointed if she stopped. But so far, every Thursday she goes, like an angel! Be there at six o'clock."

"We bought her a beautiful new dress. Don't tell her anything, Bubbee. We want it should be a surprise."

"She could use a new dress. Don't vorry. I say nut'ting."

Rebbitzin Weiss bit her lip, tears gathering in the corners of her eyes.

"We'll make it up to her, Bubbee."

"You owe her," the old woman remonstrated.

"Hurry Tateh, Pearl. We need to catch the subway. It's already five-thirty."

"I just need my hat," he answered, putting on his big, black homburg in front of the hall mirror. As he smoothed down the felt brim, he smiled at his reflection.

"Pearl, stop fussing with your hair already. Enough! How many times have you changed hair bands? And what have you got in that bag?"

"It's . . . just some of Rose's stuffed animals. And her barrettes."

"She doesn't need it. Put it away . . ." she scolded, but Rabbi Weiss raised his hand warningly. "This is very kind of you, Pearl. I'm sure your sister will appreciate your goodness. I'm sure she misses you as much as you miss her."

"Thank you, Tateh!" the child said happily, clutching the bag of treasures for her sister, into which she had secretly added many of her own new hair bands and barrettes. Not the prettiest ones, but still ones she liked very much that were almost brand-new. Did Rose even think of her at all? she wondered. Did she still hate her? Was she still angry?

"Why is your hand shaking, Mamaleh?" her father asked as they walked through the streets to the subway.

She looked down, surprised. Her whole body was shaking.

They arrived at the entrance to Beth Abraham at a quarter after six and waited.

"Maybe she's already inside?" Pearl said when they had been there more than half an hour.

"The child is right. Go check, Mameh."

"All right. And you two go inside; wait in the lobby. Sit down and rest, Tateh."

They waited patiently another fifteen minutes. The elevator opened, and Rebbitzin Weiss walked out toward them, her face fierce with anger.

"She's not here. I spoke to the woman in charge of volunteers, a very *eidle* woman. She says Rose never comes on Thursday nights."

They were waiting for her in the living room, crowding her grandmother's small apartment, sucking out the oxygen. When she opened the door, her parents jumped up, while her sister Pearl sat up on the couch, where she had been dozing.

"WHERE WERE YOU!" her mother screamed, raising her fists.

"Stop, Mameh." Her father restrained her. "Think about the child!"

Pearl sobbed hysterically, running into Rose's arms.

"Rosie! I brought you this!" the child sobbed, trying to put the bag into her sister's hands. It fell forgotten to the floor.

"Go away from her!" her mother screamed, forcefully separating the two.

"Maybe there is some explanation, Mameh! As it is written, 'judge each man leniently.'"

"Shoshi, sweetheart, vhere did you go? Your parents vanted to surprise you. They missed you. Your sister missed you. They bought you a present. They vaited at Beth Abraham."

"YOU TOLD THEM! But Bubbee, you promised!"

"You are complaining to your *bubbee*? You liar!" Her mother tried to grab hold of her, but her father stopped her. "*Sha,* Mameh! Think about the neighbors."

That immediately quieted her down.

"Silence! Everyone. Come into the kitchen, Rose." Her grandmother and mother started to walk there as well, but he turned to them, holding up his hand. "I am going to speak to my daughter. Alone."

He closed the door. Rose looked at her father across the table the way she would have looked at a stranger whose photograph she was about to frame. The white, sweating forehead beneath the heavy, old-fashioned black hat; the thick, dark beard flecked with gray, the calflike, pleading eyes. As she put her fists on the table, it wobbled. A fitting metaphor, she thought wryly, for their relationship. Lying to him was amazingly easy.

"Where were you, child?"

"I went to visit a sick friend instead tonight. It's no big deal," she said sullenly.

"The woman at Beth Abraham, an *eidle* woman, told Mameh you only come once a week, on Tuesdays. So where do you go every Thursday, child?" He spoke quietly, reasonably.

She hesitated. The truth was out of the question.

"I don't know who told Mameh that, but it's not true. I swear it!"

"It's forbidden to swear!"

"*Bli neder.*"

He looked into her eyes, wanting so much to believe her. "Are you telling your *tateh* the truth?"

She looked down. "Yes, Tateh."

The door to the kitchen flew open. To her horror, she saw clutched in her mother's hands her latest photographs and her new camera.

"Enough! You brazen-faced liar! Don't say another word."

Her mother took her father back into her bedroom. There on the bed were her library books, her receipt for tuition, and her canceled bank book.

He gave Rose a questioning look, then looked down at the floor. His heart was broken.

"Bubbee, get me a bag," her mother said fiercely. "A big bag, a shopping bag."

Rose watched wordlessly as her mother carelessly stuffed her books, her camera, her photos, film, and her receipts into it. "Pearl, go take this downstairs and throw it into the garbage can!" she ordered, handing it to her.

Rose grabbed her sister by the shoulder, shaking her, then turned to her mother, leaning in close. "Mameh," she whispered without a trace of emotion, "if you do this, I swear, I will kill myself."

Her mother took a sharp breath, looking at her, frightened, Rose's calm determination more effective than any tantrum or tears, which would have sailed past her mother like a ship in the night. But this . . . this *composure,* it was unnatural. This was no longer a child in front of her, but an adult, she saw, realizing the limits of her power. She felt helpless.

Rose discerned all this in the deep lines that bloomed on her mother's forehead and the downward pull of her determined lips. I have won this battle at least, if not the war, she told herself, rejoicing as she ripped the bag out of Pearl's clutch, leaving behind a sharp red welt as painful as a knife cut.

Pearl pressed her lips together, determined not to cry out, determined to do nothing ever again that would call her parents' negative attention to her sister.

12

Everything had to be done quietly, with the utmost discretion, her parents decided. It was the only way to avoid scandal. The cover story was simple. Rose had come down with pneumonia and would be out of school and back home with her family in Williamsburg for the six weeks needed to recover. By then, the school year would be over anyway.

She was moved back into her old room, while Pearl was given a curtained-off alcove with no window just off the kitchen. There was no choice, as the other bedroom housed the boys: Duvid, Shlomie Yosef, and Mordechai, when he was home from the yeshiva.

The Honored Rav was not consulted about these changes. Indeed, no one—not even Rose's brothers—was let in on the truth, lest word of her scandalous behavior leak out like dark ink from a faulty pen, indelibly staining the family's linen-white reputation.

This was not a choice, but a necessity. Anything else would put Morde-chai's and then Shlomie Yosef's *shidduchim* at risk, and down the line Pearl's and even Duvid's! As for Rose, under the circumstances her *shidduch* must happen much sooner than they'd planned.

Neither of her parents was happy about that. But what else could be done? Clearly, the Honored Rav's advice had backfired. They had sent away an erring child and received back a sinning, wayward, and defiant adult. The only way to smooth things over was to hide this information from any future groom and his family and allow him to inherit the problem.

Not that they liked the idea of having to hide things from matchmakers and prospective sons-in-law and their families. Indeed, it went against everything they believed in as well as their innate sense of decency and fairness. But blood was thicker than water. Why should their blameless offspring suffer because of one bad apple in the barrel? God would surely give Rose the husband she deserved, and vice versa. It wasn't in their hands.

The modern world was a strange, new place, they had to admit. They felt baffled, heartbroken, helpless, betrayed. She had proved herself a wild horse. If she was not reined in by a husband and children, who knew where her incorrigible rebelliousness might lead her? In any case, the sooner she was out from under their roof and no longer their responsibility, the better for everyone.

This being the case, they understood that they had no choice but to negotiate with Rose about beginning the *shidduch* process. If she cooperated, they agreed to let her keep her camera and—after many furious arguments—even caved in and agreed to allow her to continue her photography classes. She was clearly determined, and, frankly, they were not sure they could stop her. Moreover, she'd already paid an outrageous sum in tuition up front. Why should it go to waste? Besides, whatever bad influences she had encountered there had already done their destructive work on her character. No use trying to nail closed the barn door now. They also agreed she could continue to take out books from the library. Their agreement had two nonnegotiable conditions: number one, in September, she would not be allowed to continue her education in school; and number two, she would have to cooperate fully in the process of finding her a husband.

Rose readily agreed about school: since Bais Ruchel didn't actually have a senior year, most of the girls getting engaged and married by the end of their junior year, and since Bais Yaakov would never take her back, what big choice did she have? She knew better than to dream about joining Michelle at a coed yeshiva like Flatbush or Ramaz. She might as well have yearned for a trip to the moon. Besides, over the past year she'd become accustomed to teaching herself. As long as her parents allowed her to continue taking books out of the library, her education would continue. The photography class was really what mattered most to her anyway.

As far as *shidduchim* were concerned, the truth was she was ready to start dating, even if it had to be done through a third-party matchmaker. Her shy conversations with Professor Giglio and some of the male students in her photography class had helped to nurture her blooming womanliness, her sexuality unfolding within her like a gentle bud pulling back its petals for the first time.

And so it began. Her mother took her on shopping trips to clothing stores, where she was introduced as a *kallah moide,* setting the saleswomen buzzing around her like killer bees. The dresses they urged on her all had high necks, sleeves that reached below her elbows, and skirts that fell modestly past her knees. (They even made her sit down in them so her mother could judge their length exactingly. It was surprising how many dresses looked fine as you stood before the mirror, only to become scandalously revealing the moment you innocently sat down and crossed your legs.) She cooperated, delighted by the promise of new clothes after months in horrible Satmar uniforms, but only up to a point, insisting on exercising her own taste. She chose stylish, pretty dresses in bright colors (except for red, the forbidden color of the harlot) that fit her slim figure flatteringly.

And when it came to shoes, she picked out high heels that made her legs seem longer and more shapely. Only a girl going out on *shidduch* dates could get away with wearing such attractive shoes. When a girl was about to marry, the rules relaxed. After all, men were men. Even their world recognized that.

Despite the fact that she was clearly aware of her mother's ulterior motives (i.e., to dump damaged goods before anyone found out and the price went down on everything the factory produced), she still enjoyed the time they spent together, which harked back to a more convivial and comforting part of her childhood. Indeed, in many ways it was better. For the first time, her mother was no longer the all-powerful seat of judgment, but simply a middle-aged woman doing her best to further what in her mind was God's will. Rose could accept that.

Pearl tried hard to dwell on the joy of having her sister Rose back home, of having her own guilt assuaged. But while she grasped that the decision to move her out of her room had come from her parents and not Rose, still, she felt an irrational sense of personal rejection from her sister. Not only her room had been usurped by Rose but also that special place at the center of her parents' attention she had comfortably occupied in Rose's absence. But it was the shopping trips for Rose's new wardrobe that were the last straw.

"Why can't I come, too?" she wailed.

"Your time will come, child. Now it's your sister's turn," her mother answered implacably. The less time her youngest daughter spent with her eldest, the better. As for Rose, while she'd forgiven Pearl, she wasn't about to lobby for her to tag along when she would only get in the way.

By the time Rose had "recovered" from her "illness" and was ready to date, she had a fully stocked wardrobe that presented her in the most favorable light possible. The matchmakers had already compiled their lists of eligible young men, and the phone started ringing. Her mother fielded the calls, writing down the information in a little notebook bought especially for that purpose. In there, she jotted down the name, age, education, family lineage (*yichoos*), and geographic location of each prospect, as well as their monetary demands on the family of any prospective bride. Usually, the financial demands were in direct proportion to the boy's desirability as a future son-in-law.

Mental illness, family scandals of any kind, a reputation for stupidity or laziness put the groom in no position to ask for anything at all. Indeed, in such a case, the bride's family could expect to get off scot-free as the anxious boy's parents coughed up an apartment (purchased in full or, at the very least, with a mortgage the parents agreed to pay off), car, and monthly stipend to keep the young couple afloat until such time as either bride or groom got a job. But on the other hand, if the groom was from a highly respected family, had a reputation as a serious Torah scholar, and came highly recommended by his Talmudic instructors, the bride's family would basically face bankruptcy to haul in such a prize.

Rose, by her behavior, had lightened this burden in advance for her parents. For no family with a Grade A son who did a minimum background check would consent to take her. On the other hand, depending on how much information had been leaked, the Weisses might find themselves held hostage financially by even the parents of a son little better than a yeshiva bum. It was their hope, however, that Rose's natural charm and attractiveness, her lively personality and independence might be alluring to a certain type of good yeshiva boy, the kind who these days were demanding to go out only with girls who had been to college. If such a misguided boy could be found, he would be perfect, Rebbitzin Weiss thought, her reasoning being that while Rose hadn't even finished high school, her attending photography classes (which of course the boy and his family could never know about) was certainly equivalent in its inappropriateness, hopefully giving Rose the same status and level of desirability.

There was a rocky beginning, in which the matchmakers tried to unload all the damaged goods in their warehouses: a boy with annoying tics and a terrible, pimpled complexion; a young man who was so deathly shy he could hardly say a word; a boy who stammered horribly; and, last but not least, a man in his early thirties who was still single for whatever reason, the mere fact inexcusably damning except if the girl was the same age, in which case he'd be elevated to a prime catch. The problem was, he wanted a girl nearly half his age.

Annoyed, bored, and ready to rebel, Rose put a moratorium on these awful, time-consuming exercises in futility, concentrating instead on photography projects. Now she had decided to take photos of Hassidic brides, even ones she didn't know. Since men were not allowed to mingle with the bride and the other women either before the marriage ceremony or after, it was the perfect opportunity to capture scenes that few had been privileged to see. And the brides' families were only too happy to agree that a *frum* girl take family photos free of charge.

"Some of these are amazing," Professor Giglio told her, fingering the prints. "You've got real talent, kid. And, better yet, you have access to an unseen world. That is the combination which gives birth to great photographs. And great photographers."

She held his words in her heart like an amulet as she plowed through her days. How quickly things changed was astonishing.

13

His name was Shimon Yisasscher, but his family called him Shimmy, and to his friends he was known as Boomie, after his penchant for idly banging rulers against his desk. Anyone paying attention to him from the time he was young would have seen that phlegmatic Boomie was not Talmud-scholar material. Unfortunately for him, and fortunately for his parents, those who noticed were not motivated to reveal this fact, believing that every Jewish boy who spent his days in front of a Talmud, his eyes nominally open, was going to save the Jewish people from disaster with the merit of his learning.

And so his rebbes passed him from grade to grade, inwardly groaning, but forever in possession of the pious hope that one day a teacher would reach the child's heart and brain, inspiring in him the desire to imitate Rabbi Akiva—the greatest Jewish scholar of all time—who until the age of forty was famously an ignorant shepherd. Each tried sincerely to deluge him with knowledge in the hope that by sheer volume a few drops would land inside.

He grew up tall, handsome, and charming, adored by his family and friends, and looking forward to the day when he could pursue his real inter- ests, whatever they might turn out to be. He was in no hurry to find out, the life of the all-expenses-paid yeshiva student suiting him perfectly. He got to the study hall late, took many coffee and phone breaks, and left early, secretly spending hours wandering the city, enjoying himself in ways innocent and not so. Luckily for him, he came from a well-to-do family with an unassailable reputation, who were willing to support their handsome son in all ways necessary to maintain his and thus their own reputations.

Although his father and grandfather were not scholars, they were the next best thing: kosher butchers who owned a chain of shops with impeccable rabbinical certification trusted by even the most fastidious Hassidim in Williamsburg. But if there was one thing Boomie was even more sure of than not wanting to be a Talmud scholar, it was not wanting to be a butcher. And so he kept up pretenses, doing the minimum necessary to avoid getting thrown out of yeshiva, which would end his parents' enthusiasm for financing his Torah-scholar lifestyle, and which might lead to demands that he put on a white apron and get behind the counter.

Family life, which would make still further demands on him, he put off until scandalously late, agreeing only at the age of twenty-two to begin looking for a wife. His needs were simple: a cute, fun-loving girl who would pretty much leave him alone.

His parents, of course, had other ideas, a laundry list of qualities they demanded in both the fortunate future bride and her family. She had to be pretty (no one wanted ugly grandchildren) and healthy (i.e., fertile) and to have been accepted into Bais Yaakov High School, and therefore scandal-free. Whether or not she graduated wasn't important to them. They preferred hardworking to scholarly, piety to intelligence, obedience to charm. Fun-loving was not on their list at all, and it was their list that went to the matchmakers, along with many hints at the extravagant rewards a successful match would earn. All the matchmakers in Williamsburg, Borough Park, Monsey, Lakewood, and Spring Valley were in a tizzy of competition to find the girl whose foot fit that shoe.

But one after another, their hopes were dashed against the breakwater that was Boomie. While all the girls liked him, he had no interest in any of them. The really beautiful ones intimidated him, as did those who were learned and intelligent enough to ask him with real interest about his Talmud studies, or how he expected to bring up his children. Right, that's all he needed! An Inquisition! Most of all, they seemed overly anxious to please, their hands and foreheads moist, their eyes adoring, their voices high and brittle. Their very eagerness made him wary. Why would any of them agree to marry him, let alone approach the idea enthusiastically, if they were really as religious as they pretended to be? And if they weren't, then they were fakes and phonies. And who wanted to be married to a fake and a phony?

Inevitably, by sheer process of elimination, Rose was pushed to the top of the list.

"He comes from an excellent family with means, who won't be squeezing you dry," the matchmaker, Mrs. Yachnes, explained to Rebbitzin Weiss. "It doesn't matter that she didn't graduate. He doesn't want a scholar, just a *frum,* fine girl from a good family."

She didn't mention "pretty" or "healthy." That would be vulgar. Besides, she could see for herself that Rose Weiss had fine hips and a good complexion. She didn't need a doctor's note. As for beauty, well, she wasn't as beautiful as the younger sister (who would be in great demand when her time came), but, as the Torah says of the matriarch Leah: "She had beautiful, soft eyes."

And so, arrangements were made. They would meet informally first, so that Boomie could get a look at her, and she at him.

"Aside from money, what does he have to recommend him?" Rose asked her mother point-blank.

"He is in a prestigious yeshiva, from an excellent, highly respected family." She didn't add "beggars can't be choosers," but it was in the air.

Rose shrugged. "I'm taking photos at the Erenreich wedding on Tuesday night. Tell him to come to the reception."

"What if he's not invited? Really, Rose!"

"Tell him to come to the chuppah then. The ceremony will be held outside. Who's to know if he happens by? Besides, in a black suit and a beard, he'll look like every other guest they've invited. Tell him I'll be the girl with the camera. But how will I know who he is?"

"You'll know," her mother said cryptically.

She was curious, she admitted that to herself, even a bit excited by the fact that someone would be looking her over with romantic intentions. She put on a pretty lavender dress that hugged her slim figure and stiletto heels that were going to kill her feet by the end of the evening.

The pre-ceremony reception was lively, held in two separate halls, one for men and one for women. The women danced around the young bride, who was seated in a large wicker chair decorated with fresh flower arrangements. She looked positively terrified, Rose thought sympathetically, her head bent over a book of Psalms, her lips moving with silent urgency as she turned the pages, hardly looking up. What was she praying to have, or to avoid? Rose wondered, wishing she could talk to the girl privately. That, of course, was impossible. She didn't even know her, and her mother and mother-in-law, sisters and sisters-in-law surrounded her like bodyguards.

Finally, the music started up. The groom was coming for the bedecking, the ritual of checking out the bride's face before covering it with the heavy veil, a precaution inspired by the unhappy experience of the patriarch Jacob, who wound up in the marriage bed with the older sister when he had toiled seven years for the younger.

Rose stepped aside as the women's chamber was invaded by men, led by the groom and his father and father-in-law. The bride, her lips still moving, her eyes still lowered, just sat there as the groom looked down on her, until, finally satisfied, he pulled the veil over her face.

Rose, who had been to other weddings, was shocked. Usually the bride was all smiles at this point, exchanging happy, meaningful glances with her young groom, who looked at her adoringly. She was very young, this girl, maybe her own age. Who knows what pressures had been put on her to agree? Who knows what had transpired in prewedding meetings between the two? What if she'd changed her mind? Tough luck. There was no escape clause, especially if a *vort* had been held previously in which an engagement contract had been signed. Those were harder to get out of than a marriage contract! She felt her skin prickle as she looked around at the large assembled crowd of hundreds. It would take inhuman courage for the girl to balk at this stage. She was stuck. When the men turned to leave, heading toward the marriage canopy, the bride followed discreetly behind with the women, literally supported on either side by her mother and mother-in-law, who linked arms with her, keeping her in place. Mercifully, it would soon be over, and whatever doubts the girl had would be left behind. Or not.

It was a warm June night. A soft breeze wrapped the thin material of Rose's silk dress around her legs, outlining them. She lifted her camera to her eyes, scanning the crowd.

And there he was, staring at her: a head taller than everyone else, darkly handsome, his black suit a little more stylish than the other men's, his hat worn at an angle with a slight swagger.

She quickly lowered her camera, hiding in the depths of the crowd, as she waited for the bride, who soon appeared, blinded by the veil, stumbling down the aisle, supported by smug, bewigged matrons in their wedding finery. Following their lead, she circled the groom seven times until finally being set down firmly beside him.

Mrs. Yachnes called the very next morning. "Yes, he's interested. Very, very interested," she sang in triumph.

Her mother held the phone at arm's length, covering the receiver with her palm. "*Baruch Hashem!*" she whispered. She brought the phone back to her mouth. "So, what's next?"

All Rose heard was a series of "hmms" as she waited impatiently for her mother to hang up.

"When?" she asked, filled with excitement and dread.

"*Baruch Hashem,* tomorrow evening at seven. He's coming over with his parents."

"Oh, I don't know about that. Why can't he come over by himself first? What if I don't like him? Or he doesn't like me? Why should we get his parents involved so fast?"

" 'Won't like' . . . 'doesn't like' . . ." her mother mocked her. "Why be so negative? God willing, you'll like, he'll like, they'll like. It's all arranged in heaven forty days before you were both conceived."

"Right." Rose shook her head. She was wasting her breath.

"You have something to wear?" her mother asked anxiously.

"You should know." Rose raised her eyebrow.

"But maybe something new . . . ?" Her mother bit her lip.

"Everything I have is new . . ." Rose pointed out.

"Still . . ."

So they went shopping, again. This time, her mother took Pearl along as a special treat, perhaps feeling that Rose already had one foot out the door, and thus her pernicious influence was under control. Or perhaps she was feeling a bit nostalgic about her own engagement days, when the shopping was done with the accompaniment of a crowd of female relatives and friends. They took the train to the city and went directly to Lord & Taylor.

These clothes were a different class altogether, Rose thought, fingering the rich materials and feasting her eyes on the stylish designs. She chose a sophisticated two-piece suit with a black silk skirt and a dark gold jacket with bold black fleur-de-lis embroidery at the wrists and around the bottom.

"Never," Rebbitzin Weiss shook her head.

"But why, Mameh?" Rose pleaded, even though she knew the answer full well.

Although it covered up everything that needed to be covered, there was no avoiding the fact that it was sexy. There was something about the way it fit that accentuated her tiny waist and curvy hips. It was worlds away from the style of the average Williamsburg *kallah moide*.

"It looks very pretty on Rose," Pearl suddenly joined in. "And it has long sleeves, and a high neck, and covers her knees . . ."

Rebbitzin Weiss looked again. This was all true. Why pick a fight when this child was almost safely out of her hands? "Well, all right then."

"Thank you, Mameh!" Rose said, kissing her mother's cheek in gratitude.

But on the way home, the suit on a hanger in a plastic bag, chills went up Rose's spine as she thought about wearing it for the darkly handsome young man who had stared at her so intently across the crowd.

The following night she was in her bedroom when she heard the door open and her parents' warm greetings float through the house. She waited tensely behind the closed door until she heard her mother knock.

"It's time," she whispered.

Rose gave herself one last look in the mirror. More American wife than Marilyn, she thought, pleased anyway. Her long hair was tied back with a ribbon, tendrils gently framing her warm, olive complexion. Her eyes, accentuated with liner and mascara, shone out of her chiseled, narrow face, her full lips, dabbed with a colorless moisturizer, fading into the background unless a person focused on them. She wondered what he would focus on.

Led into the living room, she faced him and his parents, who smiled, shuffling awkwardly as they exchanged polite greetings.

"Why don't we sit down by the table and let the children get acquainted," her mother suggested.

The parents smilingly settled themselves in front of the calorie-laden desserts, while Rose and Boomie found their way to the living room chairs on either side of the coffee table, in full view of and hearing distance from their parents.

Rose bit her lip, furious.

"Something's wrong?"

He noticed. One point for him, she thought.

"Well, it's kind of hard to get to know you like this."

"What do you mean?"

Minus one point.

"I mean, with your parents and my parents looking us over like that."

He chuckled. "Yeah. Pretty ridiculous," he whispered. "So why don't you and I take a walk around the block or something?"

Up three points.

He stood up. "We're going out for a walk."

His mother's mouth fell open, but his father grinned.

"Good idea," Rose's father said.

"Don't be too late," her mother warned, squinting at the two of them in alarm.

Downstairs and out in the street, she wondered if he would head toward the lighted main street or in the opposite direction. He went the opposite way.

Two more points.

"So, you take pictures," he said affably.

"I want to be a photographer, Shimon."

"Call me Boomie. All my friends do."

"Boomie? Are you a drummer in a band?"

He laughed. "No, I just like to make noise." He quickly changed the subject. "Picture taking . . . I hear there's good money in that. Weddings, bar mitzvahs. These guys charge a fortune."

"I don't want to be that kind of photographer," she said emphatically, dashing his hopes.

"What other kind is there?"

"Doisneau, Henri Cartier-Bresson, Ansel Adams . . ."

There was a short silence.

Minus four points.

"Oh, you mean like the kind that take pictures they put in museums?"

She nodded. "And what about you? What do you want?" The question caught him up short. He was used to, "And what are you learning?" "And what *kollel* are you planning to go to?" But not, "What do you want?" That was oddly personal, even sexy, he thought.

"I'm not sure yet," he said honestly. "I only know the things I don't want."

"Which are?"

"I'm not going to be either a Rav or a butcher."

She laughed. "What then?"

"I don't know. Maybe go into business one day, I guess. Open a clothing store, or a delicatessen. I will never be poor. That's the third thing I definitely don't want."

She walked beside him, slowing her pace, thinking.

"And what do you want from a wife?" she asked.

He shrugged. "Nothing special, you know. The usual. Cook dinner, keep the house clean, take care of the kids. She wouldn't have to work, unless she wanted to. I mean, unless she liked working in a store and wanted to be behind the counter . . ." He looked up at her hopefully.

"And what if she doesn't? What if she wants to be a famous photographer?"

He stopped short. "You're *serious* about that?"

She stopped counting.

"I certainly am," she told him.

"Wow. I mean . . . I don't know. Would you take pictures that would be shameful? That would disgrace the family? My parents are very *frum*. Their business depends on their good reputation."

"It's hard for me to tell you now what kind of photographs I might be taking in the future."

He looked at her, surprised. Another girl would have immediately caved in, sworn up and down how *frum* she was, how God-fearing her intentions. She might even have put on a show of being shocked and insulted at the very question. Rose was really different. Cute, too, with a pretty little waist, an ample bust, and nice hips. And he liked that outfit. It too was different, classy. He was sick of *frum fatales*. "Well, I guess, then, the both of us will have to take a chance." He nodded affably.

She wasn't so sure about that. "So, what now?" she asked.

"So, you want to go out with me again?"

She looked him over under the street lamp. He had a slim body with broad shoulders; thick, curly black hair; and a very masculine face. His beard had been trimmed short so that you could clearly see the outline of his full lips. He didn't seem either a religious fanatic or a control freak. She could do much worse.

"Why not?" She shrugged.

14

Day after day, Rose expected the call from Mrs. Yachnes, not exactly with joy, but with resignation. He was just an ordinary guy, she admitted to herself, one of those yeshiva-student guests that had been seated around their Sabbath table ever since she could remember. To his credit, he seemed honest and had a sense of humor. But as a prospective groom, he had one thing going for him, she thought: he wasn't terribly pushy, which was her greatest fear.

But the phone call didn't come. She was surprised, her pride and self-esteem devastated.

Finally, her mother called Mrs. Yachnes.

Rose curled her hair around her fingers nervously before asking, "So?"

"So, he was willing, but the parents . . . they looked into your background. It's not for them."

"What's 'not for them'? What exactly did they find out?"

"Don't be smart. You know."

"What? That you took me out of Bais Yaakov because a girl's father loaned me a book? You sent me away from home and put me into Bais Ruchel, then yanked me out of there? What's to find out?"

"Oh, so it's your parents' fault, yes?"

"And the Honored Rav's . . ."

"I should wash your mouth out with soap."

She shrugged. "The truth is pure."

"They found out about the pictures."

"Since I met him taking photos, they didn't exactly have to be Sherlock Holmes," she said drily.

"So smart you are. So smart. You see where that gets you now."

"Never mind."

"This is not a joke, my fine daughter."

"I wasn't crazy about him anyway. He's not even really *frum,* you know. He's just passing time in yeshiva until he can open a delicatessen and put me behind the counter, so *he* won't have to be there."

"It's not about him! Don't you understand anything? This picture-taking *narishkeit* . . ."

"Photography."

"Whatever you want to call it, it's got to stop. *Farshteist?* No *frum* boy or his family will tolerate it!"

"I thought you and Tateh agreed?"

"We made a mistake!"

She sat on her bed in silent defiance. What now? She felt her hopes sinking. What exactly were her options?

Her mother sat down beside her, putting an arm around her shoulders. "God willing, when you are a wife and a mother, you won't care so much. You won't have so much time on your hands like now . . ."

Rose shrugged her off. "Leave me alone."

Her mother put her hands in her lap. "Mrs. Yachnes has another boy in mind. But you have to keep the *narishkeit* to yourself, you hear?"

Rose didn't answer.

"Look Rose, once you are married, you and your husband will decide what's acceptable to you both and what's not. It will be out of our hands."

Rose looked up at her mother. She looked old, tired, and aggravated. And what she said was true. The only way out was to get married to someone as soon as possible and to hope for the best. It was the only door left open to her.

"All right."

"All right what?"

"All right. I'll meet the next victim."

" 'Before collapse, a person's heart swells with pride,' " her mother replied warningly.

His name was Yankele, and he was neither good-looking nor blessed with even a minimal sense of humor, however she doggedly searched. And his parents were even poorer than her own! That didn't stop them from having monetary demands: big, enthusiastic, hopeful ones based on their assumption that their son, a "good learner," deserved to be supported until who knows when. Mrs. Yachnes, who was no dummy, checked out their claims, informing them that, according to his teachers, their precious boy was not really in the top echelon of his yeshiva. Quite the contrary. Informed of this, they lowered their expectations but didn't cancel them altogether. He was a sincerely pious boy who had never been involved in even a whiff of scandal. That was worth something.

The young couple sat in the corner of the living room under the watchful eyes of both sets of parents.

"It's hard to get to know you with everyone watching," she tried.

" 'Never sated are the eyes of man,' " he pontificated, shrugging.

The silence between them lengthened. He lifted off his heavy black hat, wiping the sweat from his forehead with a pudgy hand, which he then rubbed against the upholstery of his chair. She watched him, disgusted.

"How do you plan to cover your hair?" he asked her suddenly, out of nowhere.

She knew a trick question when she heard it. "Why? How do you think I should cover my hair?"

"My rebbe doesn't like wigs. My rebbe thinks women with wigs are sinners. He believes hats or scarves are best. But if you must wear a wig, then only with a hat on top of it."

"And what do *you* think?"

She could see the question confused and appalled him. "I mean, what do you think about the way women dress in general?" she quickly improvised.

"I don't look at women. Of course, my mother and sisters are very strict and modest in their dress."

She could see his eyes wandering over her body. She was wearing a pretty dark pink blouse with a high neck and long sleeves and a plain black skirt that, when she sat down, reached close to her ankles. He exhaled, looking troubled.

"What?"

"That color. As it is written: 'And red is the color of licentiouness.'"

"I'm not wearing red."

He seemed startled to hear this.

"It's pink, an acceptable color, at least to my parents."

"I would not want my wife to wear that color."

I wish the poor woman well, Rose thought, groaning silently to herself.

"And what kind of tablecloth will you use for the Sabbath?"

What the . . . ? She recovered. "I haven't thought about it," she answered politely.

"In our family, we only use white. Colored cloths are too *prust,* my mother says."

"How interesting!"

When the points reached minus two hundred, she stopped counting.

"And what do you expect in a wife?" she asked him, dreading the answer.

"A woman of valor, who is happy to share in my *zchus* of learning by supporting me, taking care of the house and children so that I might be free to reach my full potential in the study house. And of course, a good cook. My mother is a very good cook."

She looked him over. It showed. If he was busting out of his belt buckle at twenty, what would happen at fifty?

This went on, and on, and on. It was horrifying.

Finally, his parents got up from the table. Like locusts, they left not a crumb behind.

"The financial arrangements need to be settled . . ." his mother began.

But her husband shushed her. "All in good time, all in good time," he said, smiling, shaking the crumbs out of his beard.

He extended his hand to Rabbi Weiss. "It should be in a good hour," he said.

"Amen, amen. In a good hour." Rabbi Weiss smiled.

"So we'll wait for Mrs. Yachnes?" Rebbitzin Weiss asked.

"Yes," they all agreed.

Finally, the door saw the back of them.

Her parents sat down by the empty table, exhausted.

"We will have to take out a second mortgage to meet their demands on top of the loans to pay for this wedding," her mother said morosely. "Hashem only knows how we'll pay it back."

"Mameh! NOT in front of Rose."

"There's no way you are taking out any loans to pay for *this* wedding. He's an idiot," Rose announced.

They looked up at her in shock, shaking their heads.

She looked back at them in surprise. "You can't be serious! I'm sorry, Tateh, Mameh. It wouldn't last. Your money would be down the drain."

Her father stood up. "You have no idea what you've done, do you?" he exploded, his face turning a deep crimson. "Whatever it costs, it would still be cheaper than having you on our hands for the rest of our lives! Cheaper than ruining your brothers' and sister's chances for good matches! Who knows how much we'd have to pay for them to be able to marry after it gets out that you aren't married because no God-fearing family would agree to have you!"

Rose felt herself going into shock. Her kind, loving father. She had never, ever seen him so angry. "Tateh!"

He pushed his chair back. It scraped angrily against the floor. His steps were heavy as he stomped out of the room.

She felt her heart beating so rapidly she felt sure she was going to black out.

"You won't be happy until you give us both a heart attack," her mother spit out at her venomously.

"Mameh!"

"You better pray to God that this boy and his family are willing to take you, you understand? Pray! Now close your mouth and go to bed."

Fully clothed, she jumped into bed, pulling the covers over her head to create a private little space that blocked everything else out. She sobbed wildly into her pillow.

"Rose, Rose, don't cry, Rose."

She felt Pearl's soft hand on her cheek.

"I love you, Rose, don't cry. It will be all right, Rose. I'll pray for you that it should be all right."

She took Pearl's soft childish hand, bringing it to her lips, kissing it.

"*Sha*, Rose, *sha*. It will be all right."

The next two days, she stayed in bed, unable to eat anything, her stomach nauseous and heavy with dread. She had nothing to look forward to. It was the end of July, and Professor Giglio's classes were over. It was too hot to walk to the library to change her books. Besides, what was the point of reading about other lives, other places, when all roads were closed to her? On the morning of the third day, her mother barged in, pulling up the shades with a decisive whack! The sunlight poured over her, blinding her. She rubbed her eyes, sitting up heavily.

"Open your eyes, *maideleh*. I have some news!"

Oh, no! she thought.

"What are you so afraid of? It's *dafka* good news!"

"What's good news for you may not be good news for me."

She waited for her mother's harsh response, but instead she heard her laugh. She opened her eyes, focusing.

"Mrs. Yachnes called. You'll never guess. They both want!"

"What do you mean?"

"Both of the men, both of their families, they want the *shidduch*!"

"Boomie, too?"

"Who?"

"I mean, Shimon."

She nodded happily. "Yes, him too!"

"But I thought . . ."

"Your *tateh* went to talk to the Honored Rav."

"When?"

"Early yesterday morning, in shul, right after prayers. He explained the situation with Shimon's parents and the *shidduch*. Told him you had learned your lesson, that you were a good girl. The Honored Rav agreed to speak to the boy's parents, to convince them to reconsider."

"Tateh did that? Talked to the Honored Rav? For me?" She felt hot tears well up in her eyes.

"You have your sister to thank. Pearl nagged and nagged and nagged Tateh until finally he couldn't stand it. You are lucky the Honored Rav is a saint and was willing to get involved, after all he knows about you. The parents were ready to listen. Apparently, the boy too wore his parents down. He refused to go out with anyone else."

Really? she thought with wonder. "So, what does this mean?"

"What does it mean? It *means* you have your pick. Which one do you want?"

"What? I have to choose between those two, right now?"

"You . . . you . . . ungrateful little witch! After all you've put your family through! After Tateh swallowed his pride and involved the Honored Rav himself, just so you should be happy . . . ! May God not punish you! Have a little shame!"

She inhaled deeply, her mind a whirl of confusion. Shame she had. More than a little. She tried to focus on the bottom line. They would not force her to marry Yankele, with his head scarves and white tablecloths. As for Boomie, he seemed like a live-and-let-live kind of guy. *And he wanted her, fought for her!* She smiled secretly. Maybe it would be possible to have some kind of life together that suited them both. If only it was not happening so fast! She couldn't think.

After that, the pace only picked up. They wanted to have the *vort* and sign the engagement contract to make it official. To this she absolutely, hysterically refused.

"NO ENGAGEMENT CONTRACT! NOT UNTIL RIGHT BEFORE THE CHUPPAH!"

"Why not? It's not respectable! It's what everyone does!" her mother screamed back. "And his parents will pay for everything, all the cold cuts, the pastrami, the potato salad!"

"Leave her alone, Mameh," her father interrupted, suddenly at her side. "I'll just tell them that's our custom. They can have a party, but the *tenaim* will be signed at the same time as the wedding contract, at the wedding."

"Thank you, Tateh," she breathed.

"I've learned better than to argue with you," he cut her off curtly, walking away.

For the engagement party, his parents bought her a beautiful diamond engagement ring with a large stone that glittered on her finger and a delicate gold watch with a diamond-encrusted band. Her family bought him an expensive watch, a set of Talmud, and a tallis with a heavy sterling silver chalice sewn around the neck.

She wore an off-white suit with crystal buttons. The event was a swirl of color, faces appearing with big smiles, some familiar, others not. In the corner, other gifts piled up. A blender, a hot plate, silverware, a mixer.

She looked at the ring and smiled. She felt beloved, accepted, everyone congratulating her as if she'd won a coveted award. Pearl never left her side, her eyes shining.

"You are happy now, Rose, aren't you?" she asked anxiously.

Rose bent down to kiss her. "God willing by you someday, Pearl! And thank you for your help."

The child beamed, squeezing Rose's hand.

After that, the shopping began in earnest. The trousseau: linens, towels, feather beds, tablecloths (all colors). It was Rose's idea to borrow a wedding gown from a free-loan *gemach* instead of buying one. It had a tight-fitting lace and seed-pearl bodice that covered her completely, reaching up to her throat and the back of her neck and down past her wrists. The lace had been lined with white satin so that not a glimmer of skin peeked through. It had a train trimmed with the same lace. She looked at herself in the mirror, her heart skipping a beat.

This is no dream. This is really happening, she thought, feeling sick. She quickly took it off.

"How is that?" the attendant asked.

"It's fine, fine," she muttered.

"Maybe try on a few more?" her mother suggested.

What for? They're all the same.

"No, Mameh. I love this one. It's perfect."

"Well, if you're sure." She smiled back, delighted. That was easy.

"I wouldn't like that, a used gown you have to give back after the wedding," Pearl said as they were leaving, wrinkling her nose in disapproval. "Mameh, maybe we should go to a store and—"

"Mameh and Tateh have enough expenses as it is." Rose cut her short.

"Oh, it could have been much worse, *maideleh.* Much worse. Your in-laws—*Baruch Hashem!*—have been so generous. They have a little apartment set up for you, the downstairs of a two-family house they own and rent out in Borough Park. And they're not asking us to contribute anything to your upkeep. They'll continue with the monthly stipend indefinitely, until their son decides to leave *kollel*."

"Still, there's the wedding—the food, the hall, flowers, a band, a photographer . . ." Rose insisted.

"Don't worry, Rose, his parents have connections in the catering world. All the meat is at cost, and the rest . . . the best price possible. And his parents are sharing in that, too. It's a blessed match," her mother exulted, squeezing Rose's hand affectionately.

It was wonderful to see her mother so happy, Rose thought. Years seemed to have sloughed off her since the engagement. She squeezed her mother's hand back.

"Now the only thing left are shoes."

"Do we have to do that now?" Rose sighed.

"The sooner, the better. It's hard to find wedding shoes once the summer is over."

They went to a store in Borough Park owned by a distant relative, a cousin of her *tateh*.

"What about those?" Rose asked, pointing to a plain white pump in the window with a round toe and a sensible heel.

"It's ugly," Pearl declared. "What about these?" She pointed to one with a stiletto heel with crystals embedded in the material that made it glitter.

"I'd fall flat on my face in those, Pearl." She smiled, shaking her head.

"What about these?" the cousin-storeowner said, crouching in front of her with a box.

The shoes were embossed white patent leather with a lacy design, pointy toes, and a high heel.

She tried them on. They killed her feet, the heel cutting into her ankle, the toes pinching, the arch achingly high.

"Oh, very nice," her mother said.

A bewigged stranger looked over, giving her opinion, "It's beautiful on her foot. So delicate, yet stylish, too."

"Yes, Rose. You look so pretty!" Pearl agreed.

"You'll never find a better pair," the cousin said. "And afterwards, you can get a lot of wear out of them. Not like the crystals."

She walked, hobbling, around the store.

"You have to break them in, of course," the cousin said. "This is true of all shoes. But it's real leather. It gives."

"So you'll wear them a week before, a few hours every day," her mother advised.

"All right, fine," Rose agreed, sitting down and taking them off, happy to see them disappear into a box that she would not have to open for many weeks.

She let the planning go on, not really participating.

"But what colors do you want?" Pearl demanded.

"What do you mean?"

"The tablecloths and napkins and the bridesmaids' dresses."

"Do you really want your dress to match the tablecloths, Pearl?"

"But that's what everybody does!"

"So you decide."

"Really, Rose?" She was ecstatic.

Rose smiled. At least someone was happy. As for herself, she felt distanced, as if it was all happening to someone else. Still, it gladdened her to see smiles on her parents' faces, to see all her relatives turn up at the house making such a joyful fuss. What a fortunate match! they told each other, wide-eyed and incredulous. After all she's put the family through. *Baruch Hashem!* She'll have such an easy life. He could have had his pick. So many girls from wealthy, *frum* families wanted the match, and he chose our Rose.

It made up for a great deal.

The days swirled around her like cotton candy on a stick in one of those machines, thickening day by day with activities and emotions until she felt positively suffocated. At night, when she tried to sleep, the vision of that little bride in the wicker chair being elbowed toward the marriage canopy popped into her mind. And sometimes it was not a bride, but a dog led by a leash or a bear in a cage being flogged by a circus trainer in red pantaloons. Whack, whack, whack, the sharp, biting pain of the leather cut into her flesh, until she woke, screaming, her pillow wet with sweat.

While the generally accepted custom among the Orthodox is that bride and groom have no contact at all seven days before the wedding, their families had decided on an extra stringency: for the purported sake of "modesty," Rose and Shimon should not meet at all until two weeks before the wedding, and then for the final time before meeting under the wedding canopy.

They met in the park during the morning hours, her mother watching from a distance.

"So, how do you feel, Rose?" Boomie asked her.

He looked a little different than she remembered, his beard a little wilder, his eyes shifty. He was smoking.

"When did you start that?" she asked, surprised.

"I've been smoking since I was fourteen." He shrugged.

She actually liked it. It made him look world-weary, like a fictional hero involved in dangerous, daring deeds for a good cause.

"I'd like to try that, too." She smiled.

He looked shocked. "That isn't acceptable. Women don't smoke!"

"They don't take photos either." She smiled.

He didn't smile back, throwing his cigarette to the ground and viciously crushing it with his shoe. "Look, Rose, we need to get something straight."

A sick wave of apprehension wafted through her stomach.

"Okay."

"You have to stop taking photos. You have to get rid of your camera."

"What?"

"This was the deal, don't you know that? This is what your father and the Honored Rav promised my parents. It's the reason the *shidduch* went through."

There was a long pause as she considered all the implications of this betrayal.

"No one told me!"

"It was thought best to leave telling you until after the chuppah. But I'm not comfortable with that. I thought you should know up front."

"But once we're married . . . you and I can decide . . . right?"

"Let me be honest with you. I don't have any money! My parents support me. And they don't want their daughter-in-law prancing around the neighborhood calling attention to herself. A glatt kosher butcher can't have a nonkosher daughter-in-law. Their business would be kaput. Besides, some of their customers consider photographs graven images."

"WHAT? Graven WHAT?"

"As it is written: 'Thou shalt not make any graven image of man or animal . . .' or something like that."

"And these people, these 'customers,' have no family photos from Europe, right? They don't hang framed posters of saintly rabbis on their walls! Such hypocrites."

He lit another cigarette and inhaled deeply. "I know. It's a stringency-of-the-week kind of thing. You know how it goes in our community. Keeping up with the Cohens. Whoever finds a way to deny himself more things that are permissible to everyone else, wins."

She was encouraged by his sarcasm. "But surely, Boomie, you're not like that? That's not the life you want?"

"No. But I'm stuck. As long as my parents are paying my bills and I'm living in their house . . . Look, it won't always be this way . . ." he added quickly, seeing her devastation.

"What's going to change?"

"I told you. One day, I'll have money of my own. My own business . . ."

"Where will you get the money to start it?"

"Well, my parents have money. They'll help. But they think I should stay in yeshiva a few more years. Until we have too many children to manage."

She leaned back on the hard park bench, her future flashing before her. Life in Borough Park in the basement of a mother-in-law apartment. The pregnancies, one after another. The new wigs and the stylish, overpriced, pious new clothes; the expensive jewelry they'd pick out for her for every major holiday. The circumcision ceremonies and the Passover seders, the endless High Holiday meals, the prayers in the synagogue as she tried to keep the children quiet . . . Bitterly, she saw her life and youth draining away, her dreams like shards of shattered glass beneath her feet, wounding her at every step as she played her part in a vast, false drama, an actress with nothing to say but lines written for her by others.

In short, it was her mother's life, except with much more money and far greater comfort. Not a bad life for a woman, she admitted. For someone else, it would be all they needed for happiness. But such a life with a husband who wasn't sincerely religious like her father, whose piety was all outward show to please social convention, a weak man who would never in his life make a bold or honest decision for himself—such a life, with such a man, for her, was impossible.

15

The day before the wedding, Rebbitzin Weiss accompanied her daughter to the ritual baths. Even though the entire subject of sex and purification rites had been avoided, the task given over to the official bride teacher, who was experienced in initiating bashful young brides to be into their religious duties and obligations, as well as some of the more delicate points of physical intimacy, it was the custom for mothers to personally take brides to the mikveh.

It was the first time for Bracha Weiss. She felt proud, emotional, even a little frightened. Her daughter would soon go from a virgin to a wife. It was not an easy transition, she knew. Even though Rose had been to a bride class, from her own experience Rebbitzin Weiss knew that nothing could prepare a young virgin for what a man did to her in bed.

"You are so quiet, Rose. Are you scared? Because there is nothing to be scared about. Every kosher bride goes through this. You will join your *choson* under the chuppah in purity. You know, a wedding day is just like Yom Kippur. God forgives the bride and groom all their sins. You will start fresh, a new, clean page, the beginning of a blessed life." She kissed her on the forehead. "As for the other, what happens after"—she lowered her voice—"it is all God's will. No matter how difficult, you must remember that and surrender to your husband. The blessing you receive will be beautiful, God-fearing children."

"Yes, Mameh. Thank you, Mameh," Rose said in a tired monotone, with no emotion at all.

Her mother looked at her, her brows knitted, the crease between them deepening. Rose had been like this ever since her last meeting with her groom. Passive, untalkative, agreeing to everything about the wedding without a single argument. Even at the food tasting she didn't put a single morsel into her mouth, not even the samples for the wedding cake! She had lost a lot of weight, too. But that was true of all brides. The dresses always had to be taken in. If only the brides' mothers had the same problem! she thought, patting her stomach and shaking her head. She thought about her own lovely dress, brand-new and fit for a queen! And the hairdresser had done a beautiful job on her wig. As for the wedding itself, the groom's parents had insisted no expense be spared. There would be an extravagant smorgasbord for the reception that would choke an elephant, not to mention a Viennese table afterward with every kind of cake, cookie, and dessert. No matter how stuffed people were from the prime ribs and potatoes, they would pounce on it and fill their plates again. She smiled to herself, imagining the stampede. And since the groom's parents were paying, why should she object? It was going to be a wedding the community and her family would never forget, she thought, tingling with excitement.

Oh, Hashem was good, so good, so compassionate! After all they had gone through, He had seen fit to arrange for them such a just reward.

The mikveh attendant was waiting for them.

"Such a beautiful bride! Mazel tov!" said the attendant, a poor, pious Sephardic Jew in a *tichel* low down on her forehead. The attendant saw the mother smile but noticed that the girl did not. The girl didn't do anything. She was like a wind-up doll that had run down, the attendant thought, not duly alarmed. This was not uncommon among such young brides. Mostly, they were terrified, pushed into agreeing by their parents, although sometimes you saw a bold girl who was mature for her age who was the real mover and shaker, the parents simply going along. She preferred the frightened ones to the brazen ones.

"Now, come along. You'll see how pleasant it is to do such an important mitzvah. You have the bride's room all to yourself for as much time as you need, so don't rush with your preparations. You know what you have to do, right?"

Rose said nothing.

"She knows. She's been to bride class," her mother interjected quickly. "She's just a little nervous, that's all. You'll remind her?"

"Of course, of course. And there's a whole list on the wall, step by step, of how to prepare the body for immersion. She'll have her own private ritual bath, so she won't even have to put on a bathrobe and walk down the hall after she makes her preparations. Come, child." The attendant beckoned kindly.

Rose, expressionless, didn't move.

"Would you like your mother to come with you?" Sometimes the very young ones did.

"You want I should go with you? Say something, Rose!" her mother finally exclaimed, exasperated.

Rose shook her head, and walked forward.

"Fine, fine. I'll sit here and wait. Go!"

She emerged an hour and a half later, a look of shock on her face, her long hair dripping wet, her blouse soaked.

"What took so long? I was starting to worry."

"She took a long shower afterwards. Washed and washed. Put on her clothes while she was still wet!" the attendant whispered confidentially into Rebbitzin Weiss's ear. "There are hair-dryers in the next room, *maideleh*, with makeup, eye shadow, hand creams, everything you could need," the attendant said cheerfully to Rose, who walked out the door, her mother hurrying to catch up.

Later that evening, the attendant told her coworker: "But she just looked at me. Stared with a funny look in her eyes, like she was a match and I was a Shabbos candle she couldn't wait to set on fire. Looked at her mother like that, too. And when she was inside the mikveh, she put her head under the water for so long, I thought she was trying to drown herself. *Gotteinu* how she coughed when she came out! I'm telling you, I'm glad I'm not going to that wedding!"

"Young girls and their *narishkeit*," said the other woman unsympathetically. She had four girls of her own, each with their own *mishagas*. No wonder they were trying to marry her off so young!

"Are you hungry, Rose?" her mother asked when they came home.

She shook her head.

"Thirsty?"

She shook her head again.

"You know," she warned, "you are not allowed to eat anything tomorrow, until after the chuppah, so you should have something to eat now."

That was the custom among Ashkenazim of Eastern Europe. Both bride and groom fasted and prayed on their wedding day. Among the Sephardim, it was the opposite. They plied the girl with sweets the whole day to give her pleasure and energy. But that practice made too much sense to the Ashkenazim, who found holiness in suffering.

"I just want to go to sleep. I'm so tired," Rose finally said.

"Oh, so she can speak!" Her mother smiled.

What happened next caught Rebbitzin Weiss completely by surprise. Rose lunged toward her, embracing her and hugging her close. Rebbitzin Weiss was so astonished at this sudden uncharacteristic warmth, which had been missing in their relationship for so long, she almost forgot to hug her back until it was too late.

When Rose finally felt the pressure of her mother's embrace, she sighed gratefully, finally letting go. "Good night, Mameh," she said with a strange tone in her voice, her mother thought, almost as if she were holding back tears. Well, the mikveh . . . it was a difficult experience for a modest virgin to take off all her clothes and be examined by the attendant before immersing. But you lived through it. And you soon forgot about it after the wedding and everything you went through in bed . . . She would, too.

"And kiss Tateh good night for me when he returns from the study house, will you? Tell him . . . tell him . . . thank you for all he's done. Tell him . . . that I love him."

"I'll tell him, child. Now go to sleep; you have a big day tomorrow."

"Yes, Mameh."

Pearl was sitting on Rose's bed when she entered her room.

"Rose? I've been waiting for you. Where did you go? Why are you all wet?"

"I'm not wet."

Pearl let it go, an achy feeling in her stomach telling her this was another grown-up secret she wasn't allowed to know. "How do you feel, Rose? To-morrow, finally. Your wedding. I thought it would never come!"

She stroked her sister's long blond hair. "Pearl . . . I . . ." she sighed. "I'm very tired and I have a long day tomorrow. I have to go to bed."

Pearl jumped up. "Of course, Rose."

"You know, when I leave home, I'm not going to take any of my dolls or stuffed animals or books with me. I want you to have them."

Her eyes lit up. "Really, Rose?"

"Really. And also, my headbands and barrettes. I won't need them any-more. And you can have this room back. You'll like that, won't you?"

"Oh, Rose. I'm going to miss you. I wish you didn't have to move away."

"So do I, Pearl," she whispered, hugging her sister tightly, running her fingertips over her young back as if trying to press them into her memory. Finally, she released her.

"Come, let me tuck you in."

Pearl walked down the hall to her little alcove, climbing into bed and burrowing beneath the covers. Rose smoothed the blanket over her. Leaning down, she kissed the soft, rosy cheek.

"I love you, Pearl."

"And I love you, Rose. Good night."

"Good night," she whispered, walking out the door and closing it behind her.

She went into her room, closing the door behind her and looking around. There was her bridal gown, hanging on the outside of the closet door in its plastic bag, newly back from dry cleaning. She quickly turned her head away, opening the closet. She took out her small battered suitcase, the one she had taken to her grandmother's the day she was put into exile, grabbing a few random pieces of clothing off the hangers and from her drawers, mostly underwear and stockings. She fingered the Palm stockings, shaking her head as she left them behind and quietly slid the drawer shut. And there was the box with her wedding shoes.

She opened it, taking out one shoe and trying it on. After weeks of trying to wear them in, she felt the immediate pinch of her toes, the ache of her arch, the rub against her ankle. It was never, ever going to fit.

Standing on a chair, she reached up for her camera, film, and the portfo-lio that held all her precious prints. The suitcase barely closed. Then, she took off her engagement ring and watch and placed them in the center of her pillow, where they could not be missed.

Her eyes swept the room, looking for some souvenir of the last seventeen years. But there was nothing she wanted, she realized. Not a single, solitary thing. But then she saw her prayer book. She lifted it, opening its worn pages, so many of them waterlogged from tears. She kissed it, then put it back on the shelf. It was too heavy to take with her in so many ways.

She opened the window. Placing her suitcase on the fire escape, she climbed out, carefully closing the window behind her. Holding her shoes in one hand and the suitcase in the other, she climbed down silently in the darkness, until all that remained was a final, breathtaking jump to the ground.

PART TWO

Forty Years Later

16

Williamsburg, Brooklyn, September 2007

"Turn around."

Rivka reluctantly obeyed, her fingertips playing nervously with the edges of her long sleeves.

"*Gotteinu!*" Pearl exclaimed, reaching up and nervously tugging her expertly coiffed wig ever more firmly over her shaved scalp. "There is nothing to even talk about! My daughter is not meeting her future in-laws dressed like that!"

Rivka flounced down on her bed, pouting. "I thought it was for Cousin Bluma's *chasseneh*?"

"Yes, of course, but the Kleinmans will also be there."

"I said yes to the *shidduch*? Besides, what's wrong with my dress?"

"What's wrong? What's *wrong*? You have to ask even? Just look at yourself! Oy, I knew I shouldn't let you go shopping alone!"

"It's just fine," the girl retorted calmly, with uncharacteristic defiance.

Her mother's eyes widened in disbelief. "This is a way to speak to a mother?"

"Look, I'm sitting down. You see? Even sitting, the skirt stays way below my knees. What else do you want already?"

"So, the child tells the mother what to think? What's right and what's wrong? Your father would be very interested in such behavior. Why don't I call him?" she threatened.

"So call him. I should be afraid?"

The chutzpah! She could hear Mameh's voice ringing in her ears as if she were still alive and sitting in the room: *This is what comes from giving in to her all the time! First, it was the cell phone, then the computer, and finally letting her put off meeting prospective bridegrooms until she reached seventeen, a whole year later than all the other girls!*

Pearl gnawed her lip nervously. "Zevulun, could you come here a minute?"

He was sitting at the dining room table studying the Talmud. At his wife's voice, he looked up. It was unusual for her to disturb him while he was learning. He lumbered, concerned, into the bedroom.

"Something happened, Pearl?"

"Give a look at your daughter!"

He looked. "*Kaynahora!* Queen Esther." He shrugged, beaming.

Pearl looked heavenward. "Zevulun! That dress!"

He looked again, stroking his long, graying beard, his eyes measuring with almost clinical precision how many inches the skirt fell below the knees, if the collarbone was covered, and if the sleeves not only covered the elbows as required by law, but were not overly wide so as to fall back when she lifted her arms, indecently exposing them.

"Kosher, Pearl, kosher. A kosher girl in a kosher dress."

Pearl blinked in astonishment at this pronouncement from her learned husband, proving that for all their Talmud study, men were dismally ignorant when it came to the actual practice of their religion, especially when it came to women. "It's a sleeveless, low-cut, practically backless dress with silver sequins . . . !"

"So, that's why you wear a long-sleeved shirt underneath!" Rivka challenged, raising her voice.

"Rivka!" His kind eyes widened. "Where is your respect for your mother! I'm surprised at you," he said softly, clicking his tongue.

She shrank from his gentle rebuke, her bravado gone. "I'm sorry, Tateh. But this is the style now! All the girls are dressing like this! You don't want me to look like some old *bubbee,* do you?"

He smiled, smoothing down her bright, golden hair with an indulgent caress. "Mameh, leave her be. Everything is covered."

Pearl wrinkled her noise in disgust. "It's got . . . the smell of the street . . ."

But Rivka had prepared for that. "I bought it at Elzee on Thirteenth Avenue in Borough Park," she said triumphantly, waving a bag from the well-known clothing store like a victory banner. "The saleslady there said Rebbitzin Klein's daughter Mirelle just bought the exact same dress also with a shirt to go underneath."

Could this possibly be true? Pearl thought, taking the bag and examining it as if it held the answer. Elzee was *the* go-to dress shop for the most fastidious, pious, and well-to-do ultra-Orthodox girls and women in Borough Park—wives and daughters of Hassidic rabbis and wealthy Haredi businessmen. Could such an outfit *really* be considered acceptable?

"I can't believe it," Pearl said firmly, despite the unmistakable splash of doubt already corroding her iron resolve.

"All right already. So I'll take it back. Anyway, I don't want to go."

"Not go? To your cousin Bluma's *chasseneh?*" He was shocked.

"For what should I want to go, Tateh? All the relatives will stare at me like I'm the red heifer. They'll pinch my cheeks and say: 'God willing, God willing, God willing by you . . .' like I was thirty, not seventeen! And then the Kleinmans will look me over like I'm a melon in the market . . ."

"You should be so lucky they should not only look you over, but pick you!" Pearl told her, exasperated. "He's the finest Talmud scholar in the yeshiva. Everyone says so!" she said, turning to her husband for support. "If she says no now, she'll lose him to another girl, a richer girl whose parents can afford to support him for many years. Right now, he only wants her."

Her father stroked her bright, smooth cheek, smiling. "He has eyes in his head."

Bluma, his brother's daughter, had gotten engaged at sixteen and would be barely seventeen when she married with both her parents' and the Haredi community's joyous consent. A tiny pain pierced his heart at the thought that his youngest, his baby, would also soon be leaving him for another.

Rivka. She had always been such a pretty child, with her mother Pearl's big blue eyes and golden hair, hair so beautiful it was painful to cut. Her tight braid reached down now almost to the backs of her knees.

The matchmakers had noticed. They had been calling now for a year. At first, he had put them off with one excuse after another, happy his youngest daughter was in no rush. But finally, he began listening to what they had to say, agreeing to a match. He had no choice. The Kleinman boy was special, a wonderful person from a generous and well-respected family. Pearl was right. He was in great demand. If Rivka made him wait much longer, the matchmakers would get discouraged and tell him to forget about Rivka for a more willing young lady from a family with much more to offer than a simple, pious bus driver like himself. She—and they—would have to settle for what was left. As her father, he couldn't allow that to happen.

"In my day, you met once, twice and decided. Now, the girls and boys are choosy, particular. It's not enough for them that the parents want. They also have to want."

Rivka set her jaw stubbornly.

"Leave her be, Pearl. She is a good and pious girl, our Rivkaleh. She will make the right decision, about the dress, and God willing, about her *choson*."

Rivka sat on the edge of her bed, pasting a charmingly girlish smile on her face, her legs crossed modestly as she casually swung her foot up and down.

It was then Pearl noticed the shoes—such high heels! In such an eye-catching sparkly silver shade . . . !

"Those shoes!"

"They match the dress, Mameh!"

Shoes the store wouldn't take back. Not in Borough Park. Pearl's shoulders slumped in defeat. Was Rivka telling the truth? Were all the girls of marriageable age dressing like this now? It was, after all, the one time in a woman's life she was encouraged to look as attractive and stylish as she could. What did she know? Unlike some of the richer rabbis' wives, who bought their clothes in Manhattan and on trips to Europe, she was no fashion expert, buying her clothes from the inexpensive local shops whose styles never changed.

"Take it off," she told her daughter, sighing.

Rivka froze.

"So you won't have to iron it again before you wear it to the *chasseneh*." Pearl knew a lost battle when she saw one.

"Yes, Mameh," Rivka said, her long eyelashes sweeping her cheeks, her face demure. "Thank you, Mameh, Tateh."

As soon as her parents had gone, she swiftly locked the door behind them.

Kicking off the shoes, which were already killing her feet, she pulled off the outfit, flinging it on a chair. She wasn't even that crazy about it anymore with that stupid shirt underneath! She'd found it on sale in Filene's Basement in Manhattan, a designer dress with the label cut out. Without the shirt, though, it looked stunning.

Exhausted, she lay down in bed, her arm flung across her eyes. She was so tired of these constant battles. And it was only going to get worse. As soon as her cousin's wedding was over, the yenta matchmakers would be calling day and night trying to arrange the *vort*.

Honestly, she didn't have anything against the Kleinman boy. From the one time they'd met, she'd found him pleasant, interesting, handsome even. And if she'd wanted her mother's life, she'd have said yes in a minute. But she had other plans. Big plans.

She smiled to herself, thinking of the secret letter in the white envelope already making its way through the world to the destination that would change her life. What if it got lost? What if the postman dropped it, or left it lying in the bottom of the postbox? Or the rain ruined the address, or the address was wrong to begin with? She shuddered, picking up her cell phone.

"Malca? They're letting me wear it. Thanks for the Elzee bag. It saved me! So tell me, what's new with the Sephardi?"

That's what they called him, the tall, handsome, dark-skinned Israeli who worked behind the counter at the kosher pizza place they went to. He wore a knitted skullcap, not a black homburg, and had a charming, jokey way about him that made you laugh and blush at the same time. Malca, who for months had been riding around and around on the matchmaking carousel, had been the first to notice his potential.

"He's very different from the boys I'm getting fixed up with. Either they don't have a word to say, or they never shut up. But even the ones who like to talk don't talk to *me*. Most of them don't even *look* at me. It's like I'm in shul in the women's section behind the *mechitzah*. Everything is so, so . . . holy!" she'd complained.

"Oy," Rivka commiserated.

Then, Malca dropped a bombshell. "He's asked me out."

"NO!" Rikva shouted, stunned. Meeting a boy accidentally was one thing. But deliberately arranging to meet him again behind your parents' backs was only slightly less sinful than a married woman committing adultery. In both cases, the consequences were unthinkable. Still, how thrilling to have a boy actually pick you out all by himself instead of having some money-grubbing matchmaker talking him into it.

"The chutzpah! Of course, you can't go," Rivka sighed.

"Why not?"

"You wouldn't . . . couldn't!"

"What could be so bad? No one has to know."

"It's *meshuga*! You know what could happen to you . . . !"

"So, what can they do to me that's worse than what they're already doing?"

She had a point, Rivka thought, changing the subject. "Can you get away this week?"

"To go where?"

"I was thinking the Museum of Modern Art."

"Rivka! We went there two months ago, remember?"

"I know, but I have a special reason . . . I don't want to tell you. I want it should be a surprise."

And was Malca ever going to be surprised, she thought, hanging up. You see those photos hanging on the wall? she'd say. Well, guess who took them? My aunt Rose!

Malca would *plotz*.

Imagine, having a close relative who had her photos hanging in a museum! Her mother's own older sister! Afterward, maybe she'd tell Malca about her own plans, her secret, dazzling, equally wild plans. Or maybe not. When the time came, Malca would be the first person they'd contact. She was her best friend, but she was no hero. She'd talk. In the meantime, Rivka lay back, closed her eyes, and dreamed.

17

Murray Hill, Manhattan, September 2007

Hannah Weiss Gordon leaned back on the black sofa, trying to find a comfortable position. But it was a mission impossible. Either some former tenant had stained and disposed of the bottom pillows, leaving behind barely covered springs, or the Chinese-immigrant slumlord who squeezed rent out of naive and desperate college students like herself had found it in a junk pile like that, hauling it up the five flights anyway just so he could advertise the place as "semifurnished."

She slid to the hardwood floors, from which, at least, one knew what to expect. Just as she'd adjusted her earphones and got her computer settled in the perfect center of her lap, the phone rang. She ignored it. But it rang and rang and rang, until finally she heard her landlord's antediluvian answering machine pick it up.

"Hi, honey, it's me. Got a minute?"

She wasn't expecting that. She lunged for the phone.

"Mom? When did you get back from London?"

"Oh, hi, sweetie. Late last night, but I didn't want to wake you."

"How is everybody?"

She heard her mother sigh. " 'Grandma Rose,' the kids told me, 'our parents aren't divorcing us, just each other.' So I guess the message has been delivered consistently and often. Actually, there isn't much anger that I can see. Your brother Jonathan and his wife are like polite distant cousins at a family reunion that can't wait to leave. . . . Let's hope that attitude will be enough to get them and the kids through this without anyone falling apart. And since it is Jonathan, I suppose we'll all have to trust he's doing the right thing for everyone."

Jonathan, unlike her, had followed their mother's footsteps into the creative arts, and he enjoyed a growing reputation as a set designer. This gave him, as far as their mother was concerned, creative license with his life as well. Had it been she getting rid of a perfectly good spouse, there would have been hell to pay, she thought resentfully.

"Tell me the truth. How do the kids look?"

"Sad. She bought them a dog."

"What?"

"You heard me. A black-and-white mongrel from the pound."

"So their father moves out and a dog moves in. I'm glad I'm taking women's history and not psychology. Grandma and Great-grandma's generation had quite a different take on splitting up families."

"Which is why I moved out of Williamsburg forty years ago and never went back," Rose snapped at her daughter.

"Something you *never* let us forget," Hannah murmured, barely audibly. She took her mother's abhorrence of anything remotely bourgeois personally, considering herself a staid and sensible member of that much-maligned class, her hopes pinned on a tenured college professorship with a steady income. With a father who was a legend, and a mother who was also famous, her goal was a calm, normal life out of the spotlight. For that reason alone, her mother's family interested her. Although they couldn't be considered "normal," they were certainly more down-to-earth than either of her parents. "I never understood why I could never even meet your family."

"Oh, that again . . . Trust me, it was the best thing I could have done for you."

"I'd like to discuss it with you anyway. Can we meet soon?"

"Well, that's odd! What brought all this up just now? Besides, I have nothing to add to what I've already said over the years. I saved you from the Taliban, believe me."

Her mother was prone to exaggeration for effect. Hannah had learned not to take her literally. "It's hard, Mom. I'm a women's history major, after all. That's what I do all day, research the way different women lived their lives. I think it would be interesting to meet them."

"You are assuming, aren't you, that one of them wants to meet you?"

"Well, actually, I've gotten a letter . . ."

"From one of *them*?"

"It's your sister Pearl's daughter, Rivka."

"What does she want, your kidney?" she joked, trying to hide her confusion. Pearl's daughter! It had been so many, many years. She felt overwhelmed with conflicting emotions.

"That's low!"

"Okay, okay. I give up. What?"

"I'll show you the letter when we meet." She hesitated. "Mom, in all these years, your family *never once called you*? *Never once* wanted to meet your children?"

Rose wondered how much of the shocking, heartbreaking aftermath of her escape from home to share with her inquisitive and demanding daughter. For now, at least, nothing seemed the perfect answer. "When do you want to do this?" she asked reluctantly.

"Tomorrow? Lunch?"

"Oh, I don't know . . . I've got all these new negatives to work on . . . What about early next week?"

"This can't wait a week."

"Why not? It's waited over forty years . . ."

"This isn't about *them*; it's about me, your daughter! Why am I always the last one on your list of priorities? After work, self-fulfillment, friendships, fame, travel . . ."

Not for the first time, Rose heard the pain in her daughter's voice. Some of it, she knew, was justified. She was not going to win Mother of the Year. But she had done the best she could under the circumstances, she comforted herself. As Hannah's father always said: everyone had the right to screw up their children in their own way.

"Okay, okay! Tomorrow it is."

"Thanks, Mom. I appreciate you taking some time off from your busy schedule . . ."

"Are you being sarcastic?"

"No, not at all. . . . I really do appreciate . . . So meet me at NYU at Chik-fil-A in Weinstein Hall."

"Oh, does it have to be on campus? All those chatty students, all that noise . . ."

Hannah exhaled silently. "So what about Blue Hill Farm on Washington Place, right near the West Fourth subway station?" she said as politely as she could.

"Okay, see you tomorrow."

"Dear Cuzin Hannah, may G-d let you live long," Hannah read above the din of the lunchtime crowd. *"I am your couzin Rivka, the daughter of your aunt Pearl. Maybe you are shocked to get such a letter from a person you don't know? I am very sorry I never met you. The daughters of two sisters who come from the same mother, this is* very *tragic. I do not know how this thing happened or who we should blame. And so I write to you, a stranger, and hope you will show some* chesed *to me."*

"What does that word mean, 'che-sed'?" Hannah asked her mother.

"First of all, it isn't pronounced like the past tense of cheese . . . It's like clearing the back of your throat when you are getting ready to spit! 'Chhhhe-sed.' It means a pure good deed, a favor you do with no desire or expectation of reward."

"Got it." She continued: *"I am a Bais Yaankov girl, seventeen years of age. I am an excelent student, my teachers all say this, and I very much long to continue my learning. Emes? . . ."*

Hannah paused. "What . . . ?"

Rose got up and walked around, looking over her shoulder at the page. "It means 'to tell the truth.'"

"Emes? I want to be a doctor! But my parents—may they live long!—forbid me even to think such a thing, because in a secular college they are afraid I will lose my purity and faith and intermarry. Instead, out of this fear, they have found me a man they say I must marry in the next few months.

"*I have met this young man twice, and my parents are already arranging the vort.*

"What's that?"

"It's like an engagement party, only it's the kind of engagement you can never break. It's easier to marry and get a divorce."

"Gee whiz!" Hannah shook her head, looking down at the paper and continuing to read: "*I am desperate! I have a right to live my own life. Everybody has that right!*"

Rose shifted uncomfortably, coughing, the words eerily familiar but unplaceable. "Wow!"

"Yeah. I know," Hannah said, without looking up.

"*I wish to run away from home before this happens, but I have no wear to go. Please couzin, I don't know who else to turn to. Everyone in my family is against me! No one understands. Please call me on my cell phone 9 - - - - - - - - -*

"*Rivka.*"

Hannah folded the letter up, slipping it back inside the envelope and handing it to her mother over the small table in the crowded restaurant. Rose lifted her palms in horror, drawing back.

"Honey, if you call this poor girl back and offer her assistance, your life will become a living hell. And so will mine."

"That's a bit dramatic, isn't it?"

"It's not the half of it."

"Mom, even if she was a total stranger, we should want to help her! But she's blood. How can we just turn our backs?"

Rose hesitated. "Listen, I'm not saying I don't have tremendous sympathy for her. But as my mother used to say: 'You don't need sharp teeth to eat borscht!'"

"Come again?"

"In other words, you don't need to be a genius to figure this out. First of all, imagine what would happen if I facilitate another runaway bride from the house of Weiss? They'd have the final proof—not that they need it!—that the awful things they've believed about me all these years are true. That I made the choices I did not because I was different, but because I was evil."

Hannah was flabbergasted. "Mom, after all this time, you still *care* what your family thinks about you?"

Rose hesitated. "You don't, can't, understand what it's been like for me, Hannah. Besides, it's dangerous."

"Now you're being ridiculous. They're just old-fashioned Jews, not good-fellas. What can they possibly do?"

"Oh, my little naive princess, are you ever clueless! They will send their thugs here and put you and me and little Rivkaleh into the hospital."

"Give me a break. Thugs?"

"Oh, you better believe it! You think you can't bash someone over the head with a crowbar if you wear a skullcap and a black suit? You think their beards interfere with their fists? Think again. Don't imagine that stuff is just made up about them having modesty patrols that roam around beating people up. It's for real. And they do it all for the sake of heaven."

She actually looked scared, Hannah thought, shocked. This was nothing like the fearless woman she knew as her mother. "Well, *you* left, and you are still here to tell the tale."

"But I never told you anything about what I went through," she answered with uncharacteristic bitterness.

Hannah shook her head slowly. "When I got this letter, I thought that you, of all people, would sympathize and know what to do. After all, doesn't she remind you of someone you once knew?"

"Yes, and that's just the problem. I *know* what's lying ahead of her if she goes through with this. She doesn't, and neither do you. Besides, as you can see from her letter, she's naive and impulsive. She wants to be a doctor? She can't even spell!"

"But you had the same horrible education and look at what you've accomplished with *your* life! We could help her to go back to school, Mom. We could guide her. I'm sure she'd be so grateful . . ."

"Yes, grateful, at the beginning, until the tug of the family kicks in. . . . It's like the pull of the magnetic field over gravity. We'll take her in, try to help her, and then she'll get discouraged and homesick and look down that long, lonesome road ahead among strangers in an unfamiliar world. She'll have guilt dogging her every step, thinking God is going to punish her for having a brain and wanting to make her own choices. Then, she'll blame us for everything and go back home and get married. Maybe she'll invite you—certainly not me, the *scandalous aunt*—to the wedding. But you better not go, because your crime of trying to help her will be viewed as so unforgivable that even Yom Kippur will be wasted on you. My family believes some crimes can never be forgiven, and some people are so low they can never repent. And you will be one of them right alongside of me."

Hannah looked stricken, Rose thought, brushing her daughter's dark curls out of her serious, dark eyes, her heart aching for her sensible, kind, liberal daughter who gave money to refugees in Darfur and bought bag ladies lattes in Starbucks. She was so much like her father. "I know you want to do the right thing, honey. But sometimes, it's not so obvious what that is. Do you really need this in your life right now?"

In *my* life, Hannah thought, the faint hope she'd secretly harbored that her mother might somehow rescue her by offering her own spacious apartment as an alternative slowly slipping away and the reality of another person intruding into her tiny, private space becoming dreadfully real. Where would she sleep? Not on that couch. . . . With midterm exams coming up and a bunch of papers to write, did she really have time to deal with this?

Besides, maybe her mother *was* right. *Not* getting involved would force her young "*cuzin*" to rethink the whole thing before it was too late. Or was that just a rationalization on her part, a selfish but prudent desire to bar the doors of her ordered life against strange and uncontrollable forces?

"Okay, I hear you. But one day you are going to have to tell me everything."

"One day . . ." Rose smiled tepidly, her mouth dry.

Hannah stuffed the envelope back into her handbag, the way she did unsolicited mail from various worthy charities, hoping to delay both the disappointing answer to their requests and her conscience pangs. In the meantime, she hurried to classes.

The course was Women in European Society and Politics. The lecture hall was filling up. She scanned the room and saw Jason looking over his shoulder at her with a roguish smile, always at least half a flirt, if not a whole one. He waved.

She squeezed past dozens of knees to get to the seat he had saved (for her or Stacey or Deidre . . .). His long legs were snugly outlined in worn jeans with strategically placed fashionable rips. His thick, navy blue sweater with the little polo player smelled of fabric softener, the way his blond wavy hair smelled of conditioner. But nothing could drown out the reek of testosterone that oozed from his every pore, at least in her imagination. In a room full of women, he was like a lighthouse.

"Hi. Have you seen this?"

It was a printout of the new Web site for NYU's Center for the Study of Gender and Sexuality.

Proposals are invited for a panel to be entitled "Documentary Techniques in Pornographic Film and Video" . . . a panel of three presenters will explore a recent and profound trend that appears across pornographic genres: the emphasis on capturing "real" sex through narrative techniques typically found in the documentary film tradition . . .

"This is the reason I switched to history. Tell me, is everyone in your department a pervert, or just the vast majority?"

He snorted with laughter.

For months, he had been playing at something that she had yet to figure out. On the one hand, he had never asked her out, but on the other, he saved her seats and could talk to her for hours whenever he ran into her. Once, he even showed up at her apartment. He'd sat there eating her potato chips and sipping her beer until finally hinting he'd like to spend the night.

As if. What did girls who said yes to these kinds of proposals do the day after? Ignore it? Exploit it? Forget it? And were they really capable of doing any of the foregoing without feeling embarrassed, stupid, or used?

Still, she didn't blame him for trying. She was even a bit flattered. Everybody wanted something. As far as she was concerned, the only unforgivable crime was seeking her friendship just to meet her famous mother.

All her life she had had to deal with those kinds of opportunists: girls in high school who became her best friends in order to get her mother to give them tickets to gallery openings. Teachers who befriended her and then got her mother to give free talks to their favorite charities. Boys who introduced her to friends as the daughter of Rose Weiss, *the famous photographer*.

Given that he wasn't guilty of that, and the fact that there wasn't a great selection of men in women's studies, she kept hoping against hope something worthy might develop.

"Busy tonight?" he asked.

"What did you have in mind?"

"Well, we've got that midterm coming up . . ."

Of course. What else? Free tutoring.

"Sorry," she murmured, hiding her disappointment.

"Really?"

"Yeah, Jason. Really."

She settled back, annoyed, waiting for the lecture to begin.

She'd taken up women's studies to be inspired. Instead, the more she learned about the lives of women, the more depressed she felt. She'd always held on to the belief that feminism had transformed the world. Yet as much as things had changed, when she studied the modern world in light of what she was learning about the medieval world, the more she realized that they had stayed the same. Men still ran the world, initiating relationships and controlling them.

Take the medieval concept of *Kinder, Küche, Kirche*. Didn't every fundamentalist sect today have the same "barefoot and pregnant" attitude toward women? And in the name of multiculturalism, was this attitude not now receiving respect in the Western world, which it didn't deserve?

Among Jews, though, there was an interesting twist. While fundamentalist Jewish society also glorified the stay-at-home housewife whose "pride is within her four corners," it also, rather ironically, threw women out into the working world, insisting they support their families so their husbands could sit and learn the Talmud. And so even hundreds of years ago in the shtetel, pious daughters were taught to speak, read, and write in several languages, as well as to do rudimentary math in order to sustain the family business.

Predictably, social custom had risen up to ensure that women didn't get too uppity, defusing the explosiveness of a society filled with educated women married to unworldly men. Yes, they let their girls learn how to run a store, or teach—or, nowadays, become an accountant or a computer programmer. But, God forbid, they would not be allowed to go to college or become a doctor or lawyer or artist. For how could an unworldly, uneducated yeshiva boy cope with a wife like that?

She thought of her cousin. Perhaps that was why they married off their girls so young, before they had a chance to look around and get ideas into their heads? And when that didn't work, social custom ensured that breaking an engagement and getting a divorce were major hurdles completely under the men's control.

A sudden vision of Rivka's letter tossed carelessly between the leaking pens, half-used tissues, lipsticks, and dusty change in her overstuffed bag made her ache with guilt. *Isn't it my obligation as an enlightened woman to reach out a helping hand?* Almost immediately, the thought was countered by a backlash of annoyance of equal intensity. *How did she find my address?*

"What did I miss?"

She looked up to her left. It was that new guy, Simon Narkis. She felt the butterflies flap their tiny wings inside her stomach. He was a transfer student from Chicago. He had long, straight dark hair and Trotsky eyeglasses and wore a black leather jacket over a vintage T-shirt in some wild sixties print. Today he had a well-worn copy of *Madame Bovary* sticking out of his pocket—one of her all-time favorites.

There was something intense and appealing about his lean face, Hannah thought, studying him as nonchalantly as she could. While he certainly didn't have the sex appeal of a Jason, he seemed to have . . . something else of equal attractiveness. Mystery maybe? He was a Judaic studies major, minoring in Jewish literature, which also piqued her interest. His smile was shy, almost secretive, making you feel it wasn't shared with just anyone. He was definitely someone she was interested in getting to know.

"Late again, Simon?" Jason said, leaning over her to look at him, a touch of rivalry in his pose, which delighted her.

"Yeah, don't I know it! I'm working in a bookstore on Second Avenue and the traffic is sometimes impossible."

"Well, it's just a wild suggestion, but have you ever considered using that car your parents bought you—or even the subway—instead of your bike . . . ?" Jason smirked.

"Fossil fuels . . ." Simon shook his head.

"Fossil fools . . ." Jason said under his breath, rolling his eyes.

"Now, now, boys." Hannah smiled.

Jason leaned back, whispering in her ear: "So, how are your party plans coming along?"

"Oh, that," she answered, flattered he even remembered. She'd mentioned it once, casually.

"What was that about a party?" Simon asked.

She looked at him and smiled. Why not? A party after finals where she could laugh and drink soothing alcoholic beverages and forget about saving all the oppressed women of the world . . . She'd invite them both.

"I'll let you know soon," she said, reaching into her purse for her lipstick.

The white envelope inadvertently came with it, dropping silently and unnoticed to the floor.

18

Murray Hill, Manhattan, December 31, 2007

"We can use another pitcher of margaritas. Can I do the honors?" Jason asked.

The party was in full swing. Every space in Hannah's tiny apartment was filled with sound: laughter, favorite songs playing at random from her iPod, and earnest, beer-fueled debates.

"Sure. Thanks, Jason." She smiled at his California good looks only to be distracted by the unsettling vision of Simon, the intellectual, deep in earnest conversation with Stacy. She followed Stacy's glossy, manicured nails as they flipped back her shiny blond hair. Were Simon's eyes shining, or glazing over from boredom? Hannah moved anxiously toward him to get a better look.

The doorbell was ringing again.

"Do you want me to get that?" Simon eased himself off the couch, turning away from Stacy rather quickly, Hannah judged, hopeful.

Stacy nodded toward the door. "He's calling you."

Simon was looking out into the hall, a strange smile on his face. He turned to Hannah: "She won't come in. She says you're her *'cuzin.'*"

Hannah hurried to the door.

Rivka stood there, a shy, hopeful smile on her rain-soaked face, her ugly gray raincoat covered in melting snow, her chilled feet in horrible, opaque, seamed stockings and laced up black old-lady shoes.

"Cuzin Hannah," she said softly. "You got my letter?"

Simon stared from one to the other, his eyebrows raised, waiting.

"Thanks, Simon. I'll . . . be right back." Hannah pushed him gently inside, closing the door behind her.

"Rivka?"

She nodded. "I waited so long for you to call. But then you didn't. So I thought . . . maybe . . . the letter . . . it maybe got lost."

"Why are you here, Rivka?"

"I've run away!"

"You've got to be kidding!"

Her bright blue eyes filled with tears. "I can't wait anymore! If it's not good, I can go . . ."

She picked up a small battered suitcase, then turned toward the stairs and began to climb down.

For a split second, Hannah watched her go. Then, she ran down after her.

"Rivka! Where are you going?"

The girl sat down on the steps. "I don't know."

Hannah took the suitcase out of her cold, bare hand. "Come on."

She led her back up the steps and into her noisy apartment. She could see the girl's eyes widen in surprise bordering on shock at everything she saw.

"It's your birthday?"

Hannah turned to stare at her. Was she serious? "Honey, it's New Year's Eve!"

"A Rosh Hashanah party? In December?"

Was she for real? "Oh, wow! Never mind. These are some of my friends from college. Would you like to take off your coat and join us? Have a drink? I can introduce you to everyone."

"Oh, no!" the girl said in alarm, shaking her head.

Hannah exhaled slowly. "Well, come into my bedroom then. I'll close the door. You can have some privacy."

Hannah hurried Rivka through the crowd without stopping to make introductions, taking their stares in stride and answering with a shrug. A couple she barely knew was sitting on her coat-covered bed, making out.

She coughed. "Sorry, guys. Family emergency."

When they were gone, she locked the door behind her.

"Cuzin, maybe I'll go . . ."

"Rivka, take off that soaking-wet coat and sit down! I'm not letting you go anywhere in this weather and certainly not on New Year's Eve at this time of night! By the way, where do your parents think you are? They could call the cops!"

"They have no right to force me to stay and get married . . ." Her voice was almost hysterical.

"Look, calm down! I agree with you! But if you are under eighteen, they still have some legal rights over you."

She sat down, suddenly quiet. "And after that?"

"You'll be an adult."

Her face brightened. "Cuzin, in two months I'm eighteen! Could I just stay by you until then? *Imyertza Hashem,* I won't make any trouble." She looked around hopefully. "Since the time I'm little, I cleaned the whole house, washed dishes, peeled potatoes, cooked."

Hannah felt her heart melt as she listened to this eager offer. *Poor thing! What a life!* Nonetheless, her mother's warnings still echoed in her head. "Did you at least leave your family a note?"

Rivka jumped up, shaking her head violently, braced to flee. "You don't understand, Cuzin! The second they know where I am, they'll come and get me and make me go home to do what they want!"

"All right, then. *Don't* tell them where you are. Just make sure they don't think you've been kidnapped or murdered. Anything else would be just too cruel."

Rivka sat down. "I could ask my friend Malca in Bnei Brak to call them. She could say I was there with her and that I'm fine."

"What or where's that, Benny Barack?"

"It's in Israel. Near Tel Aviv."

"So, this friend will cover for you?"

"*Vus is dus,* 'cover'?"

"Huh?"

"What means that word, 'cover'?"

"Oh. It means will she agree to lie, to say that you're there?"

She nodded eagerly. "Since we know each other, we lie for each other."

This admission took Hannah aback, clashing horribly as it did with the stereotype in her head that people who dressed like Hassidim must also be honest and kind and truthful, that it was a package deal that went together, like Malibu Barbie and her beach accessories. She had to stop thinking in clichés.

"Well, call her then."

"Ah, Cuzin. I don't have a phone anymore. . . . I left it home. My parents could maybe trace it."

She had shrewdly thought of everything, Hannah realized, seeing her in a new light. "Well, mine is right on the night table. Call Malca and tell her to call your parents, immediately."

"But Cuzin, it's four in the morning in Bnei Brak!"

"Oh, right. Well, then call her in a few hours."

"It's long distance."

"Whatever!" Hannah replied, exasperated. "It has to be done, Rivka. You understand? You can't stay here without telling your parents you're fine."

"And then you'll let? Until I'm eighteen?" she wheedled, suddenly straightening her back.

Who was she, really? A little bird who had just left the nest on her first attempt to fly? Or a master manipulator? Hannah wondered, studying her more closely.

She seemed so fragile and *so very* young and trusting, like Little Red Riding Hood on her way to Grandma's house, Hannah thought, gripped by a sudden pity, her cynicism fading into a sense of shame. Had her *cuzin* really been a little bird, there was no question she'd have picked her up and nursed her, accepting all the complications and messiness that entailed, hoping only to help get her strong enough to fly out again into the wild.

"Let's just take this thing one day at a time, shall we? Are you hungry, thirsty? Would you like to come out and meet my friends?"

"No, no, no! Thank you. But I'm very . . . tired. Could I just lay down here for a little while?"

"Sure." Hannah pushed aside the coats, making room. "And, *please,* don't forget to make that phone call later, will you?"

"Don't worry, Cuzin. I'll tell Malca to tell my parents I'm on my way to her in Israel."

"And when they call to speak to you the next day, then what?"

"She'll say I'm not talking to them, that I'm mad on them . . . Don't worry, Cuzin, we'll think of something. Anyway, parents like mine, they don't start with the police. They call them 'the Cossacks.'"

A shudder went down Hannah's spine at the idea of people so far removed from anyone she could imagine in America. "And what if they call that other group, the Modesty Patrol?"

"Vus is dus?" She shrugged.

Was she being disingenuous? Or sincere? Hannah couldn't tell. "Okay, then. I'll just close this door, but don't lock it, because I'll have to come in and get the coats when people leave. I'll just tell everyone not to come in."

"Thank you so much, Cuzin Chana. You are a *tzadakis.*"

"Whatever," she sighed, glancing behind her with a deep sense of unease before closing the door.

"Who is that?" Stacy whispered.

"My cousin Rivka."

"Your family, really?" Jason said. "She looked very nineteenth century."

"More like the Amish," Stacy giggled. "Those clothes, really. And the braids, the stockings."

"If you must know, she's from one of those ultra-Orthodox families in Brooklyn. My mother's family."

"Ooops." Stacy grinned.

"She's run away from an arranged marriage," Hannah blurted out impulsively, wanting to wipe that stupid smile off Stacy's face.

"Married? She looks, like, twelve," Jason murmured.

"She's almost eighteen. But she's very naive and innocent. I can't let her wander around Manhattan."

"Eighteen?" Jason repeated, causing Hannah to wonder at his interest in this particular point.

"That's really kind of you, Hannah. But it sounds like it might get a bit messy," Simon pointed out.

"Yeah, her parents could call the cops," Stacy yawned, downing the last of her drink.

Although she herself had said and thought exactly the same things, Hannah found their warnings annoying. "She wants to study for her college entrance exams. She's interested in being a doctor," Hannah answered, none of it sounding very plausible, even to her.

"Well, if she needs help, I used to tutor for the SATs," Jason offered.

"Oh, you can count me in for that, too," Simon cut in earnestly. "I'd be happy to tutor her, Hannah. I think what you're doing is beautiful."

"Right," Stacy said under her breath, rolling her eyes. "I'll bet. And the fact that she's a blonde, completely innocent and virginal, and almost legal age has nothing at all to do with it, guys, huh?"

"Not all men think in those terms, Stacy," Simon said stiffly.

But Jason just grinned.

The next morning, Hannah made her way through the postparty debris, her head a bundle of jangling nerve endings throbbing with exhaustion. No, it wasn't a bad dream. There she was, her *cuzin,* spread out on that awful sofa.

Her tiny body looked lost in the old-fashioned flannel nightgown that covered her from head to toe, giving her the charming, old-fashioned air of one of those bonneted daughters from *Little House on the Prairie.* Her cheeks were a soft pastel pink, like a flushed baby's. She had not a speck of blush or eyeliner or powder on her. Her incredibly long hair pooled on the floor, its polished gold without artifice or ornament.

Poor thing, Hannah thought, then wondered if it was herself she was really feeling sorry for. It was so much easier to keep your charities at arm's length. To buy bag ladies lattes was one thing. To invite them to move in with you quite another.

As quietly as she could, she cleaned up, emptying ashtrays, disposing of paper cups, and sweeping cookie and potato chip crumbs into neat piles that she scooped up and disposed of. Before leaving, she taped an extra key and a long note full of instructions and explanations to the inside door of the apartment. Full of misgivings, she hurriedly locked the door behind her, hoping that the farther she went, the more the stranger on her sofa would fade from her thoughts into a soft blur.

———

Rivka got up around noon, the sunlight baking her head, making her squint. "Oy!" she whispered, caressing her aching back. When the party was over, she'd insisted on giving Hannah back her bed, choosing the sofa over the sleeping bag her cousin offered. It had been a terrible mistake.

"Cuzin?" she called out, but the house was quiet except for the ceaseless thrum of New York traffic noise. She made her way to the bathroom, staring at her face in the smudged old mirror. She smiled. "Free," she whispered, shaking her head in amazed delight.

The phone call to her friend in Israel had gone well. Poor Malca! She'd been caught out on her very first date. Her parents had been outraged, swiftly marrying her off to the Sephardi, a boy she hardly knew. Although he wore a skullcap and was observant of the Sabbath and holidays, her parents had been heartbroken, having dreamed of an Ashkenazi Torah scholar for a son-in-law. Soon after the wedding, wishing to put the whole debacle out of sight and thus hopefully out of mind, they'd shipped the couple off to Israel. They'd been married now barely three months.

"So, how is he?"

"He's very different than my father," Malca had whispered over the phone. "I never saw him open a Talmud. He goes to work during the day, and we even have a television in the house. But he expects me to cook him couscous and kebab, and won't eat gefilte fish . . . What do I know from couscous and kebab? Don't worry, Rivka. I'll call your mother and swear you're on your way here. But she won't be happy."

"For sure. You think I don't know?"

There was a pause. "Why'd you do it, Rivka?"

"You need to ask? They're pushing me."

"So, what's the plan?"

Rivka was silent for a few moments. "I know? I'll be all right, Malca. I'll do what I always dreamed of doing."

Only when she hung up did she allow herself to fully imagine the heartbreak and fury Malca's call would bring her family. But it couldn't be helped. She didn't want a husband bossing her around, explaining her duties to her when she moved out of her parents' house and *they* stopped telling her what to do. She didn't want to be a pleasing and obedient wife and daughter-in-law, one who would cater to her husband's physical needs and help him to fulfill the mitzvah of procreation. All she could feel as she'd looked ahead into the future they envisioned for her was a growing sense of dread, the world and its possibilities desiccating, shrinking into a tiny cell that she would be forced to crawl into, a space hardly big enough to breathe, let alone grow and move and explore.

There had to be more!

Her whole life she'd been subjected to numerous warnings about the fate of girls who did not measure up (that is, submit to their fate), warnings meant to terrorize and instill fear. They'd backfired, especially those whispered about the terrible fate of her glamorous aunt Rose.

For the first nine years of her life, she had been barely aware of her aunt Rose's existence, gleaning vague scraps of information from low, excited whispers in Yiddish that stopped the moment her presence was sensed. But during her grandmother's shiva, the floodgates had burst. Her aunt Rose had been practically the only thing people talked about: How she'd shortened Granny's life (she was eighty-seven). How she hadn't even had the decency to come to the funeral or to pay her respects with a shiva call! How the *shandah* she'd created would brand the family for decades.

The community was still talking about it: the unused wedding hall and the uneaten food her grandparents had been forced to pay for. The disgrace to the groom a brilliant, promising scholar from such an important family— who had been shamed before the community, becoming the whispered subject of ill-founded, gossipy conjectures. Even worse, though, was the fact that she'd rebuffed every attempt of the family to bring her home, going on instead to live the shameless life of a shunned outcast. She was Delilah, Jezebel, the Midianite whore . . . !

But the most horrible sin of all—as far as the gossiping women were concerned—was the difficulties her mother, Pearl, had faced as her younger sister. In wake of the scandal, no decent family would agree to accept her as a *shidduch*. As a result, at the advanced and almost unmarriageable age of twenty-two, Pearl had had to give up her dream of marrying a Torah scholar and settle for a bus driver, a widower with a small child. *That* could never be forgiven.

Rivka had taken it all in, angered, amazed, terrified. But when she was fourteen she came across some shocking information that radically changed not only her opinion of her aunt but her view of her own life as well.

She yawned and stretched, getting into the shower. She touched her cousin's dainty soaps and creams with pleasure, letting the hot water stream over her aching limbs for a long time. After drying off, she dressed once again in the same midcalf pleated blue skirt and long- sleeved blue shirt that she'd arrived in the night before—her school uniform.

She'd brought almost nothing else with her, hoping in that way to gain a few more hours before her mother's eagle eye spotted something amiss. The only other clothing she'd brought with her was a fancy blue satin suit meant for weddings and holidays that had been sitting at the cleaners.

She found a clean cup, filling it with water and pouring it over her lightly clenched fists three times to rid herself of the ritual impurity left behind when her spirit left her body in sleep. She took out her well-worn prayer book and began her morning prayers. When she came to the Eighteen Benedictions prayer, which must be said facing east toward Jerusalem, she wondered which way to turn. The sun set in the West. So, the opposite . . . But it had already been pitch-black when she came. So, she twirled around asking God to point her in the right direction. She stopped and faced the window. Taking three steps back and then three steps forward, she bowed deeply, then began to pray.

Every word struck her deeply.

God, the God of Abraham, Isaac and Jacob; great, and awesome and terrible, God of endless mercies, repay our kindnesses and in love bring redemption for Your name's sake to our offspring. God, You help and protect; You bring life to the dead, nourish our lives with compassion, supporting the fallen, healing the sick, releasing the imprisoned, and keeping faith with all those who lie in dust. Who is like You, King, who nurtures life and salvation?

She felt two fat tears make their way down her cheeks to the corners of her mouth. She licked them away. They were delicious.

Her growling stomach led her to her cousin's kitchen. She searched through the cabinets hoping to magically distinguish which cutlery and dishes were for food containing milk and which for meat, as her cousin's note had left out such vitally important information. To her shock, there seemed to be only one set, the plates, bowls, and cups lying on top of each other in careless abandon. The cooking utensils proved the same: only one frying pan and one large and small pot, all of them one inside the other.

She found some disposable plates and bowls left over from the party, along with some plastic spoons, then hunted for cereal with a rabbinical stamp of approval. Luckily, she found a box of Kellogg's Corn Flakes with the stamp of the Orthodox Union of Rabbis. Under normal circumstances, her family would not have relied on this organization, which wasn't Orthodox enough as far as they were concerned. But in her present circumstances, it was certainly better than nothing. Eagerly, she opened the refrigerator, looking for milk. But it was Gentile milk, with no rabbinical stamp at all.

The phone rang.

A chill crawled up her spine. Then, she calmed herself. No one could possibly know she was here. Besides, maybe it was her cousin.

"Hello?"

"Hi, is this Hannah's cousin, Rivka?" a deep male voice asked.

"Who are you?" she demanded, alarmed.

"Wow, slow down! Um, I'm your cousin's friend from the university from last night. I heard your story . . ."

"Who told you about me?"

"Well, your cousin said . . ."

"She shouldn't have told you anything!" she shouted.

"Listen, baby, I'm on your side! I think what you are doing is very brave, and I told Hannah that I'd be willing to help you pass your entrance exams and go to university. I used to tutor kids for SATs. I'm an expert," he said with soothing calmness.

She hesitated. "Cuzin Hannah, she told you to call me?"

There was a pause. "I'm not doing this behind her back, if that's what you're getting at." He sounded offended.

"Oh, I didn't mean to . . . I'm grateful . . . really . . ."

"Look, I don't have time to waste. If you really are interested, then let's start now. What are you doing?"

"Trying to get breakfast together and not getting very far," she admitted.

"Well, what about I pick you up in front of Hannah's building in fifteen minutes?"

Her stomach rumbled. "Maybe you know a place that sells kosher food?"

"There's a place not far from my apartment. A supermarket. It's sure to have something . . . And after, we can start some work."

"Thank you very much!"

"See you soon."

As soon as she hung up, she began to dial her cousin's cell phone number to discuss this with her. Then, she put the phone down. She didn't want to be a nuisance, especially if Hannah had gone out of her way to arrange this whole thing. And if she didn't know anything about it, she might not approve, not that it was any of her business. It's my business, she thought. My own, personal business.

She thought of Bluma, her obedient, round-faced cousin who'd married the second boy she had ever spoken to and taken up life in a tiny apartment in Borough Park downstairs from her in-laws. She'd work as a secretary in her father-in-law's import business until she had her first child. She'd grow fatter and more content with every passing year, watching her life relentlessly unfold with no place to get off or turn around until she reached the end and died, never once stopping off along the way to visit her own dreams.

That could have easily been my life, too, she thought with a shudder. If she hadn't been on a fanatic Passover cleaning binge, she'd likely never have even noticed that box pressed up into the far corner of the wall under her mother's bed. Of course, she'd opened it. What would her mother ever need to hide?

It was filled with a stash of fading sepia photographs of obscure relatives. She was just about to replace the cover and put it back, when she noticed an envelope addressed to her mother. Inside was a letter.

January 10, 1976

Dear sister Pearl,
Even though you said some terrible things to me in your letter, I was still happy to get it. It's been so long. Why did you finally break the family's code of silence?
To answer your charges, I called the police because the family left me no other choice. But don't think it was easy for me. I can appreciate how embarrassing it was, especially for Mameh and Tateh. I understand you are angry and hurt. But I am hoping someday you and the family will accept my choices. I have a right to live my own life. Everybody has that right!
I understand you are going to be married. I realize that even if you wanted to, you couldn't invite me. Mazel tov. I am sad I will miss your wedding but happy for you. I know it hasn't been easy for you to find a husband since I left.

I also have a mazel tov coming to me.

I'm enclosing a newspaper clipping about the award I just received. Be happy for me, can't you, even if you can't be proud? Always your loving sister,

Rose

She'd shaken the envelope, and a yellowing news clipping floated out. It was from *The New York Times,* dated November 24, 1974. "Young Photographer Wins Top Honors" was the headline. She studied the grainy photo of a slim young woman dressed in an ankle-grazing hippy dress, her dark hair falling long and straight around her shoulders. She had a long, narrow face with high cheekbones and large eyes that looked sad even as she smiled into the camera, accepting her silver statue. The caption read: "Rose Weiss Wins Distinguished Junior Photographer of the Year Award."

Rose the Outcast! A famous photographer!

That was the moment she realized that life could be unexpected and wonderful. She smiled to herself. And now it's happening to me! My life is beginning!

She tried to remember the young men she had seen at her cousin's apartment, but they were a strange blur: men without skullcaps, in formfitting shirts and pants, with longish hair and white teeth . . . men who looked like the people she saw in *goyish* magazines and movie posters.

She looked at herself appraisingly in the full-length mirror. Without giving herself any explanation, she opened Hannah's closet, flipping through the hangers until she came across a pretty blue sweater that matched her eyes and a slim, short blue skirt. She tried them on. The skirt barely dusted her knees. She could have been any one of those girls drinking beer and laughing at her cousin's party the night before. Looking at herself questioningly in the mirror, she neatly folded her own clothes, hiding them away in her suitcase before hurrying down the steps.

19

"Pearl, have warm drink!" Zevulun begged her.

She was lying prostrate with grief on her bed. In the living room, their eldest son and daughter-in-law manned the phones while their six small grandchildren ran wild.

"How can I swallow when my child has been taken from me! I'm choking!"

"The police . . ."

"The police!" she said disgustedly. "You know what they'll say: Maybe she ran away, they'll say. She is a big girl, they'll say. *Goyish heads!* Go explain such a thing is not possible. That your child would never, ever think to do such a thing to her parents . . . has no reason to do such a thing! How we spoiled her, Zevulun. Gave her everything, more than all the other children together! And the fine boy we found for her, the envy of all our friends. And how patient he's been, waiting all this time! No, some maniac must have swept her off the street into a van. A white van. You read so much about such things . . . Oy, *Gotteinu*! My baby!"

"No one in Williamsburg would do such a terrible thing!"

"Oh, what I could tell you about your holy Williamsburg! Why, when I was a child, an innocent little girl, some Hassid came up to me . . ." She closed her eyes, her voice failing.

Zevulun sat down heavily on the bed next to her. His hands were shaking. She looked up at his face. It was completely drained of color.

"Aach, Zevulun, I'm sorry. You are not well." She pulled herself up and sat down next to him. They leaned against each other, shoulder to shoulder, propping each other up.

He took her hand gently in his. "We must trust in God, Pearl. He is kind and compassionate . . ."

She nodded, her heart burdened with the knowledge of every lapse, every slight infraction and minor sin she had ever committed. She had gossiped about a neighbor and not asked forgiveness from her before Yom Kippur, as was required. God could forgive you for sins you committed against Him, but not against others. She had accused a cleaning girl of taking some silver forks, and later found them. While she'd apologized, the girl had quit anyway, offended, disappearing. She had made that innocent girl suffer needlessly, and now it was she doing the suffering. Measure for measure. This was God's way.

The ringing phone made their bodies suddenly stiffen. It would be just like their dear God to hear their prayers and answer so swiftly! Oh, Blessed Be His Glorious Name Forever!

Their eldest son knocked on the door. Zevulun ran to open it.

"It's her friend, Malca. Calling from Bnei Brak."

"Malca?" Pearl repeated. That girl who'd disgraced herself? Who'd been shamefully married off to some half-*shegetz* Israeli and banished to Israel to save the family honor? Rivka had been forbidden to even speak to her! Why would she be calling? "Give me the phone!" Pearl gasped, filled with a terrible foreboding, and yet at the same time some measure of comfort. A friend, calling from Israel with news. Not a policeman who had found a body, God forbid!

"Malca?" She held the phone steadily, listening intently as all eyes were upon her. For many minutes she said nothing, and then: "Are you sure? Is this the truth?" Again, she said nothing, nodding silently to the voice on the other side of the world. "Give me your number." Zevulun hurriedly handed her a pencil and paper. She scribbled it down. "Tell her she must call us as soon as she gets there. We are sick with worry! But thank you for calling, Malca. God bless you." She hung up, gnawing at her lips until she drew blood.

"Pearl, what?" Zevulun asked hoarsely, his voice strangled with tension.

Pearl turned to her son. "Go close the windows and pull down the shades. Don't say anything." Then, she went to her bedroom window, staring out for a moment as if expecting every window to be filled with staring, accusatory eyes. She slammed it shut, pulling the curtains closed.

"But Mameh . . ." her son entreated.

"Listen to your mother," Zevulun murmured, putting a gentle hand on his son's shoulder and squeezing it encouragingly as he led him out the door, locking it behind him.

"She's run away! She's gone to Israel to be with her friend! She didn't want the *shidduch*. Her friend says she thinks we were pushing her . . ."

"PUSHING HER? I pushed her? She never said she didn't want . . ."

Pearl sat down, wringing her hands, a terrible sense of déjà vu washing over her. "Oh, the shame of it! What shall we tell her brothers and sisters? The *shadchan*? The boy and his family?"

"This is what you are worried about?"

She looked up at him, amazed. A great smile had broken out on his face.

"This is nothing to laugh about."

"You and your white van . . . Yes, I can laugh. My daughter has made a foolish mistake, but she is young. She is not hurt. She is alive and well. Think of it, Pearl. Just think of it." He put his arms around her and both of them wept, the tears falling into his beard and to the top of her head covering.

20

"Hello? Anybody there?" Hannah called out. It was early evening and the house was pitch-dark. When she put on the light, her jaw dropped. There were grooves in the old carpet, which had been vacuumed within an inch of its life. When she lifted her eyes, she realized that the entire apartment had been scrubbed and polished and vacuumed. Even the big living room window, permanently tattooed by city debris, had clearly been attacked if not completely vanquished by someone with equal parts endless determination, foolish optimism, and bottles of glass cleaner.

She wandered from the freshly made-up bad to the spotless bathroom to the gleaming kitchen. Even her characteristically empty fridge had been stocked with juices, fruits, vegetables, and dairy products. She took out a yogurt. It was a strange brand called Mehadrin, which was twice the price of other brands. She shook her head wonderingly, putting it back.

She flopped down on the couch. And the girl had done all this on no sleep, because how in heaven's name could anyone sleep on this thing? Gratitude and guilt coupled with a vague irritation coursed through her. The door suddenly opened.

"Oh. You're home," Rivka said. She was breathing heavily, her cheeks a red burn of cold. Beside her was a large sack of laundry. "I took it down to the laundromat," she said, trying to catch her breath.

Hannah got up, walking over to her and taking the bag. "Rivka, look at your hands!"

They were chapped and red, with deep grooves in the palms.

"It's nothing. Rubber gloves I should have used. Next time, the bag will be lighter . . ."

"Rivka, Rivka, what am I going to do with you?"

"I did something wrong?"

She tried to compose her thoughts. "I didn't ask you to do any of this, did I?"

"No, but I thought, a favor . . ."

"I took you in because it was the right thing to do. You don't have to kill yourself trying to pay me back with housework. And all that expensive food you bought!"

"Cuzin, there is nothing to eat in this house."

"I'm . . . I eat out mostly. Were you hungry?"

"I also ate out," she said without elaborating, afraid of tainting her morning's experiences by hanging them out for even more of her cousin's withering disapproval. "I didn't know which dishes were for milk and which for meat."

"Like most people, I only have one for both. Are you going to need two brand-new sets of dishes?"

"No, no! I don't want to make you trouble. I can use plastic, paper."

"But what about pots and pans? I've got only one set of those, too. You won't be able to cook anything . . ."

"I'll manage, Cuzin. Don't worry about me."

"But that's just it, Rivka. All day long, I sat doing just that. Worrying. I couldn't concentrate on anything else."

"Do you want I should leave?" Rivka asked, holding her breath.

Hannah hesitated. "Look, Rivka, as you can see it's a bit crowded here. But I can't have you wandering around New York City." Like prey, she thought, but didn't say. "I hope you realize that it can be a very dangerous place out there for young women."

Hannah's young, but she talks like an *alte kocker*. She's as bad as my mother, Rivka thought. But she said, "Good you are, Cuzin, to care about me! But I know what's what. This is why I'm coming to you first instead of riding around all night on the subway."

"What? That was your plan B?"

Rivka shrugged, a foolish smile spreading over her face.

Hannah shivered. "No more housecleaning, okay? You clean up after yourself, and I'll clean up after myself. And I will do the laundry once a week in the basement."

"But . . ."

"And no more food shopping for us both! You'll go broke buying all those superexpensive brands. Explain to me why you can't eat yogurt that costs half the price?"

"Unless a rabbi watches, the farmer might add pig's milk, or camel's milk, and then it would not be kosher."

Hannah's eyes widened in astonishment. "All dairy farms are under government supervision. It's all mechanized, like a factory. You know how much work it would be to milk a pig? Or to find a camel?"

Rivka couldn't think of an answer.

"Look, Rivka, I'm not trying to interfere with your religious beliefs. Goodness knows, my mother made sure I'm completely ignorant about that subject. All I'm saying is, shouldn't you at least understand what you're doing and why? Especially if it's costing you a fortune?" Hannah exhaled, trying to calm herself. "Now let's talk about something else. You didn't leave home to wash my floors. You left for a reason, right? We need to start preparing you to start school."

"But, I am . . . you know . . ." Rivka began.

Hannah's eyes widened. "No, I'm afraid I don't."

Rivka put her hands on her suddenly hot cheeks. So, Hannah had nothing to do with this young man's phone call! For reasons that were not entirely clear even to her, Rivka decided to keep it that way.

Hannah watched, bewildered, as a furious blush rose up Rivka's neck. What have I said now? she wondered helplessly. The girl was a strange creature from another culture. She needed to respect that. Perhaps all the natives in Rivka's tribe ran out and bought bowl cleaner and scrubbed the floors every time someone did them a favor? Perhaps it was embarrassing to them to be asked questions at all?

Hannah tried again. "Rivka, what is it you really want?"

"To be free," she whispered, almost to herself, the realization clarifying her motivation for keeping secrets from this well-meaning but clueless stranger to whom she was now beholden.

"What does that mean?"

"I need a job."

"But you're so young!"

"I need money for my own place! Please don't be offended, Cuzin, but I don't like living here."

Hannah swallowed hard, mortified. "Why? Have I been inhospitable? Do you feel I'm pushing you out?"

"No. It's because I have no place to sleep."

Aah. Of course.

"And not you and not me will have any privacy. I don't want you should take the place of my *mameh*."

Fair enough, Hannah thought, understanding but feeling surprisingly wounded. It was like feeding an alley cat who turns around and scratches your face. "Why don't you go up to the employment offices at Lord and Taylor or Macy's? I'm sure they are looking for help to get them through the January sales. But they'll all ask for references. Do you have any?"

"Vus is dus?"

"Um, have you ever worked anywhere? Would your employer be willing to say nice things about you?"

She shook her head. "Sometimes, I babysit. But no one must call people I know. They would right away tell my *mameh* and *tateh*."

Hannah hadn't thought of that.

"Also, my *mameh* and sisters they shop in Lord and Taylor and Macy's."

That was true. Hannah often saw Hassidic women buying modest, fashionable clothing in upscale department stores, especially during sales. She brightened: "There are some hip clothing stores near my mother's gallery in Chelsea. I doubt the women in your family would ever set foot in one of them. My mother might even know the owners. Do you want me to call and ask her?"

"I don't know . . ." Rivka hesitated.

"What's the problem?"

"Your mother . . ."

"I've been meaning to ask you about that. Why did you show up on my doorstep and not hers? She's got a much bigger place. And she is your aunt, after all."

"I just couldn't . . . It would have been like calling Rabbi Elisha ben Avuya . . ."

"You've totally lost me now."

"Well, Cuzin, this is the *gantse megillah* . . ."

"Rivka, can you please talk English?"

"Oh, sorry. It means 'the whole story.' About two thousand years ago, during the time when our Holy Temple stood in Jerusalem, four rabbis said the secret, holy name of God and ascended to Paradise. When they got back, one went crazy, the second one died, the third—Rabbi Akiva—returned safe and sound. But Elisha ben Avuya came back without his faith. He became a heretic, and so he is called the Other. He's a legend."

"My mother is a legend?"

"You have no idea . . ." Rivka shook her head.

"But not exactly a folk hero." Hannah smiled drily. "By the way, what exactly did he see up there that turned him off, this Elisha ben . . . ?"

"Avuya. He saw an angel sitting down, writing up Rabbi Avuya's good deeds. The rabbi was shocked. 'I have always taught my students that in the World to Come there will be no eating, drinking, or sitting.' The angel got into big trouble for letting a mortal see him misbehaving and was punished. But to make him feel better, the angel was also given permission not to write down Rabbi Avuya's good deeds anymore, which would keep Rabbi Avuya out of Paradise when the time came. When Rabbi Avuya heard this, he decided then and there that if all his good deeds and Torah study would earn him no reward in the World to Come, he might as well . . . 'live it up,' I think you call it? in this world."

"And that's how you see my mother?" Hannah asked, wondering if she should laugh or be offended. "A heretic who's abandoned all morality and is 'living it up' in this world as if there is no tomorrow?"

"No, no! Not me! It's just that . . . in our *mishpoocha* . . ."

"Rivka, English!"

"Sorry. In our family, she is like such a legend. But I myself admire her. She changed my life. She's the reason I'm here. I never believed all the terrible things they said about her. I don't think my *mameh* did either. Why else would she keep your mother's letter, and the clipping about her from the newspaper?"

"What did my mother's letter say?"

Rivka was silent.

"Rivka?"

"That she was sorry she'd called the police on Bubbee and Zaydie."

Hannah was speechless.

"Your mother never mentioned . . . ?"

"Oh, sure, of course," Hannah lied, mortified at how little she knew. "And the clipping?"

"For Best Photographer. In the picture, your mother is getting this prize. It made me think: if she is such a sinner, why would God reward her like that? No, He would have punished her with a terrible disease, or an accident. But she looks so young, so happy, so pretty. That's when I understood that all my life, I'd been told lies, when I understood that it wasn't impossible."

"That what wasn't impossible?"

"To choose your own life, no matter what anyone else thought about it. Do you have any idea how strange that idea is for people brought up like me? You asked what I want. That's all I want, Cuzin, the very same thing. To choose!"

Hannah's eyes softened. "Look, tomorrow, I'll get you one of those blow-up mattresses. They're very comfortable. Then, I'll ask around about classes for GED-equivalency exams, and also jobs. Don't feel like there's any rush. You can stay here as long as you need to."

Rivka reached out, hugging her. "Thank you, Hannah. So much. You can't imagine how much."

Hannah stepped back, embarrassed. "Well, that's okay. Don't mention it. Now you go get some rest after slaving away all day to clean up this dump. I'll sleep in the sleeping bag tonight."

"I can't let you do that!"

"Yes, you can and will. I'll be fine." Hannah gave Rivka's hand a small, intimate squeeze, then watched as she tiredly entered the bedroom, closing the door behind her.

21

"Hannah darling! To what do I owe this?" Rose said, opening wide the door to her studio. Hannah never came here, complaining that the chemicals gave her a headache, something Rose's therapist had long ago interpreted as the continuation of Hannah's childhood resentment and jealous rivalry toward the pursuit that took up so much of her mother's time and passion. "Aren't you going to be late for classes?"

"Mom, you'll never guess who's shown up at my doorstep."

"Prince Harry?"

"This is not a joke. Rivka."

Rose looked at her blankly.

"Your niece!"

Rose shook her head, stunned. "After everything we spoke about . . ."

"I didn't call her. She just showed up, soaked to the bone, on New Year's Eve . . ."

"She's been at your house two weeks . . . ?"

"Look, Mom, I knew how you felt about it so I tried not to involve you . . . to figure this out myself . . ."

"Two weeks! Before you say another word, tell me this: where do her parents think she is?"

"They think she's with her friend in Israel, a girl who has promised to lie for her."

She thought of her sister Pearl's anguish and fear, the feeling sinking deep into her stomach like a stone. But then something else took over. "Are you sure no one else knows she's with you? Because the Modesty Patrol is going to be banging down your door at four o'clock in the morning with iron bars!"

"If they were coming, they'd have been here already. Besides, she claims she's never heard of such a thing."

"Either she's really that naive, or she's a liar. Let me think a minute . . . I have to . . . I'm in the middle . . . just wait, okay?"

She walked into her darkroom to wash and hang up the last negatives still soaking in fixer. When she'd finished, she pulled off her rubber gloves and turned off the light, closing the door behind her.

"When are you going to switch to digital photos and banish these carcinogens from your life?"

"When I lose my self-respect and gain the invaluable photographic knowledge of how to whiten yellow teeth and remove wrinkles."

"Can I say something?"

"No. Please don't."

Hannah was silent. When her mother got like this—which was not very often—there was nothing to be done. She waited patiently.

"I can't think in here. Let's go out for a walk."

Hannah followed her dutifully. A light drizzle was falling, making their heads sparkle with raindrops.

Rose turned to her daughter. "What are you really asking of me?"

"Mom, this is *your* family! I'm sorry you don't want to be involved, and I tried my best not to involve you, but give me a break! What am I supposed to do with her? I don't understand anything. She won't eat my food, refuses to touch my dishes or silverware, and is sleeping on the floor on a blow-up mattress. The day after she moved in, she nearly killed herself scrubbing my entire apartment from top to bottom . . . !"

Rose looked at her, a bit horrified, then suddenly grinned. "So, what, exactly, is the problem?"

"Be serious! I, unlike you, am willing to help her. I just don't know how.

She says she wants a job, but she has no qualifications. She says she wants to study for her SATs, but she doesn't even have a high school diploma. She left school in eleventh grade . . ."

Rose shook her head.

"Don't you dare say, 'I told you so.'"

"What do you want me to say, Hannah? 'Darling, send her over to me, I'll take care of her'? Is that it?"

"I never said that! Besides, I'm not even sure that's a good idea."

Rose felt a prick of discomfort bordering on insult. "Why not? She'd have a decent bed, and her own room with a bathroom . . ."

"My old room?"

"Ah, jealous already?" Rose laughed, chucking her daughter playfully under the chin. "What are you afraid I'll do to her?"

"For starters, yell at her and wind up throwing her out when she doesn't listen to you. Or try to convert her to your secular beliefs, which are just as fanatic as any her parents hold . . ."

"Really, Hannah! I'm not an evangelist of any religion or nonreligion . . ."

"Or somehow use her to settle all your old scores . . ."

Rose exhaled, wounded. "I don't deserve that."

"I'm sorry. You're right. Frankly, it *would* solve all *my* problems."

"So, that *is* what you came here for."

"It doesn't matter. What matters is that I'm not sure it would solve *hers*. She's in awe of you. Apparently, you took the part of Elisha ben Avuya in all the family's tales of wickedness."

Rose chuckled. "A great honor."

"Also, there is some letter you sent her mother? Something about calling the police on her grandparents?"

Rose suddenly felt cold. "Let's go back to my studio."

She made two cups of hot cocoa, then sank in beside Hannah on the sofa.

"I'm surprised her mother showed her that."

"Is it true? Did you call the cops on your parents?"

She sighed. "It's a long story, Hannah. But first, I'm curious. What did she say about it?"

"It's sort of strange. On the one hand, she'd been brainwashed to think of you as the ultimate bogeyman. But she said reading the letter and, especially, seeing the press clipping opened her eyes to life's possibilities, to the idea that you could actually defy everyone, choose your own life, and get away with it."

Rose suddenly stood up. "Tell her to come to me."

Hannah was both immensely relieved and strangely sad. It was like giving away a bothersome but lovable puppy to a better home. "Are you sure, Mom?"

"Yes, I'm sure."

"If she'll agree . . ."

"I can't do anything about that. All I can say is I understand this girl better than she understands herself. Certainly better than you. I'll do the best I can to help her get her own life. However she feels about me, she'll just have to grow up and get over it."

"And if she can't?"

"There is only so much you can do to help a person if they refuse to help themselves."

They hugged.

"You're a good person, Mom."

"I'm not sure that's a compliment. Your father's friend John, whose parents were missionaries in Africa, was fond of saying: 'If you see someone coming towards you who wants to do you good, shoot them.'"

Rose left her studio early, unable to concentrate. It was still early afternoon when she got home, the dimming sunlight throwing a kaleidoscope of colors over the walls as they hit the crystal vases and light fixtures. She watched them with pleasure as she hung up her wet coat and shook out her umbrella. *My beautiful, well-ordered apartment on the Upper East Side!* she thought. No matter what pundits wrote about the empty-nest syndrome, she, and almost all of her friends, agreed that it was absolutely wonderful to come home to a clean, quiet, empty house that embraced you in its sheltering, private arms. She couldn't imagine sharing it with anyone else again.

She wandered listlessly through the charmingly decorated rooms and hallways, stopping at the wall of photographs that covered the living room wall almost to the ceiling. Her photos, lovingly chosen, framed, and hung by Henry the day they'd moved in. He'd made her close her eyes before letting her see them.

"But, there's not a single one of yours!" she'd protested, stunned.

"First, I thought we'd hang the art. Then, if there's room, we can put up some magazine covers," he'd said with his usual dismissiveness toward his own work. That was so like him! He never considered his own photographs anything other than illustrations for newspaper and magazine stories, even after he won a Pulitzer. "Just a lucky break, being in the right place at the right time," he'd said with a shrug. And afterward, amid the unopened crates and moving boxes, they'd opened a bottle of warm champagne, drinking whatever was left after it exploded, raining down on them and their belongings like confetti.

She looked at the huge, blown-up photograph from her most famous collection, *This Side of Heaven*. She'd gone back to her roots, photographing life in Williamsburg, Borough Park, and Crown Heights, creating a collection that had variously been called "insightful," "harsh," "groundbreaking," and "moving."

The Hassidim themselves, however, had decided to "honor" her with a lawsuit for "stealing" their images without their permission, complaining her work was that of a Peeping Tom interested in hanging out the community's dirty laundry. They wanted her photos banned and her books taken off the shelves, and, failing that, they wanted all her royalties. The suit, which was meritless from the get-go, was eventually thrown out of court, but had still managed to generate lots of negative publicity, as well as costing her a bloody fortune in legal fees.

She looked at one of her favorite and most famous photos, a black-and-white image of women in the synagogue during *Simchat* Torah. While the men were dancing and singing with joy as they passed around the sacred Torah scrolls, the excluded women and girls crowded around each other behind the high *mechitzah,* standing on chairs jockeying for a position from where, at best, they could catch just a brief and partial glimpse of the goings-on. Their faces were somber, bored, joyful, preoccupied. Her Haredi critics deemed it "antireligious, feminist propaganda" and were furious that she had "desecrated the holiday and their sacred space" with her photographic equipment (which she had carefully hidden inside a black shawl, knowing full well the consequences of being caught with a camera in a synagogue in Borough Park during a holiday).

Her defense had been simple. "I'm a mirror," she'd said in response. "If you don't like your face, change it. Don't complain to the mirror. I show what's there. You create your world. I just document it."

And now she was renowned for these very same photographs, which had made her reputation. The numerous awards she had received for this collection spoke of the "compassion and integrity in her moving black-and-white images, which confront the difficult aspects of Haredi society." She had been praised for her decades of "quiet, watchful, passionate observation of this world." Words like "gentle" and "respectful" were used to describe her photos, which "do not speak to the cliché perception of outsiders, but present demanding and compelling revelations about a society steeped in tradition as it is forced to confront modern times."

Seeing her photos hung up and celebrated that way by the man she loved and admired had given her perhaps the greatest moment of satisfaction she'd ever felt in her work. For, although she had published ten books of photographs and won two Nikon Book of the Year awards, the Kraszna-Krausz Award for Photographic Innovation, the International Center of Photography's Infinity Award, the Women in Photography International's Distinguished Photographer's Award, and a Guggenheim fellowship, among the people who mattered to her most, she was considered a vile traitor, a festering wound that would not heal. She had no choice but to live with that knowledge. It was a chronic pain.

Had she betrayed her own world? Or had she illuminated it, bringing out all its facets of good and evil? Why did they judge her so harshly?

So as not to judge themselves, Henry once told her.

Henry.

He had been gone so many years. But this was still their house. He was everywhere.

She sat down on the couch with a glass of wine, downing it in two large gulps. Then, she put up her feet and closed her eyes, listening to the rain falling wildly against the windowpane, remembering everything with a startling clarity that made it feel like the present, not the past.

22

London, 1987

Cold, depressed, lonely, she feels her feet dragging along the nasty, wet pavement on Great Portland Road as if wearing weights. Her eyes roam desperately, looking for some shelter from the bitter London cold. There. The handsome wooden storefront. The door is heavy and solid as she opens it, expecting to be enveloped by the warm vapors of a tea shop. But there are no tables, no waitresses in uniforms, she realizes as she unbuttons her soaked raincoat in confusion and disappointment. Instead, the walls are hung with photographs.

A photo gallery! She hasn't come across a single one since arriving, and now, by accident, she stumbles into one! She steps in closer, staring. She sees a photo of a young girl carrying a baby through the rubble of a destroyed village. Her eyes are large, dark—already old. They stare directly into hers, filled with fear, hope, and a simple resignation that challenge her pity. "What is your pity worth?" the girl's face seems to say, the baby close in her arms as she steps through disaster toward an unknown future.

I cannot move, she thinks, mesmerized.

"I don't know why they insist on hanging up such rubbish."

The voice is deep, rude, male. It wakes her, dragging her back to the present, giving her frustration an outlet.

"Excuse me? This just happens to be a work of genius! One of the most heartbreaking photos I've ever seen!"

His eyes open wider, amused, surprised.

He is tall and muscular with a soldier's straight back and cautious stance. His hair, a dark, curly brown, is cut short; his eyes, a deep, earthy brown surrounded by deepening laugh lines, gaze unflinchingly into her own.

"I suppose it's not bad, for an amateur, that is. But anyone wandering around a war zone could have managed it."

"You don't know what you're talking about!" she says through gritted teeth, her native New York–ese coming to the fore in a primitive rage. "I just happen to be a professional photographer myself—an *award-winning photographer*—so perhaps I can appreciate a little better than you what kind of talent went into this! Just look at the lighting; it's surreal! And the graininess, the contrasting shadows just over the child's head—it's almost a metaphor for the horror of the situation and the hopefulness of life injected into it . . . And that child's expression, her eyes! Why, they're . . . they're . . ." To her horror, she feels the tears welling up, her throat constricting, choking her.

"I'm so sorry, I had no idea . . ." he says softly, the ironic grin replaced by sincere concern. "Here, take my handkerchief. It's the least I can do."

"A handkerchief? You've got to be kidding!" she answers rudely, searching desperately through her handbag for a tissue with which to remove as quickly as possible the embarrassing liquids spilling down her face.

"Well, if you feel that passionately about it—the photo, that is, not the handkerchief"—he grins wickedly, shrugging—"I just happen to know where you could see a lot more of this stuff."

She blows her nose, her passionate interest overcoming her antagonism and her embarrassment. "Where?"

He pauses (perhaps a bit theatrically?) and then says, "At my house."

She says nothing, a sunset-red blush climbing up her throat that paints her cheeks scarlet. She takes a quick step toward the photograph, searching for the signature. Henry Gordon. She swallows hard, afraid to look up.

The world-famous war photographer whose work is a staple in *Time,*

Newsweek, and the *National Geographic.* Hadn't he almost been killed or something a few years back? Haiti? El Salvador?

Slowly, she raises her head, catching the ragged scar across his forehead peeking out beneath the short bangs. How could she have missed that before?

"I . . . I . . . that is . . ." she stutters, mortified.

"Please don't feel uncomfortable. I'm so sorry. It was terribly wicked of me! I was just 'taking a piss,' as we louts in London are fond of saying. And I actually meant everything I said about that photo."

"You must think I'm an idiot."

"On the contrary. I think you are delightfully kind. But I guess we'll just have to agree to disagree about these pictures of mine."

"You can't really feel that way about your work . . ."

"How I feel about my work is complicated, Miss . . . ?"

"Rose . . . Rose Weiss."

He offers her his large hand. It is brown and full of old scars. She takes it timidly, feeling lost yet at the same time encompassed and safer than she has ever felt.

"And you say you also take photographs? *Award-winning photographs?*" he teases.

She nods, lowering her eyes. "I'm here on a Guggenheim fellowship for the year."

"Impressive! A real artist. Who are you working with?"

She rattles off the names, her teeth suddenly chattering.

"They're the best! And you're freezing."

"I actually came in here to warm up. I thought it was a tea shop."

He laughs, a full-throated, joyous sound that holds nothing back. "It was, not so long ago. Unfortunately, a friend of mine who mistakenly thinks photos are more beneficial to mankind than hot tea bought it and insists on putting mine up on the walls. I don't know why. I think they look out of place outside a newspaper."

"No, they are amazing. This one, of the little girl . . . Where was that taken?"

"El Mozote, in El Salvador," he says, his face suddenly grim. "The government killed a thousand villagers in one day. I just happened to be nearby . . ."

She can see clearly now the deep lines that etch his face with age and experience, the face of a man used to danger who has seen and been part of things she cannot even begin to imagine.

"Allow me to make amends. We can't send you home to the colonies thinking we Brits have no manners at all. Would you permit me to invite you to high tea?"

"Oh, I don't want to be a bother . . ."

He smiles. "And I don't want to accost unwilling young women."

"I'm willing, I'm willing . . ." She smiles back. "Like Barkis," she adds, following him outside.

"Ah, David Copperfield. So, you're a fan of Dickens?"

"I adore him. In fact, all the English novelists: Lawrence, Forster, Woolf . . . I think the novel form was actually invented in England. And your theater. There's absolutely nothing like it, even on Broadway . . ."

The conversation flows without end, the awkwardness disappearing. When the taxi deposits them in Mayfair, they are upset by the interruption, almost sad to step out of the intimate, private space.

"The Brown's Hotel. Just the thing." He rubs his hands together, ushering her up the marble steps.

The place is a Georgian mansion out of the last century. Cakes, scones, and little sandwiches are piled high on Victorian cake stands. Wedgwood china cups and plates are set on the white tablecloth along with polished silver spoons and forks. There are teakettles wrapped in chintz cozies, and little bowls of clotted cream, strawberries, soft butter, and deep red jam.

He nods toward the huge fire leaping and crackling in the old-fashioned grate. "That should warm you up!"

It does, the snapping logs sending their comforting heat throughout the room, helping the radiators dry her moist, chilled skin. That and a pianist dressed in a tuxedo playing Chopin make her feel like an extra on a black-and-white thirties movie set. She half expects to see Ronald Colman and Olivia de Havilland stroll by.

"Thank you, this is lovely."

He smiles, pleased. "It's a bit run-down; I hope you don't mind. I could have taken you to Claridge's or the Dorchester, but that would have meant tie and jacket. Very posh and very not me."

"Nor me!" She laughs, noticing for the first time how he is dressed: the ragged edges on his hand-knit sweater, the khaki pants with endless pockets, perfect for storing camera batteries, lenses, film. "I'm just a poor girl from Brooklyn."

His face relaxes, the lines disappearing, the mouth wide and friendly. "And I'm a poor lad from Manchester. My parents and grandparents were in the *shmatta* business."

She looks up at him sharply. Could it be? But Gordon is such an English name. And plenty of Gentiles used Yiddish words nowadays. They'd become part of the English language.

"So, how do you like our fair British Isles so far?" he asks, breaking her reverie.

"Love it! I've been an Anglophile all my life. The books I read as a little girl seem to come alive here."

"So nice to hear. But the truth is, I have to disagree. London is a bleak, dark, gray miasma with unspeakable weather! Give me New York any day! It's so brash and full of life, energy, and color! Here, we are all weighted down with the dust of the past, like those horrible antiques crowding the Victoria and Albert Museum . . ."

"Still, you do live here, don't you?"

"Around the corner, unfortunately. In a moment of insanity, I splashed out on a large, posh place in a posh building no less. The evils of capitalism! But I'm not home much of the time. My work takes me to the four corners . . ."

She plucks up her courage, asking him something that has been bothering her, something that might be inappropriately intimate. "What did you mean before when you said that your feelings about your work are complicated?"

He ignores her question, his head turned around, searching for the waitress. "You've got a choice of seventeen different blends of tea, including one invented by Mr. Brown himself."

She looks down into her teacup silently, wondering if she should be offended, or if she's offended him.

His hand, gentle and persuasive, reaches over the table to touch hers. "Pardon me, but did I miss something? My hearing in one ear is gone and people sometimes think I'm ignoring them."

"Oh, I'm so sorry!" she answers tenderly, relieved, impulsively threading her fingers through his.

He leans forward, his face flushed. "Please don't pity me! I don't have any complaints. I made my choices with my eyes wide open."

"I know what that feels like," she whispers. "But you torture yourself anyway with the 'what might have beens,' don't you?"

He sits back, putting his hands into his pockets, staring. "Spoken like someone who has been there."

"I have. But my wounds are on the inside." She sees his eyes soften.

"I've got plenty of those, too."

There is a moment's thoughtful silence as they take each other in, each suddenly seeing something new.

"What didn't I hear?" he asks her.

"Ah, I just . . . what did you mean before when you said your feelings about your work are complicated?"

"Oh, that." He shifts uncomfortably. "Ever since I can remember, I've hated injustice, big kids bullying little kids. I wanted to save the world. I started by volunteering to be a soldier, which is how I lost my hearing . . . It's a long story . . . After that, the army gave me a choice of an honorable discharge, or training in their photographic unit. I took the latter, and continued afterwards on my own. But somewhere along the line taking my thousandth photo of some horrible atrocity, I began to feel like a fraud. What was I doing just standing by and watching the horrors unfold? Yes, I took that photo of the little girl in El Salvador. But I did nothing to help her, or her family . . . Just like those people in Europe who had stood by watching what was happening to my family had done nothing."

She was stunned. "Your family? Are your parents survivors?"

"Holocaust, you mean?" He shook his head. "They left long before that. But my grandparents always talked about how they and their parents hid in barrels to escape the pogroms in Dvinsk the year there was an assassination attempt on the czar. Those who hated the czar and those who loved the czar both blamed the Jews! Their families and communities were decimated by atrocities. They arrived with only the clothes on their backs and spare change in their pockets."

"You're Jewish."

It was stunning news.

He nodded. "Like you."

"How can you tell?"

"Weiss . . . ? Brooklyn? The lovely dark eyes and hair . . ."

"But not religious?"

"My grandparents were very religious, the cornerstones of the Manchester Jewish community. But, alas, religion is something that tends to get diluted with the generations. My parents were free thinkers, and I'm . . . I don't know what I am."

"My parents were ultra-Orthodox."

It was his turn to be stunned. "Like those Jews in Golders Green and Stamford Hill?"

She nodded, noticing his eyes glance over the food she'd put on her plate. "But you no longer observe?"

"I ran away from home the night before my wedding. I was seventeen. I've been running ever since."

He reached over the table once again, squeezing her hand gently, his thumb caressing her forefinger. "Who's chasing you?"

"No one, not anymore. My conscience maybe? I ran toward freedom, and once I'd found it, I used it to make so many bad choices. My first husband, for one."

"Aah. Yes. The pitfalls of freedom! I was also married once, long, long ago, to a very beautiful girl who was also intelligent enough to divorce me in the middle of still another six-month assignment. If memory doesn't fail me, I think I was in the Congo at the time. I couldn't blame her. Still, it broke my heart," he says with a brave little laugh.

"Any kids?"

He shakes his head. "You?"

"A son."

"Where?"

"In boarding school in the States. I miss him terribly, but I'm away so often. It just wasn't fair to drag him out of school to follow me around the world."

"Is his dad involved?"

"Yes, he does his best. But he's got a new family and lives in California. They see each other over the summers."

"A child. I envy you that. It's one of life's greatest joys. I missed the boat."

She looks up at him and smiles. "Are you sure?' "

He smiles back. "I used to be, Rose . . . Rose Weiss. I used to be."

Something small and electric brushes through her heart then. Her ears and fingertips tingle as if she's been drinking wine, not tea. It is she who reaches over now, boldly, taking his hand in hers.

"You promised to show me some photos."

23

When she opened her eyes, the living room was dark, shadows playing tricks on her mind as they floated around her, the whispered words and sights of the past flitting through her like fireflies. She made herself a light supper and sat alone in the kitchen eating without appetite. Hannah hadn't said exactly when she was bringing Rivka over, but she might as well get the room ready, she thought, putting her dishes in the sink, suddenly filled with a new energy.

She took freshly ironed linens out of the closet, making up the bed, the scent of the lavender water the maid put in the iron rising to her nostrils as she stretched over the bed, smoothing down the sheet and duvet.

Provence. Their honeymoon. The lavender fields of the high plateau in Sault at the base of Mont Ventoux. That photo he'd taken of her standing there, knee deep in purple blooms. Afterward, hiding from view, making love, their skin drenched in the intoxicating scent.

She plumped up the pillows, looking at the lavender walls of her daughter's old bedroom, smiling. Nine months later, Hannah had been born. The color had been their private joke as they put together her nursery. No matter how many times they'd repainted it, they never changed the hue.

She took some flowers from the living room, transferring them into small crystal vases, which she filled with fresh water and then arranged on the dresser. On the nightstand, she placed a selection of magazines and books she hoped might interest her niece.

As an afterthought, she went into her own bedroom, opening the closet and reaching toward the top shelf. She took down a small yellowing box. The brittle tissue paper flaked in her hands as she unwrapped the silver-backed comb and matching brush.

Heathrow, about to board the plane back to New York, while Henry was off to another assignment. He handed her the box. "Start looking for an apartment for us in New York. And don't use these until I get there," he'd whispered tenderly, smoothing back her hair with his hand.

She brought the brush to her temple, running it through her hair, just as he used to. Tears stung her eyes. She took the set into the guest room, laying it down on the silver tray of the antique vanity.

It was time to share it, to let it live again.

For years, she'd guarded her home and her privacy with the ferocity of a jungle animal, rejecting all well-meaning advice that she be practical and sell (apartments on Park and Seventy-third were worth a small fortune), or at least find someone with whom she could share it. Over the years, there had been no shortage of men eager to apply for that position. But even though she'd tried, it just never felt right.

This was her home, hers and Henry's. She'd sealed it off in the vain hope of keeping what was left of their life together from seeping out and evaporating. It was her bulwark against the complex intrusions of life, a place where she could select music from her wall of CDs and saturate the place with sound at any time, day or night, a place where she could pile up books on the coffee table, watch movies and eat pistachio ice cream in her pajamas on the couch at two o'clock in the morning. A place where she could—without the intrusion of any judgmental eye—invest countless hours painstakingly building and furnishing the dollhouses Henry had taught her to love, places where her imagination could take flight, living whole other lifetimes. So far, there was the beach cottage, the New England farmhouse, the Tudor townhouse, and a block of old-fashioned Victorian stores. She put in all the furnishings, but never a miniature family. That would make it seem like child's play, she told herself. The truth was, she couldn't bear it, the mother and father and little ones sitting around a table . . .

Then why this strange elation about opening her home to welcome in this stranger, this girl she had never set eyes on? What would they talk about, she and this refugee from a world she had been cut off from for four decades? It made no sense. And yet . . . she had to admit, it meant the world to her to have her family back in her life again.

Only now, as she entered the last part of her life, could she finally admit to herself things she'd been too frightened to face at the beginning: that the empty wound created in her heart when she jumped off the last rung of that fire escape and ran out into the night would never fully heal. It was a dark hole, and it was bottomless. No matter what she'd filled it with—work, awards, lovers, children, friends—the gap stayed open. Only with Henry had she found some peace. Losing him had ripped the wound open again, bringing back those nights when she'd cried her eyes out, wondering if she was going to survive the terrible loneliness of her existence.

Many times, she'd wanted to reconcile with her family. But they'd made it impossible, resorting to behavior that she would never have imagined in her wildest dreams.

Was Hannah right, then? Was taking Rivka in a way to take revenge? Do I want her to like me more than she likes my sister? Is that it? Some kind of sick competition?

She shook her head.

The only thing she knew for sure was that the time had finally come to open her home, and open her heart.

24

"Rivka?"

But there was only silence. Hannah walked through the empty house. Could she have somehow guessed she was going to be offered another place to live and taken off, insulted? Hannah sat down on the rocker, rubbing her temples. Talk about irrational! Besides, if she *was* a mind reader, she'd also know I had no evil intentions. She'd know that I very much want her to have what she wants out of life, that it matters to me.

While at the beginning studying women's history might have been just a career path, she found she could no longer view it with dispassionate, academic interest. Every woman helped or saved or elevated was a small victory that made her own life more comprehensible and worthwhile.

At 2:00 A.M. she heard the key turn in the lock. She rubbed her eyes, walking into the living room. She glimpsed Rivka standing at the half-open door, her back turned, saying good night to someone Hannah couldn't see.

"Who's that?"

Rivka turned around, her face red, then white, quickly closing the door. "Nobody."

"Where have you been until this time of night!"

Rivka straightened her back stubbornly, her mouth a thin line of defiance. "You're not my *mameh*."

"I was just worried, that's all. I feel responsible for you."

Rivka's face grew doubtful. "I'm sorry, Cuzin. I know you try to help. But Hannah, I am . . . I am happy!"

Her smile was infectious.

"Really? What happened?"

"I have . . . friends, and a job I may have, and a place to live . . . It's wonderful, no?"

"Yes, but that's awfully quick, isn't it? Who, exactly, are these 'friends'? Where did you meet them? What kind of job are they offering you? And where will you live?"

"Hannah, you are my *cuzin,* and I love you and appreciate all your help. But I can't say nothing . . . No, I don't *want* to say nothing. I want to do whatever I want to do when I want to do it! That's what it means, to be free, no?"

Offended, worried, hurt, relieved, it took a while for Hannah to respond. "I just don't want you to get in over your head, that's all."

"What does that mean, 'over my head'?"

"It's an expression that comes from going into the water when you don't know how to swim and finding that you've taken one step too far out into the ocean and you're drowning."

Rivka, who didn't know how to swim, said nothing, biting her nails nervously. "I know what's what."

"Good, then there's nothing to worry about." Hannah turned her back stiffly, heading toward her bedroom.

"Cuzin." Rivka put her hand on Hannah's shoulder, turning her around.

Hannah looked into her pretty, sweet young face. It was full of hope and excitement and newly found joy. "Don't worry so much for me."

Hannah exhaled, kissing the soft blushing cheek. "Okay. I'll try. But I want you to know that I spoke to my mother today. She says you can move in with her, and she'll help you to achieve whatever you want with your life. You'll have a beautiful room of your own with a bathroom. It used to be my room."

"You told Aunt Rose about me?"

"Yes, and she really, really wants to help you."

"That's so kind of her!"

"We'll talk about it in the morning, okay?"

"Yes, in the morning, we'll talk." Rivka yawned, unbraiding her hair and running her fingers through it sensuously, as if she had just discovered it. "We'll talk. I'll tell you everything. All my secrets."

Secrets, Hannah thought, on her way to bed, turning to look at her cousin one last time, her words striking a small chord of fear. In the morning, she found Rivka's bed deflated. On top of a neatly folded pile of linens was an envelope with her name on it.

My Dear Cuzin Hannah, may you live long,

Thank you very much for all your chesed. You took in a stranger who was very lost and tired and heartbroke. But I have to go now. After you went to bed, I spoke to my friend in Bnei Brak. She said people came to the house looking for me. My parents' rebbe sent them. They threatened her and her husband and she had to tell him everything. So now my mameh and tateh they know the truth, that I never left the country. But don't worry. I never told Malca where I was staying, or for sure she would have told them that, too. Hannah, I don't want to get you or your mother mixed up in my tzurus, so it's best if I leave right away. Sorry we couldn't talk, but I was planning on going anyway. I have made a good friend who will, God willing, take care of me. I will never forget how kind you were! May God bless you, and may my parents never find out.

Rivka

Hannah sat down heavily on the couch, looking at the letter in her hand like someone looks at a huge bill from the IRS when expecting a refund. She crumpled it in her fist, throwing it across the room, a deep sense of failure gripping her heart. Then, angry, confused, and afraid, she hunted it down, smoothing it out and reading it once more.

Finally, she picked up the phone. "Mom?"

"Hi, honey. Don't worry, I'm not changing my mind. In fact, I fixed up a room for her last night . . ."

"She's gone."

Rose lay down on the bed, closing her eyes, the phone at her ear, listening to Hannah's explanation. The girl, her niece, her family, would not be coming after all. She hung up the phone, devastated, memories flooding over her once again, like a tidal wave.

25

Borough Park, Brooklyn, August 1970

The sidewalks were vaporous as they sautéed in the summer heat. She hated the summer. She hated Brooklyn. But most of all, she hated the feeling that came over her as people glanced her way. Did they recognize her? she wondered. Or were the looks generic, directed at any alien venturing inside their tight-knit community? And was it really so obvious that's what she'd become?

It was her first time back after running away from home three years before. She studied her reflection in a storefront window that displayed white Sabbath tablecloths and black velvet challah covers, closing the last remaining buttons on her light-blue summer blouse and rolling down her sleeves to her elbows. She tried tugging down her skirt—a boring navy blue polyester with pleats she'd bought especially for the occasion—but succeeded only in getting them to knee-grazing length. Styles were so short these days.

But it was no use: the blouse was too thin, the bra faintly visible beneath, and the skirt might just as well have been midthigh, failing as it did to reach acceptable midcalf levels.

Oy vey! she'd thought, her childhood clamping down on her like a giant stapler, puncturing her newly found joy, attaching her to her past. She pressed her lips together, a rush of memories making her furious, exhaling bitter air. The thought: Let's get this over with, shall we?

Turning the corner, she'd searched for the address Pearl had given her over the phone, the first time they'd spoken in years. Just hearing Pearl's voice had left her in tatters, tearful and filled with an agony of longing and regret.

The place had been easy to find. Outside, elderly Hassidic men with long snowy beards and black skullcaps sat in wheelchairs, their eyes closed, their hands idle. Ultra-Orthodox women, looking very self-important and judgmental—or so it seemed to her—in their turbans and wigs held the hands of young girls in braids and ankle-length skirts, both buttoned down to their wrists and up to their chins. Their combined gazes, equal in intensity and criticism, stuck to her like chewing gum in hair.

She'd climbed the steps and opened the door.

"Where can I find Shaindel Weiss?" she'd asked the swarthy, bareheaded man behind the reception desk—no doubt a Gentile tolerated for his usefulness in turning lights off and on during Sabbaths and holidays. He looked up, slowly taking in her shape, her full breasts pressing against the light summer fabric, her dark eyes, and the exuberant cascade of dark brown hair unconstrained by any pins or bands that highlighted the creamy whiteness of her young skin.

"Room 327," he'd told her, smiling as if they'd shared a secret.

Years later, perhaps she might have been flattered, might even have smiled back. But at that time, in that place, to reciprocate would have been the last straw, worse than short skirts and bare arms. To expose a shameless row of sparkling teeth toward a male and a Gentile would have crossed her over into a territory where even she had not yet dared to venture.

He'd shrugged, turning back to his work. It was probably what he'd come to expect from Hassidic women, although at first he probably hadn't taken her for one. It would have surprised him to learn that once she had worn braids and dark stockings and a stare of disapproval as judgmental as the others.

As she'd climbed the stairs, the odor of what passed for cleanliness in institutions had assaulted her with its combination of disinfectants, air-conditioning, and floor wax. The remembered smells of Friday morning in her grandmother's tiny Brooklyn walk-up had suddenly washed over her: rugelach dripping with chocolate and cinnamon, sweet kugel of noodles and raisins, and a cholent bubbling on the stovetop, the potatoes already dark brown, the meat succulent with fat.

She'd thought, How Bubbee must hate it here, the ugly beige walls, the fake plastic wainscoting, the generic artwork! She'd searched for a spot she still hoped was in her to sympathize with the old woman's pain as she walked down the long corridors punctuated with occasional mock-leather chairs, weighing scales, and adult diaper pails. The smell had gone from merely foreign to distinctly foul. It was the smell of sickness and helpless old age that clothed the bony specter of inevitable and irreversible decay standing patiently in the wings waiting for one and all.

She'd stopped, suddenly weak, remembering how her grandmother's stern face would melt into a smile as she handed her rugelach still warm from the oven, watching her lick off her fingers. But like the rest of her family, her *bubbee* too had sided against her.

It all came back to her: that last look around her old bedroom—the wedding dress in its long, white zippered bag; the short, dark wig on its stand for after the chuppah; the one white shoe on its side, where she had left it after trying it on, its mate still in the red shoe box, untouched. Something about the way that shoe had felt on her foot, the way it pinched and tortured her toes, had given her the courage she needed, reminding her of how her mother, sister, and aunts had all assured her they would eventually stop hurting, that eventually they would be a perfect fit. She remembered how she hadn't been able to speak up, couldn't say no, the way she couldn't say no to the match they'd found for her. Her mother and sister and aunts had all thought that he too was a perfect fit.

This was the first time she'd had any contact with her grandmother. Not that she hadn't wanted to visit her in the hospital after her stroke, but people—Pearl had insisted—said the shock of seeing her might do her grandmother even more harm, broadly hinting that the stroke itself had somehow been her doing as well.

So, she'd waited. And now, finally, her grandmother had asked Pearl to arrange a visit.

She saw a Puerto Rican orderly standing in the corner smoking a cigarette. Yes, she thought, taking out her pack and lighting up, the taste and smell of the tar and nicotine, the smoke dancing up to the ceiling, erasing for a moment the ugliness of this terrible place and her mission in it.

No one deserves this, she thought. Not even my mother. And certainly not my grandmother, who had only been following orders . . .

The old woman was lying in bed, looking oddly like herself, the short, strawlike wig drawn low over her forehead, almost touching her still-dark brows, her pristine white nightgown opaque and modest. Her eyes were closed.

"Bubbee?" she ventured softly. Perhaps she was sleeping so deeply she wouldn't wake up, Rose had thought almost hopefully, imagining sneaking away and forgetting this ever happened.

But the brown eyes, so like her own, opened slowly, turning in her direction. Her grandmother raised her hand, pointing at Rose's legs in dismay.

"Well, good to see you, too," she'd whispered to herself, annoyed. "How are you, Bubbee?" she'd said out loud.

Her grandmother had sat up painfully, revealing to Rose the terrible knowledge that the whole right side of her face was sagging and immobile. Her right hand too seemed unable to move. She uttered sounds with painful effort, but they were unintelligible.

"Wait, here's a pad and a pen. Can you write, Bubbee?"

Her grandmother had nodded, reaching out for the writing instruments with her left hand. Her laborious efforts were painful to watch. Finally, she put down the pen, gesturing to Rose to read.

"No stockings. Shameful!"

Rose looked down, suddenly wanting to laugh. Of all her crimes! Here was another one: bare legs in sandals that revealed the cleavage between her toes! She smiled, stroking the old woman's forehead. "Have a heart, Bubbee! It's too hot for opaque, flesh-colored, seamed stockings. God will forgive me."

She saw her grandmother sigh and nod, giving a lopsided smile.

More than anything else, that smile filled Rose with sorrow and pity. "I would have been here sooner, but they thought it would upset you . . ." Rose began.

Her grandmother put up a hand, shaking her head with effort, taking up the pen once again. She labored over the paper for what seemed like forever.

"Good you came. Need to tell you," Rose read out loud, struggling to

decipher the spidery, whispery pen jottings. *"Go home before it's . . . some-thing, something."*

Her grandmother gestured urgently once more for the pen, and Rose watched over her shoulder as she carefully printed the words *"TOO LATE!"* in capital letters, underlining them twice.

Rose had felt a chill slither down her back.

"I had no choice! I couldn't marry a man I didn't love. A man I didn't even know . . . I want other things, a different life . . ."

Her grandmother pressed her lips together, stubbornly pulling herself up to a sitting position. "You will never be able go back, *maideleh,* never," she said with sudden, frightening clarity. Then, she closed her eyes and sank back down again, exhausted, the pen dropping inside the folds of her sheets.

"Bubbee? Bubbee?"

She'd sat by her side uneasily, the words echoing in her ears, wondering if these would be the last words her grandmother ever spoke to her, wondering if they were true, and if it mattered.

Now, a grandmother herself, she knew.

26

Rivka stood by his door, shivering from the cold, her body soaked through with icy sleet. While the skies had been clear when she left Hannah's, the deluge had come without warning, the heavens opening up above her with what seemed like deliberate malice, the way the earth had opened beneath Korah when he rebelled against Moses. Was the universe itself now conspiring against her, siding with her family to return her to the fold? She shivered with more than just cold at the thought.

Her plan, which had been so clear, now seemed muddled and ill-timed. It was barely 5:00 A.M. Would he even be up at this hour? she wondered, realizing how little she really knew about him. But it was too late now. She knocked softly, putting her chilled ear to the door to listen for sounds of life. But there was nothing. She rested her forehead heavily against the door, feeling stupid and desperate. "Please!" she cried, gripped by a sudden panic, banging on the door with both fists.

"Okay, okay, keep your pants on . . ." She heard a voice shout from the other side of the door.

She saw the peephole darken and then heard a hurried fumbling with locks until, finally, the door opened.

"Rivka?"

"Oh, Simon!" She rushed in, laying her cold, damp head on his bare chest and wrapping her arms around him in relief.

"Whoa," he said, instinctively trying to detach himself, then thought better of it. Her body was voluptuously soft as she lay limply against him, her luxuriant blond hair unbraided for the first time, shining with moisture, the long eyelashes dark and wet against her fair skin. He put his arms around her softly, astonished.

For two weeks, he had been faithfully tutoring her in the mysteries of the SATs (and not getting very far), careful to keep his hands to himself.

Not that the idea of seducing her hadn't crossed his mind. It had, deliciously and often. But except for tentative and casual attempts entirely from his side that had been firmly rebuffed, this was the first time she had ever indicated any physical interest in him at all. He didn't want to jinx it.

"You'd better take off those wet things," he said, trying to be avuncular. "Do you have some dry . . . ?" It was then he saw the small valise. He stared at it.

"Yes, thank you, Simon." She moved out of his arms, picking up her things and retreating into his bedroom.

He stretched out on the sofa, his arm flung over his eyes, calculating the myriad possibilities afforded by this current, interesting turn of events, as well as a few of the unfortunate pitfalls.

"Simon?" Her hand shook him gently.

"Oh." He rubbed his eyes and yawned. "I must have dozed off again. Sorry."

She was dressed in her Sabbath best, looking like something out of *Fiddler on the Roof.* "Did you and Hannah have a falling out?"

She shook her head. "No. Hannah's been very kind. But I can't live with her anymore." She didn't elaborate.

"Oh." Well, that explained the damsel in distress with a suitcase. He made no suggestions, waiting.

She shifted uncomfortably, finally breaking the silence. "Simon, maybe . . . you wouldn't mind . . . if for a little while I could . . . ah . . . maybe, stay with you?"

What was a "little while" and what did "stay with you" mean, exactly, in addition to taking up room? He wondered. But he said only: "Are you sure this is what you want?"

She nodded earnestly. "I wouldn't be any trouble."

"Um, Rivka, what about your family? All that stuff you told me about how they hunt people down and force them to do things—"

"They don't know I'm here!" She interrupted him hurriedly. "And neither does Hannah. I haven't told her anything about the two of us."

He exhaled, relieved, making some rapid calculations. "I guess, in that case, sure, why not? For a couple of days at least . . . until we figure this out . . ."

Her face fell. "A few days, yes. When will happen the job at your friend's?"

He looked at her blankly. "Job?"

"Your very good friend with the art gallery? The one who might need a secretary/assistant or a salesperson?"

"Oh, right, sure," he said, vaguely remembering something he'd casually said on the spur of the moment. "But there's no rush."

"But I want to pay. I don't want charity."

"Yeah, sure. I understand completely." He yawned again, at a loss, wondering when he was going to be able to go back to sleep.

"Do you want I should make you breakfast?"

"It's kind of early for that . . ."

She looked ready to cry.

Oh, Jesus! "Sure, Rivka, that would be great!"

She went into the kitchen, opening and closing closet doors. "Your frying pan, it's new?"

His mother had come in with a box of things she'd unpacked into his kitchen cupboards. Since he never cooked and hardly ate anything other than cold cereal at home, he had no idea what was in there, just that it had never been used.

"Everything in there is new: the dishes, the utensils, the pots."

"Are you sure? Because if they've been used, even once, I have to know which is for meat and which is for milk . . ."

"Yeah, sure. I get it . . ." He lay back, his eyes closing.

"Your refrigerator. It's empty."

"You don't say?"

"No eggs, milk, butter, bread, fruits, vegetables . . ."

He groaned softly. "I wasn't expecting company. . . . Look, I'll pick up some stuff on the way home from school."

"Maybe I'll go to that kosher store now." The first morning she'd come to him, he'd taken her by bus to a glatt kosher minimarket.

"Oh, that's kind of far from here and they probably don't open until eight. But there's a twenty-four-hour supermarket right down the block. I don't know how much kosher stuff they carry, though."

"Don't worry. I'll find something." She put on her coat, hesitating, embarrassed. "Simon, I have no money."

"Oh, right." He found his wallet and took out a twenty. It felt strange giving her money. He could see she felt equally uncomfortable accepting it. It was as if some clear barrier had been breached. "Knock yourself out!"

"What?" she asked him sharply.

"It's just an expression. It means 'have fun.'"

"Oh." She relaxed. "And maybe you have a bag and an umbrella?"

"Ahhh . . . wait." He reluctantly hauled himself upright once again and went searching for them. When he came back, she was standing by the window, looking out. She looked so adorable, so young, so lost, he thought, his grouchiness mellowing. He handed her the items silently, twining his fingers through her hair, running his thumb down the side of her soft cheek until it rested on her lips. Then, he drew it slowly over her chin and neck, until it rested just at the place where the buttons of her blouse began.

She felt a chill run down her spine that had nothing at all to do with the weather.

What have I done? she thought, as she rounded the corner and found the store. The words throbbed through her like a mantra, opening up a new consciousness of dangers and thrills, new forms of good and evil, all sifted together like ingredients for a recipe she'd never tried. And what will be the result? she wondered. Would it be good, tasty, worthwhile? Or brutish and nasty and possibly harmful to her health? In either case, who was she to judge? She knew nothing.

She was a lost soul, she mourned, unlinked to her past and moving rapidly toward an uncertain future, like a child on one of those giant slides in water parks, both dreading and loving the velocity and the eventual drop into something that was definitely going to be—as Hannah had warned—above her head. Was it still possible to stop herself? she wondered. Or had she cut her ties? Could she go back now if she wanted to?

Her parents would be thrilled. But they would still only agree to take her back on their own terms. They might even decide to punish her, restricting her movements even more and keeping a greater watch over her for a while. The thought of that, in itself, didn't really bother her. After all, it wouldn't be that different from the life she'd always known, where the whole community acted as watchdog, one's slightest deviation reported with diligence to all the powers that be. Like an animal in the zoo, one's cage was nominally open, but the portal led only to another cage, hemmed in by a thousand watchful eyes.

Eventually—sooner rather than later—the bridegroom parade would begin again. This time, if her wanderings had made it out to the gossipmongers, her stock would have fallen. The male merchandise available to her would be diminished in quality, if not in quantity. Like her mother (although in her mother's case it had been through no fault of her own) she would get the misfits, boys who were the third or fourth choices of the heads of their yeshivas; the fussy cousins or male relatives of neighbors who had been on the market a bit too long for one reason or another, none of them good. She would find herself moving rapidly toward those girls who had been pushed out of the respectable bride pool and were now floundering in the rapids, hoping for a marriage proposal, any proposal, before they went over the falls.

Rather than being in a position to accept or reject, she would be one of those unfortunate creatures who dressed carefully for each blind date, hoping to please, rather than to be pleased. From there, it would be only a few short steps down to desperation, where her parents would need to assure the groom that they would take out loans to buy him an apartment and furnish it and provide him with a living for the first five or six years of his marriage, bankrupting them.

She couldn't do that to them, knowing as she did that their sacrifice would be in vain. She could never stay happily married to a yeshiva boy, any yeshiva boy. From the small sampling she'd been exposed to, they all seemed like children. They'd never traveled or opened a novel or seen a movie.

While they didn't say it outright, they all believed a woman was inferior to them and was there to serve them, for why else would they thank God every morning for not making them one?

In contrast, Simon seemed like the most exciting man in the world. He had been to India and had hiked up and down mountain trails in far-off places in America. He had strange ideas about music, art, religion, and politics, which she could not understand and which, in their very foreignness, were thrilling. In this place, alone with him, was the adventure she had dreamed of when she'd decided to run away, she told herself, fingering the buttons of her blouse nervously, reliving his touch and how her whole being had responded with a deep, sonorous vibration that made her shiver with delight.

She was hungry for experience, wanting so much to feel all those things that until now she had only read or heard about. Once, years before, she'd accidentally overheard a conversation between her older, married sister and her sister's newly married friend. The girl had confided that on her wedding night she'd locked herself into the bathroom, terrified of what her groom might ask of her. And in the end, she'd whispered, it had felt like rape.

Never, she'd promised herself then, will I let that happen to me! *I* will choose the man who will transform me from a girl to a woman, a man for whom I will feel desire and love. But the older she was, the more she realized how impossible that would be. The whole system of her community and their religious stringencies worked against such feelings, making sure love could only come after marriage.

But what if it never came? What if she was forced to live with a man she could never learn to love, who would have the use of her body, forcing himself on her whenever he pleased for as long as she lived? What if it always felt like rape?

The more she thought about it, the more she convinced herself that there was no justification at all for anyone to be involved in so intimate a choice. The stakes were too high, and they involved only herself and no one else. Her mother and father, the rabbis, the matchmakers, what had they to do with her private, soft flesh and the intimate secret recesses of her heart? The public part of it, that which involved the community, with its rituals and its ceremonies, seemed like some monstrous intrusion, forcibly insinuating itself into her very womb. They had taken for themselves the power to justify and sanctify what was done to her body. But it did not belong to them! That power was hers and hers alone. But if she wrested it from them, claiming it as her own, she would never, ever be forgiven. She would lose the self she knew and everything that was right and familiar to her, winding up instead in some strange place that frightened as much as it fascinated.

Either way, whatever she decided, it would be irrevocable: once back home, she would never again have the courage to leave; and once she gave into her passion, they would never agree to take her back.

She took a shopping cart and began to put things inside. Nothing here was available in her special brands. She fingered the milk, surprised to realize that she no longer believed it mattered if a cow was rabbinically supervised. A cow was a cow and milk was milk, yogurt was yogurt, and butter was butter. Cheese, which might have animal-based rennet in it, was another matter, so she avoided that. She piled the items into her cart before she could change her mind. As they touched the metal bottom, she felt something inside her that had been whole smash to smithereens. She had embarked upon a path that had led her so far from her old life that there was no way to redeem herself or find her way back. So she threw the minor sins to the wayside on her road toward the major ones.

When she returned to the apartment, Simon was sleeping on the couch, still dressed only in pajama bottoms. But something was different, she realized. It was the scent. He had splashed on some men's cologne. It smelled musky and dangerous.

Slowly, she put down the groceries. Then, she took off her coat, hanging it carefully in the closet. "Do you want eggs?" she asked him, helpless with the knowledge that she had come to a turning point.

He got up from the couch, walking toward her with slow, silent steps, as sinuous and dangerous as a panther, she thought. He put his arms around her. "My sweet angel," he said, enfolding her, resting his cheek against her neck. His lips pushed aside her blouse, finding her bare shoulder.

"Simon," she whispered, breathless, trapped in her own confusion and desire. "It's a sin."

"Are you married?" he murmured.

"No."

"Engaged?"

"No."

"Then why?"

"We aren't married."

"Where is it written that single people have to get married before they can have sex?"

She could not think of an answer. It was like the Jewish milk, she thought. More things she'd been taught that made no sense, added on to her religion by people who wanted to make life difficult, not pure. But there was one thing she was certain of. "I have to go to the mikveh first."

"Those ritual purification baths?" He shook his head skeptically, smiling.

"I must." She shook her head adamantly.

"Okay . . . if that's what you need. I respect that," he said, loosening his arms. "But I have to ask you something. Do you have some protection?"

Now she was totally confused. "From what?"

"Okay. I guess that means I'll use something."

"Something?"

"A condom."

She blushed scarlet. "No, no. You mustn't use anything! It's a sin. Like spilling your seed on the ground like Onan. But you don't have to worry about it. I won't get pregnant."

He didn't probe. "So you *are* using something."

"I won't get pregnant, Simon," she repeated.

"All right, then. I guess I'll go get dressed and get to work."

She watched as he turned, his beautiful body moving away.

27

A week later, Rivka walked down the unmarked path toward the door of the mikveh. Opening her purse, she took out the shiny, five-dollar ring and slipped it on her finger; then, she tied a scarf around her head, tucking in all her abundant hair.

She had traveled an hour and a half by subway to Far Rockaway in order to visit a ritual bath where hopefully no one would know her. Sick with apprehension that the mikveh attendants—who had a reputation for unrelenting piety and strict supervision of the area under their control—might somehow sniff out the scandalous truth, she shook as she rang the intercom, aware of the blinking video cameras recording her every move. Finally, she was buzzed in.

The waiting room was full of women of all ages. Some, certainly past menopause, had no doubt decided to come simply for good luck, as was the custom. One or two looked like frightened young virgins clinging to their mothers. But the majority were overweight and harried young mothers who seemed pleased to have a reason to sit and do nothing. They looked up briefly and curiously as she took her place among them.

From across the room, she looked into the open door of the "salon," where women who had finished their ablutions were now using high-powered hair-dryers to style their hair, as well as availing themselves of the nail polish and makeup left on display for their use. While strict religious adherence usually looked askance at such displays of vanity, the opposite was true of those preparing for their rabbinically sanctioned postmikveh encounters with their husbands.

From the time a woman's period commenced until seven days after it ceased and she immersed in the mikveh, married couples were forbidden any physical contact. Nonobservant people, she realized, could never understand what kind of passion this abstinence evoked. She remembered the way her mother would come home with wet hair but fresh lipstick, something she hardly ever wore. The way her father would speak to her mother in an especially soft tone of voice. She squeezed her hands together nervously at the memory. The practice of attending mikveh was meant to encourage intimacy between married couples, who would produce the next generation of pure souls. What would they say of her, though, a single girl prettying herself up for an illicit romp with a boyfriend?

Can I really immerse in the holy waters, say the blessing, and then desecrate myself? *Was* sex a desecration when it was between two consenting, unmarried people? According to the Torah, she knew, it was hardly a sin at all. Well, it was severely looked down upon by Jewish custom, but nowhere was it written that it was strictly forbidden. In fact, Jewish law even considered it a legal method of contracting a marriage. But having sex without immersing in the mikveh was unforgivable. The punishment for such a transgression was "*karet*," meaning "being cut off," a supernatural punishment brought down on you by heaven. Some said it was being cut off from your people forever—both here and in the World to Come, while others said it was to be cut off from life—dying young or without children.

But custom was stronger than law, she knew. If anyone here even suspected the truth, it would start a virtual riot, and she'd be thrown out unceremoniously in front of all these strangers! She felt tears rise to her eyes for what she was about to do and, contrarily, at the thought that something might prevent it.

"Just had a baby?" a young woman sitting next to her asked, pointing to Rivka's long nails.

Rivka hurriedly clenched her hands into fists, attempting to hide them.

Why, oh why, hadn't she cut them at home? They were a dead giveaway. There were only two reasonable explanations for such nails: that you were finishing up a long pregnancy and birth, and thus hadn't been to the mikveh for months, or that it was your first time. Since she'd walked in with her hair covered and a ring on her finger, the latter was no longer possible. I am a very bad liar, she thought, forcing a smile and a nod.

"I had my first baby a few months ago," the woman chatted on. "So I'm back to no nails. But I don't care. Who has time for manicures with a newborn crying day and night? Are you new in the neighborhood?"

"I'm . . . actually visiting . . . with . . . that is . . . we are visiting . . ."

"Oh, who are your friends? Or is it family?" she probed, continuing the friendly game of Jewish geography that made Rivka want to cut and run. Luckily, her interrogator's name was called and she soon disappeared inside before Rivka needed to make up an answer.

Soon after, it was her turn. "Room number four," the mikveh attendant told her, handing her a towel, washcloth, and bar of soap. "Do you need anything else?"

Rivka, who had no idea, shook her head, walking into the room and locking the door behind her. Everything looked clean and pleasant, she saw, relieved. There was a sink and a bathtub with nice pink bath tiles. On the counter were nail clippers, cotton balls, nail-polish remover, and makeup remover. Luckily, there was also a sign listing all the things she needed to do to make herself ready for immersion. It went on forever.

Slowly, she hung up her coat and unbuttoned her sweater, hanging them on a hook. She unbuttoned her blouse and unzipped her skirt. Her slip was new, a pale white silky material with lace over the breasts. She hung it beneath her coat, hiding it along with her new, matching lace bra and panties, horrified by the idea that the matronly attendant should see them. Naked, she felt suddenly vulnerable and frightened. She quickly wrapped a towel around herself, turning on the faucets of the bathtub.

As she waited for it to fill, she lifted her leg up, resting it on the rim of the tub, examining her toes and using the nail clippers to shear off her toenails, carefully gathering the shards and disposing of them, as was the custom. Then she switched legs, repeating her actions. Then she turned to her fingernails, cutting them so close to the nail bed that her skin began to bleed, determined to convince the mikveh attendant of her piety.

Done, she hung up the towel and got into the bath, looking down at herself. She couldn't recall a time when she had been forced into such intimacy with her own naked body for such a long time. She had never taken baths, an unheard of, selfish indulgence for a member of their large family given that they all shared a single bathroom. No one would have dared waste so much expensively heated hot water on themselves! Bathing—along with everything else they did in that room—was a hurried affair, completed as soon as possible.

Lying back in the warm water, she drew the soapy washcloth over her pink, smooth arms and shoulders, finally reaching down to her plump young breasts, embarrassed at the nipples that stood out so firmly. But why should you be embarrassed at your own body? she asked herself, boldly examining them as if for the first time. They were like two soft, plump fruits, not rounded, but conical with a dark pink circle at the center with its own tiny bud. She lifted them and they filled her hands, pressing against them with luxurious, heavy softness. She ran the cloth over her firm rounded hips and flat stomach, her slim thighs and calves. Following the written instructions, she shampooed the hair of both her head and lower body, blushing as she rinsed both carefully.

Then, she stepped from the bath, reaching for a towel to cover herself. In the corner of her eyes, she caught a glimpse of her naked body in the mirror. As if sleepwalking, she moved closer, standing shamelessly before it.

OH, oh. Could it be possible? All those pieties, and yet, underneath the heavy opaque stockings, the midcalf skirts, the long-sleeved shirts, there was . . . this! She looked at the voluptuous curves of her breasts and hips and thighs, the blond triangle where her legs met. This, this was what she was. Not a prayer sayer, an obedient, modest girl filled with spirituality . . . but this. She felt almost angry, as if this truth had been deliberately hidden from her, this amazing revelation, with all its intoxicating power.

She felt suddenly hot, almost dizzy with the vision. Slowly, she took a comb and ran it through her hair to remove any tangles. And when she finished with the hair on her head, she reached down to the blond triangle below.

She had never spent any time at all thinking about it, and had never in her life stood like this examining it. That powerful place where life began, where babies pushed out into the world. And yet, not just a factory. A place too of magic and wonder, a vortex of pleasure. This was where she felt Simon. Not in her head, or even her heart. But down here, in this place, the place she liked to call her belly. But she could see now that it was not. It was a different destination altogether.

Was she ready to go there? To take him?

For one panicked moment she considered fleeing. It was not too late to rush back into her parents' arms, to put off this decision for months, even years. The terrible idea came to her that, whatever she did at this point, her life might not turn out to be all that wonderful anyway. Was it really worth it, then, to sacrifice her honor, all she still believed in? And was it really her honor, and did she really still believe in all those things she had been brought up to believe?

You have no idea what your life is going to be like, a voice inside her scolded. *Stop being a spoiled brat! Did you really think it was going to be so easy? Have courage to follow your dreams, or die trying!*

The voice was harsh, intimidating, and convincing, much more so than the pale threats from her parents that her imagination conjured up, annoying reminders of her duty to the Torah and to the family's good name. Since she was the youngest and her other siblings were all married, she was spared the most convincing threat of all: that her wantonness would destroy her siblings' chances for good matches, as her aunt Rose had destroyed her mother's. That threat, she knew, kept most of her friends in line.

Scrubbed, clipped, and painfully combed, she modestly covered herself with a towel and rang the bell for the attendant. Soon someone was knocking on the door, trying to get in. She quickly unlocked it.

"Ready?"

Rivka nodded.

"Your hair! It's so long! Didn't your husband make you cut it when you married?"

"My husband likes it long," she said in a small voice.

The woman shook her head. "No wonder it took you so long to get ready for immersion! And all the stray hairs . . ." she tsk-tsked, examining Rivka's bare shoulders and back. "It's impossible. Come, show me your nails."

Rivka held out her brutally manicured fingertips and the woman gave her a bright smile of approval, somewhat placated.

"Very good. But next time, don't damage the skin. You can't immerse if you're bleeding." Then, the woman was silent, waiting. Finally, she said, "The towel, child."

"What about it?"

The woman gave her a long, searching look. "You act as if this is the first time for you in a mikveh . . . ?"

"No, no, it's just that where I usually go . . ."

"So tell me, how does the mikveh attendant check your body where you usually go if you keep it covered with a towel?" Her tone was polite but skeptical.

Rivka felt herself blush from head to toe as she opened the towel and let it drop to the bathroom floor. The woman looked her over matter-of-factly, picking off stray hairs with a tissue, all the while peppering her with questions: "Did you remember to clean out your belly button? Did you use Q-tips on your ears? Did you wipe the corners of your eyes? Did you brush your teeth?"

All the while, Rivka stood, exposed and mortified, all the joy of her secret exultation stamped out and destroyed. Stupefied, she nodded wordlessly.

"Fine, fine." Again, the woman waited, finally handing her the terrycloth bathrobe that had been hanging on a hook, still slightly damp from the last woman who had used it. Rivka cringed.

"Are you sure this is not your first time?" the woman asked again, this time with added sharpness.

Rivka, disgusted, suddenly gave up. "Yes, it's my very first time here! I have no idea what to do!"

"But you are married, aren't you?" the attendant demanded sharply. "We don't let unmarried girls use the mikveh."

She felt the moment of truth had arrived. She could tell and be honest and one with her soul, accepting her punishment of public humiliation and facing Simon's disappointment and anger, or she could continue to lie, weaseling out of the unhappiness that was her due in order to reach the illicit joy looming tantalizingly in her imagination.

"Yes, I am married and even have a child," she said with a shy smile, shocked at how easily the words came to her. "But I am newly religious."

"*A ben niddah*," the woman gasped, shaking her head. "A child born in impurity! But at least now you are trying to do the right thing. And your husband, is he supportive of your efforts to serve God?"

"Not very," she said sadly.

"Never mind," the woman comforted, patting her shoulder. "You must be determined, and then the man will follow. It is the woman who builds her house or destroys it, *maideleh*. Come, follow me."

The attendant opened the room's back door, which led down a long, narrow corridor ending in the mikveh itself. It was a small pool of deep, clear water. Under the woman's watchful eye, Rivka took off her robe and hurried naked down the steps into the water, anxious to hide her body. It was pleasantly warm and came up to her neck.

"How many times do you *toivel*?"

Rivka, pretending to be secular, couldn't very well admit she knew the word *toivel* meant "dunk." She shrugged helplessly.

"It means to immerse in the water. Girls usually follow the custom of their mothers in the number of times they immerse. Some do it seven times, and some only once."

While she was sure her family had a custom, it was one she had not yet been privy to. She felt saddened by this knowledge, knowing she was the loose loop that had broken the chain of tradition. "How many times do you think?"

"Twice for good measure."

"Twice then." Rivka nodded, wanting to get this over with. She waited, confused.

"Bend your knees, then plunge into the water until it covers your head completely," the woman instructed her patiently. "The water must cover the top of your head. Don't clench your eyes or mouth or hands. Keep them gently closed. When you come up, cross your hands over your breasts, and I'll hang down a towel to cover your hair. Then, say the blessing."

Rivka closed her eyes, taking the first plunge.

"Not deep enough! Try again!"

Choking back the water she had breathed in, she did as she was told. Drowning, she thought. She felt her chest clench in anger, holding her breath even as she emerged.

"Kosher!" the woman exclaimed, hanging the towel over the side until it touched her head. "Now repeat after me."

Rivka crossed her arms across her bare breasts: "Blessed art Thou, O King of the universe, on this immersion," she repeated in Hebrew after the attendant, ashamed to be evoking God's name in this sorry enterprise. Far from purifying her spirit, she felt soiled and damned, as if she had deliberately dropped a prayer book into the mud.

Since the Holy Temple in Jerusalem had been destroyed, everyone in the world was impure, she knew, profaned by death and sin with no way to purify themselves. Immersing in the ritual bath was one of the few things left to Jews that provided such purification. And she had now sullied that experience for herself forever.

She felt like crying.

She immersed twice more, then walked up the steps. The mikveh attendant held out the robe, averting her eyes in modesty. Rivka slipped it on, feeling like nothing could cover her nakedness. She had been exposed, now and forever.

She hurried back to her room, showering off the mikveh water, feeling she had stolen every drop. Anxious to leave, she quickly pulled her clothes on over her still-damp body, dropping the wet towels into a laundry basket. She paid the attendant her small fee, adding a generous tip. Securing her scarf over her damp hair, she escaped into the night.

Around the corner, Simon stood waiting, a broad smile spreading over his face when he saw her. He reached out to take her hand, but she pulled away.

"What's wrong now?" he asked, annoyed.

"Nothing. I'm still wet. It's cold."

"Well, let's get you home and warm you up." He grinned.

His levity made her feel sick to her stomach. She couldn't bear to even look at him.

The subway platform was outdoors, and the air was freezing cold. She shivered, wondering if she would get pneumonia and die. It didn't seem too harsh a punishment to her. In fact, if she had been God, that's exactly what she would have done to a sinner like herself. *Midah keneged midah.* Measure for measure.

Finally, the train rolled in and they got on.

"I was thinking maybe next weekend we could go up to my parents' cabin in the Adirondacks, get in a little skiing. Have you ever skied? It's not difficult to learn. I could take you to a little slope I know that's perfect for beginners. I'm starting a new course next semester about Hassidism. I expect you to help me with all my homework . . ." He went on and on, as if trying to deny her steady, morose silence. But all she heard was the rapid beating of her guilty heart and the rumble of the train moving relentlessly forward.

It was hours before they finally got home. She was thoroughly chilled and coughing. Simon seemed oblivious, unbuttoning her coat and tearing off her head covering the moment they walked through the door.

She didn't resist. He put his hands beneath her sweater, pulling it up over her head urgently as she obediently raised her arms. But when he touched the buttons of her blouse, something about his cold hands at her neck reminded her of the mikveh attendant. A flood of disgust and violation washed over her. She couldn't breathe.

"Don't!" she whispered, pulling away.

"C'mon!" He smiled. "Just relax, honey."

He got the first button undone, then started on the second.

"*Don't!*" she screamed, loud enough for the neighbors to hear, wrenching herself away from him.

He dropped his hands, flustered, angry, bewildered.

"Just leave me alone!"

He put his hands into his pockets and backed away, furious. "Okay, Rivka. Whatever you say . . ." He turned his back.

"Simon. Please . . ."

Mollified, he turned back, holding out his arms. "Tell me what's wrong, babe."

"I . . ." But the words dammed up in her throat. She grabbed her coat and put it on, then made for the door, slamming it behind her as she rushed down the steps to the street.

Outside, it was very dark and beastly cold. She looked around her, terrified of the strange men who picked up their heads as she walked by. Too late, she realized she had left her purse behind. She didn't even have money for a subway token or to make a phone call. What difference did it make? Where would I go? she asked herself. Who would I call? Hannah? My mother? How could she explain to either of them her lies, her disappearances, her actions, all the things she had been desiring and pursuing? And what would they say to her? Both would talk her out of going back to Simon, of doing what her whole body and heart longed to do.

I am in hell, she thought, more frightened than she had ever been. She wanted to pray, but didn't feel worthy. Every choice she had made was wrong. Every independent idea she had formed, mistaken. She had made her choices, and now, when the time had come to pay for them, she was trying to back out. But the universe would not allow it. She must go back. She must bear it. She must allow herself the joy of it.

She turned around. And there he was, walking toward her. She ran into his arms. He held her tightly. "Rivka, Rivka."

She lifted her chin and looked into his eyes. No one had ever said her name that way. In his voice, she was another person, that Rivka. He had come after her, afraid for her, she told herself. He cared about her. He loved her.

He held out his hand, and she slipped hers inside. It was warm against her icy skin. They walked slowly back to the house, all the while a current of fire flashing through that place she had so recently discovered.

In the elevator, she stood with her back against the wall, her hands held tightly behind her, the fingers squeezing together with punishing fierceness. He stood apart, looking at the floor. And then, suddenly, he looked up, taking one step toward her, reaching out and holding her chin, his thumb making a soft, circular motion on her cheek. She closed her eyes, counting the number of times it moved up and back over her face, feeling the movement intensely. She moaned.

He held her head between his hands, his fingers soft as they met in back of her neck, pulling her mouth to his. He pressed his lips against hers, and she felt her entire body flow toward him, electrified, almost drunk with abandon.

They staggered, kissing, to the door. She waited as he detached himself from her, fumbling for the keys, all the while keeping one hand at the back of her neck with an insistent pressure. Inside at last, he quickly closed and locked the door.

They stood facing each other for a moment, as his hand slid around slowly to her throat, his thumb caressing the beating pulse that led to her heart. Slowly, he unbuttoned her coat, pushing it off her shoulders. She watched passively, letting it slip to the floor.

He leaned in, his breath in her ear. "Help me, Rivka," he whispered, a suggestion, a command, a plea.

Obediently, she found her fingers undoing the buttons of her blouse, then pushing it down off her arms.

"Turn around."

She stood with her back to him, feeling his hands pull down the zipper of her skirt, his fingers slipping now and then, touching her back, each touch a small, almost painful, electric jolt. She closed her eyes. The garment barely grazed her body as it tumbled to the floor.

His hands pressed her naked shoulders as he turned her around to face him once more. "You are so beautiful, Rivka. So very young and beautiful," he whispered in awe. "Will you . . . ? Or shall I . . . ?"

"You," she answered, as if in a dream, lifting her arms above her head.

She felt the silky brush of her new slip as he pulled it over her face, blinding her for a moment, the straps tickling her arms. His hands were behind her back now, undoing the hooks of her pretty new bra, letting her breasts spring free. He rolled down her dark panty hose, her legs white and smooth beneath them. She stepped out of her shoes, trampling down the last shreds of her stockings, freeing herself.

Standing there, almost naked, she had her first rush of shame. She crossed her arms over her breasts. "*No!*" she pleaded, ready to kill him if he touched her.

He did nothing, said nothing, waiting patiently, his hands at his sides, as the silence grew. Finally, he whispered, "Do you want me, Rivka?"

She could not answer, her voice strangled by her education, upbringing, and beliefs. But then the vision of her body in the mirror at the mikveh returned to her. A song without words overwhelmed her heart, bursting through the man-made bands of social conventions, a force of nature contained in her blood that could not be held back. Its time had come, the rushing flow of her primitive blood instincts, which no man-made dam of rules and regulations could hold back. She dropped her arms to her sides and took a step toward him.

He lifted her as he would a tired child, and she flung her arms around his neck, burying her mouth and nose in the soft material of his shirt, inhaling the clean, manly scent that made her blood surge, her cheek pressed against his stubble. He laid her gently on top of the bedcovers, leaning over her. And then, as she held her breath, terrified, she felt his hands slide up her thighs, finding their way beneath the last separation between their bodies, a flimsy bit of white cotton lace

"Are you cold?"

She was shaking now, with desire, a fear of the unknown, and an acknowledged fear of sin. She shook her head no, her arms rising once more to cover her breasts. He reached out and stopped her.

"*No,* no Rivka. There is nothing to be ashamed of. Nothing to hide."

"You are still dressed," she said accusingly.

He smiled, swiftly tearing off his clothes.

The room, lit only by the street lamps below, filled with the sound of their breathing, the far-off whine of traffic, the soft murmur of the bed springs, and the whispered answers of the bedcovers moving beneath them.

She pulled up her legs, foraging beneath the covers for shelter, to restore her sense of decency.

He crawled in beside her.

"Are you sure, Rivka?" he whispered.

She put her mouth over his, desperate to stop him from speaking. *No more questions!* she wanted to shout. *I have no answers! Leave me alone!* she cried out silently to some accuser who hovered nearby, waiting to rob her of joy.

She felt him caressing her, just as he thrust his tongue inside her mouth. And it was sweet, and shocking. An explosion like fireworks went off inside her. He grasped her hard, and in his hands she felt how young and smooth and desirable her hips were, how they bloomed from her tiny waist. She tried to imagine herself as him experiencing her, and the idea filled her with almost unbearable passion. And then she stopped thinking altogether, the shock of new experiences building each upon the other at a frenzied pace. It was impossible to absorb them all.

He nudged her legs apart, and it was a shock to feel herself handled this way by hands other than her own, a will other than her own. She resisted. But he was stronger, his desire out of control now as he pushed inside her. She wrapped her legs around his back, horrified, and then all at once the horror was over, the pain was over. A new feeling, like circles of infinite light, wound around each other, lifting her higher and higher until she felt she would burst if she didn't have release.

And then it came, like nothing she had ever felt before, a joyous pain, a feeling of ecstasy that overwhelmed all her senses. She wanted to tear his flesh apart with her teeth, to grind into him like an incubus, possessing him. She wanted it to go on forever.

28

So, this was love, Rivka thought as she sat waiting every day for him to come home; waiting for the moment when his key would turn in the lock and his body would fill the room, bringing with it the whiff of cold leather and the chilled fibers of his jeans; waiting for the moment when she could slip her hand beneath his clothes to reach the smooth, hard bones of his shoulders. She wanted him to hold her, to feel his body surround her and enfold her, taking away all separateness. She didn't want to feel like herself anymore, but like a new creature with two heads, two hearts, and one enrapturing desire.

It was an obsession.

At first, he was happy to accommodate her, smiling slowly, ready at a moment's notice to drop everything he was doing to lose himself in her. But then, one day, a day that was the same as every other day, he shrank away and said: "Rivka, I've really got to finish this paper. Can't you find some other way to amuse yourself?"

Walking into the bathroom and closing the door, she turned on the faucet and wept as quietly as she could, devastated. For a few days, she kept her distance, wounded to the core, until finally he noticed.

"Come here, babe," he said, opening his arms. She was only too happy to run back into them, reveling in his acceptance, the terrible panic and fear and sorrow lifting from her as if they had never been.

"It's not good for you to be cooped up all day cleaning and cooking me meals, babe," he said, patting his rounding stomach. "I've gained about ten pounds in the last few weeks. My pants are getting tight on me. And please, please stop ironing my undershirts and my sheets!"

"I want to be good to you. I love you so much!"

At the word "love," he seemed to flinch. It was subtle, but visible. "You are a good girl, Rivka, but you are trying too hard to please me. Think about yourself, won't you? I thought you wanted to get into college. Have you done those SAT practice sheets I left for you?"

The truth was she'd stared at them, confused and bored, noticing the streaks she'd left on the windows when she'd cleaned them and the dust in the corners of the ceilings. She didn't want to admit to him that she had no clue at all how to answer any of them. But she took his scolding to heart, trying harder.

"Jean Piaget, a Swiss psychologist, and the first scientist that made systematic studies of how children learn."

What followed were five alternative sentences, one of which, supposedly, was a better way to phrase this idea. She tried to figure out which little bubble to fill in. But all of the sentences were equally incomprehensible to her, and equally boring. Besides, what was wrong with the original?

The math was even worse:

The stem-and-leaf graph above shows the distribution by height, in inches, of pines in a grove. What percent of the pines are over 45 inches tall?

(A) 15%   (B) 25%   (C) 30%   (D) 40%   (E) 75%

She could not make heads or tails out of that one either.

In the evenings, he tried to help her, patiently going over the material, until they both finally had to admit it was hopeless. Her education had not been very thorough to begin with, and she had stopped it early. There were enormous gaps that needed to be filled in. It simply wasn't possible to get a terrible education, not to mention skipping over two years of high school, and go straight to college.

"Why don't you enroll in some GED classes where you can get your high-school-equivalency certificate? There's plenty of time for you to study for college."

"You think I'm stupid!" she cried. "But I know more than you will ever know! You're completely ignorant about your own religion. Why, you can't even recite the simplest prayer, *Shma*. What will you do when you are about to die? That has to be the last thing a Jewish person says!"

"I'll recite the 'Star Spangled Banner,'" he deadpanned, annoyed. "You knew when you moved in with me I wasn't religious. So what's the problem now?"

She began insisting that they have a traditional Friday-night Sabbath dinner, with Sabbath candles and wine. Wanting to keep the peace, he reluctantly went along with her, because the sex was great, and his house had never been cleaner. And truthfully, he had affection for her. She was like a little kitten, soft and cuddly and defenseless. Even when she tried to be wounding, her claws barely made a scratch.

"Here, you recite the kiddush over the wine." She handed him a siddur.

He broke his teeth forming the Hebrew words.

She laughed. "You sound like a white skullcap."

"What is that supposed to mean?"

"You know, those white skullcaps they give out at bar mitzvahs for Jews who know nothing."

He was not amused. "Where is all this coming from, Rivka?" He was weary.

"Maybe I didn't learn much in school, but I know better how to live than you! How can you treat every day the same way, with no Sabbaths, no holy days? It's monotonous and dreary (words from the SATs!). What do you believe in? Anything?"

"I believe in love. I believe in beauty."

He might as well have said he believed in Coca-Cola and good movies. "Love? Beauty? Were you created by love and beauty? Did they form you in your mother's womb? Do they stop planes from crashing, babies from being born with deformities? Who do you pray to?"

"I don't pray. I meditate."

"What does that mean, really, except to look at your stomach and think no thoughts at all?"

"Are you unhappy with me, Rivka?" he interrupted, his voice calm but his jaw clenched. "Because no one is forcing you to stay, you know."

She straightened her back, bunching her lips together defiantly, but soon collapsed, lowering her head and weeping into the steaming chicken soup. "I feel like such a failure, Simon. I feel stupid and worthless and sinful."

He took her in his arms, whispering lovely things to her, and, as always, they wound up in bed. It was the only thing she could give him, the only value she had, she thought.

He began coming home later and later, with one excuse or another. And when she complained, he felt trapped. She was in his house, in his bed, with no place to go. If only there was the human equivalent of the ASPCA where he could drop her off, he sometimes thought. But the more responsible and obligated he felt, the more he wanted out. His eyes began to wander.

"So, tell me about your cousin Hannah. How was it living with her?"

"Why do you want to know?" she asked, her eyes narrowing.

"Oh, just curious. I'd like to know more about your family."

"Why, because my aunt Rose is famous and rich?"

"Is she?"

"Hannah never told you?"

He shrugged, pretending indifference.

"Rose Weiss, she's a famous photographer! She had a show in the MOMA museum just last year and they still have many of her pictures in their collection. You should go see them! They're wonderful! You never asked Hannah about it?"

"No. But I will."

"You talk to Hannah a lot?" Her voice was strained.

"I see her in class, Rivka, that's all."

She couldn't put her finger on it, but after that conversation, things began to change. He seemed more distracted when they were together and spent more time out of the house studying, or so he claimed. She too began to change.

"Where have you been!" she shouted at him when he walked through the door.

"Oh, just in the library."

"Until midnight?"

"So I went out with a few friends . . . Gee, Rivka, chill out!"

She immediately felt guilty. "It's . . . I just get so lonely when you're gone."

He held her, brushing away her tears, wondering how he was going to extricate himself from all this suffocating drama.

"Maybe you could take me out with you, to meet your friends?"

He felt sad for her and guilty. "Sure. What about tomorrow?"

He took her to a local pub, a college hangout. The air was thick with the smell of alcohol and boozy laughter. She downed one drink after the next, until she too felt like laughing. The next morning she felt sick, throwing up in the toilet until her heaving finally went dry.

Simon was sympathetic, but also a bit amused, which infuriated her.

"You'll be fine by tomorrow," he told her. "And next time, drink Shirley Temples."

She didn't ask what that meant. But the next day she wasn't fine. She felt ill, the nausea growing worse and worse. She spent her days roaming from bed to bathroom. He was concerned.

"I've made you an appointment at the health clinic at 2:00 P.M."

"Are you going to be there, too, Simon?"

"I would, babe, but I've got classes. Call me and tell me what the doctor says. Take care of yourself, honey!" He hurried away.

She got dressed and ready to go too early. Then, she sat on the edge of the bed, waiting. For some reason, a passage she had read in one of her SAT questions came to her. It was from a novel written in 1899. A woman's overbearing husband, wanting attention, wakes her up in the middle of the night complaining that one of the children has a fever, insisting that she is a bad mother for sleeping through it. While she checks her perfectly healthy child, her husband falls asleep. Now, unable to go back to bed, she sits out on the porch:

An indescribable oppression, which seemed to generate in some unfamiliar part of her consciousness, filled her whole being with a vague anguish. It was like a shadow, like a mist passing across her soul's summer day. It was strange and unfamiliar; it was a mood. She did not sit there inwardly upbraiding her husband, lamenting at Fate, which had directed her footsteps to the path which they had taken. She was just having a good cry all to herself.

She wept, not even knowing why, feeling ill and ill used and unreasonable. She put on her coat, getting ready to go, when, for no reason, she turned back, looking up. Sticking out on top of the bookcase was the glitter of red wrapping paper.

A gift, she thought, all her anguish lifting like smoke. He had gone out and bought her something to make her feel better. Simon! She climbed up on a chair and reached up. It was a large, heart-shaped box. She shook it gently, and it rattled with tiny thumps. Delighted, she envisioned exquisite little chocolates in silvery paper. There was a card. Carefully, she eased it out of the unsealed envelope. As she read it, her hands shook. She replaced it, wetting the edge of the envelope with her tongue and sealing it closed, replacing it and the box where she had found them.

Walking into the bedroom, she packed her suitcase. It seemed heavier than when she had first come, weighing her down. She opened the front door, then locked it behind her. As she walked toward the subway, she saw a public mailbox. Opening it, she threw the key inside.

29

The phone call from Hannah came at 2:00 A.M. "Mom, I thought you'd want to know. Rivka has finally called."

"Oh, Lord! It's been over two months. Is she all right?"

"I don't know. But she says she needs our help. She sounded desperate." There was a brief silence.

"Hannah?"

"I'm not taking her in again, Mom," Hannah said flatly.

Again, there was a pause as Rose gathered her wits about her, throwing off the last vestiges of sleep. "I thought she went home."

"So did I. But apparently not."

"So, where has she been all this time?"

"Why do you care?"

The sharpness of her daughter's response to so innocent a question convinced Rose not to probe further. "Did she hint she wanted to move back in with you?"

"She wasn't really clear on what she wanted. She sounded high . . ."

"Oh, no!"

"Okay, not exactly high, but pretty incoherent."

"Did you *offer* to take her back in?"

"No," she answered curtly.

This wasn't sounding at all like her kind, compassionate daughter, Rose thought, confused.

"I offered her your house instead. I hope you don't mind. We did talk about it."

"Yes, but that was months ago . . ."

"I'm sorry. But I didn't know what else to do with her. I simply can't have her moving back in here with me, all right?"

"Did something happen between the two of you?"

Hannah didn't really answer, mumbling something vague and unconvincing about needing her own space, then hanging up the phone.

Oh, God, Rose thought when she opened the door. Rivka stood there silently, looking like a survivor of some natural disaster, a hurricane or a tsunami. There were dark circles under her eyes and her long hair was matted and unwashed. As for the clothes, they seemed beyond the powers of dry cleaner or washing machine.

"Rivka?"

"Aunt Rose," she said dully.

"Well, I guess you'd better come in," Rose said awkwardly, her heart torn.

She walked in without a word, putting down her small valise.

Rose stared at it. *The small, battered suitcase dragged on subways and off buses that had once held all she owned in the world.* She felt a lump growing in her throat. "Do you want to take a shower, change clothes?"

"Aunt Rose, can I have something to eat first?"

"Right," Rose said quickly, hurrying into the privacy of her kitchen. She leaned forward heavily, gripping the counter with trembling hands; then, she took out the kosher food she had purchased early that morning: corned beef on rye, coleslaw, potato salad, and a Dr. Brown cherry cola.

Rivka took an eager bite, then stopped, picking out the meat with her fingers, then ravenously digging into the rest of the meal.

"It's glatt kosher," Rose murmured, holding out the packaging she had

brought along from the kitchen, having expected to be cross-examined before the waif would agree to touch a bite. But she didn't even glance up.

"Oy, it's not that. It's any meat . . ." Rivka said, finishing off the potato
salad and coleslaw.

"Are you a vegetarian now?"

"No, I . . ." She tried to speak, but her mouth was full of food.

Rose watched her, appalled. Her hunger was ravenous and pitiful. "I
bought you a piece of chocolate cake, too, from the kosher bakery on Broadway," Rose suddenly remembered, hurrying to get it and placing it in front
of her. "Would you like a cup of tea to have with it . . . ?"

But before she could finish, Rivka had already polished off the cake, not
even asking if it was parve and thus permitted to be eaten along with meat,
something any observant Jew would have surely asked. Had she lost her
faith? I won't ask, Rose thought. I don't want to know. "Well, if you want
anything else to eat, just go into the kitchen," Rose said, barely able to speak.
"Your bedroom is the second door from the left down the hall. There's a
private shower, towels. Make yourself at home. We'll talk later."

Rose went directly to her own bedroom. Closing the door and stretching
out on the bed, she parted her lips swallowing huge gulps of air as she tried to
clear the enormous lump in her throat. But it was no use. Silent tears rolled
down her cheeks as she remembered those first terrible, hungry days after
she'd run away from home, riding the empty subways downtown and uptown
all night long, the rancid smell of the cars screeching along the filthy subterranean tracks, the gnawing sense of doubt about where her next meal would
be coming from when the little money she had ran out. She'd survived that
way barely two days, the end coming with frightening intensity at 2:00 A.M.

She hadn't thought about that in years and years. What was the point? It
was over. She'd survived. And so would her niece. They had both made their
choices, and there was no turning back the clock, no way to integrate your
new life with your old. Their parents and society would not allow it. Once
you left, they wanted you to know you could never return except entirely on
their terms. For her, that would have meant transforming into the docile
seventeen-year-old she had never been, willing and able to marry a weak and
foolish man she didn't even particularly like just to please her parents and
the rabbis.

But perhaps for Rivka that might still be a realistic option. Rose didn't know her well enough to judge. It would certainly save her a great deal of heartache. Chagrined at this rare and sudden show of weakness, Rose wiped her eyes, heading back into the living room.

Rivka was curled up fast asleep on the sofa in the fluffy long bathrobe Rose had left for her. She looked like a tired child, her face rosy and well-scrubbed, her hair loose and wet. Rose took a light crocheted afghan from the bedroom, covering her gently. Then, she sat down across from her, waiting.

"How are you feeling, Rivka?"

She smiled, still half-asleep, stretching.

"Why didn't you lay down in your bed?"

"I don't know. It looked so clean . . . Anyhow, I thought I'd just sit here a minute. I guess I must have conked out." She looked out the window, surprised to see that the street lamps had already come on. "I didn't know I was so tired," she said with a sheepish grin.

"Here, I brought you some tea and cookies. All kosher, don't worry."

"A *treife* cookie should be my biggest sin, Aunt Rose," she said, her lower lip trembling. "My life is ruined. I've ruined it. I'm going to Gehenna!"

"From the looks of you when you arrived, I'd say you've just come back. I've been there myself," Rose added gently.

"No one has sinned more than me! I'm so ashamed!" She hid her face in her hands.

Gently, Rose pried them loose. "Here, have something to eat and drink. In the meantime, I'll tell you why you're wrong. My story is way worse than yours, kid."

"I heard a little bit here and there, mostly from Bubbee Weiss. Mameh didn't talk about you."

"And what did Bubbee Weiss say?"

"That . . . that you'd disgraced the family," Rivka said softly.

"Bubbee Weiss was absolutely right. I did. I ran away, leaving my poor parents to deal with furious in-laws, an embarrassed (if not exactly heartbroken) groom, unpaid caterers, and hundreds of disgruntled wedding guests making their way to Brooklyn, who were cheated out of their million-calorie Viennese table . . ."

"You did the right thing."

"Don't be so forgiving, child. Everyone paid a terrible price."

"Sometimes, a person has no choice."

Rose stared at her, startled by her answer. She wasn't the cliché she'd imagined, the flighty teenager throwing a short-lived fit. She'd thought this all out. "What else have you heard about me?"

"My *mameh* said that you always wanted to be the center of attention, even when you were little. You even insisted on saying kiddush in front of all the men Friday night . . ."

"Your mother has that a little confused. It was *she* who wanted to make kiddush and wound up spilling wine all over herself and Tateh . . . Never mind. We were both little kids, and it was a long time ago. What else?"

"They said that, just like Pharaoh, you'd reached the forty-ninth level of degradation, a place where—"

"No explanation necessary," Rose cut her short, feeling surprisingly hurt. "I don't suppose they ever mentioned that for the first sixteen years of my life, I was the perfect Bais Yaakov girl . . ." Then, suddenly, she laughed. "Well, not exactly. I did a few things behind my parents' and teachers' backs."

"Like what?" Rivka asked eagerly.

Misery loves company, and sinners want to weigh their transgressions against those of others, hoping theirs weigh less, Rose thought, smiling to herself. "I took a course in photography when I was supposed to be cheering up sick, old people. That's when my parents thought they needed to find me a husband who would do a better job of reining me in. I thought dating would be fun. We were both wrong. I remember how one boy looked at the carpet the entire time we were together, trying to prove he was too pious to look at women! How these guys have ten kids I'll never know."

"Eyes are not involved, Aunt Rose," Rivka said demurely.

A slow smile spread across Rose's face. She was beginning to like this kid. "Was that also your experience?"

"The boy they picked for me was really very nice." She blushed. "He told me about how exciting it was to him to learn all day. How he loved it. We even talked about medicine, about being a doctor, and how difficult that was, but what a great mitzvah it was to heal the sick. He was not so bad. To tell you the truth, Aunt Rose. I . . . I even liked him. It wasn't his fault. I just didn't want to be a wife and a mother. That is, just yet. I wanted a more interesting life. What's going to happen to me now?" She wept.

"Well, you are certainly having an interesting life," Rose murmured, handing her a tissue.

Rivka laughed through her tears.

"Look, kid, you can become anything you want . . ."

"No, no! You don't understand. It's all over. It's horrible."

"You'll get through the horrible. Trust me."

"Aunt Rose, how did you survive?"

"It wasn't easy." She paused, weighing the pluses and minuses of reliving her story for the edification of her young niece. The girl needed a reality check. It had to be done.

"The night I left, it was really dark, and the streets were deserted. I'd never been outside at such a time of night, let alone all by myself. I remember shivering, wishing I'd worn something practical and ugly and warm under my winter coat, instead of dressing in my Shabbos best. I was relieved when I finally got to the subway. I remember listening to the clacking of my shoes against the hard concrete as I ran up the steps, thinking it sounded so loud that even at such a distance, it was sure to wake my parents! I kept looking over my shoulder expecting them to catch me at any moment and drag me back to that borrowed bridal gown and those white shoes that didn't fit me any better than the life that would come along with them."

Her throat was suddenly parched. "I'm going to get a drink. Do you want something?"

Rivka, her eyes wide, shook her head.

Rose poured herself a half glass of whiskey, gulping it down. She ran her tongue over her parched lips. "The subway car was almost deserted except for a half-asleep elderly black man and a young couple who were all over each other. Station after station passed, and the rhythm of the car felt almost like the rocking of a boat that was lulling me to sleep. I was exhausted. The humiliation of standing naked in front of the attendant at the mikveh murmuring blessings, all the while planning my escape . . ."

"Oh!" Rivka exclaimed, holding her face.

Her reaction puzzled Rose. "Well, at least you were spared that . . ."

Rivka said nothing.

"But I'm sure you too must have felt the tension between making plans and having to keep them secret, the fear of discovery. Then, there was the guilt of betraying everyone I loved. Even though in the past I'd done things they wouldn't have approved of, they were nothing like this; this was on such a grand scale!

"I was drained. Dozing on the subway all night was as good a plan as any for the moment. In fact, that first night, it worked out just fine. But the next night, about two in the morning, something woke me up. Laughter." She tipped the glass into her mouth greedily, swallowing the last remaining drops.

"There were five of them, all dressed in leather jackets and tight jeans."

Sleeping beauty, one of them said, and the others laughed. Hey, honey, are you rested now? Yeah, we wouldn't want to bother you if you're tired. No, for what we've got in mind, you'll need plenty of energy, won't she, guys? Squeezing back into her seat, her eyes darting desperately around the deserted car. It was only her and them.

"I told them to go away," she said. "And they looked at each other as if they were surprised."

Now, that ain't polite, is it, guys? Especially when we was trying to be so friendly? Yeah, it was downright unfriendly. Now, I think we need to teach her a lesson, don't you? Yeah, a lesson in being nice . . .

"One of them tugged on my coat, pulling it off, while another reached out, snapping open my blouse."

One by one, the buttons fell to the floor.

"Oh, Aunt Rose!"

"I screamed."

The fist pressed brutally into her mouth. The fingers tickling their way up her thigh like roaches. The vicious tugging at her panties. The prayer: Please God help me!

"But then, out of nowhere, a policeman showed up."

Like a miracle. HEY! It was another voice, older deeper. The hands retreated. WHAT'S GOIN' ON HERE? The boys scattered, running into the next car. HEY, come back here! But she grabbed his arm. Please don't go after them! Don't leave me here alone! she begged. How he looked down at her, concerned. Sobbing uncontrollably, she never let go.

"The cop took me to a homeless shelter. But that turned out to be the kind of place where the worst people you meet on subways all *lived*!"

"How interesting for you," Rivka said wickedly.

It was Rose's turn to laugh. "Oh, that's for sure. Finally, I got so desperate, I called home. My mother answered."

"What did Bubbee Weiss say?"

"She said if I came home and got married immediately, all would be forgiven. And if not, she never wanted to hear from me again." Rose felt the vicious, sharp edge of that memory, which even time could not blunt.

"I can guess your answer."

"They left me no wiggle room."

"*Vus is dus?* Wiggle room?"

"It was all or nothing. I'm not good with ultimatums."

"So, you too . . . were also out there . . . homeless, penniless . . ." Rivka twisted her fingers nervously.

"Is that what you've been doing for two months? Riding the subways, eating out of trash cans?"

"I don't want to talk about it. Not now. Please, finish. What did you do?"

"Look, I'm prepared to tell you, but not because I'm proud of it." Rose paused, wishing she had a cigarette, or at least something to do with her hands. "I got the phone number from information of one of the photography teachers of the course I'd taken. He'd always been so kind and rather fatherly to me. He said he remembered me and listened to my sad tale. 'Come over, honey' were his exact words.

"I was seventeen, and he was a renowned photojournalist and teacher. Now I know you'll understand me when I explain this to you: maybe I had rebelled, but, deep down, I was still a good, religious girl like you, taught to respect her elders, to be pliant and good and listen to what she was told." She took a deep breath. "When I got to his apartment, he offered me wine. I didn't know how to say no. It was the first time in my life I'd drunk a glass of nonkosher wine. He was so experienced. He had been married twice, and was then either divorced or separated. There were pictures of children around the apartment. And that night when he'd tucked me into his spare bed, he was so kind to me, and I felt so lost, I began to cry . . ."

She cleared her throat, staring deeply with unseeing eyes into her empty glass. "He leaned over and took me in his arms as if I was a little girl. And the warmth of his arms, his body, felt so comforting, like a father's . . . until . . . it . . . wasn't."

"Aunt Rose!"

She got up, pacing nervously. "Now, don't get me wrong. It wasn't rape. Not exactly. To have been rape, I should have pushed him away. I should have known what my rights were and insisted on them. As it was, I had never actually been informed by anyone that I had any rights at all in this world. And after days on the street and in the shelter, where my choices were worse, I was ready to pay almost any price for protection and guidance."

Rivka's eyes glazed over. "Yes." She nodded dully.

"We settled into a routine based on his time schedule and needs. I cooked and baked and helped out in the darkroom and did what he wanted in the bedroom. He wasn't kinky or very demanding. It felt like a business deal. Only later, when I grew older and wiser, did it feel shameful. But I always told myself it was the price I had paid for my freedom. After all, if I'd stayed home and gotten married, I'd have been in bed with someone I liked even less! At least Vincenzo and I had the same interests. For whatever else he was personally, he was a superb professional. What he taught me made the life I wanted possible."

"Did you . . . love him?"

She gave it a moment's thought. "You probably didn't see that movie *The Lover,* did you? No, I didn't think so. Never mind. It's about a young girl involved with an older man, and she also thinks she's in some kind of adventure/business deal. And when it's over, she realizes that there had been love, but it had gotten lost, like water absorbed in sand. Did I love him? He wasn't young. He wasn't attractive. But, as I said, he was kind, that is, most of the time. He had a temper, especially when he drank . . ." She shook her head and was silent for a few moments. "Anyhow, it didn't last long. One day, the Modesty Patrol showed up at the door wearing black Hassidic garb and carrying metal pipes. They forced the door open and hit him so hard they broke one of his legs. Then, they smashed the entire house to bits, thousands of dollars of furniture and equipment. Luckily, I wasn't home.

"Vincenzo was furious. To his credit, he didn't immediately throw me to the wolves. He called the police, lawyers, and his insurance company. But we both knew it was over. He handed me over to Milly Gerhardt, a fellow photographer looking for an assistant for a *National Geographic* shoot in Costa Rica. She became a wonderful friend and mentor. Here, see this?"

She took a framed photo off the wall and handed it to Rivka, pointing to a slim, tall woman—tanned and self-confident—wearing shorts and a wide panama hat, posing against a backdrop of wild jungle growth, a parrot on her shoulder. "That's her. That had to be one of the best years of my life. Here I was on a tremendous adventure, shooting pictures like a pro . . . It was a dream come true." Her thumb fondled the photograph; then, she hung it back up in its place of honor.

"Was she married? An old maid?"

"Such an ultra-Orthodox question! If you want to know something about a woman, that's the information that will tell you her true worth, no? Rivka, I have no idea about her sexuality. All I can tell you is that she had many friends, both men and women, and she never attempted to climb into bed with me."

Rivka blushed.

"When we got back to New York to Milly's apartment, it took only three days before I picked up the phone and found my mother on the other end. Despite the fact that she said she never wanted to hear from me again if I didn't come running home to get married, I guess she had a change of heart. She begged, cajoled, then threatened and shrieked that I was a whore who was ruining the entire family's reputation. I packed up my things immediately. Milly was so sorry, but we had no choice. They obviously knew where I was, and I couldn't risk Milly getting hurt, too. She helped me find and furnish a little studio apartment, loaning me money for the deposit and the first few months' rent. I continued to work as her assistant, and then she helped me land a few lucrative freelance jobs at various publications. Eventually, I set up my own studio.

"But my parents weren't finished with me yet. They soon found out where I lived. Various relatives showed up at the door at intervals to threaten me. At a certain point, I had had enough. I filed a police complaint and took out a restraining order. My parents were hauled down to the Williamsburg police station. And there, among the dope pushers and prostitutes, I imagine they were fingerprinted and photographed, an experience for which they never, ever forgave me. After that, they left me alone."

"It must have been so terrible for them!" Rivka said.

Rose looked at her, annoyed. If she loved her family so much, why didn't she throw herself into *their* arms and eat *their* food?

Rivka seemed to sense it. "She was always kind to me," she said apologetically. "They both were. They're both gone now, you know."

Rose nodded. She had been sent word when her mother died, along with strict instructions not to dare show up for the funeral or to pay a shiva call. She'd come to the cemetery anyway. No one had said a word to her, and some of her brothers had wrapped a tallis around their children to shield their eyes so they wouldn't—God forbid—look at her. "Before my *tateh* died, I saw him in the hospital. I waited for everyone to leave, then sneaked in. He didn't know who I was, so I was able to sit there and hold his hand, and give him a drink . . ." Her voice cracked. "After he went, I had no contact with my family at all, until you."

"Aunt Rose?"

"Hmm?"

"Was it good?"

"Was what good?

"Your life, Aunt Rose. Was it worth it?"

She thought about how to answer that. "Sometimes," she finally answered with painful honesty.

The Sabbath, the New Year's, and Passover holidays were the worst, the loneliness heightened and exaggerated by echoes from past family gatherings noisy with the laughter and talk and songs of cousins and aunts and uncles sitting around huge tables groaning with food.

But then, out in the city, taking her photos, experiencing absolute freedom, the joy of discovery, the excitement of claiming her little place in the world, she could not have imagined any greater happiness.

"It was the life I had chosen, the life I wanted," she elaborated. "But it was no picnic. Every lifestyle, every culture, has its good and bad points. It's a trade-off. You're the only one who can decide what you need, what you can and can't live without. So, if you still feel you have a choice, maybe think it over again? It's not as easy or simple as it looks to run away from your life and replace it with something better."

"Aunt Rose, when I found those things about you under my mother's bed . . ."

"Under her bed?"

"They were hidden, in a box."

Rose nodded, understanding dawning. So, Pearl hadn't shown it to her daughter! Rivka had discovered it, by accident. Well, at least Pearl hadn't thrown it away. That also meant something.

"I looked you up on the Internet. Then, I found your books in the library. I went to see your pictures at MOMA last year. Such an inspiration you were to me! If not for you, I don't know if I have the courage to do any of this!"

Hannah had been telling the truth! Rose thought, equally flattered and appalled, resentful at being put into such a position, one she'd never asked for. "My life has nothing to do with yours, Rivka," she said with unintentional harshness.

The girl looked stunned, as if she'd been slapped. "You're wrong, Aunt Rose. It has everything to do with mine! We took the same train out of Brooklyn, looking for a life to call our own! But, not like you, I moved in with a man because I loved him. I didn't sell myself for a bed to sleep in."

Touché, Rose thought, her eyes watering from the sting of the well-placed insult. "Who was he?"

"Someone I met at Hannah's house who was tutoring me for the SATs. His name was Simon Narkis."

"Hannah's boyfriend?"

Rivka looked ready to cry. "He wasn't Hannah's boyfriend when I met him that first night at Hannah's! At least, Hannah never said. And the next day when he called me, he said *Hannah* told him I needed a tutor. He said he wanted to teach me . . . to help me . . . I thought it was *her* idea."

Rose paced furiously around the room. "And Hannah knew about all this?"

She hung her head. "I told her last night."

"Ahhh, I see." It all made sense now. Hannah's cold unconcern, her quiet fury. "You and Simon got together behind her back."

"I didn't think it was anybody's business but mine, Aunt Rose! And when I found out they were dating, I left him. But I don't think Hannah believes me!"

Right before her eyes, the kid seemed to be growing older, her rosiness fading, her face thinner.

Rivka stood up. "I don't feel so . . ."

"Rivka . . . Rivka . . ."

———

Someone was patting her face. She opened her eyes and saw her aunt's mouth moving, but heard nothing. She lifted her head off the carpet, then wobbled unsteadily to her feet. "I have to throw up!" She ran into the bathroom. Rose heard her heaving. When Rivka made her way back to the living room, she was clutching the walls for support. She flopped down on the carpet, leaning her back against the couch, suddenly letting out a wild sob, her whole body shaking with grief: "I loved him so much!"

Rose put her arms around the girl. "Oh, my poor kid," Rose whispered, sitting down next to her and gathering her into her arms. "My poor, poor kid."

Rivka snuggled against her like a small animal seeking shelter.

"Look, I can't promise you I know how this is going to end, but only that it will end. And you'll be all right. I know you can't imagine that now, but that's the truth. At some point, it will be all right."

Rivka looked up into the eyes of this woman she hardly knew, whom she had been taught to fear and loathe, and saw herself reflected there. She put her arms around Rose's waist, resting her tired head against her knees like a lost child, wanting to believe someone had the power to save her.

30

NYU, Manhattan, April 16, 2008

Hannah saw Simon sitting in the lecture hall doodling idly in a notebook, his whole body stretched out with the relaxed calm that she had always found so appealing, attributing it to superior understanding and a clear conscience.

"Hannah, over here!" Jason called to her from the other side of the room.

Simon looked up, turning his head slowly in her direction.

If he smiles or waves, I will have to kill him, she thought.

She turned away quickly, walking toward Jason.

"Hey, what's wrong?"

"Not now." She cut him off curtly.

He shrugged, surprised.

The lecturer was one of her favorites, always so lively and engaging, making the past come to life. Halfway through, a sudden burst of laughter startled her into the realization that she hadn't heard a word.

Ever since Rivka's call, she'd felt sick, her stomach in knots, her head aching. Against her will, she'd been pulled inside a vortex that was spinning out of control and that was taking her and everything she once thought she knew about herself with it. Her self-image as a kind, liberal, open-minded person lay in pieces all around her like the aftermath of a tornado. Her emotions were equally fierce, running the gamut from deep betrayal to envy, hatred, and a crass and despicable desire for revenge. She had no idea who this person she had become was.

When the lecture ended, the movement of the students toward the exit distracted her from her prison of evil thoughts

"Want to go someplace for lunch?" Jason offered.

"No," she said bluntly, picking up her books and moving swiftly out of the auditorium, leaving an astonished and wounded Jason staring at her back in disbelief.

She'd had enough of him, too! Enough of men.

"Hey!"

She felt her arm tugged and looked up, startled. "If you want to live, Simon, you'll let me go."

He looked stunned. "What have I done?" He put his hands into his pockets. "Can't we at least talk about this?"

"What topic do you have in mind, Simon? How you seduced my innocent little cousin? Or how you seduced my innocent little cousin behind my back while dating me?"

He looked around swiftly to check if her words had carried.

"I'm willing to discuss this privately," he whispered stiffly.

"How privately, Simon? Because, for your own sake, you better have witnesses."

He gave her a look, half-entreating, half-fearful, then gestured toward the door of an empty classroom. She followed him reluctantly. He closed the door behind them.

"At least sit down."

"Talk! Or I'm out of here," she warned, bracing her back firmly against the wall.

"First of all, she came on to me . . ."

"Oh, right! She called you."

"No, I called her, but just to help her out. I did it for you."

"You were only thinking of me? Get real, you turd!" She turned away furiously, her hand on the doorknob.

He hurriedly blocked the door. "You said she needed help with the SATs! I met with her the next day after the party."

She turned around. "The very next day?"

"Yes! What? She didn't tell you?"

She shook her head in disbelief.

"We met every day for two weeks. You mean to say the little, innocent virgin never mentioned what she was doing when you were out of the house?"

She bit her lips, her fury mounting. Little bird! She'd done it all behind her back.

"She was the one who brought over a suitcase and decided to move in. It wasn't my idea, believe me."

"Why should I believe anything you say? Besides, she had no idea what she was doing. You took advantage of her innocence!"

"Do you know she insisted on going to the ritual baths for purification so we could have sex properly? That also wasn't my idea."

Hannah felt stunned. "She went to a ritual bath?"

"She insisted. Listen, I never forced myself on her. She could have left at any time if she was unhappy. Once, she actually did walk away. But it was late at night and she deliberately didn't take her purse or her phone. I couldn't let her leave like that! I went after her just to make sure she was okay, and she fell into my arms."

"I'll bet!"

"It's the truth! She came back willingly. She *wanted* me! You've got this totally screwed-up image of her. She knows what she wants, and she's used both of us to get it."

Hannah's thoughts ran around in circles, trying to put the pieces together. Why did Rivka do what she did? And what had she gotten out of it? There was so much Hannah didn't, couldn't, understand. "Then why did she leave you now? Why did she call me? What happened?"

"I don't know. Women." He shrugged.

"How could you ask me out when you were sleeping with my cousin?"

He paused, wetting his lips nervously. "It's true she and I were . . . but we both decided it wasn't going to be long-term. We weren't right for each other. She moved on. And so did I. I don't know why you are all that upset. She needed tutoring; I tutored her. She needed a place to stay; I let her move in with me. She wanted to experiment sexually; I accommodated her . . ."

She felt her fury wane. From the very first day, Rivka had been seeing him and had deliberately kept it from her. All those times they had talked, the subject had never even come up. The two of them deserved each other.

"Well, maybe you're right. Maybe Little Red Riding Hood isn't any better than the Big Bad Wolf. I wash my hands of both of you."

"Hannah, please!"

"You know what, Simon? I thought you were something special. That behind those Trotsky glasses and long hair was a person with values, an intellectual . . . I thought you cared about me."

"I do, Hannah!" he said warmly.

"You are such a fake!"

"You know what? You shouldn't be so quick to pass judgment on others," he said pointedly.

"Meaning what?"

"What was your cousin doing on my doorstep in the first place?"

"I didn't throw her out!"

"Maybe not physically, but you sure as hell must have passed on the information that she was persona non grata. If she came to me because she had no other place to go, shouldn't you be asking yourself why?"

"I never threw her out!" she repeated, shouting passionately.

"So, she's with you now?"

Hannah let out a long sigh, her body losing its defensiveness and rigidity. She sank down into a chair, shaking her head. "I refused to let her in."

"Because of me?"

"Because you both lied to me! But I didn't know it had been a lie from the start."

"I never lied."

"No. You just neglected to tell the whole truth."

"Did you ever once ask me?"

"Why should it have even occurred to me?"

"And why should it have occurred to me that you *didn't* know?"

That was true! She felt her anger shift toward her cousin. Not a wounded sparrow at all, but a scavenging vulture. She had been conning her and everyone else from day one.

"How did you find out about us?" he murmured.

"She called me a few days ago. Wanted to move in with me again. Said she'd been living with you and that she couldn't anymore."

"A few days ago? I haven't seen her in two weeks."

She was shocked. "Really?" She'd been out there on her own doing God knows what for weeks before she finally brought herself to pick up the phone! And I told her off. I told her no. Her heart felt heavy, filled with fury at Simon and at herself.

"Did she tell you why she left me?"

She searched his face carefully. "Are you telling me that you really, really don't know?"

He put his hand over his heart. "It's the truth! She didn't even leave a note. Never even returned my keys!" He smoothed back his hair calmly. He'd had to change the locks. "But hey, it was her choice. She wasn't in jail."

Something in the words and gesture made her see red.

"Yeah, you said that already. But I'll tell you something, Romeo, you just might be."

"What?"

"Statutory rape. She wasn't eighteen when you did her the big favor of joining her in bed."

With a sense of satisfaction, she saw her words had hit the mark, the blood draining from his face, his hands shaking. "I just . . . thought . . ."

"Well, you thought wrong."

"Um, you know, I'd really like to talk to her, Hannah. Maybe apologize. Can you tell me how I can reach her?"

"Oh, so now suddenly you want to reach her? What's the matter, Simon? Afraid Little Bird is going to sing to the cops, or her parents, who might have a problem with the idea of *her* seducing *you*?"

His face turned colors. He gnawed his lip, thinking of his parents and the generous allowance they deposited in his account every month. If they ever . . . "Do you think she would?"

"You're asking the wrong person. Apparently, she doesn't tell *me* anything. We'll just both have to wait and see now, won't we? If she needs to talk to you, she's got your number. And, believe me, so do I. So this is what is going to happen. Listen carefully." She paused. "You don't know me. You don't see me. You don't wave, say hello, sit next to me . . . You're like Patrick Swayze in *Ghost,* invisible, got that? And if you ever make contact with

Rivka again, I won't wait for her to get the guts to go to the cops. I will go myself."

He pushed his glasses back up as they slid down his sweaty nose. He said nothing, walking to the door and out into the hall. He did not turn around.

31

They sat down to breakfast like an old married couple, wordlessly passing each other the jam and butter. It had been a week since Rivka arrived. Rose, who had pretty much let her be, finally felt compelled to broach the subject of the future.

"So, what's going to be with you?"

Rivka shook her head. "Whenever I decide something, all the reasons not to do it jump up and start yelling."

"Well, anything is better than nothing. Aren't you bored stiff?"

"When I was with Hannah, all the housework I did. But you already have a cleaning lady. In your house, I could eat off the floors." She hesitated, suddenly shy. "But maybe . . . I could go and watch you work? I could help even."

"Oh, I don't know . . ." Rose hedged. That's all she needed! It was bad enough this waif was in her apartment all day and all night! But then she gave it further thought. Maybe it wouldn't be so bad. Her assistant had dumped her the week before to head out to Las Vegas with her petty criminal/artist boyfriend. She could actually use a hand.

"Well, we can try it. But if you don't like it, you have to promise to tell me, okay? I'm working on a book about life in different ethnic neighborhoods in New York City. I think I'm going to head over to Chinatown this morning. I'm warning you, though, it's hard work. There's lots of heavy equipment to haul, and lots of time on your feet waiting and waiting for the clouds to move and the light to change . . ."

Rivka's eyes lit up. "It would make me very happy to help you."

"Good. And maybe in the process, you can have some fun taking some photographs yourself."

Rivka hesitated. "Some people say that cameras are forbidden because they make 'graven images.'"

Rose sighed. "Really, things are getting out of hand over there in Williamsburg! Soon, nothing will be permissible. No food will be kosher enough—everyone will learn to live on *shmurah* matzah. No clothes will be modest enough, except maybe a burka. And a man and his wife won't even be buried side by side anymore because of 'immodesty.'"

"Oh, Aunt Rose. Men and women *are* already buried in separate sections of the cemetery . . . because of immodesty."

"You're kidding!" She shook her head, smiling. "So, what do *you* say?" Rose challenged her.

"I don't agree. I'd love to learn how to take pictures like you, Aunt Rose."

"Good. Come get dressed, then."

She came out wearing her Sabbath best: a long blue skirt with a long-sleeved white shirt and a jacket. The material was pilling, the buttonholes frayed, and the shirt had a dark red stain on the cuff.

"Maybe if we have time afterwards, we'll stop off and get you something to wear?"

"I don't have any money."

"Never mind. I do. And if you are going to be my assistant, you deserve a salary."

She hung her head, dwarfed, almost crushed, by her aunt's unending kindness and generosity. What a naive, brainwashed little twit she'd been to listen to and believe all those terrible things they'd said about her aunt!

She lugged the equipment, learning how to set it up, how to wait with endless patience until her aunt was satisfied that she had the perfect natural lighting for a particular shot, how to hurry when her aunt was rushing to capture someone or something in the passing parade of human activity. Despite the sheer hard work and the tedium, she found herself loving every moment. She felt a sudden stab of envy for her cousin.

"Hannah's probably done this with you a million times."

Rose was quiet. "Actually, Hannah . . . well . . . she wasn't very interested in my work."

"How could that be? If I was your daughter, I'd make you teach me everything you know."

Rose smiled. "Would you now, really?"

"I would, Aunt."

They took a short break for lunch in a kosher restaurant outside Chinatown.

"You look green," Rose told her.

"It's the smell of the meat!"

"Are you sure you're not a vegetarian?"

"Believe me, I'm not."

"Maybe you have a stomach virus?"

"I don't have fever or any other symptoms."

"If you don't feel like yourself soon, I'll make you a doctor's appointment. In the meantime, get some soup."

"Just not chicken soup!"

After she ate, Rivka felt better, but very tired.

"You look wasted! I think we can call it a day. But before we go, I want you to take some photos yourself."

Rivka protested. "No, Aunt Rose! I could drop your camera! Besides, I don't want to waste your expensive film!"

Rose ignored her, putting a camera strap around her neck. "There, it can't possibly fall. And there is no film, kid. You're thinking of the Kodak-moment fifties. Today, it's all digital. Only crazy people like me still use film. And even die-hards like myself are secretly exploring the joys of digital photography."

Rivka felt herself fill with adrenaline as she held the camera in her hands.

"This will be easy for you to use. It's a digital automatic. The camera will adjust itself to lighting conditions. See that little screen? Just think of it as a picture frame. All you need to do is fill it with something that interests you.

This was the first thing I learned about photography. I've never gotten better advice."

"Something beautiful?"

"Not necessarily. Ugliness has equal strength in a photo, and is sometimes much more fascinating. Remind me to show you a book of Diane Arbus images when we get home. Just look around for a person, a moment, a scene that has meaning for you, something you want to rescue from oblivion in order to look at it again and again."

It couldn't possibly be that easy, Rivka thought. But the camera did feel comfortable in her hands as she slid her palms around the compact metal and plastic. She looked through the lens. It was exactly as her aunt had said: an empty picture frame waiting to be filled.

She walked down the street, losing track of time and of her tiredness, clicking away, trying to capture the moment when a baby was lifted in her mother's arms and smiled through her tears, the moment the greengrocer's face rose above a box of bright red tomatoes he was carrying, the expressions on the faces of two old men who turned to look at a beautiful teenage girl walking by.

"Having fun?" Rose smiled at her.

"It's amazing how many things you can see through a camera lens you would never have noticed with just your eyes."

"Yes, isn't it? Like carving away at life until you reveal the form and meaning inside it."

"Like a sculptor, right?"

"Right!" Rose answered, impressed. "Who but Michelangelo knew there was a David trapped inside that ruined chunk of Carrara marble the church fathers were getting ready to throw away?"

Rivka handed Rose back the camera. "Thanks so much!"

"Why don't you hold on to it for a while, kid?"

"I don't want to use it up. You might need it."

She laughed. "It's impossible to 'use it up'! It has a memory card that holds hundreds of photos."

"Hundreds!"

"Yeah, and when that fills up, we'll just download all the photos to the computer and free up the space again for hundreds more!"

For the first time since they'd met, Rose got to see how her niece Rivka looked when she was happy. She felt her own dark place open for a moment, nourished and warmed.

"I think we're done for the day. The light is all wrong now. Why don't we drop all this stuff off at the house, then go shopping for some clothes? Stores are open late tonight. Unless you're too tired."

She wasn't tired. She was exhausted. But the idea of shopping with her aunt's credit card was too delicious. "Oh, thank you, Aunt! That would be wonderful! But I can't go to any of the big department stores. My family shops there!"

Later that afternoon, Rose took her to some little upscale boutiques near her studio. They were throbbing with rock music. Mannequins dressed in tiny skirts over leggings and transparent tops looked at them bewitchingly.

"Oh, I don't think . . ." Rivka shook her head.

"Okay, there's a Talbots near my apartment. They are very conservative, and they have a whole petite department."

That was better, the atmosphere dainty and subdued, and the mannequins charmingly chic. Rivka went through the racks with a practiced hand, concentrating on the merchandise on the reduced racks. But even then, she found the prices shocking.

"Thank you very much, Aunt Rose, but it's not *shayich*."

It had been so long since she'd heard that word, Rose chuckled. It meant "not connected to, not part of, irrelevant, a waste of time." It was a word that peppered the sentences of ultra-Orthodox Jews in a wide variety of ways: Some things were permanently not *shayich*, like movie theaters. Some things were situationally not *shayich*, like Sephardic boys in a Hassidic groom pool. And some things were temporarily not *shayich*, like the present too-high prices of Talbots' clothes, which even on sale did not begin to compare to Macy's or Lord & Taylor's seventy percent off with coupon sales.

"We could get the same clothes in Borough Park for half the price!"

"Aren't you afraid you'll be discovered if we go there?"

"No, no," she said. Her family didn't shop in Borough Park unless a holiday or wedding was looming. Still, it was a risk. But she just couldn't resist. She couldn't stand overpaying.

She took her aunt's arm, and soon Rose found herself hurtling toward Brooklyn in the subway.

She had not been back to such a neighborhood since she'd visited her stroke-felled grandmother in the nursing home. She looked around. It was forty years later, but nothing had changed. The same bewigged and turbaned matrons with their long-sleeved, thick-stockinged little girls looking at her suspiciously. The same men in black satin waistcoats with black hats avoiding looking in her direction at all. You were either conspicuous or unwanted. Your existence was never just accepted, unless they knew you and you were just like them. In that case, either you needed them or they needed you, and so it was worth it to be friendly.

She bit her lip. No, that wasn't fair. Whether they knew you personally or not, if you looked and acted the part of a member in good standing of the community, you would benefit from endless friendship and caring love from every quarter. You'd never be alone, never without help or companionship. Whatever you needed, be it food, clothing, extra chairs for Seder night, antibiotics when the drugstores were closed, the community would see to it that you got it. She'd found nothing remotely similar outside the Haredi world.

The store was a long, narrow strip stuffed with women's clothing. Religious women pawed through the piles of clothing bearing carelessly chopped-off designer labels. They were probably designer samples, the sizes ranging from zero to four, with a rare and occasional six or eight. The prices were ridiculously low.

"Go ahead, try something on," Rose urged her.

Rivka brought basketfuls of clothes into the makeshift dressing room, but soon opened the curtain wearing her old, frayed suit. "Let's go, Aunt Rose."

"What! Didn't you like anything?"

"It's not *shayich*."

"What's not *shayich*?" she asked, beginning to hate that word.

"New clothes, size two. I'm gaining weight so fast. I don't know why. Nothing fits me anymore."

She saw there were tears in Rivka's eyes.

"Listen, kid, gaining weight is nothing to cry over! Otherwise, we women would be weeping nonstop until the grave! Just get a larger size. It's not the end of the world to go from a size two to a size four!"

"But it's a waste of money! At the rate I'm going, I might outgrow them in a month!"

"So, get some skirts with an elastic waistband and some peasant blouses. It's very stylish now. I suppose I won't be able to talk you into wearing slacks or jeans?"

She shook her head, scandalized. "*No!* This is *assur.* 'Women shall not wear men's clothing.' It's forbidden by the Torah."

"Who's talking about men's clothing? I'm talking about slacks made especially for women."

"But they would be immodest, showing everything."

"You could buy a tight skirt that would show everything, too. I'm talking about a nice-fitting, modest pair of trousers with an elastic waistband that would leave you a little grow room. It's what photographic assistants usually wear. With all that bending over you'll be doing—it's much more modest than a skirt."

Rivka thought about it. It was like the yogurt. Her aunt's words made perfect sense. "But we can't buy women's slacks here. They don't sell them."

"So, let's go back to the subway."

After a hectic day, they arrived home full of packages. Rose prepared a light supper of eggs and cottage cheese and salad. Rivka made no objection to eating food cooked in questionable pans and served on suspect plates with suspicious utensils, Rose noticed. Maybe she was just overtired? Or maybe she was changing? Rose wondered how she felt about that.

"It's been a long day, kid. Go take a rest. I'll take care of the dishes."

"No, let me, Aunt! And thank you. For everything."

"*Thank you,* for all your help."

Rose decided to give in, tucking her legs comfortably beneath her on the sofa and opening the day's mail. She sliced through the most delicious envelopes first. Invitations to showings, invitations to speak, and a proposal to do a retrospective at a photography museum in Paris!

She stretched out, flinging her arm across her eyes. Her usual pleasure and excitement in all these things seemed diminished somehow. All she could think about was Rivka.

What, she thought, if the situation had been reversed? If Hannah had decided to leave her life and her family and had shown up in Williamsburg at her sister Pearl's looking for a life as a newly born Jew? What if Pearl had not only taken her in, but had kept it a secret, never once calling to inform her where her daughter was staying and that she was all right? It was unthinkable! No, this had to end. As much as she'd come to like the girl, Rivka couldn't stay with her if she wasn't going to call her family. She felt guilty she hadn't thought of all this immediately. Obviously, her mind had blocked it out for good reasons. Calling her family with this news was definitely going to bring them roaring back into her life. But since her home address and phone number were unlisted, they'd only have access to her gallery. Sheena, her assistant, was careful to buzz in only people she knew.

There was nothing else to be done. She'd have to take a chance, not only for her own conscience, but for her niece's sake as well. Perhaps there was something there that was still salvageable? Oddly, mixed in with the dread, she experienced a strange sense of excitement and curiousity at the idea of making contact with her family after almost forty years. Her friend and childhood companion, her little sister. Pearl.

Rivka shed her sweaty clothes, taking a long shower. Her stomach was definitely a tiny bit more rounded now than it had been yesterday or the week before. She would have to watch what she ate from now on. Those two weeks she had been homeless and not eating regularly had left her constantly hungry. She'd eaten all the wrong foods: rye bread and knishes and kishke and kasha varnishkes and soda and cake. It wasn't healthy. It was no wonder she was throwing up every morning and every evening. She felt nauseous almost all the time.

She thought of all her nice new clothes. She would take her shower and then try them all on, even the pants. The idea of putting on pants was thrilling and dangerous. But they were pants made especially for women, as her aunt pointed out, and they covered her legs much more fully than even the most opaque tights, so why was that immodest?

Thinking for herself about religious issues was a new experience for Rivka. It was amazing the conclusions one could come to if you opened your mind.

Life was going to be wonderful, wonderful.

32

The next morning, Rose waited for Rivka at the breakfast table. By nine, she gave up.

"Rivka? Can I come in?"

"Sure, Aunt Rose."

She was sitting up in bed wearing one of her new outfits, the tears staining her face, but no longer falling in fresh streams.

"What's wrong?"

"I don't know, Aunt Rose. I don't feel good. Not sick exactly, just so strange."

"Is it that same stomach flu?" Rose asked, alarmed. "It's gone on much too long! You need to see a doctor, today. I'm sorry we waited."

"No, no, it's not necessary."

Rose looked at her strangely. "Are you afraid of doctors, Rivka?"

She was afraid of something, Rivka thought, but couldn't decide what. "No. It's just, I don't like to make a *tzimmis* over nothing, to waste money . . ."

"Let me worry about that, will you? So long as you're under my roof, you must let me take care of you as best I can."

Rivka gave in, relieved. "Thank you, Aunt Rose."

"But that's not the reason I came in here. You look very nice, by the way. Stand up, let me see."

Rivka got up dutifully.

"Now turn around slowly."

What a transformation, Rose thought, pleasantly surprised. She was wearing jeans and a pretty green and pink blouse. She looked like one of Hannah's young college friends. Her parents probably wouldn't recognize her. They'd be furious.

"Beautiful! Now come into the living room and sit down. There is something we need to discuss."

Rivka followed her, tense and alert.

Rose took a deep breath. "Rivka, I've been thinking about this all night. You really *must* speak to your parents."

Her eyes went wide with alarm. "No, *no!*" She shook her head.

"What's so terrible? Explain it to me."

"But you, Aunt Rose, of everyone should understand by yourself! Hannah didn't. The day I ran away, she also wanted me to call them. I left Hannah's when my friend in Israel told me they knew I wasn't there. I didn't want them coming to bother her. Two weeks it only took them to send someone to Israel to check out the story, to find out the truth. They're looking for me all over, all the time, to make me go back and get married!"

Rose sighed. "I *do* understand, believe me! And as long as you are here with me, I promise I won't let anyone force you to do anything you don't want to. But you have to try to understand me, Rivka. Your mother is my little sister. I can't do this to her, and I know she would never do anything violent or hurtful to you." Even as the words left her mouth, she felt uncomfortable. It had been so many years. What did she really know about Pearl, who she had become or what kind of a man she had married?

"But what if they send people . . . threaten you?"

"Don't think I haven't thought about that. Whatever happens, I promise to stand by you, Rivka. But however they might react, it's inhuman for us to let your parents worry like this any longer. If it was Hannah who had run away, I'd be crazy sick with worry."

If she had been hoping to instill guilt or conscience pangs in the girl, she had failed miserably, Rose realized as the girl shook her head adamantly. "Never! Please don't make me!"

"Do you want me to talk to them for you?"

Rivka looked up with sudden hope. "Would you, please, Aunt Rose?"

Against all her experiences of the past, all her reasonable desires to distance herself as much as possible from this mess, Rose found herself agreeing. It was as painful a task as she could have imagined for herself, but exhilarating, too. After all these years . . .

She picked up the phone. It rang four times, each unanswered sound stretching her nerves to the breaking point. Finally, someone picked up.

"Hello? Is that you, Pearl? This is your sister, Rose."

There was a long pause where only the sound of breath coming in short, heavy gasps was audible.

Finally, she heard her sister say: "Shoshi!"

"No one has called me that for forty years," she whispered, tears coming to her eyes. "I'm so happy to hear your voice, Pearl."

"Is everything all right? Has something happened to you?"

"No, not to me or mine. It's about your daughter, Rivka."

There was a stunned silence.

"What do you have to do with my Rivkaleh?"

"Nothing, nothing. Well, actually, many things, but don't worry; she's well." Rose coughed, beginning to feel serious misgivings.

"Oy, Oy, *Gotteinu*! How long do you know about her! Is she there by you?"

"She wrote my daughter Hannah asking if she could move in with her. My daughter didn't answer her, but she showed up at her door anyway." Rose could hear a great commotion in the background, her sister hysterically repeating everything she said to a third person.

"We want to come over right away to get her . . ."

"Whoa . . . listen, that's not a good idea. I know you must have been crazy with worry, but I can't tell you where she is without her permission."

Suddenly, her sister was gone . "This is Zevulun Meir, Rivka's father. Vat did you do to her?"

"And hello to you, Brother-in-law. What did *I* do to her? What did *you* do her that she ran away in the first place?"

"It's been months . . . Do you know vat *Gehenna* that is for a mother and father . . . not knowing?"

"My daughter insisted she couldn't stay until she let you know she was all right."

"We heard some *bubbeh mayseh,* a fairy tale, from a friend in Israel. A girl who lied to us."

"Well, you can hardly blame me for your daughter's friends . . ."

"How long was she by your daughter?"

"A few weeks, and then she ran away from there, and no one knew where she was. We actually thought she might have gone home. In any case, I had no information to share with you. But now she's back. I was the one who insisted we call you. Please don't make me regret it."

His voice rose. "She needs to come home. Ve are her family."

"You'll have to talk to her about that. Hold on, I'll put her on the phone."

Rose held out the phone to the frightened girl, who edged away. Then, finally, at Rose's stubborn insistence, she reached out and took it.

"Tateh?"

Rose watched the girl's face go from fear to hopefulness to concern to despair as the sound coming from the other end of the line grew louder and louder.

"*No, no,* you can't tell me what to do! I'm eighteen. I can do whatever I want! I *do* honor you and Mameh, but that doesn't mean you can ruin my life." Rivka paused, listening intently, her breath coming in short, agitated gasps. "God is already punishing me, Tateh, don't worry!"

She extended the phone back toward Rose. "He wants to talk to you."

She listened incredulously to his angry tirade, finally cutting him short. "Look, Zevulun, I know what you think of me, what the family thinks of me, but this has nothing to do with me. She was on the street, and I took her in. Say thank you, can't you?" She shook her head. "In what way am I responsible? What do you mean 'drop her off'? She's not a suitcase! Yes, I know she's your daughter, but she's also a human being, and she's of age . . . I know that you go by your own rules, but I go by mine. Wait a minute, is that a threat? No? I misunderstood you? I'm glad to hear that, really, because if I thought it was a threat, you know I have no problem calling the police. Good-bye. And tell my sister I said she can wait another forty years for my next call."

She slammed down the phone

Rivka looked at her, appalled, and then suddenly they both started to laugh. They laughed and laughed and laughed until their bellies were sore with shaking, their throats dry, and their cheeks wet with tears.

"Oh!" Rivka suddenly said, her voice small with surprise.

"What is it?"

"I don't . . ." She got off the couch. There was a large, red stain.

"Rivka, I've got some sanitary nap . . ."

"*Oh!* Aunt Rose!"

The panicked girl fell into her arms.

33

Rose waited in the gynecologist's office for Rivka. They'd come straight from Dr. Brand, her family physician. She was still in a state of semishock. Ohgod, she kept thinking. Ohgod, ohgod, ohgod.

She looked around the office listlessly, glancing at the other women, then averting her eyes from their reciprocal gazes. She picked up some magazines, but they were filled with photos of pregnant women and smiling babies, everyone so milk-fed and rosy-cheeked. Such beautiful fantasies. Perhaps this was what she loved so much about photography. You could find anything you wanted through the lens and ignore the rest, so much pain and so much ugliness.

What if, Rose thought, what if . . . It all made too much sense: the nausea, the weight gain, the stomach pains, the spotting. She felt like an idiot not to have picked up on it immediately. But maybe it is natural for our minds to avoid going to places we are terrified to be. Pearl and Zevulun are hysterical now. But what if . . . ? She couldn't go there.

Ohgod, ohgod, ohgod.

Had the girl known all along and been playing dumb? She did say that first day that her life was over. Rose had taken it for drama. But . . . what if . . . ? Now the whole mess would be in her lap. They'd never believe she hadn't known.

Maybe something could be done. It wasn't, after all, the end of the world the way it had been back in her day when a girl in trouble had to risk her life to get out of it. But what women tended to overlook was that, even now, without the physical dangers, abortions were still life-changing experiences. The knowledge that you'd destroyed potential for a whole human life, your own flesh and blood, was nothing short of traumatic. Her body felt chilled.

The door opened and the nurse came out. "The doctor would like you to come in."

She got up slowly, walking reluctantly inside.

He was a young doctor, the kind who probably had a pretty blond wife and three healthy kids, the kind who loved delivering babies into the arms of ecstatic new moms. She looked around for Rivka.

"Your daughter is getting dressed," he said. "She'll join us in a minute."

Should I correct him? Rose wondered. But she held back, the chilling thought going through her mind that she might very well have to pretend to be Rivka's mother for all kinds of awful reasons.

Rivka came in, sitting down in the chair next to hers. She looked like a badly shaken ten-year-old who'd fallen off her skates and banged her head and scraped her knees.

The doctor looked from one to the other, smiling encouragingly. "The bleeding wasn't serious. I think a few days' bed rest should do the trick. And no heavy lifting! You are definitely still pregnant, and I can't see any reason why you shouldn't carry to term."

Rose stared at Rivka, who avoided her gaze, her eyes stoically focused on some far-off spot on the wall, her face giving away nothing. Noting this, he paused, a strained expression passing over his handsome features. "You were aware, weren't you, that you were pregnant?" He looked at the girl, then, getting no response, turned toward the woman.

Rose shook her head slowly from side to side, and Rivka stared at her hands without moving. Two red spots had suddenly appeared on her cheeks, making her look feverish.

He leaned back heavily in his chair. "Oh, I see. Well, then, would you like me to explain your options?" He waited for some reaction from the girl, but there was nothing.

"Yes, please, Doctor," Rose interjected, still trying to catch her breath.

"You can, of course, terminate. It's a simple procedure since we're fairly early. But you might also want to consider adoption, which would be a blessing to some wonderful, childless couple."

Rivka didn't look up. Rose wondered where her head was and if she had heard a word.

"Or . . . you can keep the child and raise it. One-parent families are fairly common nowadays. That is, I'm assuming—which I shouldn't be—that the father doesn't wish to be involved?"

Rose looked at Rivka sharply. "Yes," Rivka said decisively, speaking for the first time. "I mean, no. He doesn't."

He pushed away from his desk lightly. "I can see that all this is apparently a shock to you both. Why not take some time to think it over? But not too much time. If you are going to terminate, the sooner, the better. In the meantime, I'm going to write a prescription for some vitamins. I'll call you with the blood- and urine-test results, but I'm not expecting any complications. You come from a large family and are in good health, and you're young . . ."

The silence lengthened.

Most of the time, you could pretty much guess the outcome of these mother-daughter surprise-pregnancy diagnoses. You could tell who would be back within the hour to make an appointment to terminate and who would be keeping the baby—for better or for worse. Sometimes people surprised you, though. There was a strange vibe about these two that left him clueless.

The woman had not reached over to touch the girl, but she didn't seem angry or put out either. He got a lot of those—the mother furious, the girl weeping. In the scenario before him, he had a woman filled with concern and sympathy, but distanced somehow. The girl looked bruised and sullen, like a child brazening it out after being caught red-handed. She had given her age as eighteen, but he wondered. She seemed so childish. And her apparent cluelessness—if it wasn't simply an act—seemed more appropriate to a younger girl.

"Thank you, Doctor," the woman finally said, reaching out to take the prescriptions.

He waited for her to add something more substantial, but she did not enlighten him further. She got up, and so did the girl. He abruptly followed suit. "So, please feel free to call me if you need more information about any of the things we've discussed. And talk to my nurse about your next appointment."

Rose nodded, taking Rivka's arm when she saw how unsteadily the girl was walking. And then, without warning, Rivka just crumpled.

When she came to, a woman was leaning over her, taking her pulse. "Wow, you took a bit of a tumble there, young lady! How do you feel now?" an energetic, smiling nurse inquired

Rivka shifted uncomfortably, feeling the carpeting prickling her skin through the shirt on her back. She looked up at the small crowd of strangers gathered around peering anxiously into her face. She blinked, but they were still there and so was she. It was no nightmare. It was really happening.

Pregnant!

Oh God!

"Rivka, here, drink this." Rose put an arm under her neck and raised her up, putting a paper cup of orange juice to her trembling lips.

Rivka drained the cup, wiping her mouth with the back of her hand and slowly lifting herself into a sitting position. She attempted to get up, but her legs would not hold the weight. She put a hand over her stomach. Another person was in there! Growing every day a little bigger, taking over her body, pushing out her stomach for all to see!

"*No!* Don't even try to get up yet. The doctor will be right back," the nurse admonished.

Eventually, they were in a taxi on their way home. Rose respected the girl's silence. As soon as they were inside the apartment, Rose put her to bed, checking in on her anxiously every half hour, allowing her to sleep until evening.

"Rivka."

She opened her eyes.

"I brought you some food. Here, it's on a tray."

"I can't! I feel so nauseous!"

"That's because you are overhungry. It happens at the beginning of a pregnancy until your body adjusts. It means it's a healthy pregnancy."

"I can't be pregnant . . ." She shook her head. "I just can't."

Rose sat down on the edge of the bed. She smoothed down the girl's long bright hair. "Why not, kid? Why can't you be pregnant? Were you having sex?"

The girl nodded, ashamed.

"Were you using birth control—taking pills, inserting a diaphragm?"

She shook her head no.

"Well, was the boy using a condom?"

She looked up sharply. "No, I wouldn't allow that, Aunt Rose. It's the sin of Onan, who spilled his seed on the ground."

"Well, then," Rose said patiently, trying to be kind, to keep the exasperation out of her voice. "You know about the birds and the bees, don't you, kid? Then, why can't you be pregnant?"

"Because a child is a blessing! And what I was doing was a sin! God could not have blessed me with a child!"

Rose took the shaking girl into her arms. "Oh, my little Rivkaleh. Oh, my poor little kid."

Rivka let herself be rocked. Eventually, she pulled away, wiping the tears from her eyes, getting up, and pacing the floor. "Everything I did—running away in the first place—was to avoid this! And now, I'll be a mother at eighteen! Exactly what I didn't want!"

"No one is going to force you to have this baby if you don't want to."

Rivka's eyes widened. "You want me to be a murderer?"

"Rivka, I once had reason to look into this. Jews don't believe abortion is murder, that the fetus is the same as a baby. Unlike Christians, among Jews the mother's life comes first. If a fetus is endangering the mother in any way, abortions are permitted under Jewish law."

"My life isn't in any danger!"

"But you could be mentally and emotionally scarred. A rabbi would consider that if you wanted to get an opinion."

"I couldn't face a rabbi!"

"What about adoption, then?"

"Give it to strangers, my own flesh and blood? And then wonder for the rest of my life where my child is, and how they are being cared for?" She shook her head. "Never."

The girl was a strange combination of a pious fundamentalist mixed with dollops of adventurous sinner. Rose tried hard to get into her mind-set, to speak to her in her own language. "That doesn't leave you much wiggle room, honey. You've said no to everything but having a child and raising it yourself. If that's the case, what about getting married to the baby's father?"

"He would never marry me."

"Never mind that. We can always deal with that. Do *you* want to marry *him*?"

She hesitated. "I'm not sure, but I don't think so. It's not the life I want. Nothing is holy to him. I miss the Sabbath. I miss the holidays . . ."

Rose thought she was one of the very few people who could understand how someone running from a Haredi family could still feel that way. She sympathized.

"What, exactly, *do* you want, kid?"

Rivka shook her head helplessly. "I don't know that, either."

Rose could understand that, too, but it wasn't helpful. "Well, that *is* a big problem. You have to figure that out first before we do anything."

"If my parents find out, they are going to kill me—and him."

"That's just an expression. People don't actually kill over things like this. I think you'd be surprised at how your mother, your parents, would feel. This is, after all, their grandchild."

"It doesn't matter how they feel! No one will care how they feel! This will finish off the family's precious reputation unless they find some way to cover it up, like sending me some place far away where I can give birth and then getting rid of the baby so that I can come back to them ready to jump into the bride pool again."

"Are you so sure that would be such a terrible idea?" Rose was shocked to hear herself say.

"I'm not sure of anything, except that I'm a wicked, foolish girl who has ruined her only chance at having a real life. I wish I was dead!" She threw herself facedown on the pillow, sobbing.

"Oh, Rivkaleh! Don't say that, kid. Don't ever, ever say that! Life is the most wonderful adventure! You've taken a bit of a wrong turn down a challenging path, that's all. You'll find your way again. You've got so many fantastic experiences ahead of you! And you're not alone. I'll help you. I promise."

Rivka raised her hand and Rose clasped it in hers warmly.

"Now try to rest. You heard the doctor."

There was one more question, a vital one, Rose wanted to ask her, but she decided now was not the time. There is no good solution to this, Rose realized, closing the door softly behind her. Any path she chooses, she will meet up with heartbreak and ugly moral compromise. All I can do for her is make sure she is allowed to choose her own way freely while recognizing the consequences; all I can do is stand by her side and wait.

Freedom *is* a birthright. But it is also a great responsibility. Who knew better than she did that girls in her world were given no tools to own their freedom and exercise it responsibly? From earliest childhood, at each step they took there was a parent or rabbi or teacher hovering over them, telling them which way to point their toes. Cut off from that, they had no training in how to deal with the euphoria and blessing of independence.

A little while later, Rose checked in on her again. This time, Rivka was sitting up, her face pale and tear-stained. But at least she was no longer sobbing.

"Rivka, perhaps we should arrange a meeting with your parents. You need to discuss this with them face-to-face."

"*Oh no!* How can you of all people tell me to do that? You know what will happen!" Rivka shouted, absolutely horrified at the thought.

"We can't be sure," Rose continued calmly, undeterred. "Anyhow, it's still the right thing to do. If I was your mother, I'd want to know. I'd want to be given the opportunity to help."

"My mother is a good person. I love her. But she can't go against the family. She can't go against the community. And in their eyes, what I've done is pretty much unforgivable."

"But Rivkaleh, you yourself said a child is a blessing from God. I grew up with your mother in the same house. Yes, we were brought up strictly, but we were also taught to respect life and to love God and to respect His decisions. He's decided to give you a child, a little blessing. Oh, so it's not the most convenient time. Oh, so it's not what you thought would happen. In fact, this is what you thought you were running away from . . . But you know the saying, 'Man proposes and God disposes.'"

"*A mentsh tracht un der Oibershter lacht*," Rivka replied.

"'Man plans and God laughs.' Yes, well, that, too." Rose smiled. "Are you really so afraid of your parents?"

"No, not of them personally . . . But I've heard stories about what's been done to other rebellious girls."

"What stories?"

"They are kidnapped and brought to Haredi psychiatrists who give them drugs or commit them to mental institutions if they don't do what their parents want."

"Sounds pretty much like a made-up horror story to me!" Rose protested, skeptical.

"No, Aunt Rose. It's true! If you don't do what they want, then you must be crazy. They have a system to deal with girls like me."

"Rivka, you are letting your imagination run away with you! Listen, honey, I know you're scared, but you have to remember that this is your *tateh* and your *mameh* . . ."

Rivka lifted her head, stricken.

". . . Who've loved you all their lives and wanted what they thought was best for you. They deserve at least to speak with you, to know what you are going through."

"But Aunt Rose, *you* never came back! *You* never spoke to your parents! So why are you forcing me?"

I deserve that, Rose thought, chastened. "No, I never did. And for the rest of my life, I will regret it. My parents deserved a chance to talk to me."

Rivka listened, stricken. "But you must promise me you won't leave me alone with them! That you'll be by my side the whole time!"

"I promise."

"Well, then, if you think it's for the best."

"I do. Now, I don't want you to worry anymore." She lifted the tray, which had hardly been touched. "I'm going to bring you dinner. Anything you like, but you have to try to eat. What would you like?"

"A pizza and a Diet Coke?"

"Sure. But make it a regular Coke, okay?"

Rivka smiled. "Aunt Rose?"

"Hmm?"

"You're a *tzadakis*. And you're all I have in the world," Rivka said, kissing Rose's hands.

Rose felt her heart flutter at the touch of the girl's soft lips. She looked so much like Pearl.

Later that evening, when she was sure Rivka was fast asleep, she picked up the phone. "Hannah, do you have a moment? There is something we need to discuss."

And so Rivka's journey begins, Hannah thought, listening in shock and amazement to her mother's revelations, marveling at the strange parallels between her young cousin's life and that of her own mother. It was almost eerie.

34

They were sitting at Faye's Café at NYU. It was noisy and crowded, but the only place Simon had agreed to meet them. This time, Hannah thought, he really does want witnesses.

"I'm not sure what I'm doing at this meeting, Mom. It's very uncomfortable for me, to say the least. Why didn't you just bring Rivka?"

"Because she isn't strong enough to face this herself, Hannah. But it has to be done, because we are meeting with her parents tomorrow, and I have to know for sure what kinds of options are open to her."

"You don't need a meeting for that. Where Simon the Sleaze is concerned, there is no option. Believe me, it's a blessing. To be married to him would be much worse."

"But I thought you liked him. Weren't the two of you even dating?"

Hannah winced. "Let's not get into that, shall we? I told you, I don't want to be involved in any part of this."

"Well, it's not that easy, young lady. You did, after all, introduce the two of them . . ."

"Now, wait one friggin' second, Mom! I was having a party and she showed up uninvited and moved in, which I allowed out of the goodness of my heart! I was not playing matchmaker! In fact, I had no idea they even knew each other. Simon called her behind my back the very next day, and Rivka met with him, also behind my back, without saying a single word to me about it."

"Yes, I know. And if it helps, Rivka is extremely sorry about it. She didn't know you two were dating. She left him as soon as she found out."

"So she says . . ." Hannah replied skeptically. "I cannot for the life of me understand why *you*, Mom, are taking her side! After everything you said to me! And now you are up to your eyeballs in this mess."

"*You* sent her to my house, remember?"

"And I thought if anyone would know how to get rid of her, it would be you."

"Well, surprise. Blood *is* thicker than water, and I, apparently, was some kind of role model for this misguided and unfortunate kid."

Hannah shifted uncomfortably. "It's so weird."

"Okay, weird, maybe. But you know what? I'm surprised to find that I really like her. She's smart, and she has guts and a good heart, although she's very naive, and she's made appalling choices. We have actually had fun together. I took her along with me on photo shoots. She was very helpful. And so eager to learn."

Hannah felt a sharp stab of jealousy pierce her heart. "Oh, so now you've got the daughter you've always wanted!"

"Don't be ridiculous!"

"I swear, she's got a talent for doing whatever she wants, then finding people to help her out of it by making them think they have some responsibility for her actions. Well, I'm not buying in. She's made her bed with no help from any of us."

"I wouldn't go that far," Rose murmured, watching a tall young man with long dark hair weave his way between the tables toward them.

"Sorry, I'm late . . ."

"Simon, meet my mother, Rose Weiss Gordon, Rivka's aunt."

"The famous photographer." He smiled.

Hannah glared at him. So, he'd known all along! Was that what their whole relationship had been about, then?

"Thank you for coming," Rose began politely.

"Oh, Mom, please! Spare us! You got her pregnant, you bastard!"

He slumped, astonishment taking root in his eyes, which before had merely been wary.

"Really, Hannah," Rose protested. Then, she sighed. Perhaps it was just as well to put all the cards on the table at once. "Young man, now that you know the story, what are your plans?" Rose demanded.

He exhaled, feeling panic-stricken and flattened. He had expected some unpleasantness, but leavened with civilized niceties, a little small talk. He was good at small talk.

"Mrs. Gordon, I don't know what to say. I'm in shock! What is it Rivka wants of me?"

"That's not important right now, is it? She's in no position to make any demands on you. She's terrified and confused and heartbroken, and this close to being suicidal . . ."

Hannah gave her mother a sharp glance. Rose inclined her head slightly, raising an eyebrow. Okay, an exaggeration, Hannah surmised, leaning back.

He slumped, raising both hands helplessly. "What can *I* do?"

"Well, for one thing, how about offering her some financial support?"

"As you know, Hannah, I'm just a student. I don't have any money . . ."

"You have a very nice car and well-off parents . . ."

He suddenly sat up. "I don't want my parents involved in any of this!" Now it was his turn to be demanding. "If you contact them, I'll deny everything. And they'll believe me."

"Until the DNA results come back," Hannah pointed out.

"I'll take my chances with that," he replied, suddenly belligerent. "You might be surprised at the results."

Rose stared at him. Rivka *had* been wandering around by herself for quite some time. It wasn't impossible. "Why don't we all just calm down? I have no reason to involve your parents at this stage," Rose said. "What I wanted to know from you, Simon, is, do you have any feelings for my niece at all?"

The question took him by surprise. He hesitated. "Sure, she was sweet . . ."

"And innocent . . ." Hannah threw in.

"That's not what I asked." Rose shook her head. "Do you *love* her?"

"Oh, *Mom,* please." Hannah rolled her eyes.

"Hannah, be quiet! Answer the question, Simon."

"I'm not sure what that word means," he said.

"How convenient! It means caring for someone more than you care about yourself. You know that possibility exists, don't you, Simon?"

"Please, Hannah!" Rose begged.

"Even if I did love her, I don't think Rivka really wants *me*. It wouldn't work out anyway. We're just too different."

"Okay. That's the first thing I had to make sure of. Secondly, do you want anything to do with this child?"

"If it's mine, you mean . . ."

Hannah clenched her fists.

"Yes, of course," Rose continued, annoyed but keeping her voice businesslike.

"I think . . . in the long run . . . this was all just a big mistake. I wouldn't want to be a child born into such a mess."

"So, you think she should abort?"

He nodded. "For everyone's sake, especially Rivka's."

"Right, it's her you're worried about." Hannah slammed her fist down. The table shook.

"Hannah, dear, maybe you should just go? I'm sorry I dragged you into this."

"Too late, Mom, I'm not going anywhere. I want to see how this plays out."

"And in the case she decides to go forward with the pregnancy, do you want to be part of their lives?"

"Well . . ."

"Just tell the truth, Simon. That's all I came here to hear. I'm not judging you," Rose murmured quietly, trying to diffuse the tension and reach the bottom line.

"Well, no, I don't. I'll have a family of my own one day, one I choose to have. This was just an accident. It's foolish for me to pretend otherwise."

"So, you will sign away custody if she gives the child up for adoption?"

"No problem."

"Don't you even want to see it, your own child?" Hannah interjected, appalled.

"Look, if you don't have any more questions, I've got classes . . ." He got up, avoiding Hannah's eyes.

"Sit down one more minute, young man. I'm not finished," Rose said firmly.

He sat down.

"Did you force her to have sex with you?"

He shook his head emphatically. "No."

"Did you threaten to throw her out on the street if she didn't go to bed with you?"

"She would say that! Look, she took me all the way out to Far Rockaway so she could dunk in some ritual bath where no one would know her, and then, when we get home, she suddenly has no interest in me at all! I admit I was ticked, and maybe a little drunk, too. But I didn't rape her! I just didn't want her wandering around in the dark!"

"So, you brought her back. And she came back to you because it was dark and cold and she had no place else to go . . ." Rose said softly, as if to herself.

"It didn't happen like that! She wanted me, and I wanted her, at least then . . ."

Hannah picked up her coffee cup, flinging the dregs into his face. He jumped up, choking.

"I'm sorry." Rose handed him a napkin. "Temper, temper, Hannah."

"We're done!" he sputtered.

"Almost, Simon. One more thing. Right at the beginning, why didn't Rivka tell Hannah she was meeting with you? Why didn't you?"

He was furious, wiping off his leather jacket, which now had a permanent stain. "I'm not a mind reader. Hannah wasn't her mother. She'd run away from her mother."

"And that's what you told her, right?" Hannah asked with sudden insight.

"I hope so! Can I go now?"

"Yes, but we are meeting with Rivka's parents tomorrow. I can't promise you that you won't be hearing from them."

He groaned, then turned and walked away.

Hannah sat there. For a few moments, she didn't move.

35

❦

On the morning of the meeting scheduled between Rivka and her parents, Rose awoke when it was still dark. She turned on the light, looking at her watch. It was just after 5:00 A.M. Throwing off her covers, she walked into the living room. To her surprise, Rivka was sitting on the couch, already fully dressed.

"How long have you been up? Our meeting isn't until eleven, you know."

"Good morning, Aunt Rose. I didn't sleep at all. I finally decided I might as well get up and get dressed."

Rose looked her over. She was wearing one of her new outfits, a blue corduroy skirt that skimmed her knees and a colorful T-shirt that proclaimed: BORN TO BE FREE. And she had worried the kid might be intimidated!

"Well, you look ready for war."

"You know, Aunt, there aren't going to be any surprises at this meeting."

"Would you care to expand on that? Or, as you like to put it: *Vus is dus?*"

"My parents will beg me to come back, but only on their terms. They'll even let me keep the baby, but only if I agree to get married to some old widower who will promise them to keep me in line the rest of my life." She shook her head. "I'm not going to agree to any of that."

She might be young, but she was no dummy, Rose thought. "So, you think it's a waste of time to speak to them?"

She shook her head. "I didn't say that. They are my parents. I love them. And they tried, in their own way, to be good to me."

"That's very mature of you, Rivka. I must admit that when I was in the middle of my war of rebellion, I hated them all."

"Really? Hated?" Her eyes looked surprised and envious, as if she had never given herself permission to even imagine such a thing.

"Well, maybe that's too strong a word. But I didn't feel I owed them anything. I thought they were bent on ruining my life."

"They don't know anything else. It's all about power and honor. My needs will always come last." She shrugged. "That's their problem, not mine. I'm not afraid to stand up for myself anymore."

Rose looked her over. It was true. She wasn't that trembling, weeping child of two weeks before, crumpling at the thought of facing the music. Was that a good thing or a bad thing? she wondered. Courage or shamelessness? "Then what?"

"I still don't know what it is I do want, only what I don't want. And I don't want this baby."

There, it was out in the open. And it wasn't pretty, Rose had to admit. She felt breathless. "Rivka, there is something I've been wanting to ask you, something I need to know."

The girl looked suddenly wary.

"How long have you known you were pregnant?"

"When I left Simon's, something wasn't right with me. He actually made me a doctor's appointment. It wasn't for sure—my periods, they never come on the same day, and sometimes they skip a month, two months. It's always been like that with me. The morning I left Simon's, I was on my way to my doctor's appointment. But just as I was leaving, I found this box of chocolates. It had a card, which said: *'To Hannah, the most special girl in the world. Love, Simon.'* He left it right in the living room, like he wanted me to find it! I was . . . just . . . so . . . *farmisht.*" Her eyes misted.

"I can just imagine . . ." Rose murmured. "Go on."

"So, then I had to leave, you understand? And once I knew Simon didn't love me, I couldn't let myself be pregnant. So I talked myself out of it."

Rose felt her knees go weak. She was such a child! Such a child! "Rivka, I also got pregnant when I wasn't married."

Rivka slumped into a chair, astonished. "Really?"

Rose nodded. "And I kept the baby, and married the father."

"Hannah's father?"

"No, my son's father."

"You loved him?"

She hesitated. "He was a good man. But no, I can't say I ever really fell in love. We met in Central Park walking our dogs. I was very, very lonely. We divorced when our son was four."

"So, Hannah has a different father?"

Rose nodded.

"And were you in love with *him*?"

"With all my heart."

"Then what happened?"

"He was killed when Hannah was ten. He was a war photographer working for *Newsweek*. He was trying to talk soldiers out of shooting up a school bus in Kosovo." Finally, he had just not been able to stand back and watch.

"Oh, Aunt Rose!"

"Yes, yes, well . . ."

She didn't like to talk about it, her life's greatest tragedy. With Henry, she had finally found a true home, which she had learned was not a place but a feeling. Wherever he was, that was where she lived, really lived. She had expected to see his dark curls turn gray, his face turn wrinkled and leathery from the sun . . . They would be like those handsome old couples walking hand in hand you sometimes saw, the kind who travel the world loving every minute of it as they turn seventy and eighty . . . That was the plan.

Their marriage had coincided with the most successful and productive time in both their careers. They'd spent so much time apart, always making a list of things they would do together when they both finally retired.

And now she would have to do them alone.

She couldn't bear to think about it. Experiencing such a passionate love had been the greatest gift, and also the greatest risk she had ever taken. She couldn't imagine ever having the courage to risk that again.

"I don't think I could ever marry a man I didn't love." Rivka shook her head. "It would feel too much like what I ran away from. What's the point of trading one lifestyle for another if the bottom line is losing your freedom either way?"

"Rivka, this idea you have of freedom . . ."

"Yes?"

"What does freedom mean to you?"

She was silent for a few moments, surprised by the question. "It means doing what I want."

"But you do know that with freedom comes responsibility? You can do anything you want, but that doesn't mean you can avoid the consequences. And everything a person does has consequences, wherever you live and whatever you believe in."

Rivka blinked. "Aunt Rose, are you trying to talk me into getting married? Into having this baby?" Her voice rose in alarm bordering on hysteria.

"Is that what it sounded like to you, Rivka?"

"Yes," she said, her face closed and sullen, like a spoiled child's.

Uh-oh, Rose thought. What have we here? "Do you think there are no consequences?"

"How *you* say it, it sounds like you're yelling at me, just like my parents! No one can make me do anything I don't want to do! Not you, and not them!"

She ran into her bedroom, slamming the door.

Rose sat down on the sofa, rubbing her tired eyes, remembering the famous punch line from Laurel and Hardy: "Well, here's another nice mess you've gotten me into." Oh, why didn't I follow my own very good advice in the first place and refuse to get involved? Well, it's too late now. I *am* involved, over my head.

She knocked softly on Rivka's door. "May I come in?"

She heard a small, muffled response that sounded like a yes, so she risked opening the door. Rivka was sitting on the bed, her legs folded beneath her, clutching one of Hannah's old teddy bears. She looked like eleven-year-old Pearl that day when she'd begged someone to walk her to school. Rose's heart melted.

"Rivka . . ." She sat down on the bed next to her, taking her hand.

"I'm just so . . . scared, Aunt Rose. I don't know what's going to happen! I have this . . . thing . . . inside me . . ."

"A baby . . ." Rose corrected her softly.

"It doesn't feel like a baby. It feels like some *dybbuk* that's invaded me and taken me over, making me do all the things I don't want to do! I never wanted this!"

"Well, you seem to have made up your mind about how to put things right, then. The doctor told you, it's still early."

Rivka looked up. "Will it hurt?"

Now, that was a mature question if she'd ever heard one! Rose thought, shaking her head in frustration. Rivka took it as an answer.

"Then, that's what I'll do, then! That will solve everything! Then, I'll be free again. And next time I'll be a lot more careful, Aunt. Believe me!"

Unfortunately, I do, Rose thought. You'll behave the same way, except take better precautions so as not to pay any of the consequences. And you'll do it in my house, with my help. But this was not the time to bring these things up. She didn't want to upset her any more than she obviously already was. She wanted this parent-child conference to take place as planned without any hysteria that could be avoided.

Who am I kidding? It was going to be hysterical from the get-go on all sides! She dreaded it.

"Rivka, have you had some breakfast? Otherwise, you'll be feeling nauseous very soon."

"I'll make myself something," she answered, relieved that they weren't fighting anymore. She couldn't take much more. She was glad she'd made the decision to abort. It felt right. No one wanted this child, not its father, or mother, or grandparents. There would be no one to care for it or support it. Who would want to be born into such circumstances? It was the right thing to do. She felt a sudden surge of relief and happiness. Now her parents would not be able to blackmail her! She would be able to keep going down the road she'd started on. She'd become a famous photographer like her aunt Rose! And she would marry some mysterious stranger she'd fall madly in love with, and if it didn't work out, she'd divorce him.

Life could be beautiful!

She went into the kitchen, suddenly hungry.

"Hannah."

"What's up, Mom?"

Rose sighed into the phone. "Do you think you could possibly find it in your heart to come to the meeting this morning with Rivka's parents?"

"As I vaguely recall, we already discussed that, Mom. I said no, and you said okay."

"Hannah, she's very upset! I don't know what to do with her!"

"What do you mean?"

"She's got this idea in her head that she can just abort this baby and keep living with me, and all her childish dreams will still magically come true . . ."

"Won't they?"

"There are consequences!"

"Only if people insist on imposing them."

"No, there are natural consequences that can't be avoided. You can't have an abortion and go on as if nothing happened," Rose insisted.

"Some people do just that. Isn't what you're really saying is that *you* won't be able to go on like nothing happened?"

She forgot how sharp Hannah was. "Yes, I guess I am."

"You can't stand the idea of her getting away with this scot-free."

"It's not right! She says she'll be more careful *next time*."

"So this is going to be a lifestyle?" Hannah muttered.

"That's what it sounds like."

"She's just a stupid kid. She has no idea what she's saying."

"I don't want her to think I approve of this."

"So, Mom, you feel you haven't been judgmental enough with her? Hasn't she had enough of that in her life?"

"She's under my roof."

"So what? You can't control her, any more than you can control your own kids . . ."

Rose was quiet, thinking. "I don't want to control her . . ."

"But you want her to live by a moral code, preferably your own. So how are you any different than her parents?"

That hurt. "Listen, Hannah, all I want is for her to make a mature decision, that's all. She's holding life and death in her hands, and it doesn't matter how young she is. That's an enormous responsibility, and she can't just shirk it."

"Can, and will, if possible."

"Her regrets will come ten years down the line, when she's old enough to understand what she did!"

"That's her business, not yours."

Rose was surprised. Considering everything that had happened with Simon, she hadn't expected Hannah to undertake the role of her cousin's lawyer. But Hannah was right, she had to admit to herself. Besides, there was no way to make her own argument stick, except by the crudest possible means: letting Rivka know that she'd be kicked out if she decided to go through with an abortion. She'd grow up in a hurry, then! The question that remained was whether she, Rose, was capable of that kind of ruthlessness? And if so, how was she any different from her own parents, or from Rivka's?

"Will you come, Hannah?"

"Sure, why not? I'll come and hold your hand."

She felt foolish that it meant so much to her. "Thank you, sweetie."

Hannah hung up the phone. What was the point of fighting it? It was like quicksand: the more she struggled against it, the deeper it would suck her in. She might as well just take it easy and go with the flow. For in the end, none of it was any of her business.

Her cousin would have a baby, or not. She would stay with her aunt Rose, or go back to her parents, or not. She would live a wonderful life, or not. She had flown into her life uninvited and unexpected, fouling everything she touched. And now, thankfully, she had flown out, taking Simon with her. And good riddance to them both.

He was a cad, but no different from any other undergraduate male she knew. None of them would have behaved any differently. And you couldn't really blame them. Settling down with a wife and family would mean dropping out of school, and then where would they be? No one expected college men to be celibate, just to be careful. And Rivka had pretty much thrown herself at him and, in some ways, even deceived him. She had to take some responsibility for the pickle she was in, innocent or not, virgin or not. She'd gone to the mikveh, which meant it wasn't a sudden burst of passion, but something carefully thought out, calculated even.

Maybe she *would* be better off back with her parents! She seemed to need a lot of looking after. For all the strictness of her upbringing, she seemed to lack any self-discipline.

It would be interesting to be at this meeting. She'd never met any of her mother's family. It would almost be like some kind of anthropological field trip! Besides, it was only fair, seeing as she'd been the catalyst who had brought Rivka into their lives in the first place. Had she not run after her down the stairs that first night, neither she nor her mother would be involved now. So it really was the least she could do. Anyway, it was—what? Two hours of her time? Maybe less. And then, it would be over—as far as she was concerned—for good.

36

Williamsburg, Brooklyn

Pearl woke up the morning of the meeting with her sister and runaway daughter feeling as if she had just discovered a lump in her breast and was on her way to a doctor to hear a horrifying diagnosis. Her adored youngest had stabbed her in the heart, running away from home and thus announcing to the community (those who knew about it, who at present were thankfully few) that her parents had failed in instilling in her the Torah values of respect for parents, modesty, and faithfulness. That she had chosen to flee to her own sister, Rose, who had broken her heart and who for years had been a thorn in their sides and a source of shame, compounded her daughter's sins exponentially, twisting the knife. Were any of this to become widely publicized, it would tarnish the family name for generations, making it more difficult for grandchildren to find suitable marriage partners, get into the best schools, or find jobs in the yeshiva world, a heartbreaking situation that would no doubt shorten her husband's life and her own.

Poor Zevulun Meir! He could hardly hold up his head since the child left. In the yeshiva where he ran the bus service, picking up and dropping off the younger children every day, a scandal like this would make it impossible for him to continue demanding the respect he needed to continue functioning. How long would it be before they fired him? And then what would he do? What would they do? As ungenerous as his salary had always been, they had managed to scrape by on it. Anything extra he earned from tutoring or performing circumcisions went to support their many sons and sons-in-law, all of whom were in various institutions learning Talmud, struggling to make ends meet on miniscule stipends.

It had been a difficult situation before the latest troubles, but one they had shared in common with most of their friends and neighbors. Wealthy and successful businessmen were rare in their community, looked up to like princes, despite having put Talmud learning aside for more secular pursuits. That was the strange irony, but the reality.

She washed her hands ritually, carefully covering her nearly bald head with a scarf, then took out her prayer book. Every year since becoming a bride, she had cropped her long blond hair shorter and shorter. Long hair was heavy and suffocating inside the traditional wig, and almost impossible to hide beneath hats. The less hair a truly pious married woman had, the easier it was to fulfill God's commandment to keep it hidden even from the walls of one's own home.

Turning her face east, in the direction of Jerusalem, she prayed silently. Among the many entreaties and words of praise and thanks—including thanking God for straightening the backs of those bent in sorrow and for giving strength to those weakened by care—she prayed for the well-being of her family: "May You have mercy on my sons and daughters and grandchildren, my sons- and daughters-in-law. May You forgive Rivka, and give us the wisdom to bring her back to us. May You fill our daughter's heart with sincere regret for her sins and accept her desire to do penance for her shortcomings."

As always, when she kissed her prayer book and put it away, she felt lighter.

As she prepared her simple breakfast of toasted bread—which had been prepared and baked under strict rabbinical supervision—spread with butter supervised by rabbis from the time it left the cow, and jam that rabbis in her community had thoroughly ascertained contained no hidden substances contrary to the laws of God, she tried to imagine a best-case scenario.

Little Rivkaleh, she thought. Her beautiful baby girl, the last of her children. She had felt more like a grandmother to her than a mother, her firm hand softening in her upbringing. Unlike the expectations she held for her other six children, she had not set Rivka heavy chores, like washing floors or carrying heavy shopping bags from the grocery. She had given her the unheard-of luxury of her own bedroom and had dressed her in clothes purchased new from clothing stores, rather than hand-me-downs.

When she tried to pinpoint where she had gone wrong, she found herself focusing on these indulgences, and many more, which had given the child the idea that she was special, exempt from the harsh realities that so clearly marked the lives of her siblings and parents. Worst of all, these luxuries had afforded her much privacy and free time in which to explore all kinds of forbidden passions, including secular novel reading and watching videos on her computer.

None of her other children had even dreamed of either a computer or their own room, not to mention the spare time in which to get up to mischief! Only after her daughter had fled had she and Zevulun Meir watched with horror some of the DVDs she had left behind: movies in which immodestly clad women went to forbidden colleges and had unchaperoned liaisons with men they chanced to meet, all by themselves, in all manner of places: bars, college campuses, office buildings—God protect us! In one, the heroine was a small blond girl who looked a little like Rivka, played by an actress with a strange goyish name: Reese Witherspoon. *Legally Blonde,* it was called. They had no idea why. They were shocked. They had had no idea that a computer, which they thought would help her prepare for employment in the offices of a decent religious businessman from their community, could be used to see such *shmutz!*

It was their own fault, Zevulun Meir had mourned. With their last born, they had wanted to be "modern," and for this sin God had punished them severely by taking their daughter away from them.

Only one thing gave Pearl comfort: her sincere faith that even a scarlet thread could become pure white. There was always *teshuva,* repentance, for their daughter and for themselves. But they would need to prove to God, and to their friends and neighbors, that they and their daughter had learned their lessons and were not the same sinners they had once been. They would have to redouble their efforts "to build a fence around the law," forbidding more and more things that were permitted so as not to even approach red-lines.

The world was filled with temptations, and they had shown themselves and their family vulnerable. They would need to win back their community's trust if they were to remain respected members in good standing.

For this, they needed first and foremost to deal with their prodigal daughter. In the best case, she would come home after a cover story had been spread about her semester enrollment in a strictly supervised religious girls' school in Bnei Brak. After a suitable interval in which she would be seen with her hair tightly braided, dressed in ankle-length skirts, long-sleeved, high-necked blouses, and sturdy closed-toe shoes, she would once again be allowed into the bride pool by the most respectable matchmakers.

Of course, they realized that now they would not be able to demand from the *shadchan* what they had in the past. The foremost scholars of impeccable lineage with provable saintly character traits were forever beyond their grasp, for such boys' parents would thoroughly investigate the cover story and find it wanting. They mourned this lost son-in-law they had so looked forward to welcoming, a beautiful new branch on their flourishing family tree, as if a true treasure had slipped through their fingers, falling into the depths of the sea. They blamed themselves most of all. A child had no sense, no will, no natural form of its own. It had to be prodded, molded, and directed until it took the proper shape to fit into the space allotted for it in the community. As parents, they had failed to achieve this, and they and their daughter would now pay the price.

The kitchen door opened and closed.

"Zevulun Meir?"

"Yes. It's me." His light and pleasant voice was deep and gruff, betraying his inner turmoil.

"Do you want something to eat?"

"Just a cup of tea."

She hurried to prepare it for him, putting an unasked-for but appreciated plate of cinnamon-dusted rugelach down as well. He said the blessing over the tea and then over the pastry, and then he chewed and swallowed without pleasure, as if it were a chore.

"Zevulun Meir, can we talk?"

He looked up at her, puzzled. What, after all, was there left to say? He shrugged.

She exhaled, as if making room in her throat for the words. "About my sister . . ."

His face clamped shut, his lips bunching.

"We should try to avoid conflict."

"Where there is a Delilah and a Samson, a Moses and a Pharaoh, there will be conflict! Don't fool yourself into thinking this will end peaceably!"

"You don't know my sister. She wouldn't have invited Rivka to come to her house. She hasn't been in touch with the family for forty years."

"Then how did our Rivkaleh wind up there? Magic?"

This was difficult, and truthfully, in all the time she had been married to this principled but compassionate man, this was the first time she felt a little afraid of him.

"I had a box underneath my bed in which I kept some old photos of the family. There were also some secular newspaper clippings and a letter, from my sister."

He looked at her sharply.

She hurried to finish before she lost her nerve. "The clippings showed my sister, Rose, winning an award for some pictures she had taken. And the letter, it was a mazel tov to me on my engagement . . . Maybe Rivka saw these things and that's what gave her the idea to go to my sister. You shouldn't blame Rose."

He turned to her in slow motion, heaving with emotion. "And you kept these things in our kosher home? Near our pure child?"

"You don't know anything at all about my sister . . ."

"What is there to know?"

"She was very dear to me when we were young. Such a kind, good, loving sister . . ."

"You are defending her? You! After all she did to you? If not for her, you could have married a brilliant young scholar. You could be a powerful, respected rebbitzin. Instead, you had to marry me, a broken-down widower with a child, who will never amount to anything . . ."

She moved closer to him, reaching out tentatively and touching the wrinkles on his forehead. "This was not a punishment, Zevulun Meir. This has always been my good fortune."

He took her fingers in his hands, bringing them to his lips and kissing them gently. "My *eshes chayil*," he said gently. "Please, you must not blame yourself. Our Rivkaleh didn't learn to be so *prust* and so defiant from a newspaper article or a letter. She also didn't learn it in our home or from her school or her sisters and brothers." He shook his head angrily. "Your sister has ruined our daughter, defiled her with her secular ways."

"But Zevulun, does not our holy Torah teach us to give each man the benefit of the doubt?"

"That is only in the case where there are no witnesses and the matter is unknown. You and I are both witnesses to how our daughter has changed, how she spoke to us."

She wanted to answer: but why blame my sister for this, when it is we who have raised this child for the last eighteen years? But she did not want to hurt him any more than he was already hurt. Instead, she said vaguely, "But surely there is room for repentance. As it is written, God waits for the sinner to return, even if he has fallen down to the forty-ninth degree of impurity."

"It is also written: 'A man who purifies himself after touching a corpse and then touches it again, of what avail will his purification be?' So with a person who fasts for their sins and then repeats them."

Let him take his anger out on my sister, then, Pearl thought, giving up. That way, there will be less for me, and less for my baby. "We must have faith that our child is capable of true repentance, Zevulun Meir. This is our child, our baby, our little Rivkaleh."

He hung his head in grief. "We'll see."

On the other side of the Williamsburg Bridge, in Manhattan, Rose was putting the finishing touches on her outfit. She had changed at least six times, switching from "want to please" to "want to shock" outfits and back again; from tight pants and short skirts to maxi skirts and wide culottes. She finally settled on a roomy gray dress over a T-shirt, layered with a long-sleeved violet-gray sweater. She wore a pretty beaded necklace and comfortable walking shoes. You couldn't get more covered up than that! She shook her head, chagrined yet relieved, satisfied she'd done the right thing.

She thought about knocking on Rivka's door again, but decided against it. The kid was in a state of high tension. The less they spoke, the better off they were. She called Hannah to remind her of the time, but there was no reply. Just as well. Hannah would, or wouldn't, show up. It didn't really matter that much either way, she lied to herself, wanting to prepare for disappointment. Of course, it mattered immensely, for reasons she couldn't even fully explain to herself. Maybe it all came down to just the idea of meeting her family's wrath head-on with some family of her own?

Finally, an hour before their meeting in her gallery in Chelsea—a fifteen-minute taxi ride away—she knocked urgently on Rivka's door.

"It's time to go, Rivka."

The door opened and the girl came out. She had changed into a longer skirt but otherwise looked exactly as she had earlier. She smiled tensely.

"I'm ready, Aunt Rose."

They hailed a cab and rode silently to their destination, Rivka checking for messages on her newly acquired cell phone, and Rose picking lint off her sweater.

Rose walked past the guard in the lobby, relieved to see him. "Good morning, John." She nodded.

"And how are you this morning, Mrs. Gordon? Oh, I see you have a little friend with you this morning."

"Yes, meet my niece, Rivka."

"Hello, Rivka."

Rivka looked him over: the uniform, the tall, fit body with the big black gun in the holster. She smiled broadly, relieved. "Hi, John!"

Rose then turned to the person manning the reception desk. "Michael, we are expecting some visitors today at eleven o'clock. Please don't send them up. Call me when they arrive, and I'll come down to get them."

"Of course." He wrote it down.

She exchanged glances with Rivka, trying to keep her expression as matter-of-fact as possible to promote the illusion this was something she did a dozen times a day. She could see the girl wasn't fooled. Well, whatever would happen, it would be in a safe place, she thought, hurrying Rivka into the elevator.

About ten minutes to eleven, Pearl and Zevulun walked up the steps from the subway. They had considered asking their two eldest sons to drive them, but that would have necessitated filling them in on all the sordid details, which at present they preferred to keep to themselves, wanting to spare these gentle and scholarly men they had raised, as well as to preserve the relationship between siblings. The more positive things Rivka could come back to, the more attractive an alternative it would be to continuing her rebelliousness.

While they had lived in New York City all their lives, they had never been to this part of Manhattan. At first, they looked curiously into the windows of the high-priced art galleries. They saw a grid photograph of a dozen Asian children in ill-fitting suits with large black eyeglasses, each one looking more strange and forlorn than the next. Zevulun and Pearl shrugged at each other, raising their eyebrows, their mouths twisting in derision as they examined the fantastic prices being charged for this *narishkeit*. A fool and his money are soon parted, they thought, shaking their heads and continuing on. In the next gallery, there was a skull divided by blue lines into squares, each one a sparkling piece of stained glass. They moved away quickly, disturbed. Then, they came to a photograph that from a distance looked like people in a fancy theater. But as they moved closer, they could see everyone in the photo was as naked as the day they'd been born!

Zevulun turned his head away, spitting on the sidewalk, while Pearl hurried after him. After that, they were afraid to look at anything until they arrived at the address Rose had given them. They walked past the guard and up to the reception desk.

"We've come to see Rose Gordon," Zevulun said.

"Your names, please?"

"We are her family," he answered, and the words cost him something. "Zevulun and Pearl. Can we go up now?"

"Just a moment. She told me to expect you. I'll call her."

They waited, Zevulun impatient, Pearl excited and filled with equal parts joy and apprehension at what lay ahead of them. All she could think of was her daughter, so nearby, after all this time! And her older sister, Rose.

Rose emerged from the elevator, looking anxiously ahead.

There she was. Pearl! Her little sister.

She looks more or less how I remember, Rose realized, surprised and a bit devastated as she smoothed back her own gray, wiry curls, pulling her sweater self-consciously around her to hide her girth. As was sometimes the case with Haredi women who had given birth to many children, Pearl had retained her slim, youthful shape, and her expertly coiffed blond wig hid any hint of gray. She wore a long stylish suit of dark gray with a pretty gray, white, and maroon scarf, no doubt both designer labels purchased at another one of those cut-rate stores or seventy-percent-off sales.

The opposite was true for Zevulun, whom she had met briefly only once, at her mother's funeral. He was almost unrecognizable. His once erect, distinguished figure was disfigured by rolls of fat that pressed out the sides of his black gabardine coat, the belt buckle barely making the last hole. His once black, neatly trimmed beard was almost white now and had grown to Santa Claus length. He looked like an old man.

"Rose?" Pearl said, staring at the strange woman who approached her, trying to mentally dig out in her face and body the sister she remembered. She found her in the eyes and mouth, which seemed the same, the deep brown ovals flashing with the same passion, the mouth in an ironic grin, a little flicker of the Rose who was once her dearest friend.

"Pearl, Zevulun," Rose said, finding herself surprisingly unable to hug her sister as she had hoped she would. It was mutual, both of them hanging back in confusion, overwhelmed by emotion. Zevulun nodded, vaguely, looking at the ground. Did he subscribe to the view that a man should never look at a woman other than his wife? Or was it just her? In either case, she found it insulting and demeaning.

"Where is Rivka?" he asked sullenly.

"Come, she is upstairs waiting in my office."

They walked to the elevator, then entered. Their close physical proximity combined with their emotional distance was awkward and nerve-wracking, Rose thought, willing the machine to move a little faster. The fact that no one spoke made their few seconds together seem like an eternity. When the doors finally opened, releasing her, she felt a knot growing in her throat.

Why she felt like crying she couldn't exactly explain or neatly sum up. It was a combination of anger, regret, longing, sadness, fear, and disappointment. And, yes, love. That most of all. To see her blood relative after all these years! She waited for Pearl to make some tiny, conciliatory gesture that would allow her to reciprocate, but there was nothing. They walked down the hall and into her gallery.

Michelle, Rose's gallery manager, stood on the side, having pasted on her best professional face.

"Michelle, this is my sister, Pearl, and her husband, Zevulun. We are going into my office."

"Hello, welcome!" Michelle said brightly, hiding her shock. She would never in a million years have guessed. Pearl smiled back tentatively, while Zevulun swept past her as if she was air.

The door opened.

"Rivkaleh!" Pearl cried, running to her daughter and embracing her.

"Mameh," Rivka said in a small voice. She felt crushed, her defiant resolutions dissolving like salt at the first touch of warm water.

"Rivkaleh, what have you done?" Zevulun said hoarsely. To their utter astonishment, he sat down on a chair and began to weep uncontrollably like a child, his body heaving with heavy sobs.

Rose stared at him, appalled, realizing for the first time what he must have been through. She felt her anger toward him dissipate.

"Tateh!" Rivka cried, releasing herself from her mother's embrace and sitting on the floor near him, leaning her head against his knees. He wiped his eyes and stroked her hair. "Rivkaleh, Rivkaleh . . ." he repeated, dirge-like. "Why?"

Rose could see that whatever resolve had lately strengthened the kid had now fled. She was a helpless shell. She wondered which Rivka she preferred? The determined modern girl who was ready for her abortion and her new life, or this wounded, chastised child with no will of her own at all?

"I didn't mean to hurt you, Tateh, Mameh," the girl wept.

"Why did you do this to us? Were you unhappy, *maideleh*? Did we demand things you didn't want to do?" Zevulun asked his daughter gently.

"I don't know," she answered.

Rose shook her head, appalled, thinking: This is even worse than an abortion. She's aborting herself, whatever new life she envisioned for herself. She's in over her head and she's deliberately opening up her mouth, breathing in water, drowning.

"It is time to come home, *maideleh*. Whatever you have done, we will begin again, and God will forgive us both."

With that, Rivka straightened up. She wiped her eyes and stared at the wall. And then, suddenly, she turned an imploring gaze toward Rose.

Rose cleared her throat. "Before you make any arrangements for the future, there is something you need to take into consideration."

"Was I talking to you?" Zevulun asked her threateningly. "Why do you think you have something to say? That you have a right to butt in, to put your nose in our business? This is our daughter, our family . . ."

"Zevulun Meir!" Pearl cried sharply. "Let my sister speak. Go on, Rose."

"Rivka has something she needs to tell you," Rose said quickly, offended, deciding to let her niece fend for herself for the moment.

"Please, Aunt Rose . . ." Rivka begged.

"What? What is it you need to tell us?" Zevulun demanded.

"Whatever it is, there is always repentance," Pearl chimed in hurriedly.

"Oh, Aunt Rose, please!"

Just then, the door to the office swung open. Hannah walked in. She was dressed in tight jeans, an NYU T-shirt, and a leather jacket with lots of zippers.

There was a moment of tense silence as everyone turned to stare at her.

"My daughter, Hannah," Rose said awkwardly.

"What did I miss?" Hannah said calmly, breezing into the room, giving Pearl and Zevulun a casual glance, her eyebrows raised when they did nothing to acknowledge her presence.

"So, she told you she's pregnant?" Hannah asked them abruptly, annoyed. "And what do you plan to do about it?"

"Hannah!" Rose called out, too late.

It started as a cry, then rolled into a roar of anger and grief. Zevulun got up, slamming his hand into the wall. Pearl began to wail.

The door opened, Michelle sticking her head in. "Is everything all right?"

Rose quickly went to the door, pushing Michelle gently outside, whispering urgently in her ear, "Call security!"

"*Oh my God!* Rivkaleh, it can't be true, can it?" Pearl asked, devastated, studying her daughter's stomach.

Rivka stood up stiffly with a sudden defiance that was spilling starch into her backbone, Rose noticed, relieved. "Yes, it's true!"

"This is *your doing*!" Zevulun shouted at Rose. "A shiksa, a *prutza*, dirties everything she touches. It wasn't enough to kill your own parents, now you have to destroy us also!"

Rose backed away, alarmed, then stopped, standing her ground. "I know that you never studied biology, Zevulun, but surely you know it wasn't me that got her pregnant."

He roared, advancing toward her in fury. Pearl held him back. "Zevulun, sit down!"

He sank into his chair again, breathing heavily.

"Listen, I've had just about all I can take of this," Hannah cried. "Why don't you say something, Rivka? Why are you letting my mother, who was so kind to you, take the rap for something you did?"

"It's not her fault, Tateh!" Rivka burst out. "I did this. Only me."

"You are a child. You didn't know any better."

"I'm not a child. You were trying to marry me off, remember?"

"Is that the reason you ran, because you didn't want to get married? He was such a fine boy! You would have been lucky to have him!"

"Yes, he was. He's not the reason. I wanted a different life! Something of my own. I wanted to live, not just go from being someone's child to being someone's wife. I wanted a chance to be me first!"

"*Me?* Such *narishkeit*! *Goyish narishkeit*!" Zevulun said.

"Why? Why is it foolish, Gentile nonsense?" she answered her father. "Can't a girl be a human being? Can't she try to be somebody?"

"Who do you want to be?" Pearl asked her.

"I don't know yet."

"Me, me, all the time, me! But she doesn't even know who that is!" her father scoffed, snorting derisively.

"How could you forget everything we taught you? How could you sin like this?" Pearl exhorted.

"She didn't forget. She even went to the mikveh!" Hannah burst out.

A sudden transformation came over Zevulun. His swollen, clenched face fell into smoother lines. "Is this true?" he asked his daughter with sudden calm. "Did you go to the mikveh, Rivkaleh?"

"Yes, I did. I didn't want to sin. And the boy, he is Jewish and not married. It's not so terrible," she pleaded.

"She went to the mikveh," Zevulun said to Pearl, who reached out and held his hand. "The child will not be a *ben-niddah*. It will be pure."

"Oh, so that's the point, right? Well, there isn't going to be any child!" Rivka shouted. "I'm going to get rid of it."

Zevulun reached out for her swiftly. "Never!" he said, grabbing her by the shoulders in a painful grip. "To fornicate is one thing, but to shed innocent blood, it is unforgivable!"

"No, Rivka! Your father is right! We must talk about this. Come home with us for just a few days, just so we can talk this over," Pearl begged. "There are other ways, better ways . . ."

"I am not going anywhere with you! I know what will happen! You'll drug me, and send me off to some loony bin until the baby is born, and then you'll give it away . . ."

"Maybe that is not such a bad idea!" Zevulun roared. "You are talking crazy, acting crazy."

"I am *not* crazy because I want a different life."

"You said yourself you don't even know what you want! You are a *farshimmelt* child. Come home!" Pearl pleaded.

"Don't beg her, Mameh. If she has any Torah left in her, she will not disrespect her parents! You know what the punishment is for that?" he said shaking her. "God will shorten your life!"

All this time, Rose hung back helplessly. It was a family tragedy, and something that had nothing at all to do with her. But this was a bit much. "Wait a minute, Zevulun. Take your hands off her! And don't try to black-mail her with fire and brimstone. Let her breathe. Let her think!"

"I'm telling you for the last time, shiksa, stay out of this!" Zevulun warned Rose threateningly.

"Hey, you can't talk to my mother like that! And leave Rivka be. Who do you think you are?" Hannah said, pulling his hands off the girl and standing belligerently between him and her mother.

"How dare you touch me!" he screamed at Hannah. "Oh, so the apple doesn't fall far from the tree. It was you who taught my daughter your whoring ways, and now you tell her to defy her parents?"

"I'm not telling her anything. And frankly, I don't care what she does. She's been nothing but a pain in the butt since she turned up on my door-step. But this isn't a Mafia movie, and you aren't dragging anybody away to do who knows what . . ."

He grabbed Rivka's hand. "You are coming home now!"

Pearl grabbed the other. "Yes, it is for the best, Rivka. You'll see; we'll sort it all out," she pleaded.

There was a knock on the door. "Security!"

Rose opened the door. "Is everything all right in here, ma'am?"

"This has NOTHING TO DO WITH YOU!" Zevulun screamed at the

guard, suddenly beside himself, as he lunged at the door. "This is MY child, and she is coming home with me, before anything else happens to her!"

The guard began to draw his gun from the holster.

Zevulun and Pearl stared at it, momentarily cowed, but not defeated. Zevulun dropped Rivka's hand. Pearl did the same. The girl massaged her wrists.

"It's all right, John. This is my family. It will be all right." Rose intervened.

"Okay, if you're sure," he said, putting the gun back inside his holster and staring at Zevulun. "But I'll be right outside the door, ma'am."

Zevulun sat down again, squeezing his hands in anguish. He spoke slowly and deliberately. "Rivka, I am your father. I am asking you to please come home just so we can talk this over among the family. Are you willing to do that? Please, for the love of God!"

"Yes, my darling child. Listen to your father. He and I want only the best for you. We love you! Haven't we always spoiled you, given you everything? We'll take care of you, Rivka. You can repent your sins, and wash them as white as snow."

Rivka looked from one to the other, her eyes wild, two bright spots of color in her cheeks.

Rose cleared her throat. "Think about it, Rivka. It is not easy being cut off from your family. I know."

"Mom?" Hannah gasped, flabbergasted.

"You have no idea what it's like to be alone like that, Hannah!"

Rivka flashed Rose an inscrutable look.

"You see, even your aunt agrees," Pearl urged her, nodding at Rose gratefully. "Come, Rivkaleh. I'll make you your favorite foods. And we'll visit with your brothers and sisters and see the children. No one has to know."

"Are you coming or not?" Zevulun broke in, gripping his knees. "Will you respect your parents' wishes after all you've put them through?"

All eyes turned to the shaken girl, who stood leaning against the wall, her eyes red, her mouth a clear, thin, determined line.

"No," she said.

There was silence.

Zevulun rose to his feet. He turned to look at her, wincing. "Better I should have heard you were dead than to see what you have become! Come, Pearl. We will go now."

"No, don't go yet," Rose begged her sister. But Pearl shook her head, following silently behind her husband. They opened the door, walking past the guard, whose arms were folded over his chest. He followed them to the elevator, riding down with them, ensuring that they left the building.

"I'll go after them," Rose said.

"What for, Aunt Rose?" Rivka asked, astonished.

"Because they didn't mean those terrible things they said. In their own way, they care about you, Rivka!"

"Who are you kidding, Mom? They are exactly the way you described your family to me years ago when I asked you why you weren't in touch. Do you remember what you said?"

"Actually, I don't."

"You said, 'To them, children aren't people. They are *nachas*-machines. And there is no warranty. Whenever they break down and stop producing things for parents to be proud of, they get thrown away. Only if they show signs they can be repaired to start working again are they let back into the house.'"

"I'm permanently broken, Aunt." Rivka smiled.

"It's not a joke, Rivka! Being permanently cut off from your family is not a joke."

The smile slowly faded from her young face. "This is not up to me, Aunt!"

"I have to agree with her, Mom. Anyhow, if there is nothing else, I have to get back to class." Hannah lied, anxious to get away. Rivka's anguished cry, "Can't a girl be a human being?" echoed inside her, more disturbing than she could bear to acknowledge . . .

She thought of the women she was researching for her thesis on nineteenth-century Jewish women's literature, women who had bolted traditional family life only to find that the enlightenment had its own brand of oppression for women, as well as no shortage of chauvinists and cads.

There was so much she wanted to say to Rivka, aside from simply venting. To laud her courage, to admit she'd done her a favor by outing Simon, to encourage her to continue fighting for herself. But they were out of each other's lives now. Wasn't it better to just leave it that way?

"So, that's it?" Rose asked, looking from her daughter to her niece. "Rivka comes home with me, and you take off? And I am left here with a problem on my hands I never wanted, and am not prepared for?"

Hannah and Rivka looked stricken.

"Aunt Rose . . ."

Rose shook her head. "You have made many bad decisions, Rivka. And now a fetus is involved, which has the potential to be a real human being. You've made the decision to abort it and throw it away. And you know what? I understand you. That's probably the easiest way out for you at this point, all things considered. But I must tell you truthfully, I can't stand the idea! I just can't stand it! And I can't look on and just let it happen."

"So, Aunt Rose, when you made your choices, which hurt so many people, that was all right? And now because it's not you, it's not all right?" Rivka cried out, deeply offended.

"I never said it was all right! I was young and stupid and selfish. I left my family holding the bag to a canceled wedding and a humiliated groom and his family. All that is true. But I never killed anyone."

"Because you were lucky . . . that's all. And I wasn't," Rivka spit out bitterly.

"Luck had nothing to do with it! I got pregnant, but I took responsibility for it, and there is a child and grandchildren in the world who are alive and flourishing because I didn't take the easy way out."

"But didn't you tell me if I asked a rabbi he would even approve of it and allow it if the fetus was injuring my mental health?"

"You told her to go to a rabbi?" Hannah asked, aghast.

"I said that was one possibility, yes! This is a moral problem and you need some moral guidance, Rivka. You should have listened to your parents and gone home with them for a while."

"You want me to suffer, is that it, Aunt? You want me to have my punishment. You are no different than my parents!"

"And you are a spoiled little brat who thinks that the world owes her something! Oh, you show up on doorsteps expecting to be taken in and sheltered and nourished. Because you come from the land of the schnorrer, a place where people don't work and expect everyone to support them and take care of them because they are so 'holy.'" Rose was furious.

"Mom, calm down!" Hannah had never seen her mother like this. "She's just a stupid kid."

"Yes, and her parents raised her that way, and now they come to me filled with complaints, calling me names! Why didn't you listen to me, Hannah? Didn't I tell you exactly what was going to happen? And now you are rushing off to school, leaving me to clean up after you! This is your mess! She never would have gotten pregnant if you hadn't taken her in and let the worthless and degenerate men you hang out with get hold of her!"

"That's your opinion of my friends? Well, gee, thanks. I never knew."

"Well, what would you call Simon?"

"He's neither of those things. Just a typical man. I'm not responsible. That's how God made them." She paused. "So, Mom, you expect me to take her back in? Is that it? Well, you can forget about it. She started this affair with Simon the day she moved in, and she did it all behind my back! She's lied to me from day one, and I'm not taking her back."

"Such a prize, this Simon! Go fight over him." Rose shook her head.

"I don't care about him! Good riddance to him! Anyway, he only developed an interest in me because of my famous mother! Like, what else is new?"

"I'm sure you're mistaken. But don't change the subject!"

"Which is?"

"It's not a question of which one of us takes her in but under what circumstances and what she plans to do from now on!"

"Well, then, why not ask her?" Hannah shouted.

Rose turned her gaze from Hannah, searching for Rivka. But she was nowhere to be found.

"Try the bathrooms, and then go outside the building and try to catch her," Rose said quickly, frightened. "I'll talk to the people in the lobby."

Hannah nodded, running out into the hall.

"John, did you see . . ."

"Your little friend? Yes, she ran out of here a few minutes ago."

"Did you see which way she went?"

He shook his head. "Can't say I noticed."

"Thanks anyway."

The streets were crowded with a lunchtime crowd looking for a place to come out of the pouring rain. Rose ran through them, searching frantically in every direction. Then, she saw her, across the street. She didn't bother going to the crosswalk or waiting for the light to turn green, crossing in the middle of traffic to the furious honks of cabdrivers.

"Got a death wish, lady?" one shouted at her.

But the moment she got close enough, she saw that it was not Rivka but a child about twelve with long blond hair. "Just a child," she murmured, filled with self-loathing, frantically trying to recall what she'd said. She couldn't remember. But my tone, my facial expression! I was awful!

Hannah was coming back down the street toward her. She was alone.

"No luck?"

She shook her head. "I even went down to the subway platform. She must have just caught a train. She could be anywhere."

Rose was devastated. "It's so wet! Where would she go? Call Simon. Maybe she went to him!"

Hannah shook her head, shivering and soaked. "Not a chance."

"Maybe she decided to go home, then?"

"Home? You mean to Pearl and Zevulun?"

Rose nodded.

"Are you prepared to call Pearl and Zevulun and ask? Because if the answer is no, they are going to flip out."

That was true.

"We could call the police."

"And tell them what? She's been missing for fifteen minutes?"

"I'd better go home, then. She might have gone there," Rose said, not believing it for a second.

"Okay, I guess I'll also stop off at my apartment and check there, too," Hannah murmured, as if she had not said all the things she'd said and that her cousin had not heard them and would be waiting at her doorstep.

"Sorry, Hannah." Rose kissed her daughter. "For everything. I'm an adult. I shouldn't have gotten so upset. It was just seeing my sister and brother-in-law after all these years. No matter what I've achieved, I'm still the lowest of the low in their eyes. I can't explain how that makes me feel."

"Don't try, Mom. It's okay. I understand. I guess we'll just have to wait."

"But if we don't hear from her by tomorrow, we'll have to call the police and her parents."

Twenty-four hours. Rivka could certainly fend for herself for that much time, couldn't she? She wasn't a cripple, or mentally deficient, or diseased, was she? Hannah thought, furious at herself, at Rivka, at Simon, at her mother's family, the long-lost, good-riddance relatives. She wasn't really worried. Rivka would simply fly into someone else's window, no?

"Yes, tomorrow," Rose reluctantly agreed.

"We'll talk later, Mom. Try not to worry. She's a big girl."

"Call me as soon as you hear from her, all right?" Rose implored.

"Sure," Hannah responded. Rivka wasn't coming back to her house, nor was she about to call. She'd bet her life on it. Where Little Bird would land next was anybody's guess.

37

It was already drizzling when Rivka reached the subway. She hurried down the steps, taking out money to buy a transit card. Twenty dollars, that's all she had in her thin wallet, she realized, money her aunt had given her the day before so she wouldn't be walking around penniless.

She hopped on the first train that came along and got off a few stops later on Forty-second Street and Sixth Avenue. She had no idea where she was going or what she was going to do. The harsh words of her parents and aunt and cousin lashed her again and again as the train swayed and rumbled through the dark subterranean passageways beneath the city's brightly lit surface.

Her stomach hurt, and her heart ached. Aunt Rose, who had been so kind to her, who had given her a camera and encouraged her! She didn't want her. She was a burden on everyone. To be free, she thought, is so expensive, so tiring. But, sooner or later, whoever pays your way has their say. The only way to be truly free was to stand on your own two feet. But how?

She walked past the kosher pizza place on Broadway and Thirty-eighth, stopping in to buy a warm, fragrant slice to stave off the insistent hunger that wracked her body day and night. She wound up buying two and washing it down with a Coke. Satiated, she thought: Where now?

Outside, the wind and rain slashed against her face, dampening her ears and nose and cheeks. She had no coat, no umbrella. She walked aimlessly, hopelessly down the streets. There was Bryant Park! And next to it, the massive entrance to the New York Public Library, with its elegant steps and stone lions. Inside, it was dry, smelling of wood and books and wet umbrellas.

She went upstairs, sitting down at a massive wood table in the main reading room. Her head felt so heavy. She leaned forward, resting it on top of her arms.

"Miss, we are closing in ten minutes," an older man said, gently tapping her arm.

"Oh, yes, thank you." Had she slept all afternoon? And now what? she thought. What am I going to do? She thought of the many people who would be happy to hear from her, happy to take her in, as long as she did whatever they wanted her to do. But she was done with that. *I'd rather die,* she thought.

She got up but hung around in the corridor, hoping she'd be able to find a quiet corner where she could spend the night, but the man who had woken her was now watching her closely, she realized.

A blast of rain hit her full in the face as she exited. She looked around her. The birds were huddled together on budding April branches, clinging to each other and sharing their warmth. But I'm alone, she thought, frightened, her hand touching the top of her rounding belly. On the crosswalk, bathed in the red glow of a traffic light, a bag lady stood wrapped in rags, her stringy gray hair tucked into three dirty woolen hats, her feet wrapped in old boots stuffed with newspapers. Behind her, she dragged a filthy beat-up shopping cart brimming over with dirty bundles.

"I have no place to go," Rivka told her.

The woman glanced up. "Oh, child," she said. "Oh, little child."

"I have no place to go," she repeated. "I am pregnant, and alone, and I have no place to go."

The woman reached out her filthy bandaged hands for Rivka's.

"Come," she said.

Gratefully, Rivka followed her.

———

Surprisingly, despite all her bravado show of complete indifference, Hannah found herself spending a sleepless night. First thing the next day, she called her mother.

"Heard anything?"

"No, nothing! I'm beside myself."

"Okay, calm down. I'll call the hospital emergency rooms . . ."

"Oh, God forbid!"

"Look, we've got to start somewhere. And then you and I will go down to the police station."

"They won't do anything! She's eighteen and she just had a fight with her family. They won't get involved. I'll have to hire a private detective."

"That's an idea, Mom. But you know first you need to call Aunt Pearl."

"I'm dreading it! I know exactly what they'll say! It will be all my fault. Again."

"But you know that's nonsense."

"Is it? I'm not so sure. I spoke as if she wasn't even in the room, like she was a piece of furniture . . . How could I do that?"

"We were both upset. I'm not particularly proud of what I said either. But you know what? We didn't say anything that wasn't true, even if it was hurtful."

"So hurtful . . ."

"I'll call you later. I want to get started."

"Bye, honey."

"Bye, Mom."

Rose hung up the phone, wringing her hands until it was positively painful. What if something *had* happened to her? It would *really* be my fault! Why wasn't I more supportive? There I was, more worried about a fetus than the human being carrying it! What right did I have to interfere with her choices? What made me do it? Rose couldn't forgive herself. But even more disturbing was the fact that she couldn't understand herself.

She wasn't one of those right-to-lifers. She'd voted a straight liberal, Democratic ticket in every election for the past forty years. She was actually in favor of giving women absolute rights over their bodies. So where was this coming from?

And then the realization struck her. She sat down heavily. She didn't think of Rivka's baby as a fetus. She had this image in her head of a beautiful little baby with a round head and soft, blond hair who had dimples and a ravishing smile, or who might even look a little like her or her precious son or daughter. Or her little sister Pearl.

It was one thing to be in favor of abortions for strangers you had never met. Quite another, she thought, when the fetus bore your genes and was your own blood.

She wanted it to live. She wanted to see that beautiful little round head and fat cheeks and dimples. She wanted to know if it had the talent to be a photographer, or a writer, or a wonderful mother. If it would like chocolate or vanilla. She wanted it to have a chance at seeing the world.

Then something else occurred to her: Rivka had once said that a child was a blessing from God. But if she had decided on an abortion, then she obviously didn't feel that way anymore. If that were true, then it broke Rose's heart to know her niece's values had been corrupted, her faith destroyed, and all under her roof! It proved true everything her family had always protested about the lifestyle she had chosen. Maybe that's where her anger at the girl had been coming from.

In any case, that didn't matter anymore. The only thing that mattered was finding Rivka and making sure she was all right.

She dialed her sister's number. Zevulun answered.

"Hello, Zevulun, I need to speak with Pearl."

"You have the chutzpah to call here, after what you've done?"

She exhaled, taking the phone away from her ear and holding it in her hand for a moment. "Please, Zevulun, this is about your daughter, and it is very, very serious."

"Serious?" His tone changed immediately, losing its confidence and anger, becoming small. "What happened to my Rivkaleh?"

"I don't know. She left the gallery soon after you did. We didn't even notice she was gone. I don't know where she is. I wanted to let you know that."

She heard him call for Pearl. His voice was desperate.

"Shoshi, what happened?"

"Pearl, I told Zevulun, and I'll tell you: I don't know. She was there one minute and gone the next."

"What did you say to her?"

Rose hesitated. "I didn't say anything *to* her; that's just it. I was speaking my mind to Hannah as if she wasn't there. I said I thought she should go home to you."

"You did? And then, what, you let her run away? How could you?"

"How could *I*? You're her mother and you walked out on her, Pearl! She's your daughter, and you allowed your husband to say to her he wished she was dead! Take some responsibility, won't you?"

She heard her sister crying. The sound broke her heart.

"Look, Pearl, can you think of anywhere she might have gone? Some friend or relative that might have taken her in?"

Pearl caught her breath, blowing her nose. "She didn't go to anyone in the family. They would have called me. Everyone knows what's going on now. After the meeting we had, we called the family and explained the situation. No one would have taken her in without calling me or Zevulun."

"Then what about her girlfriends? A teacher? A rabbi?"

"I will call them, but all these people are members of our community. No one would have taken her in without first calling us."

She has no one, Rose thought. That's why she came to Hannah, to me. To strangers. And we . . . Her stomach began to tighten into a ball of pain. "I am going to hire a private detective to find her, Pearl. Not to worry."

"God bless you. Please call me the minute you hear anything."

"Yes, of course."

"And Shoshi?"

"Yes?"

"I'm sorry for those terrible things Zevulun said. He was angry, upset. She is the joy of his life."

"You didn't agree, then?"

"No."

"Then why didn't you say something, Pearl? Why didn't you speak up? It would have meant a lot to your daughter." And to me, she thought bitterly.

"He's my husband. A woman has to follow her husband. A mother cannot teach a child to disrespect a father."

"Sometimes, Pearl, you have to break the rules."

There was a brief silence, and then Pearl said, "Sometimes, rules are all that a person has to hold on to. When you let go, you drown."

They would never agree, Rose finally accepted. "Let's hope we have another chance to talk to her soon."

"God willing!"

"Yes. Good-bye."

"Good-bye, Shoshi."

She hung up the phone and waited. As the day faded into night, the rain and thunder began in earnest, the pleasant spring weather turning unexpectedly cold. She felt sick with worry. Rivka hadn't even taken a sweater! She warmed up a little leftover soup and ate it listlessly, barely tasting it. She waited by the phone. In the late evening, it rang. It was Hannah.

"Mom, I made a dozen calls, but no one of Rivka's description matches anyone brought into a Manhattan or Brooklyn emergency room. I even called Simon. He hasn't heard anything either. I can't think of anything more to do."

There was nothing. The next stop would be the police station, and the offices of a private detective agency.

Pearl met her at the police station the next day. She seemed to have aged overnight, Rose thought, shocked, her face wrinkled and gray, dark bags edging her eyes.

The police were correct and busy. They took down the information and took a copy of the photo Rose had taken of Rivka that day in Chinatown.

"You sure she's eighteen?" the cop probed. "She looks a lot younger."

"She's been very sheltered," Pearl emphasized. "And she isn't . . . well."

"What's the medical condition?" the cop asked. He waited patiently. "Well, ladies?"

"She's pregnant," Rose finally told him.

He gave a knowing nod and a shrug, then went back to his paperwork.

"You say she has no place to go and wouldn't approach a family member for shelter?"

"We are her family. She's left her family."

"Left, or was thrown out?" the cop asked, not looking up from the form he was filling out.

No one answered.

When the silence lengthened, he lifted his head and saw the two women staring at each other with tears in their eyes.

They walked out of the police station.

"So I guess it's good-bye, then," Rose said. "I hope we'll be in touch soon with good news . . ." She turned to go.

"Shoshi!"

Rose turned back. To her astonishment, Pearl's face was bright red, her eyes swimming. She clutched Rose's hand. "Please . . . ! Can we go somewhere? I need . . . I wanted . . . to . . . talk."

Rose felt her heart beating as if she'd run a race. "There . . . I mean . . . well . . . there are no kosher restaurants around here," she stammered. "Would you agree to go into a coffee shop? You can order tea, or a Coke?"

"Yes, yes. It doesn't matter." Pearl nodded, holding on tightly to Rose's hand.

The feeling of her sister's warm skin on hers was shocking. Rose tried not to show how much it affected her, keeping pace with Pearl as they walked forward. Finally, there was a small luncheonette.

"Is this okay?"

In response, Pearl walked forward, holding open the door for her. Rose went through.

It was fairly empty. They took a quiet booth in the corner. A young waitress, pierced and tattooed, approached the table.

"Do you trust me to order?" Rose asked.

"Please," Pearl said, staring with open fascination at the girl. The girl stared back, raising an eyebrow.

"Coffee for me, unless you've got cappuccino on the menu, and a Coke for her, but don't put it into a glass, just bring a straw," she told the waitress hurriedly.

"No cappuccino and no menu," the waitress said carelessly. "One coffee and one bottle of Coke, hold the glass, coming up." She turned her back a little too swiftly, walking away.

Rose shook her head, looking after her.

"You can actually pour a cold liquid into a clean glass, you know, Rose. It's only hot coffee you can't drink out of a nonkosher cup."

"I know that. But I thought you might be stringent about it."

"So you actually remember all the laws about kosher food, hot and cold beverages . . . ?"

"It's like that commercial for Crest toothpaste they kept repeating over and over again in the sixties: 'Crest has been shown to be an effective decay-

preventive dentifrice that can be of significant value when used in a consci-
entiously applied program' et cetera, et cetera . . . It was just beaten into my
head so often, I'll probably forget my name and who my children are before
I forget certain things . . ."

"It hurts me to hear that all those things you learned as a child in our
parents' home mean as much to you as a commercial for toothpaste . . ."

"That's *not* what I meant . . . Geez. You know what? Maybe this is not
such a good idea," Rose said, digging into her pocketbook for change and
getting ready to leave.

Pearl reached out to her, squeezing her hand. "Shoshi, please! I'm sorry. I
didn't . . ."

Rose exhaled, settling back into her seat. "I expected you'd want to run
home as soon as possible."

"Why? Why would you think that?"

Rose glanced at her sideways. "After forty-odd years, you need me to
answer?"

Pearl blushed. "I'm not proud of it. So many times I wanted to call you,
to visit you . . ."

Rose's eyes widened. "Then why didn't you, Pearl? My whole life I've
been waiting for that call. Things could have been so different between us."

"You have no idea what it was like to wake up the morning of your wedding and find you gone! Mameh thought Tateh was going to have a heart
attack. She tried to call an ambulance, but he wouldn't let her . . ."

Rose bit her lip.

"And then all those phone calls! Mameh and Tateh called everyone in
the family, asking them what to do. No one knew. Some people said you'd
be back, that it often happened with a young *kallah,* that you'd come to your
senses in time for the chuppah. Only Bubbee said we should call it off, that
you wouldn't be coming home . . ."

"Ah, Bubbee." Rose nodded painfully. The old woman had known her
too well.

"One of the uncles went to speak to the boy's family. They were hysterical. They came barging into the house, made a scandal, called Tateh a
rosha . . . That's when he collapsed. That scared them, so they left. We never
heard from them again. But later, the Honored Rav called Tateh in and told
him they were asking for a huge sum of money to make up not only for their

expenses but for their shame, their loss of business. If people thought there was something wrong with their son, they said, they'd also think there was something wrong with their chopped liver. They wanted the Honored Rav to arrange for a Din Torah in a rabbinical court."

Rose felt suffocated under this overload of burdensome new information. Even though she'd imagined this—and worse—years ago, still, hearing first-person testimony like this was devastating. "What did Tateh do?"

"What could he do? He didn't have any money. As it was, he'd taken out loans for the wedding. All those matching satin dresses for Mameh and me and the granddaughters . . ."

"My own gown was rented for the day," Rose said pointedly, feeling battered. "Did Tateh go to a doctor?"

"His doctor sent him for tests to Kings County Hospital. His heart was weak, the doctors said. They warned him to be careful. Mameh went to the Honored Rav. She was desperate. I don't know what she said, but, soon after, the Honored Rav convinced the groom's father to drop his demands. He said God would bless him, his son, and his business if he showed some compassion. The Rav promised he would personally find his son a new *shidduch* and use his catering service for the shul's kiddushes for the next year. It saved Tateh and Mameh from ruin."

The Honored Rav . . . Rose exhaled. She owed him one. Or, perhaps, they were at long last even? "What was it like for you, Pearl?"

She shrugged. "It was a long time ago, Sister."

Did Pearl really need to say anything? Rose thought, a queasy ache starting in her stomach as she imagined the stares from the teachers and girls in Bais Yaakov as the news spread and Pearl became a pariah, the-sister-of-the-one-who-ran-away-the-night-before-her-wedding. "But you managed to get a good *shidduch* in the end, no?" Rose said hopefully.

"At first, the matchmakers didn't want to take me on at all. They said just mentioning my name would ruin their reputations. They said we needed to be patient, that the wound was still fresh . . ."

"But by the time you were ready to date, it must have been at least three years."

Pearl shrugged. "People in our world have long memories, Rose. Finally, someone, a cousin of one of Mameh's friends, told us about her neighbor, a widower with a small child whose wife had died—God spare us!—in childbirth. He wasn't young, or particularly learned, or wealthy, and came from a family of simple, newly religious Jews. He was in no position to be choosy, she said, and neither was I."

A flash of pain cut through Rose's stomach. "Did you like him, Pearl?"

Pearl lifted her head, looking straight into Rose's eyes. "He was a bus driver. I was twenty-two when I married, a pair of shoes left on the shelf from last season. Who was I to make demands?"

Rose choked, something reaching out for her throat and squeezing it. She tried to press her lips together, to stop herself from crying. She coughed and coughed, dabbing her mouth with a napkin.

"Are you all right?"

Rose nodded, her hand shaking as she raised the coffee cup to her lips. "It's cold!"

"And this Coke is warm."

They gave each other a small smile.

"So, is this what you wanted to speak to me about? How I ruined your life?" Rose said, trying and failing to be jocular.

"You didn't ruin *my* life! You ruined your own!"

"How dare you!" Rose asked with a flash of sudden fury. "Do I seem to you like a person with a ruined life?"

"You don't seem happy to me."

"And you're the great expert on happiness, Pearl, is that it? Your daughter obviously doesn't think so, which is why she came to me!"

Pearl looked stricken.

"Oh, I can't believe I said that. I'm sorry. It's not true!"

"Yes, it is! It's true! You were always the successful one, Rose. Our parents' pride and joy. I was always the clumsy, dumb youngest. Remember that time I wanted to make kiddush, and you wound up doing it, and everyone said how smart you were, while they sent me to my room and punished me?"

"You can't possibly remember that! You were a baby, not older than three."

"Yes, but Mameh brought it up often."

"Funny, you told Rivka a different story! Just to set the record straight: You got wine all over yourself, and I had to clean you up. Mameh whacked you and sent you off to your room, and I washed you and put you into pajamas and gave you a bottle and something to eat. When I wanted my own meal, they forced me to make it for myself because it was late and no one was left to make it for me. Otherwise, they wouldn't let me eat."

"Is that true?"

Rose nodded.

"Then I've resented you for nothing for all these years."

"You resented me? I always thought we were so close." Could it be true? Could her little sister Pearl have been filled with jealousy and resentment? And then something shocking occurred to her. "Tell me the truth, Pearl, did you make that noise on purpose when I showed you that book of photographs? Did you *want* our parents to find out and punish me?"

Pearl wrung her hands, twisting her wedding and engagement rings around her finger. "Do you know how many times I've asked myself that question? The truth is, I don't know. Maybe. Remember how I wanted you to walk me to school and you wouldn't ? The year before, a man looking like a Hassid had tried to drag me into the alley when I was playing in front of the house. I couldn't tell anyone. I was terrified to walk to school alone. And you refused to help me."

Rose leaned back, shocked. "I never knew!"

"I know that! And I couldn't tell you! But I wanted you to keep taking care of me, and instead you started high school; you started your own life. Maybe I wanted to punish you. But when they sent you away to Bubbee's, I realized I'd gone too far. I felt like a *rosha*. I stopped eating. *That* got Mameh's attention. And then—I'm ashamed to even say it—I got used to being spoiled, to being the center of attention. I was suddenly their princess. I didn't want that to change."

"And once I was out of the way, you were able to take over the crown permanently, right?" Rose said, the knowledge dawning on her like increments of light seeping through a curtain being slowly pulled up before a rising sun.

"Yes, and how I suffered for it! You have no idea. It was a terrible thing."

"Oh, my God! In what way?"

"To be responsible for all your parents' happiness? To live with two people so damaged that you could never even dream of doing a single, little thing that might upset them, or be looked at as rebellious or less than perfect? Your freedom cost me mine."

Rose was speechless. Then, slowly she lifted her head, looking straight into her sister's eyes. "Well, you started it all, my dear Pearl. Maybe if they hadn't sent me to Bais Ruchel, I might be sitting here next to you with a wig on."

"Neither of us would be sitting *here,* believe me."

Rose suddenly smiled. "Well, that would have been a real tragedy, Sister, now wouldn't it?"

Pearl laughed, lifting up her bottle of warm Coke and clinking it against Rose's cold coffee cup.

"Tell me the truth, Rose, what kind of a life did you wind up having? Have you really been happy? Has your life been what you hoped it would be?"

"Rivka asked me the same question."

"And what did you tell her?"

"I have no complaints. For the most part, I've been happy."

"I've read about all your material successes. But you don't eat kosher anymore? You ride in cars on the Sabbath? Eat bread on Passover? You don't daven or say a *brachu* on your food? Have you really found happiness living like a goy?"

Rose was stunned by the directness of her attack, which hit her in so many vulnerable places. "I've found happiness living my own life, the life I've chosen, Pearl. It's no one's business, certainly not yours," Rose said harshly, her heart aching.

Why not tell her how much you've struggled? Admit the first time you turned on a light during the Sabbath, you felt sick, the first time you ate ham, you threw up? But admit, too, that once you succumbed, it got easier to live that way, and impossible to admit you still believed in a God who had nonnegotiable demands, because believing that would have led you straight back to Williamsburg.

"What about you, Pearl? Have you been happy?"

"I've also had many blessings."

"Even though you were forced to marry a man you didn't love?"

"Why would you say something like that? However my *shidduch* came about, God blessed me with a good man, a righteous, kind, and generous man, a person with a loving heart."

"Could've fooled me."

"You don't know anything about him! What you've seen and heard is a stranger to me and to himself, a father crazy with grief for the dearest thing in his life, his precious daughter, his *bas zekunim*!"

"You love each other?"

"I never regretted my marriage for a moment. This was God's plan for me, Rose, and you helped bring it about," she said sincerely.

How generous, Rose thought, her heart contracting. If the situation were reversed, I would never, ever have forgiven her. Never.

"And what about your husband, Rose?"

"Husbands. I wasn't as lucky as you, apparently. The first time, anyway." She was silent for a few moments, studying the dark dregs at the bottom of her cup. "Raphael, my first husband, was someone I met in the park. He wasn't Jewish. All we ever talked about was politics. He was a radical social-ist determined to save the world, involved in a million organizations. That left him very little time to help me out, even when I was pregnant. He be-lieved in women's rights, just not his wife's. He thought my photography was a hobby and I should be spending my time vacuuming and typing up his political screeds. Any success I had was *in spite* of him."

"Sounds not so different from the groom you ran away from, no?"

"What?" Rose had never thought of that. The irony of it astounded her. "Well, I left him, too."

"So, you were alone with a small child . . ."

"Yes, but I was happy. My clients were sending me more and more jobs, and my reputation was growing. I began to work on my second book."

"You married again, no? Hannah's father?"

"Yes. Henry. And he was Jewish, just not very traditional. He was like me, a person who took risks, loved life. He loved me and our children . . ." To her horror, she felt the grief welling up inside her, unstoppable. She wiped her eyes. "I was widowed after only ten years of marriage. It was a terrible time for me and the kids."

"I'm so sorry! I didn't know. What happened to him?"

"He was a news photographer, and he was shot by some of the worst, most evil men imaginable. He gave his life to help some kids. It was like him."

"Were you angry?"

"What? Angry?"

"That he went off to a war, got himself killed . . ." Pearl said innocently.

"Got himself killed?" Rose felt the fury rising inside her. But then she

looked at Pearl's honest distress. She hadn't meant any harm. It was just the way she thought. A man going off like that to pursue his life without his family was utterly incomprehensible to her. "I *was* angry, but not at him. I wondered why God had done this to me. If it was some kind of payback, a punishment."

"You may have used your subway token to take your body out of Williamsburg, but if you can think that, your mind and soul are still there, Sister." Pearl shook her head sadly. "Even I don't think like that anymore. Tragedies happen, sometimes to very good people who have lived pious, generous lives. God is there to help us through them."

"Wow!" Rose nodded. "I really didn't expect to ever hear that from you. We weren't brought up to think that way."

"I also chose my own way in certain things. When I asked you about your life, I wasn't judging you . . ."

"I'm sorry I got mad. I'm so confused about so many things. I once read this story about Chaim Grade—a famous Yiddish writer who was even better than Isaac Bashevis Singer. Anyhow, Grade was teaching a course on literature at Hunter College. He had an ultra-Orthodox student in his class. Gradually over the year, the student changed, showing up first without his black suit, then shaving off his beard, and finally getting rid of his skullcap. One day, Grade pulled him aside: 'You can do anything you want,' Grade told him, 'but you'll never enjoy it.' That's a little bit how I feel."

Pearl shook her head. "I hope you don't think this makes me happy."

"Doesn't it?"

"I don't know if you'll believe me, Rose, but I always hoped and prayed you'd enjoy your life. That would have meant that at least everything the family went through had a purpose!"

Could she possibly mean that? Rose wondered, disoriented. "What was it you wanted to talk to me about, Pearl?" she said hurriedly to hide her confusion.

"Isn't it obvious?"

"Not to me."

"Why did my Rivkaleh leave us? What did Zevulun and I do wrong? What did our *mameh* and *tateh* do wrong . . . ?"

Rose gripped her empty cup tightly. "I'm not sure if I can point to any one thing. I'm not even sure that if all the things I resented had never happened I wouldn't have wound up in the same place. Maybe that's true of Rivka as well. I can't say. Because, you see, there is one thing our world doesn't and has never understood: Freedom. The right of every person to choose. In our world, the rebbes and parents and teachers think they can rub out the desire for freedom with scary stories and excommunications, but they will never succeed. You can't take that desire from a person. We are born with it; it's God-given."

"We know that! We only try to help our children make the right choices," Pearl protested.

"No. You don't. You try to convince them that there is only one right choice, that which was decided for them on the day they were born, even the day they were conceived."

Pearl was silent. "We're not like you. We love our lives. We love the small, good, perfect world where we were brought up. We never want to leave it."

"Yes, that's what they want you to believe. And they are very good at making you believe it's your choice."

"That's not fair."

"What's not fair is the idea that if a child opens a book and sees a photograph, you throw him out of the house."

"It was the Honored Rav's idea."

"*They* were my parents, not him."

"They thought they were doing the best for you."

"They were wrong."

"And you never made any mistakes bringing up your children?" Pearl lashed out.

Rose was silent. So many mistakes! Too many to count.

She had left her children more or less to fend for themselves, telling herself that the long photographic assignments in faraway places, the month-long speaking tours, had not affected her kids too much, that they had learned by example to be independent and fearless people. But every once in a while, she got an unwelcome glimpse into their hidden reserves of anger and resentment. Jonathan had married a girl from Wales and moved to faraway London. She hardly saw him. And Hannah often said things like, "It's not like I don't know how to take care of myself, Mom" or, "Motherhood is a part-time job, right, Mom?"

She too had tried to lead them into living the kind of lives she approved of. Every parent did. "Like I said, I'm not sure it made a difference in the end. I wanted a certain kind of life, different from the one they envisioned for me. The same is true of Rivka. I'm sure she loves you and Zevulun. She's young, confused, ashamed. Believe me, I tried to get her to go home to you . . . I think maybe that's why she ran away."

"Now she has no one," Pearl moaned, clutching her hands. "May God protect her."

"She's smart, and she's good. She'll be all right," Rose said hopefully, shaking inside with the knowledge that neither one of those qualities could really keep the girl safe.

"That's all I want. For her to be safe, for her life to be good. Even if she doesn't want the kind of life I've chosen. I don't agree with Zevulun. I don't even think *he* really meant what he said. I'm her mother. I'll love her no matter what. The way our mother and father loved you."

"Wish for something better for her than that! Mameh and Tateh wanted nothing to do with me after the police got involved."

"That's not true! Every Friday night, Tateh said a blessing for you and Mameh answered amen, until the day he died."

Rose felt the door to that empty room inside her suddenly swing open. It was filled with treasured memories she had not visited in decades. "I had no idea."

"But now you know," Pearl answered, sipping the last drops of liquid from the bottle, then getting up to leave. She opened her purse and left some money on the table.

"Please," Rose said, handing it back to her and laying down some bills.

"Thank you, Shoshi," Pearl said.

They walked out into the street. The late-afternoon light was gold with sunset, turning Pearl's matronly wig the color of the hair she had once had as a little girl. She was still beautiful, Rose thought. Just like her daughter. Rose reached out hesitantly, touching her shoulder. "Take care of yourself, Sister."

Pearl suddenly turned. Burying her head in Rose's shoulder, she wept.

38

New York University Campus, April 2011

Hannah sat in the NYU library, mesmerized by the photo on the book cover in front of her: the young, pretty face; the sad, searching eyes; the nineteenth-century dress. With a shock, Hannah suddenly realized it reminded her of Rivka.

That had happened often in the last three years. The back of the head of a blonde in the far end of a subway car, a *People* magazine with Reese Witherspoon on the cover, or simply any woman in a midcalf skirt. For some reason, it had happened much more frequently when Simon was still around. But since he'd left school—a year before graduation—the sightings had somehow grown fewer.

Like Rivka, no one knew what had happened to Simon either. Rumor had it that he had gone to India to study meditation, while others said he had joined his father's clothing factory, starting at the bottom. Presumably, that meant he would now be loading boxes or shoving racks. The idea charmed her.

She turned the pages. The book was called *To Reveal Our Hearts,* by Carole B. Balin, and contained a number of fascinating biographical sketches of Jewish women writers in czarist Russia. It was a real find, filled with the rare, fascinating writings of nineteenth-century Jewish women rebels, and dealt with issues that never got old. They'd waged quite a battle, taking aim at their society's most cherished and accepted norms. One of them, Hava Shapiro, had written: "A Jewish woman must stifle her own feelings a thousand times . . . whereas a Gentile woman is capable of drawing near to that which she loves [the Jewish woman] must sacrifice her soul and her freedom." Indeed, she went on to say, "ambitious and intelligent women often don't fit in anywhere, winding up . . . disillusioned dreamers . . . odd old maids . . . [or pathetic] . . . loners."

She'd found these words chillingly relevant.

She'd been resolutely single ever since the relationship with Simon had ended, paralyzed by the idea of making another terrible mistake. But to have a relationship was to take chances. There was never any guaranteed armor against heartbreak. She wondered if Rivka was in the same boat, and wondered, too, if she would ever find out.

Despite the best efforts of a very, very expensive detective, they had not been able to find her. It was as if she'd evaporated or been beamed up by aliens. At first, there had been some hope, her name appearing on the rolls of a city drop-in center for homeless women the very day she'd disappeared. But by the time they went over there, her name had disappeared, and so had she. From then on, her tracks had more or less been erased, like footsteps on the shoreline.

The girl had made so many stupid mistakes! Still, her heart went out to her cousin. Poor Rivka! Misunderstood and condemned by everyone she knew, wandering around looking for a niche in which to live her own life, flitting from one branch to the next, determined to be herself, without even knowing who that "self" was!

She had long regretted how their relationship ended, all those things she'd said and felt. While the Simon part of it had long ago become irrelevant, what still rankled was her cousin's underhandedness, her betrayal of trust. All of Simon's faults could not erase Rivka's choices to behave in the way she did.

Often, Hannah had tried to come up with exculpatory explanations to erase even that: Perhaps Rivka had simply been ashamed of her feelings for Simon? Admitting desire was never easy for women. It was always supposed to be the men who were the pursuers, the seducers. A woman cast in that role was always a villainess and a wanton. Maybe the girl simply couldn't face openly what she was planning to do?

In time, Hannah even admitted that she herself was far from blameless. After all, how could Rivka have known about her secret feelings for Simon, feelings, she now understood, that had been based on ignorance and fertilized by mystery, allowing them to bloom into an infatuation?

Her cell phone, set on vibrate, began to shake. She took it out, looking at the number. Her mother. She gathered her notes and exited the reading room, leaving the book behind on the table, where she planned to return to it soon.

"You'll never guess!" Rose said exultantly.

"Gee, Mom, you sound happy for a change. I'll never guess what?"

"The Metropolitan Museum of Art has acquired forty-three of my photographs and is inaugurating a permanent exhibition!"

Hannah was speechless. All she could say when she finally caught her breath was, "Wow! Which photographs? No, forget it. I don't even have to ask. The photos from Jerusalem."

After spending a year trying to find Rivka, her mother had finally shaken off a deep depression, traveling the globe again. She'd spent a year in Israel and a year in Jordan. The photos of women in Meah Shearim, Bnei Brak, and Amman had been hailed by critics as a triumphant return from her hiatus and praised as her best work ever.

Hannah had had mixed feelings about that. To her, the photos looked like one long search for Rivka. "I'm so happy for you, Mom. You absolutely deserve it."

"Can you put the date of the opening down on your calendar?"

"Wait a sec. Let me just get a pen." She opened her day planner, cradling the phone between her neck and chin: "Shoot."

"The exhibit will be running the whole month, starting on June sixth. The gala is that evening. Get a cocktail dress and bring a boyfriend in a tux."

"The former is possible and likely, the latter is neither."

"I'm sorry to hear that."

"Well, Mom, I've got work to do. Talk to you later." Her mother's words rankled. When she went back to her cubicle in the reading room, the book was gone.

Damn it!

She looked around the table and underneath it and on either side.

"I'm sorry, but are you looking for this?"

He was tall and very slim, with sandy-brown hair and gray-blue eyes that were bright and intelligent. He had a small trimmed beard and a mustache that looked very nineteenth-century, or very cool, depending on how you looked at such things.

"Yes, thank you."

"I saw it lying here and wasn't sure you were coming back."

"Do you need it?"

"No, no. I've got it at home. I was just looking something up. Wonderful book. If this kind of material interests you, I can recommend a few others."

"This kind of material?"

"Oh, um, Jewish women writers of the enlightenment. You know, in Hebrew there is no word for enlightened women, only enlightened men: *maskil.* But now there is a whole group of mostly female scholars who have discovered numerous overlooked women writers, poets, and essayists who were enlightened intellectuals that participated fully in the renaissance of Jewish writing and political movements of the nineteenth century. They've even invented a term for them: *maskilot.*"

Someone shushed him.

"I'm sorry," he whispered. "We'd better go outside."

She followed him out of the building, suddenly noticing the skullcap on the back of his head.

"I haven't introduced myself. I'm David Adler. I'm a doctoral student in Hebrew literature."

"Here?" She had no idea NYU had such a program.

"No. Harvard. But I did my master's here at Skirball. When I come in from Boston to see my dad, I like to use the library here."

"I'm just a lowly first-year master's student in the history department, concentrating on women's studies. My name is Hannah Weiss Gordon." She looked for a flicker of recognition, an intake of breath that would precede, "Ah, the famous photographer's daughter!"

There wasn't any.

He put out his hand.

She smiled, taking it. "So, you shake hands with women?"

He laughed, adjusting his skullcap. "Whenever I have the pleasure and opportunity," he said. "So, what are you researching?"

"I'm fascinated by early women writers of Hebrew."

His eyes went wide with surprise. "Me too! I actually fell into this whole subject. I was working on a translation of Yehuda Leib Gordon's poem 'Tip of the Letter Yud,' trying to understand where his feminism and support for women came from. That opened up the door to his correspondence with the writer Miriam Markel-Mosessohn, and then I just started researching the rest of these women writers. I have boundless admiration for them! First, the men denied them an education out of piety. And then, when women managed to educate themselves, they refused to recognize their talents.

"I have a special place in my heart for the writer Sarah Foner. When other writers of the enlightenment were throwing their faith out the window, she didn't understand why a person couldn't be enlightened and devout; why secular and sacred knowledge couldn't coexist peacefully. Too bad so many of her writings have been lost."

"I actually came across something about her on the Internet," Hannah said. "I think her great-grandnephew, Morris Rosenthal, has published her writings in translation."

"I've read his book! But he only has the first half of her novel—the first one a woman ever wrote in the Hebrew language. The second half apparently never got published because some enlightened hotshot-male-chauvinist critic blasted it so badly." He shook his head. "She died in nineteen thirty-six in Pittsburgh. I wish I could find out what happened to her papers and manuscripts."

"Yes, so do I!"

"Well, I have actually been doing a bit of research on that subject . . ."

"Really . . . ?"

They found their way to an off-campus coffee shop.

"You said you came in to visit your dad?"

"My mom died a few years back, and he took it very hard. He tends to be a bit of a recluse. He's an archaeologist and not in the country for months on end, so whenever he gets back to New York, I make it a point to come see him."

"I lost my dad when I was ten. My mom is also never home."

They talked nonstop, until the light outside faded and hours passed without their even feeling it. Finally, she looked up.

"I can't believe the time!"

Her words seemed to jog him out of some trance. He looked startled as he glanced at his watch. "It can't have been that long!" He smiled. "And I have so much more I wanted to talk to you about . . ."

"When are you going back to Boston?" she asked, feeling suddenly shy.

"Monday morning. Perhaps we could meet Saturday night, and then again on Sunday . . . ?"

They smiled at each other.

He paid the check, then held open the door for her.

She felt a small "ping" in her heart as she walked beside him, their arms gently brushing against each other.

"To be continued . . ." she said as they reached the subway entrance.

"Here, take my card."

"You have a card?"

He chuckled. "My niece had this project in Hebrew school to raise money for some charity or other by selling business cards, and she talked me into ordering them for myself. Look at the title."

She laughed. It said, DAVID ADLER: BUTCHER, BAKER, CANDLESTICK MAKER.

She tore some paper from a notebook, writing down her number. He studied it, then took out his cell phone and jabbed it in. "I tend to lose papers," he said. "I wouldn't want to lose this."

She actually blushed.

39

Metropolitan Museum of Art, New York City, June 6, 2011

The gala opening of her exhibition at the Metropolitan Museum of Art was a glittering affair. Everyone Rose had ever known in the business was there: every important photographer, all her late husband's journalist friends, all the people who had helped her and supported her along her difficult journey surrounded her with love, cheering her achievements in a meaningful way.

As she wandered around the crowded hall, she felt humbled by the accolades and excited by the interest and appreciation in the eyes of all those beholding her latest work. There *was* something special about this collection, she acknowledged. Far from being carbon copies of each other, the faces of the women with Muslim and Jewish head coverings and modest dresses were cast in fine relief by the sameness of their dress, the very drabness and uniformity of their outfits making the individuality in their eyes and expressions stand out that much more clearly: the struggle of the new Haredi mother to get a carriage on a crowded bus, the hands reaching out to help her; the suspicious stare of the pious matron guarding her world from outsiders; the natural curiosity of a charming toddler covered up in tights and a long skirt. The Muslim schoolgirls deep in avid conversations on a Jordanian bus. There were no clichés here, she thought. Each person was a world unto herself, a special world, a secret world, which each photo pried open like an oyster just enough to give the viewer a true glimpse of the beauty that rested within. It was her best work ever.

"Hi, Mom."

"Hannah!" She hugged her, then pulled back, looking her over appreciatively. Her dress was lovely, sparkling with black sequins that shone as delicately as the evening sky. "You look beautiful."

"Mom, this is David."

Rose looked him over, pleasantly surprised. He was nothing like Hannah's usual choice in men. He looked clean, studious, and respectable in his tweed jacket with the leather elbow patches. For some reason, she was glad he hadn't worn a tuxedo. It showed character.

"And this is his father, Joseph."

"I'm delighted to meet you, Mrs. Gordon. I'm embarrassed to say that as an absentminded-professor type, I'd never heard of your work. The exhibition is a marvel."

He was a tall man with a shock of graying hair and blue eyes that were searching and intelligent. He looked distinguished and cosmopolitan in his dark suit.

"Thank you so much! I'm always happy to make new fans. Would you excuse me a minute?"

She took Hannah over to a corner. "What are you doing!"

"Dr. Adler is an archaeologist and a professor at Sarah Lawrence," Hannah said, trying and failing not to sound like Yenta the Matchmaker. "He's a widower, loves to travel . . ."

Rose shook her head. "I don't believe this." But then she smiled. "And this David of yours, is it serious?"

She blushed. "I hope so."

Rose leaned over and kissed her as they returned to the two men.

"Please, won't you both have some wine?"

"They only eat kosher food, and the wine here isn't kosher," Hannah said, sounding not only respectful, but knowledgeable.

It was then Rose noticed the skullcaps. She expected to cringe, but, instead, a strange calm washed over her.

"But you can have the cocktails. Liquor doesn't have the same restrictions as wine, right? I know all about *kashrus*." She smiled, saying the word with a heavy Yiddish inflection. "I've had an interesting past, you see."

"I look forward to an opportunity to discuss it with you, Mrs. Gordon," Joseph said sincerely, extending his hand.

She stared at it, startled. It was large and brown and worn, covered with rough patches and tiny scars.

"Please, call me Rose," she said, placing her hand in his and smiling back shyly, also sincere.

She hugged Hannah again, before being overtaken and inundated by her hostess/star duties for the rest of the evening.

The next day, wanting to view the photos again in peace and quiet, she headed down to the exhibit in the late afternoon, after the lunchtime visitors had left and before the scheduled tour of the docent. In front of the photo of a little girl with smiling, curious eyes stood a young woman with thick, shoulder-length blond hair.

Rose held her breath. She had been disappointed so many times in the past, her longing and guilt providing so many mirages and false leads, each ending in heartbreak. But as she took some tentative steps forward, the woman turned around to face her.

"Aunt Rose!" Rivka said, smiling.

Rose stared at her silently. The face was the same, but the eyes were older now, the mouth firmer and less vulnerable. The long hair had been cut, but not shorn. She no longer looked like a child. She wore dark pants pilling at the cuffs and a worn pink sweater.

"Rivka? Is that really you?"

"Yes, it's me." Her smile was joyous.

Rose felt herself drowning in complex emotions that made her heart beat faster and her throat ache as she held back tears of anger and gratitude. "We've looked everywhere for you for years."

"Really?" She seemed genuinely surprised. "Why?"

"How can you even ask that! Because we were worried sick! Because we felt responsible."

"I guess sometimes a person can't make a right decision that will please everyone. I thought for certain my leaving would be a big relief to you and Hannah, and even my parents. Anyhow, I took all those things you said to me in your office that morning to heart, especially the part about me taking responsibility for myself. You were so right."

Rose felt her anger drain. "If you only knew how many times I've played that conversation over in my head, wishing with all my heart I had kept my mouth shut!"

"But why, Aunt Rose? You only said the truth. I was a spoiled brat, living in a dream world where I could break things and someone else would paste them back together for me. I was rebelling, but I wasn't willing to pay the price for it. You were very kind to me, as was Hannah. I had to grow up sometime."

"So, where are you living? What are you doing?" Rose asked, reaching out to touch her, still half in shock, afraid she'd disappear.

"I live in Brooklyn, in one of those apartments that haven't been fixed up since nineteen ten, when the greeners moved in straight from Ellis Island." She laughed. "But the street is slowly getting *farpootzt*."

Rose smiled. "I think the word is 'gentrified.'"

"That too. They have these little boutiques selling overpriced *schmattes*, and bars and coffeehouses. I waitress in one of them. Tuesday afternoons I have off. I like to go to the city and look around like when I was a teenager." She opened her huge handbag. "I bought myself a camera. It's old, but very good." She handed it to Rose.

It was a vintage Nikon without any automatic settings. "I haven't seen one of these for years," Rose marveled. "How did you learn how to use it?"

"I worked in a photo store for a while, you know, feeding those machines that print out digital photos. But the owner used to be a real photographer. He was the one who sold me the camera and showed me how to use it. He passed away a few months ago, and the store shut down . . ."

"So, you've been taking photographs?"

"Yes."

"I'd love to see them."

"Would you?" Her face lit up.

Rose nodded, sincere.

Rivka hesitated. "That would be great, but listen, Aunt Rose, you have to promise me that if I give you my address, you won't tell my parents where I am."

"They don't know you're back in New York?"

She shook her head. "And I'd like to keep it that way."

"Are you sure?"

"I'm positive."

So, there wasn't going to be a happy ending then after all, Rose thought, the family coming together and accepting each other with unconditional love. But at least there would be some kind of resolution. "I promise not to pass on this information without your permission. I do speak to your mom off and on, you know. I won't lie to you. It's going to be excruciatingly painful to have to keep this a secret from your parents, knowing how happy it would make them."

"I get that," she answered stoically and without further explanation or apology, taking out a pen and writing down her address. "Next Tuesday would be best, at about two o'clock?"

"I'm looking forward to it," Rose said, taking the note and studying the girl's hands, once so soft and tender. Now they were red, work-roughened, the once-manicured nails chipped and stained, the cuticles raw. The sight of them filled Rose with sadness.

"Can I bring Hannah with me?" she added as an afterthought. "I know she'd love to see you. She has a new boyfriend. He wears a skullcap."

"Really?" Rivka said, her eyebrows arching in surprise.

"She didn't speak another word to Simon from the day you left. He dropped out of school, by the way. No one really knows why or where he is now."

She shrugged indifferently, then changed the subject. "Aunt Rose, I have nothing against Hannah, but can we keep this first meeting just between the two of us?"

"Of course, of course, whatever you say . . ." Rose answered, disappointed. "Can I at least tell her I've seen you? She's also spent years worrying."

"Of course. But I'm not sure she and I should meet just yet. It's complicated." She glanced at her watch. "Oh, it's so late. I've got to run."

"I thought this was your day off?"

"It is, but I have other . . . obligations. I'll see you next week?"

"Absolutely. Good-bye, my dear. It's *so* good to see you."

The phone call to Hannah was short, filled with exclamation points, and ending in disappointment.

"You mean she's still angry at me, after all this time?" Hannah asked, wounded.

"She said specifically that she's not! She just said she wasn't sure about meeting you *right now.* I suppose it's a bit overwhelming for her. That doesn't mean she never wants to see you again."

"But why you and not me?"

"Because I'm the photographer, and I think she's looking forward to a professional opinion about her work."

"And I, on the other hand, can't offer her anything. Doesn't sound to me like any radical character transformation has taken place, Mom."

"Don't be so harsh! She looked poor, as if she's been working very hard and earning very little. I'm sure she's not the same girl."

"Well, take in everything. I expect a full report when you get back."

"Will do my best."

40

Brooklyn, New York, June 14, 2011

Rose looked out into the run-down street from inside the taxi, putting the strap of her purse protectively around her neck and slipping her arm around it before exiting. But when she actually stood on the pavement, the street seemed surprisingly benign.

The buildings were old but not particularly graffiti-scarred. Scattered among the run-down bodegas and dusty luncheonettes were charming little coffee shops and tiny boutiques selling trendy clothing. Young women pushed baby carriages, and men of every ethnic shade were dressed as if they were busy with some kind of useful employment. She relaxed, taking out the paper on which she had written Rivka's address.

She walked up the cracked but well-swept stoop. No security system was in place, she noted apprehensively as she pulled open the massive old lobby doors. Inside, cracking, uneven floor tiles from another century gave the place a colorful antique ambience. The walls were grimy, but not criminally scarred with slogans and obscenities, which might have frightened her enough to turn around and leave. Instead, she searched without much hope for an elevator before beginning her long trek to the fifth floor.

The name on the door was written on a piece of paper taped just beneath the peephole. It said WEISS-GONZALES. *Oh God, what now?* went through her head.

Rivka opened the door. Her hair seemed to shine with its own light in the dark apartment as she ushered Rose over the threshold. A cursory glance showed she was wearing the same frayed pants and sweater.

"You found me!" she exulted, pleased.

The place was tiny. In one corner Rose glimpsed a kitchen consisting of two parallel walls just far enough apart for a slim person to stand in sideways. It had a stained sink, an old stove, and an ancient refrigerator—all pushed together like subway passengers during rush hour. In the living room, a couch covered with a colorful African-print throw stood against the wall. Completing the "decor" was an old armchair in frayed fake leather that reminded her of Hannah's cushionless sofa, and a coffee table that consisted of a round piece of glass over an old porcelain elephant that had seen better days. The only other piece of furniture was a cheap, fragile bookcase whose shelves sagged beneath an eclectic collection in Hebrew and English: novels, biology textbooks, a prayer book, a Bible. The main decorations, as far as Rose could tell, were the walls, which were literally covered with photographs so closely hung that the wall color itself was almost impossible to discern.

"I see you've got your own gallery. It's quite a collection!"

Rivka smiled with shy pride.

Rose walked up close, studying them. There was a beggar woman on Broadway, the complicated road map of her life traced across her old face in a hundred telling lines. There was a shadow that fell across the lawn of Central Park like a picnic blanket, shielding two lovers holding hands. And here and there and everywhere, there was a baby, and then a toddler with dark, curly hair, light eyes, and a winning smile.

It was the same child, she realized, feeling suddenly dizzy. She sat down heavily on the couch. "Rivka, would you be kind enough to bring me a glass of water, please?" She gulped it down quickly, wiping the beads of perspiration from her forehead, the feeling of faintness slowly giving way to an urgent question: "Who is he, the child?"

"Isn't that obvious?" Rivka shook her head, sitting down beside her. "He's my son."

"Your son?" Rose repeated stupidly. "So you never went through with it, the abortion?"

"I never changed my mind. But my body refused to cooperate."

"I don't understand."

"I was actually on the table getting prepped when I suddenly felt this thing . . . It was like I'd swallowed a bag of cats that were trying to punch their way out with their tiny paws. They told me it couldn't be real; it was way too early to feel the baby move. They said I was imagining it. But after that, I couldn't think about the abortion as if it was some tumor that had to be cut out. It was too late . . . too late."

"Rivka, where did you go?"

"First, some horrible drop-in center in the Bronx where bag ladies go on rainy days. And from there to this home, a place for what they call 'unwed mothers.' I looked through the *Yellow Pages* for a Jewish home but couldn't find one. In the end, I went to a Christian place. They were fanatic about privacy. We were all registered under the names of saints. I was Saint Agatha! Their shame issues are even worse than the Jews! Anyhow, there were lots of crosses everywhere with poor little Jesuses suffering away. I ended up eating mostly vegetarian food. Once in a while, someone told me 'to feel Jesus's mercy.' You know what? I honestly tried! I was willing to take any kind of mercy I could get at that point. But I didn't feel anything, except . . . I . . . just felt like I was on one of those people conveyer belts that move you around in airports that don't let you get off in the middle. You have to run ahead or force yourself to go backwards to leave. I didn't have energy for either! So I just went along, waiting for God to let me off."

"You had the baby," Rose repeated gratuitously, still trying to process that information.

"Yes, I did. The labor took two hours and twenty minutes, record time for a first birth, everyone said. The doctor and the midwives joked I was the type who could have a dozen, one after the other, with no problem. I wanted to tell them that the women in my family did exactly that and there was nothing funny about it! I guess those fertility genes got passed down to me, too. Funny, isn't it? You can't run away from biology."

Rose hung her head in shame that her niece had gone through all this completely alone. She couldn't even bring herself to ask: Why didn't you call us? The answer was too clear. It was as if she were looking at herself forty years ago. "I'm . . . so . . . very, very sorry, Rivka, and so very ashamed that I let you down. Can you ever forgive me?"

She seemed amazed. "*You're* sorry? As my friends in the home used to say, 'Jesus, Mary, and Joseph!' Why should *you* be sorry? You were very kind to me, Aunt. You are a world-famous photographer, a person who brings truth and beauty to the world. And who was I? A stranger, a mixed-up kid from a family that had rejected you and thrown you out, who suddenly landed on your doorstep, demanding you take risks and expose yourself to even more abuse. And you did. You went through tons of holy crap—oh, sorry, that's also some of the other new words I learned there—all for my sake. No, no, I'm the one who's sorry."

How generous she is, Rose thought. I am not so generous to those who were unkind to me when I needed them. I will hold a grudge against every single one of them until the day I die. And yet I behaved no better to my own flesh and blood. "You are a good person, Rivka, you know that?"

The girl shook her head. "The jury is still out on that one."

"Where is he?"

"Who?"

"Your child."

"Or?"

"Or what?"

She laughed. "No, that's his name. I called him Or, which is the Hebrew word for 'light.' He's in daycare."

"Why didn't you give him up for adoption?"

"I thought about that before he was born, but never after. All my longing to be myself, to create a world of my own, and here it was, in this little creature, this little world that belonged only to me. I couldn't give him away any more than I could donate my heart to someone who needed it. I needed him more than anyone did."

"But how did you manage, all alone, with a new baby?"

She pinched her lips together, gnawing on them, then sighed. "You do what you have to do. When the good Christian ladies at the home finally gave up on talking me into signing him away for adoption or converting me, they put me in touch with social workers and city services and Jewish charities. I got some rent money and a few dollars for furniture and baby supplies. I found a job. And then I saw this ad on Craigslist for 'a spacious one bedroom, prewar'—I guess they were thinking of the Civil War!—'apartment thirty minutes from Manhattan.'"

Rose got up, looking around, peeking into the bedroom off the corridor. It had a bed and a child's cot stuffed inside with hardly room to squeeze by between them. But it was neat, with a matching ecru and rose bedspread and curtains and a few crowded shelves of plush animals and toys.

"Not much privacy."

"No. But thankfully my son and I get along," she laughed. "I don't expect to live here forever. I passed my GEDs last year, and now I'm enrolled at Hunter College. I go three nights a week."

"It shows."

"Really?"

"The last time we spoke, you would have said: 'Three nights a week I go.'"

They both laughed.

"Do you still want to be a doctor?"

She shook her head with a grin. "I've grown up a lot since last we met. But I'd like to be a medical technician. It pays good, I mean well, and you get to help people."

Rose cocked her head, incredulous. "And on top of school you work and take care of the baby?"

"Do I have a choice?" Rivka answered, her voice at once both challenging and resigned.

"And who watches him?"

"He's in a free daycare center during my working hours. And at night, I have a friend who helps babysit."

"A friend?"

"Okay, a boyfriend."

"Gonzales?"

Rivka looked puzzled, then broke out in a wide grin. "No, she's in Brazil. This is a sublet. Her mail still comes here, though."

Rose exhaled. "Tell me about him."

"He's like me. We met at the apartment of this girl who runs an organization for people like us."

"Like you?"

"Runaways from Haredi families. She got some funding. She runs GED classes, drop-in centers. We're all in the same boat: no education, no family, no place to live, no jobs, no contacts. We help each other."

"Does your boyfriend live with you?"

"No. I don't want Or to see that kind of life. I want to be very, very sure before I commit myself to a man next time."

"Do your parents know about Or?"

"No."

Rose thought of Pearl and Zevulun, pitying them for their terrible loss. "Rivka, can't you forgive them, the way you've forgiven me?"

"I told you, Aunt, with you there is nothing to forgive. But with them . . . it's complicated." She wandered around the apartment, studying the photos of her son, touching them, smiling here and there. For a long time, she said nothing. Then, she turned around and faced her aunt.

"It's not anger, Aunt Rose. I just can't risk them knowing about us. Remember Yossele Schumacher?"

It happened in 1960, but the Jewish world was still reeling from the story. Yossele Schumacher was a six-year-old boy kidnapped from his secular Jewish parents in Israel by his ultra-Orthodox grandparents and uncle. Taken abroad dressed as a girl by a woman convert to Judaism, he was kept hidden in France and Switzerland for two years, until the woman brought him to the States, handing him over to an ultra-Orthodox family in Williamsburg, who kept him, thinking they were saving his soul. Only when the crack operatives of Israeli intelligence got involved was he finally tracked down and returned to his parents.

"If they or someone else in the community kidnaps my son because they don't think I'm pious enough to raise him, I won't have the whole Mossad to help me. I just can't take the chance."

"But Rivka, that happened once, long ago . . . it's not something normal. And I'm sure your parents would never—"

"I'm sorry, Aunt Rose." Rivka cut her off. "I just can't take that chance."

Rose closed her eyes in sorrow. Frame by frame, images floated through her imagination: Her sister Pearl's eyes bright with tears embracing her daughter. Zevulun lifting his beautiful little grandson into his big arms, his long beard tickling the child and making him laugh. The family sitting together around the table, glasses of kosher wine raised in a toast. Rivka and Hannah and their two boyfriends sitting side by side, their voices happy and friendly. She and Pearl setting down steaming platters of food on a large table, while the whole extended family sat around eating, speaking, laughing, all stiffness, silences, harsh judgments suspended in time, like a video set on pause. She blinked back tears, the images disappearing into the harsh, cold light of day.

"So, you've given up on them." Just like I did, Rose thought with sorrow. "It's a terrible, terrible thing to lose your family. It was the biggest tragedy of my life."

"I can't stand to think about it that way. I think of it more like 'not just yet.' I have this dream that one day I'll have this great job, and a nice home with nice furniture in a leafy place with a big backyard, and a handsome Jewish husband. Maybe then I could see inviting them over to meet my family."

It was a modest dream, a very American dream. How far away was she from all that? Rose wondered. "Do you envision marrying this boy?"

She smiled, shaking her head. "Oh, he's not up to that. No way. He's like me. He's got no education. He's working as a dishwasher. But he also has dreams. He'd like to open up a store selling music discs. He loves music. He wants to be a famous Jewish rapper, like Matisyahu."

At this, they both laughed.

"Is he kind to you?"

Rivka seemed genuinely moved by the question. "Yes," she answered eagerly. "He is very kind. And he loves Or. And he wants me to be anything I want to be. And he is a big help. He . . . he gets it? You know? Gets everything you can't explain in a million years because he's lived through the same thing."

Rose nodded. "I'm glad for you, Rivka, that you have someone like that in your life. It's a blessing."

"Now I have two blessings. And a few years ago, I felt I didn't have any. That's good, isn't it?"

"Yes, very good. You know, Hannah is very concerned. She'd love to see you."

"How is Hannah?"

"Flourishing. She's working on her master's degree, and she's found a new boyfriend. He's modern Orthodox."

She smiled. "As my friend Malca would say, *gevalt!* Life is strange, isn't it?" She was quiet, thinking, her head down, playing with the fringes of the couch cover, tangling and untangling them from their knots. "About Hannah, I don't know what to say. I know she meant well, she really did, but she never really understood me. I was a 'cause' for her, not a person. And I . . . I wasn't straight with her either, didn't really trust her. I'm still very ashamed of myself for what happened when I was living with her. I know she was trying her best. But back then I was so . . . *farshimmelt*. The idea of facing her is not so . . . comfortable for me. But that's more my fault than hers." She lifted her head and looked at Rose with sudden hope. "Does she really want to see me?"

"I know she does! We've discussed it. Look, I have an idea. Why don't I invite you over to my house for dinner this Friday night? Come with your boyfriend and the baby, and Hannah will come with her David."

Rivka hesitated. "Aunt Rose, could we do it maybe on a Saturday night instead? And could I bring my own food, or maybe you could make vegetarian?"

"You are still observant, aren't you? Wow!" She had expected many things, but not that. "I thought you were running away from all that?"

"Life isn't so black-and-white, Aunt. Religious secular, believer-nonbeliever. When you run, you can't take heavy suitcases with you. So, some people just throw everything away. But I never did. I kept it all in this locker and always held on to the key. When Or was born, I made sure he had a bris. The Christian ladies weren't much help, but a synagogue arranged it for me. There wasn't a single person there I knew. But you know what? It still made me feel happy. I felt connected to the things that I still love and that I want to give to Or. When I moved into this place and started to think about what kind of home it was going to be for my son, I started remembering all the things I loved from my own childhood: *oneg* Shabbat games, and chulent, and songs on Friday night, and apples with honey . . ."

It was then Rose noticed for the first time the ceramic candlestick holders, the wine cup, and the menorah sitting on the bookshelf.

"I couldn't find anything out there to take their place, and believe me I looked."

"Yes," Rose admitted to herself, opening up that locked room inside her and sitting there for the first time in a long, long time. "We'll make it a Saturday-night dinner, then. And please bring your boyfriend . . . ?"

"His name is Jerme, from Jeremiah. It'll be so much trouble for you . . ."

"Hannah's boyfriend will also need kosher food." And so will his father, she thought, the idea of inviting Joseph filling her with a sudden warmth.

"And dishes and pots and silverware . . ."

"I know, I know. Believe me, I remember it all . . . I suppose I better get used to it. Those two seem serious!"

When Rose got up to go, Rivka took a photo off the wall.

"Here, for you."

It was Or, about two months old with a huge grin (probably gas) on his sweet little face. Such a beautiful baby! Rose felt tears sting her eyes. "Thank you, Rivka. I can't wait to hold the real thing. I'll call you?"

"I'd like that, Aunt."

Rose gently put her arms around Rivka. She wasn't a girl anymore, Rose realized, but a fine, strong woman, tempered and hardened by her trials. She released the young woman's slim waist. She was, in her own way, truly heroic, Rose thought. It was easy to cut yourself off from the past, to reject everything. But Rivka had taken the harder way, digging deep inside herself and finding her real nature and desires, bravely keeping connected to all those things that were really important to her, instead of slamming doors like a spiteful, angry child. I could never admit the things I missed. It was too threatening, and I was too vulnerable.

I will find some way to help her make her dreams come true sooner rather than later, Rose promised herself. And then, maybe, in time, she will feel able to include Pearl and Zevulun and her siblings in her life. But only she could decide that, Rose thought sadly, wanting with all her heart to make that phone call to her sister and brother-in-law, to share this photo with them. Being denied that felt like a gut-wrenching physical pain.

But as she walked slowly down the old stairs to the street, she found that in her heart there was still hope, hope that Rivka and her family might someday find a way to crack open the concrete barriers set up between them now like the Berlin wall of old, allowing those imprisoned on either side to break free and cross over to meet again, without recriminations and without fear. A hope that she too could sneak through the opening and salvage what was left of her connections with all the good and valuable things she missed in the world she'd left behind.

She took out her phone and called Hannah, ready to tell her everything.

Epilogue

∽∾

Excerpt from the master's thesis of Mrs. Hannah Gordon-Adler, entitled *Heaven Above, Heaven Below: Nineteenth-century Jewish Women and the Enlightenment*, June 2012.

While the struggle of most nineteenth-century women for a place in the sun was doomed to failure and heartbreak, theirs was a heroic failure that tested itself against great odds before succumbing. Each individual woman, though she stumbled and fell, nevertheless added a stepping stone for other women in the decades that followed. Like the steady work of ants climbing out of their dark holes, women followed the path-blazers up and out, into the light.

On a personal note, I'd like to say this so-called progress is far from complete, and entirely reversible. In countries outside the West, the punishment for seeking heaven on earth is often fatal for women who dare to do so. We in the West should never forget that. Even today, the path-blazers pay a huge personal price for their stubborn resistance against oppression, and for their willful determination to assert their human rights to express themselves fully and creatively.

And the question remains, especially for religious women, why does it have to be a choice? Why should you have to give up heaven above when you seek out heaven below on earth? Why do religions force you to choose between them?

With a little patience, understanding, and love, children could be taught that the two were not mutually exclusive, and they in turn could teach this to their children. And the world will become a more heavenly place for everyone.

Acknowledgments

The Sisters Weiss, while purely the product of my imagination, is about women who can be found abundantly in the real world I grew up in, in both New York and Jerusalem. I continue to live among them. The stereotypes of women, in both the religious and secular worlds, do not do women justice, as the choices all women make are complex and often driven by forces beyond their control. I am grateful for a lifetime of friendship with such women, religious and secular, Jew, Christian, and Muslim, who have, despite societal pressures, carved out a unique space for themselves in advancing all that is good in the world. To all my women friends who have provided me with the example of their tireless inspiration, my thanks.

I thank Dr. Shmuel Feiner for our many invaluable discussions on the Jewish enlightenment and the lives of women intellectuals. I would like to offer him, and Dr. Tova Cohen, my congratulations and heartfelt thanks for their pioneering scholarship in this area, which has brought the work and the lives of these remarkable women the attention they have long merited but have not until now received. Similarly, I thank Professor Carole B. Balin for her inspiring books and wonderful scholarship in this area, and for her cooperation and friendship.

I thank Morris Rosenthal for his help and for translating Sarah Foner's work into English and for allowing me access,

A big thanks to my editor, Jennifer Weis, for her ever-sharp eye and ear and good advice, and to my agent, Mel Berger, for his encouragement and good counsel. As always, my dear husband of over forty years continues to be my sounding board, most influential critic, and dearest friend. Thanks again, Alex.

Glossary of Hebrew
and Yiddish Words
and Expressions

al pi taharas hakodesh   according to the strict, holy way

assur   forbidden

Baruch Hashem   "God be blessed"

bas zekunim   the youngest daughter born when a parent is already advanced
in age

bitul Torah   time wasted that could be spent on studying Torah and self-
improvement

bli neder   a formula used to prevent a person from swearing in vain

bochur   young man

broocha on your keppeleh   "a blessing on your head"

chesed   a deed of compassion and charity

choson   groom

chulent   a dish of meat, beans, and potatoes left to cook overnight Friday
night to be eaten hot on the Sabbath, when all reheating and cooking is
forbidden

Chumash   the five books of Moses

chutzpadika   impudent, impertinent, brazen, someone showing chutzpah

chutzpah   brazenness, gutsiness, audacity

Daas Torah   a Torah scholar's personal opinion on all matters, which is considered by some to be more accurate than the opinion of others, even though the scholar might know nothing about the subject

dafka   something done out of spite or something that is said to "actually" or "in fact" occur: "She *dafka* used the sports section, which I read religiously, to clean the windows." Or: "She's a liar, but this time she was *dafka* telling the truth."

daven   to pray

Eibeisha   God

eidle   refined, trustworthy, respectable

eshes chayil   a woman of valor, a virtuous wife and mother, also the name of a song traditionally sung Friday nights by husbands to their wives beginning with those words

farmisht   confused, befuddled, dysfunctional

farshimmelt   similar to *farmisht*

Farshteist?   Do you understand?

frum   strictly observant of all Jewish laws and customs

gai   go

gartel   the belt in traditional Hassidic garb that separates the upper and lower halves of the body

gemach   a free-loan society that distributes a wide variety of goods and services as a good deed

gevalt   "Oh, no! Woe is me!"

Hashem   literally, "the name," meaning God

hechsher   rabbinical stamp of approval, usually concerning the kosher status of food

Ich farshteist?   "Do you understand?"

imyertza Hashem   "God willing"

kallah moide   a young girl ready for marriage

kashrut   food permissible to eat under Jewish law

kavanah   sincere intentions

Kavod HaRav   the Honored Rabbi

kiddush   the prayer over wine said on Sabbath and at festivals

kollel Talmudic academies of higher learning for men out of high school, usually married men

maideleh a young girl

Mameh Mommy

Mincha the afternoon prayer

moisar a despicable person who hands over a Jew for punishment to the Gentile authorities

narishkeit childish foolishness

nuch "What can you do?"

posek a respected religious authority who decides religious law

prust low-class, vulgar

Rashi a medieval commentator on the Bible

Rebbitzin honorific for a rabbi's wife

Rebono shel Olam "King of the Universe"

Satmar fanatical religious Jewish sect who reject Israel and modernity

shaine lovely, beautiful

shidduch (sg.), shidduchim (pl.) marriage arrangement

shmurah matzah ritual Passover bread in which leavening is forbidden, made from wheat watched in the fields and in storage to ascertain it is not moistened and thus leavened before being baked into matzah; this is a stringency

shmutz literally "dirt" but used to mean dirty dealings, gossip

shvitzing sweating profusely, working hard, or filled with pride

Tateh Daddy

tenaim formal engagement contract

teshuva repentance

tuchus behind

tzadakis a female saint

tzadik a male saint

tzimmis literally, a pot of fruits, vegetables, and meat; used to describe a commotion, a big to-do (usually about nothing)

vilde chayas wild animals

Vus? Vus is dus? "What?" "What is this?"

Vus mere vilstah? "What do you want?"

yichoos family connections, prideful lineage